After a career in the Civil Service, Brenda Clarke began writing when her two children had left school. Since then she has written about twenty novels, many of which were published under her maiden name of Brenda Honeyman.

Brenda Clarke lives with her husband in Keynsham, Bristol.

Also by Brenda Clarke
THREE WOMEN
WINTER LANDSCAPE
and published by Corgi Books

UNDER HEAVEN

Brenda Clarke

CORGI BOOKS

UNDER HEAVEN

A CORGI BOOK 0 552 13229 2
Originally published in Great Britain by Bantam
Press, a division of Transworld Publishers Ltd.

PRINTING HISTORY

Bantam Press edition published 1988
Corgi edition published 1989

This book is set in 10/11 Ballardvalle

Corgi Books are published by Transworld Publishers Ltd., 61–63
Uxbridge Road, Ealing, London W5 5SA, in Australia by Trans-
world Publishers (Australia) Pty. Ltd., 15—23 Helles Avenue,
Moorebank, NSW 2170, and in New Zealand by Transworld
Publishers (N.Z.) Ltd., Cnr. Moselle and Waipareira Avenues,
Henderson, Auckland.

Made and printed in Great Britain by
Cox & Wyman Ltd., Reading, Berks.

To everything there is a season, and a time
to every purpose under the heaven

Ecclesiastes Chap. 3, v. 1–8

PART ONE
1946–1949

A time of war and a time of peace
                         Ibid.

1

He found the house again, without difficulty, in a quiet tree-lined street, five minutes' walk from Marylebone station, in the heart of St John's Wood.

It was a three-storeyed house, called simply The Lodge, set well back from the road behind a high grey wall, and with a wide gravel sweep which led past a clump of cedar trees to the sturdy oak front door. A forbidding place, Henry Lynton had thought it on the only other occasion he had been there. That was during the war, not long before D-Day, when he had been an infinitesimal part of the United States First Army, awaiting the opening of the Second Front. Now, on this fine October morning, he was a free man once more; back in 'civvy street' as the British so quaintly called it; his four years of service and the chest wound he had received in the Ardennes having ensured his early demobilization. He had come back to Britain as soon as he was able, shrugging off the advice of well-meaning friends.

'You're mad, Hank! It's still all shortages and gloom over there. Don't let yourself be fooled by those pictures of the VJ-Day celebrations.'

'I shan't. But the only family I have is in England. My Uncle Stephen lives in London.'

He did not add that his uncle was head of Lynton's Chemicals, nor that his cousin, Ralph, Stephen's only child, had been killed on a bombing mission over the Rühr three years before. He was not quite sure himself yet, what those two facts added up to; but his instinct told him that some kind of opportunity beckoned, which it would be unwise to ignore.

He approached the house. There was no bell, so he lifted the heavy brass ring suspended from the eyeless gargoyle face – a replica, had he but known it, of the sanctuary-door knocker at Durham Cathedral – and knocked. There was a pause, while he had time to glance about him and experience the first feelings of trepidation regarding his welcome. When he had made the appointment to see his uncle, earlier in the week, the invitation to lunch had, he thought, been distinctly grudging. From his previous visit he recollected a rather alarming housekeeper, and as the door opened, he braced himself for the present encounter.

The young woman who stood in the open doorway was certainly not alarming, and much too young to be the redoubtable Mrs Symonds. Henry judged her to be roughly his own age, twenty-four, or possibly less, and the first thing he noticed about her was her eyes: they were hazel, with greenish flecks, a colour one usually associated with red hair. But this girl's hair was a glossy chestnut brown, swept up on the top of her head in the wartime pompadour style, and held with combs. The second thing he noticed was her legs, long and slender, their shapeliness marred by low-heeled shoes and the ugly rayon stockings worn by most British women in preference to the even uglier lisle. He thought how good her legs would look in nylons: he must get his friends to send him some over from the States. And it was at that point that he noticed the third thing: she wore a solitaire diamond engagement ring.

'You must be Mr Lynton's nephew,' she said, holding the door wide. 'He's expecting you. Please come in.'

The hall was still as gloomy as Henry remembered

9

it, its only direct source of light two stained-glass windows, one on either side of the front door. The thin autumn sunshine filtered through the coloured panes, stippling the dark mahogany furniture with lozenges of jewel-bright warmth.

The young woman smiled and held out a well-manicured hand, innocent of nail varnish. Indeed, everything about her, including her severely tailored grey suit and plain white blouse, denoted an efficiency belied by her youthful face. She was not, in any sense of the word, beautiful; her features were too irregular. Her nose was a little too long, her mouth a little too full, her eyes set fractionally too wide apart. But when she smiled, Henry found himself forgetting all these defects in the conviction that she was one of the most attractive women he had ever met.

'How do you do?' she said. 'I'm Katherine Grey, Mr Lynton's secretary. As Mr Lynton isn't going to the office today, he asked me to look in this morning to take some dictation.' Her eyes twinkled. 'That way, he's certain that I shall be occupied this afternoon when I return to Lynton House. I suppose I shouldn't have answered the door, but I was crossing the hall when you knocked.' She grimaced conspiratorially. 'Mrs Symonds won't like it.'

As she spoke, the housekeeper emerged from one of the rooms flanking the hallway; a sharp-faced, grey-haired woman in a black dress. She looked accusingly at the pair of them.

'Ah, Miss Grey! I see you've admitted Mr Lynton.' She sniffed and addressed Henry, her pale eyes expressing disapproval of his unmistakably American appearance. 'Mr Lynton senior has gone upstairs to change for luncheon. He asked me to show you into the drawing-room while you wait.'

'Sure. Fine,' Henry drawled, sensing her animosity and stressing both his accent and his casual transatlantic manner. 'In here, isn't it? I seem to remember ...' And he had opened a door on the right-hand side of the hall before Mrs Symonds could move to do it for him. He smiled winningly at Katherine Grey. 'Don't rush off. Stay and keep me company until my uncle gets down.'

Katherine glanced sideways at the housekeeper's outraged face and gurgled with hastily suppressed laughter.

'That would be very nice,' she answered demurely. 'Thank you, Mr Lynton.' She preceded him into the over-furnished drawing-room and Henry shut the door firmly behind them. 'That was wicked of both of us,' Katherine continued, grinning. 'We've upset Mrs Symonds for the day.' She moved to a table in the centre of the room. 'Can I offer you some sherry?'

'Bourbon, if there is any. I mean Scotch. Hell! I guess I should have brought a bottle. I can't get used to how difficult it is to buy things over here. American dollars seem to be the "Open Sesame", however.'

'I'm sure they are,' Katherine responded drily. 'And Mr Lynton doesn't appear to have any whisky. It's sweet sherry or nothing, I'm afraid.'

'No, thanks.' Henry threw himself into one of the deep chintz-covered armchairs and stared around him. 'This place gives me the creeps,' he said. 'It's like a goddam mausoleum.'

'Is it? I haven't really thought about it. I don't come here that often; only when Mr Lynton's ill or unable to come to the office for some other reason. But now you mention it, I suppose it is. I shouldn't think anything's been changed since old Mr Lynton's time.' Katherine looked at Henry in faint surprise. 'Of course, old Mr Lynton must have been your grandfather.'

'Old Josh! That's right. My father quarrelled violently with the old boy and was cut off with the proverbial shilling. He emigrated to the States. That would have been around 1910, when he was a bit younger than I am now. He met and married my mother in 1920 and I was born two years later, shortly after which my mother upped and left us. The shock of my arrival was too much for her, and she disappeared without trace.' Henry spoke flippantly, but a look of pain momentarily shadowed his face. Then it was gone, submerged by his engaging grin. 'My father died when I was sixteen and I've been looking out for myself ever since. Potted biographies while you wait! Well, that's my life story. Now, how about yours?'

Katherine perched on the arm of the over-stuffed couch, like a bird ready for instant flight.

'Oh, my history's very ordinary,' she protested. 'You wouldn't be interested.'

'Try me! Aren't you rather young, for instance, to be the personal secretary of the head of Lynton's Chemicals?'

She stiffened and glanced across at him, trying to detect some note or look of patronage, but there was none; only a genuine curiosity. She relaxed and smiled.

Henry was not at all what Katherine had expected when she had learned that her employer's nephew was coming to lunch. She had anticipated the long, slightly equine Lynton features, with their high forehead and narrow chin, pale hair and eyes, allied to a delicate build and a stature which generally topped six feet. Instead she saw a stocky, well-built young man, of middle height. The square face, with its freckled complexion, was crowned by red hair. The eyes, in contrast, were cool and grey, fringed with sandy lashes. It was an unusual and intriguing colour combination, Katherine reflected. Fire and ice. The main impression was of a good-looking, well-dressed young man; but there was a contained energy

12

about Henry, not immediately apparent. Once she had become aware of it, however, she was conscious of a slight acceleration in her pulse rate; an unexpected surge of excitement coursing along her veins. Katherine had seen a photograph of the late Geoffrey Lynton, and she could only assume that in looks Henry must take after his mother's family.

'Well?' he prompted, when she was slow to answer his question. He returned her scrutiny without embarrassment, enjoying her obvious interest in him. 'You are young, aren't you, for such a responsible post?'

'Am I? All right! Yes, I suppose I am, a little, but there are reasons. First and foremost, I'm very good at my job. I can speak French and Spanish as well as being an efficient shorthand-typist. Secondly, it hasn't been easy, during the war, to staff private businesses. Even now, over a year after the end of the war, a lot of women are still in uniform. And thirdly' – her eyes met his and again she gave her engaging smile – 'my family have known yours for ever. My mother's father worked in the mines, and my mother herself was in service at Chapel Rock. She had risen to the dizzy heights of head parlourmaid before she married my father and went to live in Plymouth.'

'Chapel Rock. That's the place in Cornwall, isn't it? Pop often used to talk about it. I think, secretly, he was homesick for it until the day he died.'

'I'm not surprised. It's a beautiful place.' Katherine Grey swung one admirable leg and her skirt rose above her knees. Her legs were even better, Henry reflected, the further up they went. She continued: 'It's north Cornwall, right on the Devon border. It was copper-mining country until the lodes ran out. The mines are all derelict now.'

She did not add what he must have learned from his father; that the copper had left sufficient deposits of arsenic to make the Lyntons' and other families'

13

fortunes for the second time; sold, first, to the pesticide companies of North America to counteract the ravages of the boll-weevil in the cotton fields of the southern states; then used by Joshua Lynton as the foundation of his own chemical production business. Instead she stood up, straightening her skirt and once more holding out her hand.

'I must go. I have to get back to the office and type my letters. Goodbye, Mr Lynton. Are you staying in England long? I don't suppose we shall meet again.'

Henry got to his feet. 'I wouldn't bet on that.' He enveloped her hand in his. It was a strong, firm hand, Katherine noted, with spatulate fingers: a workman's hand. 'I don't really know how long I'm planning to stay over here. It all depends.'

She had a feeling that he wanted her to ask the obvious question, so, woman-like, she refused to humour him.

'I must go,' she repeated, adding, as the door opened, 'Here's Mr Lynton now.'

If Stephen Lynton was annoyed to find his secretary idling away her time in his drawing-room, he did not show it. Indeed, it seemed to Henry that the look he gave her was almost avuncular, and he held the door open while she passed through.

'I'm glad Miss Grey has been entertaining you, Henry. I don't know what I'd do without her. What I shall do without her,' Stephen amended, and Henry remembered the engagement ring. 'A very remarkable young woman.'

The voice was quiet and extremely British: detached and empty of emotion. Henry missed the effusiveness of his compatriots – the ebullient greetings, even if, sometimes, they were insincere. He could never tell with the English if they were genuinely pleased to see him or not.

Henry thought his uncle had aged considerably since they had last met. Stephen was now sixty-five years old, and the death of his only child, born when

14

he was in his early forties, had dealt him a severe blow, as had his wife's death, just before the war. He was a typical Lynton, tall and slender, with narrow hips and delicate hands and feet. He was thin almost to the point of emaciation, the facial skin stretched tightly over the bones, revealing the skull beneath. His lips were bloodless and the eyes a pale washed-out blue. No one could have presented a greater contrast to him than his nephew, red-headed and pulsating with life.

Mrs Symonds appeared in the doorway.

'When you're ready, Mr Lynton, please! Luncheon is served.'

It was not a pleasant meal. Rationing apart, Mrs Symonds was known as 'a good plain cook', which, in her case, meant a complete absence of taste and plenty of filling, stodgy fare.

'You need a good lining to your stomach,' was one of her favourite maxims.

Today, the lining consisted of a thick, glutinous vegetable soup, steak-and-kidney pudding – 'Two weeks' meat ration,' she had grumbled to the girl who helped out three mornings a week in the kitchen – followed by treacle tart and custard. The coffee which she eventually placed before them, much in the manner of a magician producing a rabbit from a hat, was mixed with chicory and extremely weak. The real stuff was hard to come by and necessitated a certain amount of under-the-counter bargaining, in-volving time which Mrs Symonds was not prepared to spend.

Henry pushed his half-empty cup away from him and thankfully lit a cigarette, refusing his uncle's courteous offer of a cigar. He inhaled deeply, trying to recall some of the well-rounded phrases, the polished smalltalk with which he had intended to grace the meal.

It had all seemed so easy before he arrived: he

15

would simply put his proposition to his uncle, man to man. But it had not worked out like that. The room, with its dark discoloured wallpaper in a bilious shade of green, its heavy Victorian prints of dead pheasants and bloodstained hares, its plethora of old-fashioned furniture crowding him in, had proved inhibiting. And, in addition, his uncle's manner had not been encouraging, the conversation confined to the most superficial of levels.

What did he think of President Truman? The revival of the Ku Klux Klan? Had he approved of the execution of Pierre Laval? The Nuremberg War Crime Trials? Had he managed to see any shows since arriving in London? Laurence Olivier's *King Lear*, at the New Theatre, was considered to be well worth a visit. As on the previous occasion, there were no questions about Henry's parents, his life in the States; no natural curiosity about a brother whom Stephen had not set eyes on since he was thirty and whom he would never see again.

Looking at the portrait of his grandfather, Joshua Lynton, which hung at one end of the dining-room, among the gory still-life paintings which adorned the other walls, Henry could recognize the strong physical resemblance between father and elder son. He had no doubt, either, that the likeness was more than skin-deep. There was the same humourless slant to the mouth, the same remote look in the eyes. It was no surprise that his own father, who, whatever his other faults, had been warm and loving, had found his family impossible to get on with. It crossed Henry's mind to wonder how his cousin Ralph had fared.

'Sir—' he began, but was interrupted by his uncle rising to his feet.

'Shall we go into the drawing-room? I find it rather chilly in here. Fuel, you know. It's still strictly rationed, but I'm sure Mrs Symonds will have managed a fire of some sort in the other room.'

The October day was close and Henry was uncomfortably warm, in spite of the thick walls and shadowed interior of the house. Reluctantly he followed Stephen across the hall to the drawing-room, and sat as far away from the little fire, burning desultorily in the black-leaded grate, as it was possible to do without appearing rude. His uncle chose the armchair nearest the hearth and regarded his nephew warily across a low marquetry table.

Stephen had felt uneasy ever since receiving Henry's telephone call three days earlier. The news that he was in England had come as an unwelcome shock. Until that first visit, early in 1944, Stephen had forgotten that he had a nephew. There had been no love lost between the two brothers, and when Geoffrey emigrated to America, Stephen had felt nothing but relief. Life would be a lot less complicated without him.

The break had been almost total, and only three letters had been received from Geoffrey in all the intervening years. The first had been sent eighteen months after his arrival in the States, giving an address in Atlantic City; the second, after a gap of ten years, had announced his marriage to a Miss Nancy O'Halloran; while the third and last communication, in the spring of 1922, had baldly informed them that his son, Henry, had been born on February the second and that his wife had left him, within six weeks of getting out of bed, literally holding the baby.

'Irish! And no doubt Catholic!' Joshua had snorted. 'What did he expect, marrying one of them?'

Joshua had died ten months later, and with all the responsibility of taking over as head of the firm, his marriage and subsequent fatherhood, Stephen had had no time to spare for the concerns of his brother. Geoffrey's last letter had remained unanswered, and the man himself had gradually slipped out of con-

17

scious memory, until Stephen could only recall his existence with an effort. Henry he remembered not at all until that wild March day, a year after Ralph's plane had been shot down over the Rühr, when his nephew telephoned Lynton House in the West End. Henry had announced that he was stationed 'somewhere in England' and was going to spend a few days' furlough in the capital. Could he call and see his uncle?

That visit had been as brief as Stephen intended this one should be. Then, as now, Henry's mere presence exhausted him. Energy and vitality emanated from him in almost tangible waves, even when he was sitting still. There was nothing of the Lyntons about him, and it occurred to Stephen that his sister-in-law might have played his brother false. But even as the suspicion crossed his mind, some fleeting expression on Henry's face reminded the older man vividly of Geoffrey. It conjured up memories, long buried, of two small boys playing in the gardens at Chapel Rock, chasing one another down the waterfall of paths which led to the lime kilns and the quay . . .

Stephen was jerked out of his reverie by the sound of his nephew's voice and realized that he had missed the first part of what Henry was saying.

'. . . and so I was thinking that as I'm your only living relative, you might be willing to give me a job with the firm. I was hoping, not to put too fine a point on it, that as Ralph's dead, you might be prepared to consider me as your heir. After all,' Henry added, 'I am your next of kin. I'd be ready to take out British citizenship, if you did.'

The audacity and unexpectedness of the proposal took Stephen's breath away. It confirmed him in his belief that Americans were the most self-assertive and insensitive race on earth. His immediate reaction was to utter a resounding 'No!' Then he would get up and walk out of the room.

The reason he did neither of these things was the recollection of a recent interview with his solicitor, who had been urging him for the past year to make a new will.

'Now that Ralph is dead' – John Morley, senior partner of Morley, Stafford & Browne of Chancery Lane, had never been one to wrap up the truth in euphemisms – ' you need to make new provisions, Stephen. What will happen to Lynton's when you're gone? Or even if you want to retire? You were sixty-five last birthday. Let's face it, you're no longer a young or even a middle-aged man. It's a pity, a great pity, that you have no relatives. It will be a sad day when Lynton's ceases to be Lynton's, after all the hard work you and your father put into the firm to make it the success it is today.'

But of course he did have a relative, although he hadn't mentioned the fact to John Morley at the time. He looked across at his nephew and asked harshly: 'And what do you know about the chemical industry? What do you know about the manufacture of pesticides, fertilizers and the like? You've had no training as a pharmacist or a chemist.'

'You wouldn't know whether I have or not,' Henry answered bluntly. 'You haven't asked me a single question about my life – what I did before the war. As a matter of fact, your assumption is correct. I know absolutely nothing about the chemical industry, but I could learn. Not to be a chemist; presumably you employ those guys. But I don't imagine you're a qualified chemist, either. What you have to be, what all bosses have to be, is a good administrator and a good salesman.' Henry leaned forward, elbows on knees, eyes alight with enthusiasm. 'I was a salesman before the war, and I'll tell you for nothing that I was a damn fine one. Oh, on a small scale, I grant you, but I'm fairly bursting with ideas. Uncle Steve!' The older man winced at the unfamiliar contraction of his name. No one in his life had ever called him anything but Stephen. 'I could put Lynton's on the map. I know I could! I can feel it! Here!' Henry thumped his chest, vaguely aware that the histrionic gesture only embarrassed his uncle. He moderated his tone a little, trying to keep the eagerness out of his voice. 'I could turn Lynton's into an international company.'

Stephen answered coldly, in a voice in which icy rage vied with indignation: 'For your information, Lynton's is already "on the map", as you put it. It doesn't need to become any bigger.'

'But it does!' Henry banged the arm of his chair excitedly. 'Lynton's may be big in the UK, but no one's ever heard of it in the States. But they could, with the right kind of advertising over there. Don't you see, Uncle Steve, that we've been given the chance of a new beginning? This post-war era could be Shakespeare's "brave new world"! It could be another Renaissance, twentieth-century style! Technology and research have been enormously speeded up by two world conflicts in just over thirty years. During the last war alone, our knowledge advanced in all sorts of fields by leaps and bounds. Lynton's mustn't be left behind!'

'And you think you're the man who can work this miracle?' Stephen asked drily. He suddenly felt old and extremely tired. 'Lynton's own personal Messiah, sent down to preach the gospel of the market-place.'

'I could do it,' Henry repeated stubbornly. 'And, what's more, the firm would stay in the family. I don't intend remaining a bachelor.' Katherine Grey's face rose vividly before him. He remembered the engagement ring, but engagements could be broken. 'There will be other Lyntons to follow after me, and future Lyntons to follow after them.'

20

2

Katherine Grey left her bed-sitting-room in Holland Park and took the Tube to Piccadilly Circus. As she emerged into the bright October sunshine and turned into Coventry Street her spirits insensibly rose. A few moments later, she was returning the greeting of a doorman at Lynton House before entering the lift and pressing the fourth-floor button.

It was crazy, she mocked herself, how coming to work always made her feel better, no matter how depressed or under the weather she might be. But she liked her job; she liked being Stephen Lynton's secretary and the sense of importance that it gave her. But it was more than that. She enjoyed the whole atmosphere of big business, its traumas and excitements; the elation which came in the wake of a successful deal, the knife-edged disappointment when things went wrong. It was, she supposed, the feeling of being a part of that male world which she found so stimulating; a world from which, in spite of the vital part they had played during two wars, women were still largely excluded.

She went into Stephen's office and opened the engagement diary before going into her own office next door to take off her hat and coat. She felt in her handbag for her powder compact, but instead her fingers encountered the letter which had arrived from Germany that morning. Her fiancé was still there, as part of the British Army of Occupation.

'At last! I've had word about my demob,' Robert had written. 'I should be out and home by June of next year, so start making the wedding arrangements. I don't want to wait any longer than we have to. It will mean living with my parents for a while, but you won't mind that. It will be so wonderful, to be together permanently after all these years of separation.'

Katherine sat immobile, staring into space, still holding the letter. Why did the news that Sergeant Robert MacNeice of the Royal Engineers was coming home to marry her fill her with such dismay? Surely most women would be delighted at the prospect of giving up work to become full-time wives and mothers. Perhaps it was just the prospect of going to live in Edinburgh, so many hundreds of miles from her family and friends, which she found so daunting; the idea of sharing a house with Robert's parents, neither of whom she had ever seen. That must be it. Whatever other reason could there be?

She had met him during the war, at the forces' canteen where she had helped out during the evenings. He had been in London on a ten-day pass, and on his first day had come in out of the rain for a cup of tea and companionship, rather than brave the anonymity of an unknown, friendless pub. They had liked one another immediately, and, at Robert's insistence, she had pleaded illness at the canteen for the rest of his leave. But even he could not persuade her to deceive Stephen Lynton, no matter how often he taunted her that it was 'just a desk job with a private firm'.

'It's not exactly essential war work, now is it?' he had demanded, aggrieved.

'That's all you know!' she had retorted, nettled.

That was the nearest they had got to a quarrel, and by the time he went back to his unit Katherine had found herself, somehow or other, engaged. She had gone down to Plymouth to tell her father, and Victor Grey had looked at her with his shrewd blue eyes and told her not to be such a bloody fool. She had ignored his advice, however. She really was very fond of Robert MacNeice. And if, on occasions, it occurred to her that fondness was not the same as being in love, she rationalized her misgivings. Affection was a very sound basis for marriage. Grand Passion was much less common than most dramatists and novelists would have people believe.

Victor Grey's cynical and slightly jaundiced view of life had influenced his only child far more than either of them realized. An ex-Chief Petty Officer, Victor had, in his service days, been noted for his readiness to stand as Prisoner's Friend whenever there was any disciplinary action to be taken on board ship. He had been affectionately known as 'Red' Vic because of this tendency to confront authority; but in spite of his natural aggression, he had made an excellent Chief Writer and earned nothing but glowing reports from the various captains under whom he had served.

After being invalided out of the Royal Navy in 1936 with a badly strained heart, Victor's audience had dwindled to two: Katherine and his unmarried sister, who had looked after both of them since the death of his wife. Margery Grey had never had any time for her brother's radical ideas, and told him severely that she didn't hold with 'all that Bolshie nonsense!' Katherine, however, had imbibed enough of Victor's notions before she left home to make her approach to life that of an older and maturer woman than was natural for her eighteen years. Now, at twenty-three, she was still very much her father's daughter, although it never occurred to her that his opinions and attitudes had moulded her own.

Katherine found the powder compact – another reminder of Robert with the arms of the Royal

Engineers welded to its fluted lid – and powdered her nose. As she snapped the compact shut once more and restored it to her handbag, the buzzer sounded from Stephen Lynton's office. She picked up her notepad and pencil and went in.

The sight of Henry Lynton, standing at one of the windows which looked down into Rupert Street, surprised her. She really had not expected to meet him again. Behind his uncle's back he gave her a broad, delighted grin. She had almost responded with an equally welcoming smile, when she recollected herself and moved efficiently to the chair on the side of the desk opposite Stephen's.

'Good morning, Mr Lynton.' She sat down, crossing her legs, pencil poised and ready.

Stephen made a dismissive gesture.

'No, no, my dear. Put that away. I'm not ready for dictation just yet. You know my nephew. You met him last week at The Lodge.' There was a pause, as if he were reluctant to proceed. He laid his long bony fingers tip to tip, then rested them against his forehead, peering at Katherine through the arch of his hands. 'In a few days' time, Mr Henry will be joining the firm.' Stephen smiled thinly at Katherine's look of surprise. 'He will, of course, be starting at the bottom, visiting our factories, getting to know the business inside out. Before then, however, I think it would be a good idea . . . that is, he has expressed a wish to – er – see the family home.' Stephen lowered his hands and cleared his throat. 'As my nephew does not know this country very well, I should be grateful, my dear, if you would go with him. You could spend a couple of nights with your father, and during the day take Mr Henry across to Chapel Rock. If you would look up the necessary trains, you could leave tomorrow morning. Needless to say, all expenses will be incurred by the firm and you need not deduct the two days from your annual holiday.'

24

'C-Certainly.' Katherine was so astonished that she faltered over her reply. But she was pleased, too. She would be able to pay her father and aunt a visit; and, furthermore, she liked the young American. 'I shall be only too happy.'

Stephen nodded. 'That's settled, then. I'll telephone Mrs Hislop, if you'll get me the number, and tell her to expect both of you for lunch on Wednesday. Right!' He waved his hand. 'That's all for now. I'll call you in later for letters. Oh, and warn Miss Parker that I shall want her to take your place for the next three days.'

Katherine got to her feet and made for the door, then swung on her heel, hesitating. Stephen raised his eyebrows in enquiry.

'I had a letter from my fiancé this morning, Mr Lynton,' she said. 'He's being demobbed next June and wants to get married right away. That means I'll be leaving you, I'm afraid. I thought I should warn you, to give you plenty of time to find a replacement.'

'Oh dear,' Stephen sighed. 'I shall miss you, my dear. Very well! And thank you for your consideration.'

Henry moved to open the communicating door into her office.

'I'll see you tomorrow morning, Miss Grey.'

She smiled at him. 'Yes. I'll let you know the time of the train later.'

Henry leaned forward in his seat and read out loud the name of the station.

'Dawlish Warren.' He laughed. 'Hell! What place-names you have in this country.'

They had travelled on the GWR line, via Bristol and Taunton, and ever since Exeter they had had the first-class compartment to themselves. A packed lunch, provided by the staff canteen, had already been shared, and Katherine was beginning to feel that

25

she had known Henry Lynton all her life. She had heard about his early days in Atlantic City, his shiftless but charming father, the way he had worked his way through college, doing any and every evening job that came to hand. After graduation he had landed himself a job with the giant Clifford Corporation whose interests spanned everything from cars to drugs, but barely had time to get started, in spite of what he had told his uncle, before America entered the war. He had enlisted and eventually been sent to England, looked up his uncle, learned of his cousin Ralph's death and the course of his life had changed. He had not said so in so many words, but to Katherine the implication was obvious. He was Stephen Lynton's only living relative: he must see himself as his uncle's natural heir. Whether or not Mr Lynton would see it that way she had no idea, but suspected that Stephen had arranged this trip in order to free himself of Henry's presence for a few days while he considered the matter. He had agreed to take his nephew into the company. That, at least, was a step in the right direction as far as Henry was concerned, and gave him the foothold that he wanted.

In return for these confidences, Katherine had supplied some of her own, among them the fact that her parents had never got on.

'My father was away a great deal of his time, at sea, so they really never had much chance to know one another. Apart from that' – Katherine shrugged – 'my mother wasn't clever enough for him. Dad was a Devonport Grammar School boy; Mother didn't have much education. She was in service at Chapel Rock by the time she was fourteen. Her people were miners and tenant farmers. Grandfather Grey was a civil servant, and middle class.' Katherine smiled ruefully. 'You'll soon discover that the British are obsessed by class. We have as complicated a caste system as India. My mother died when I was twelve. I don't think it really mattered to my father.'

26

She also told him about Robert.

'His parents have their own bakery, in Edinburgh. His father does, I should say. Scotsmen like to keep their business life separate from their womenfolk. Wives are strictly for the home.'

'Surely not nowadays!' Henry had exclaimed, but not, Katherine noted, with much indignation.

'Life moves very slowly in these islands. It takes more than two world wars and a couple of atomic bombs to alter our way of thinking. And the further north you go, the more conservative people are.'

'Then, why marry the guy?'

But this was going too far and too fast for Katherine. That way lay dangerous ground, quagmires and sinking sands, which she was not yet ready to attempt.

'Because I love him,' she answered with finality, and closed the conversation.

Silence had reigned between them for the past few minutes, broken now by Henry's cries of delight as the train began its run along the seafront between Dawlish and Teignmouth. He lowered the window, peering out at the lovely, changeful, autumnal day; at the sunlight glinting and dancing among the waves, at the little clouds scudding across the sky in an ever-changing vista of shapes. He was like a small boy, she thought, having his first sight of the ocean; calling out to late holiday-makers on the beach, throwing a packet of chewing-gum to some startled children who were digging for crabs. Then the train turned inland towards Newton Abbot, following the course of the River Teign, and the sands were lost to view.

Henry pulled up the window and sank back once more into his corner. They were sitting opposite one another, and as he sat down, his knees brushed hers. Both were immediately aware of the contact and their eyes met briefly, before Katherine turned away to stare out at the passing scene. She was furious to feel herself blushing, and was afraid he might comment on the fact. But all he said was, 'When we reach Plymouth, which hotel do you recommend?'

'I've been thinking about that.' Her colour receded. She looked at him and smiled, having recovered her composure. 'Why don't you stay with us? I can move in with my aunt for the two nights we're there, and you can have my bedroom. I'm certain my aunt won't mind, and my father will be delighted. He can't go out much because of his heart, and he loves an audience. He can be quite entertaining,' she offered, 'when he's not frustrated and cross.'

'Well, if you're sure it wouldn't be putting your aunt to too much trouble, then thank you. I'd like that.'

'I'll telephone from North Road station and check that it's all right. But I'm convinced my aunt will say yes.'

The bungalow was in one of the outlying suburbs of Plymouth, with a panoramic view across Dartmoor and the ghostly white mounds of china clay; a rectangular lime-washed building set in a garden which had once been pretty, but which had now run to seed for lack of attention. A few bronze chrysanthemums struggled to survive against the surrounding wall, and some bedraggled Michaelmas daisies made a patch of colour beside the path. The grass needed cutting and was full of weeds.

Margery Grey was in the kitchen when Katherine and Henry entered by the back door. She was taking a batch of scones out of the oven, banging the baking tray down on top of the gas stove and muttering furiously to herself. As soon as she saw her niece, she gave vent to her feelings.

'I won't stay, you know, Kate, if he goes on like this. Showing me up in front of the vicar's wife! I won't put up with it!'

It was an empty threat and Katherine knew it. She kissed her aunt's wrinkled cheek affectionately.

'What's Dad been doing now? Misbehaving himself again by the sound of it. Darling, this is Mr Lynton's nephew, Henry. Mr Lynton, this is my aunt, Margery Grey.'

'For heaven's sake, call me Hank! Everyone does at home. How do you do, Miss Grey? It's nice of you to have me at such short notice.'

'Oh dear! How do you do?' Margery wiped her floury hands on her apron. 'You must forgive me, Mr Lynton. Hank, then! What a welcome. But really, Kate, he gets me in such a state! Telling the vicar's wife the things he did! I've never been so embarrassed in all my born days.'

Katherine gurgled with laughter. 'What has he been saying?'

Her aunt sniffed. 'Nothing I could repeat, I assure you. You'd better ask him. He does it deliberately. He hates anything to do with the Church; he always has. Says the clergy and their wives are a lot of prying busybodies.'

Katherine turned to Henry. 'Come into the living-room and meet the old reprobate himself. Then I'll show you to your room.'

Victor Grey was sitting in his armchair on one side of the empty grate. The day was too warm for a fire. He glanced up as his daughter and her guest came into the room, giving Katherine a malevolent grin.

The room itself ran almost the whole length of one wall of the bungalow, with a picture window looking out over the moors. It was light and airy, furnished in cream and varying shades of brown; a nondescript room, reproduced in thousands of homes all over the country. The two most striking things in it were a huge crystal bowl which had been crammed, higgledy-piggledy, with a mass of late, velvety, dark red roses, and a large silver-framed photograph of

Victor Grey in his naval uniform, standing beside the hot springs at Rotorua.

Katherine bent and kissed her father before introducing Henry Lynton.

'It's a great honour to meet you, sir. Please don't get up. Has anyone ever told you that you look like James Cagney?'

Victor Grey chuckled. 'Often. We're about the same height, as well.' He switched his attention back to his daughter. 'What's that Queen Mary's Gift been saying about me, in the kitchen?'

'You're not to speak of Aunt Margery in that way,' Katherine reproved him sharply. 'And you're not to upset her by being rude to the vicar's wife.'

'Prurient old cow!' Victor exclaimed viciously. He mimicked an over-refined high-pitched voice. '"I suppose there's a good deal of – er – unnatural sex in the navy, Mr Grey. You must have seen something of it in your time. Most distressing, I should imagine."'

'Oh dear!' Katherine regarded her father apprehensively. 'And what did you say?'

'I said: "Are you referring to buggery, my dear madam? There was certainly some of that about." And I told her how they used to give us regular medical inspections when we came ashore. Every man, mother-naked, had to bend over and call out the name of his ship. *Impregnable. Indomitable. Glorious. Marigold.*' Victor glanced sideways at Henry, who was convulsed with silent laughter, then transferred his defiant gaze to his daughter. 'All right! I'm sorry if I upset Margery, but not for scandalizing Mrs What's-her-name. Women like that are all the same. They want salacious little titbits, wrapped up in pretty words, so that they can hold up their pious hands in feigned horror when repeating them to their friends. They don't want to hear a spade called a spade.'

'The trouble with your stories,' Katherine said severely, 'is that I never know what is the truth and what isn't. You apologize to Aunt Margery before supper, or I'm not sitting down at the same table with you. Neither is Mr Lynton. We'll eat in the kitchen.' She turned to Henry. 'Please don't encourage him by laughing like that. If you'll follow me, I'll show you your room.'

Henry picked up his overnight case and meekly went after her across the long central corridor to one of the two front bedrooms overlooking the tree-lined road. Katherine pointed out the bathroom.

'I'm sorry about that domestic upset,' she said. Her mouth relaxed into a smile. 'He really is impossible! I don't know how my aunt puts up with him. Dearly as I love my father, I couldn't live with him all the time.'

Henry sat down on the edge of the bed. 'For Pete's sake, don't apologize. He's a great character. I like him just the way he is. How does he come to have such a dodgy heart? He's not that old.'

'Fifty-nine. I think it started when he was a Writer – that's a clerk in the Royal Navy – on board a hospital ship which was sunk during the First World War. He was in the water for several hours before being picked up. But the real damage was caused when he was in the tropics once. He was carrying a freshly made pot of tea from the galley to his mess when he slipped and was very badly scalded over his stomach and thighs. And because they were in the tropics, the burns wouldn't heal. I imagine it put a strain on his heart.' She shrugged. 'Whatever the reason, he was discharged unfit for further service in 1936. For the past ten years he's been a semi-invalid and hates it.'

Henry sent her a glinting look from beneath his lashes. 'He'll miss you when you're all that way away, up in Scotland.'

'He'll survive,' Katherine retorted grimly. 'Better, in fact, than if I were on his doorstep every five minutes. We're too similar. We both like getting our own way.'

Victor Grey echoed her sentiments during supper,

31

when he forthrightly expressed his doubts about her marriage to Robert MacNeice. Katherine and her aunt had been discussing wedding plans.

'I've told you, Kate, you're a bloody fool. Robert's a nice fellow, but he's a Scot. Women are chattels to them. That won't suit you, my girl! You're like me. Bossy.'

'Now, look here, Father . . . ,' Katherine began angrily, a spot of red burning in either cheek.

Henry, noting Margery Grey's agitation at the prospect of a family row, cut in smoothly: 'I see you've been to New Zealand, sir.' He nodded towards the photograph. 'That's Rotorua, isn't it?'

The older man put down his knife and fork and slewed round in his seat to stare at the picture.

'It is.' His eyes lit with enthusiasm. 'Wonderful place. Wonderful country. New Zealand is the second most beautiful place God made. And the girls! Gorgeous creatures! Real hot-blooded females, just like women ought to be. When we put into port, they used to be lining the quayside, four or five deep. They couldn't wait for us to go ashore.'

Henry grinned. 'If New Zealand is the second most beautiful place God made, where's the first?'

'Tonga,' Victor Grey said without a moment's hesitation. 'Paradise.' His blue eyes misted over, his voice blurred with emotion. He laid a thin veined hand on Henry's wrist. 'I tell you, if I hadn't been married, with a child, I'd have jumped ship at Tonga and followed in the footsteps of the *Bounty* mutineers.'

There was a moment's silence, during which Henry was aware of Katherine sitting tense and still.

'Well,' she remarked at last with a brittle laugh, 'ought I to be thankful or sorry that your sense of duty triumphed?'

The shadows of old memories, of unfulfilled dreams, of half-forgotten yearnings left Victor Grey's face. He chuckled richly, once more picking up his knife and fork.

'Flicked you on the raw there, my girl, didn't I?' He looked round the table. 'Where's the mustard? You can't have ham without mustard. How many times do I have to tell you, Marge? And you've forgotten the bloody salt.'

'I'll get them.' Katherine jumped up before her aunt could move. 'Where are they? In the sideboard?' She banged the mustard-pot and salt-cellar down in front of her father. 'What you need', she told him acidly, 'is a Royal Marine.'

Victor roared with laughter. 'You see?' he crowed, turning again to Henry. 'It won't do for her to marry a Scot. He won't stand for that kind of shrewishness. Try to din some sense into her, will you? Before it's too late.'

3

'Your father's right. You shouldn't marry this Scotsman of yours.' Henry stared through the windscreen at the car in front. Without altering his tone of voice, he added: 'Why don't you marry me, instead?'

After breakfast, Margery had suggested that they take her little Austin 7 to Chapel Rock.

'I only use it nowadays to go into town, and I hardly touch my petrol ration. I get extra, too, because Vic's an invalid. The tank is full.' She had searched in her handbag and produced her ration book.'Here are some coupons in case you need to fill up again.'

And so, at a quarter past eleven, the bright October day warm and still, Katherine and Henry sat in the queue of cars waiting to cross the Tamar by the Torpoint ferry. They had said very little to one another. Henry had been quietly appalled by the devastation in the centre of Plymouth, and Katherine had been forced to keep her mind on her driving because the streets looked so different without the familiar landmarks of her childhood. The temporary shops, housed in Nissen huts with concrete façades, upset her more than she cared to admit, remembering the pre-war buildings. Someone had nailed up a rough wooden cross outside the ruined church of St Andrew, bearing the single word *Resurgam*.

Devonport was no better. The dockyard had been one of the chief targets of the German bombers, and whole streets round about had been demolished.

Katherine had relaxed a little as they joined the queue of cars, concentrating on her route once they were across the river. Henry's remark, out of the blue, caught her completely off guard.

'I . . . I beg your pardon?' she gasped.

Surely he couldn't be serious! She turned to look at him. He was smiling.

'Did you think I meant it?'

'No,' she answered, blushing. 'No, of course not!'

'You shouldn't be too sure,' he said, almost to himself.

He spoke so softly that Katherine was unsure whether or not she had heard him correctly. She decided to ignore the remark. She watched the long line of vehicles streaming past her from the ferry, then inched the Austin forward in the wake of the cars in front, down the concrete ramp. Once on board she wound down her window, but refused Henry's suggestion that they get out and stretch their legs.

'You go, if you want to,' she said. She wanted to be alone, to think.

But he remained in the car with her, chatting easily and sensibly about his life in the army and all that had happened to him since demobilization. As she listened, gradually forcing her disorderly thoughts back under control, Katherine realized for the first time how extraordinarily ambitious Henry Lynton was. Now and then he would talk as if the company were already his. She suppressed an admiring grin. He certainly had nerve, or, as he would put it, neck enough for two. All the same, she was impressed by many of his plans for the firm's future, should he ever find himself in a position to implement them. She regretted more than before that she would not be around to see him in action.

'We'll be there in a moment,' she said. 'The entrance to the drive is round the next bend.'

They had driven west, then north, through

Polbathick and St German's, Landrake and St Mellion, before turning off into a maze of country lanes, where the autumn tress poured down the gullies of the hills in rivers of molten bronze. The car bucketed across a hump-backed bridge and began to climb again towards a pair of wrought-iron gates. These were open and, once through, the ground levelled out on to a metalled driveway which snaked between crowding rhododendron bushes, bringing them eventually on to the broad gravelled sweep in front of the house. Henry sat, open-mouthed, staring before him.

'My God!' he breathed at last. 'I didn't believe places like this really existed. I thought they were just products of Hollywood's overheated imagination.'

Chapel Rock was a rambling three-storeyed house, with a multitude of chimneys and gables. Its grey granite walls were clothed with creeper and trellis roses, and a formal terraced garden descended on three levels to a retaining wall in which was set a white wicket-gate. Beyond that, a riot of paths threaded through a profusion of bushes and flowering shrubs to a dovecot and water-lily pond. Below that again they disappeared into a belt of trees, through which could be glimpsed a broad expanse of shining water.

Katherine followed Henry out of the car. He was so awestruck that he forgot, in his polite American way, to assist her.

'That's the Tamar down there,' she said. 'Also Chapel Rock's private quay, the old lime kilns and trading office. I'll take you to see them after lunch. But come inside now. I expect Mrs Hislop's waiting for us.'

The housekeeper was pleased to see them, especially Katherine, whom she had known since birth.

'Your mother and I,' Mrs Hislop reminded her,

'both started in service here on the very same day. She used to bring you over to see me after she was married.' She bustled ahead of them across the lofty marble-tiled hall, pausing once to pull back some curtains of shabby brocade. 'I have to keep everything shut up all the time when it's fine. The sun creates havoc, even at this time of year, because the furnishings are falling apart. It's such a shame. But Mr Stephen never comes here, and he won't spend money on the place. One of these days he'll sell it. He's been talking about it for long enough. And then Hislop and I will be out of a job. Ah, well! I suppose we can't grumble. We've been here for forty-five years. We're past retiring age.'

Henry was still looking around him like a man in a dream.

'Is that a real suit of armour over there?' he whispered to Katherine. 'You know, old as opposed to modern fake.'

She laughed. 'Oh, it's genuine all right. It belonged to some ancestor of the people who originally owned Chapel Rock. De Sallis, I think their name was. Your great-grandfather bought it from them, in the middle of the last century.' She stopped, pointing upwards. 'You see that quatrefoil shape in the wall, to the right of the little gallery? That's a spy-hole. You can look down from one of the upper corridors and see everything that's going on in the hall below. In the same corridor there's a window which opens into the private chapel. In the old days, if you were ill and forbidden to mingle with the rest of the family, you still had no excuse to shirk listening to a very boring sermon.'

Mrs Hislop ushered them through a door covered with tattered green baize and into the servants' quarters.

'You won't mind having your lunch in the kitchen with Hislop and me, will you?' she asked. 'But it's the only part of the house that's comfortable. The rest of the place, as I said, isn't fit for company. Some of the rooms are closed up altogether. As for the rest . . . well!' She shrugged defeatedly. 'I do what I can with a duster and the vacuum but it's too much for one woman. All them evacuees during the war didn't help.'

She preceded them into a sunny room at the back of the house overlooking the vegetable garden. Bright rush mats were scattered over the stone-flagged floor–all that was left, apart from the walls, of the original kitchen. Everything else had been modernized just before the war and Mrs Lynton's death.

'She loved this place,' the housekeeper said, shaking her head reminiscently. 'If she'd lived, I reckon she'd have persuaded Mr Stephen to come back, at least for two or three months of the year. But he's never come near it since she died.'

Proudly she pointed out the new gas cooker and Aga boiler which had replaced the old blackleaded range. Rose-patterned curtains matched the cushions on a rocking-chair next to the dresser.

Hislop, to whom his wife referred simply by his surname, had not yet come indoors, and his lunch was put to warm in the oven. As he combined the jobs of both gardener and handyman, he had, Katherine surmised, plenty to keep him occupied around the estate.

Henry ate his lamb chop and green peas, followed by a blackberry and apple tart, in silence, letting the two women chatter on. The size of Chapel Rock and the extent of its grounds had taken him aback. Geoffrey Lynton had never talked much about his home, and Henry had asked no questions. He knew, without being told, that the seedy lodgings and rented apartments in the poorer districts of Atlantic City had been a far cry from the life his father had been used to in England; but, even so, he had never imagined anything on the scale of this place. Why on earth didn't his uncle keep it in decent repair? Why waste his money on that gloomy monstrosity in London? One day, given half a chance, he, Henry Lynton, would restore Chapel Rock to its former glory. His uncle, he thought contemptuously, was a fool and a philistine!

When they had finished their meal, Katherine excused herself and Henry.

'Mr Lynton is anxious to see the rest of the estate, and we'll probably drive up towards Calstock later, to look at what's left of the mines. I'm sorry we've missed Mr Hislop, but we'll be back for tea. Perhaps we shall see him then.'

'Lord love you, don't worry about Hislop!' exclaimed his wife. 'I never do.'

Katherine and Henry walked down across the terraces, between flowerbeds gay with dahlias and asters and dwarf Michaelmas daisies, Chinese lanterns and the nodding plumes of golden rod. The wall was red with the berries of cotoneaster, spattered like drops of blood among their glossy green leaves. Katherine pushed open the wicket gate and led the way through.

'Which path?' she asked. 'You choose.'

'OK. What about the one that goes past the lily-pond?'

Katherine laughed. 'A good choice. It takes us past the dovecot, as well, although it misses the waterfall and the summerhouse. Incidentally, this is called the valley garden, and all the paths eventually lead to the same place: the little fifteenth-century chapel, just above the quay.'

'Fifteenth-century chapel?' Henry looked dazed. 'Hell's teeth! Now I really know I'm dreaming.'

His mind, however, was racing. He wanted this place. It had been his father's home, and, now that his cousin Ralph was dead, it should rightfully be his after Stephen. He wouldn't want to live here. It was too far off the beaten track; too remote from the lights of the city. But he would like to know that it belonged to him. He would lavish money on it, make it a showplace, bring people – important people – down for weekends and astound them.

It was the first time he had realized that he was acquisitive. He supposed it stemmed from having had so little as a child. He wanted things: nice things. He wanted Chapel Rock. He also wanted Katherine Grey . . .

The revelation startled him. Why her? Why this particular woman? She was a pleasant girl, reasonably good-looking, but that was all. He had known dozens of females equally, if not more, attractive; at least, on the surface. Perhaps that was it. She had character, determination. She didn't bore him, and Henry was easily bored. Moreover, she possessed those fabulous legs!

They had at last reached the chapel, from which the rock where the house was perched took its name. Below them, the tree-studded bank sloped down to the quay and the derelict lime kilns. Henry could see the sunlight dancing on the river.

Katherine pushed open the chapel door, and the familiar smell of an unused building mingled with the scent of damp and decay. It was very small – Henry judged no more than about seven foot square – and completely empty except for a drift of last winter's leaves. Its only source of light was through a cruciform window set high in one wall.

'It was built in 1485, the year of Bosworth,' Katherine said. 'It's dedicated to the Cornish saint, St Hyacinth.'

The door swung to behind them, leaving them standing close together in the gloom. Instinctively, Henry's arms went round Katherine and his mouth found hers. For a moment or two she clung to him, eagerly returning his kisses; then she jerked her head back and her hands were bunched against his chest, forcing him away.

She said, very gently, 'I'm engaged.'

His embrace tightened. 'Send the man back his ring. He won't be the first person it's happened to.'

'No,' Katherine answered quietly. 'I would if I were sure that I didn't love Robert, or if I were sure that I loved you. But I'm not. I like you very much. I find you extremely attractive and I'd like to sleep with you. That, however, is not necessarily love.'

He released her with a shaken little laugh. He found her composure unnerving.

'You're a very outspoken young woman.'

She considered this, meeting Henry's eyes with her steady gaze.

'I suppose I am. That's my father's influence. He, as you may have gathered, is an extremely forthright man.'

Henry laughed again, this time in genuine amusement, as he followed her outside and down the slope of the path.

'What's a Queen Mary's Gift?' he enquired. 'I've been meaning to ask you. Your father mentioned it in reference to your aunt, yesterday afternoon.'

'Oh, that!' They emerged from the trees on to the quayside, to their right a cluster of derelict cottages and sheds, and to their left the long-disued lime kilns towering against the cliff. 'To my father,' Katherine explained, 'it means anything that's totally useless. During the First World War, Queen Mary gave a present to every serviceman: a tin containing a pen, pencil, rubber, a slab of chocolate and some other odds and ends. None of it much good to men daily risking their lives in the trenches or on the high seas.'

'They do say it's the thought that counts,' Henry offered.

'True. But that's an argument that didn't cut much ice with my father. Well!' Katherine continued, spreading her hands. 'This is Chapel Rock's private quay. The ore was brought down from the mines and loaded on barges for transportation to Plymouth. For part of the second half of the last century, the Tamar Valley was one of the most industrialized places in the whole of the British Isles. Silver, lead, copper: they were all mined around here. And all the big landowners burned their own limestone, which was brought up from south Devon. My mother's grandfather was a lime burner. It was a skilled job. He and the others used to tend their own group of kilns, going from one big house to the next.' She turned. 'Let's walk as far as the river's edge.'

It was a beautiful afternoon. The sun lay heavy and warm across their backs, like fur, and the air was redolent with the sharp crisp scents of early autumn. The trees on the opposite side of the broad running river were turning to yellow and crimson. Falling leaves drifted slowly to the ground. Insects busied themselves in the long sweet grasses. It was so still, so dreamlike, that it was impossible to imagine that the whole valley had once hummed and throbbed to the vibrant beat of industrialization. All along the Cornish bank, for mile upon mile, the crumbling stacks of brick and lime kilns, roofless cottages, decaying mine workings and broken arsenic flues stood like the rotting remains of an ancient civilization, silent witnesses to the glories which had passed.

To Katherine it was simply home; part of the area where she had been brought up. She recalled, as a small child, being taken for a trip in the ageing paddle-steamer *Empress*, which had plied between Devonport and Calstock. Her mother had been taking her to see Mrs Hislop at Chapel Rock, and Katherine remembered her bitter disappointment because the house was invisible from the river, hidden behind the towering banks of trees.

For Henry, staring about him, the place held a sense of enchantment. All the fairy stories of his childhood came crowding in upon him: the uncanny forests, the haunted woods, the magical thorn-hedges which grew around the palaces of the spellbound and the dead. Babes in the Wood; Sleeping Beauty; Snow White and the Seven Dwarfs; it had never occurred to him before how often this theme was repeated in the folklore of mankind. But here, in this valley of lush vegetation, where, except for the muted hushing of the water, the silence was almost total, he could suddenly understand why the idea of sinister, brooding woodlands had, for centuries, exercised such a powerful fascination over the minds of men.

He said abruptly, 'Let's go back. You were going to drive me somewhere. To see the old mines?'

'Yes, of course, You might as well see everything while you're here.'

They retraced their steps, climbing up past the little chapel and through the valley garden with less enthusiasm than they had displayed during the descent, half an hour earlier. By the time they reached the house they were hot and tired and glad to seek the shade of the car.

Henry demanded irritably, 'Is it usually as warm as this in October? I thought this was the land where it always rained.'

'That's because Americans never bother to find out the truth about other countries,' Katherine retorted, letting in the clutch. 'It's what makes Hollywood films about England so ridiculous. *Mrs Miniver*, for example.'

They were suddenly bickering like a couple of children, out of sorts with one another and with the world. The tender moment in the chapel might never have been. Katherine twisted the steering wheel sharply and the Austin lurched to the right, scattering gravel from beneath its wheels. Henry knocked his elbow on the passenger door. Her Scotsman was

43

welcome to her, he decided, glancing sideways at the set young profile. He couldn't imagine why he had ever thought her attractive.

Damn Yanks! Katherine thought sourly. They had been the same during the war, criticizing everything. Too hot! Too cold! Too primitive! As they drove through the gates into the narrow country lanes, she gave a bad-tempered blast on the horn.

Just as suddenly, their irritation with each other evaporated. Henry began to grin and Katherine giggled. A milk lorry, with its cargo of rattling churns, pulled into the hedge to allow them to pass. The man driving it was red-faced and sweating, and made an obscene gesture when Katherine grazed his wheels. They both laughed hysterically. They were back in the normal world again.

'Well?' Victor Grey asked brusquely. 'Did you persuade her to change her mind?'

Henry, who had packed his overnight bag immediately after breakfast, was sitting in his host's bedroom while he and Katherine waited for the taxi which would take them to North Road station. Victor had had a bad night and had been persuaded to spend the morning in bed. He was propped against a bank of pillows, looking frailer than his fifty-nine years. There was a pallor to his skin, accentuated by the harsh northerly light from the window; but even that, together with his tired eyes, could not completely counteract the healthy weatherbeaten tan, acquired in his years at sea.

In answer to the question, Henry said, 'No, I'm afraid I didn't, sir. Although I did ask Katherine to marry me, instead.'

Victor looked searchingly at his guest.

'If you're serious,' he replied at last, 'I trust my daughter had the good sense to say no!'

Henry grimaced. 'She did. But would it have been

44

such a calamity had she agreed? Or are you opposed to her marrying anyone?'

'I'm not opposed to her marrying,' the older man responded, looking more than ever like James Cagney in a belligerent mood. 'It's just that I don't think Kate's the type who ought to get married. She's too damned independent. My advice to her is to make a career for herself with your uncle. The life would suit her a bloody sight better.'

Henry was shocked. 'And deprive her of her natural function in life? All women want a home and children.'

'No, they don't!' Victor was getting worked up. 'Good God, boy! Women are like men; everyone is different. In Russia, they no longer treat women as chattels.' He tilted his head back against the pillows, fighting for breath. Then he bawled, 'Margery! Where the bloody hell are you! Where's the coffee, you stupid woman?' He stared defiantly at Henry.

Henry nodded, relieved, after this outburst, to see Victor's colour slowly return to normal.

'I see, sir, that you don't believe in translating theory into practice.'

'Insubordinate young devil! Here, give me one of those pills and a glass of water.' Victor gulped down the tablet, spilling some of the water on the sheet. 'There are women,' he explained, 'and then there are women. There are intelligent self-sufficient ones, like Kate, and there are the . . . the . . .'

'The Queen Mary's Gifts?' Henry suggested.

Victor eyed him speculatively. 'Mmm. I can see you're quick to catch on.'

'I thought it a particularly telling phrase. Katherine explained to me what it meant.'

Margery Grey came into the bedroom, carrying a tray of coffee things which she put down on the bedside table.

'You'll give yourself another heart attack, yelling

45

like that,' she told her brother severely. 'Just don't expect me to look after you, that's all.'

Katherine entered, wearing the grey suit and navy blouse in which she had travelled down. Yesterday she had let her hair tumble about her shoulders and worn a soft green dress which had highlighted its reddish tints. Today she looked remote and efficient, every inch the confidential secretary. Henry felt unexpectedly intimidated, and the sensation jarred.

'We were just talking about you,' Victor informed his daughter.

'Oh? I thought you were bullying Aunt Margery, as usual.' Katherine took one of the cups of coffee from the tray and perched on the end of her father's bed. 'What were you saying about me?'

'That in my opinion you're not the marrying sort. You're bound to make a mess of it. But, then, I've been telling you that for years . . . There's that bloody Nosy Parker from next door coming up the garden path, Marge.' Victor turned to his sister. 'If she's collecting for Conservative party funds again, sing her a quick chorus of the "Internationale". That'll send her on her way in a hurry.'

As Margery Grey flounced out of the bedroom Victor gave a malevolent grin, showing the whites of his eyes. 'Poor old girl! She can't get used to the fact that the New Millennium has dawned; that this country at last has a Labour government with a thumping great majority!'

'You,' his daughter informed him, 'are incorrigible.' A car horn bleeped. Katherine replaced her saucer and empty cup on the tray and picked up her handbag. 'That must be the taxi.' She stooped and kissed her father. 'Stop worrying about me. And don't bother to deny it, because I know you do, and I'm grateful.' She stood looking down at him for a moment or two. She squeezed the thin hand still clasping one of hers, and smiled. 'Allow me to know what's best for myself, Dad. You make sure you're fit enough to attend the wedding.' She moved towards the door. 'And stop making Aunt Margery's life a misery.'

'Rubbish!' Victor Grey scoffed, his eyes bright with tenderness. 'She loves it! She'd miss it if I didn't bully her. You know bloody well she would.'

4

Katherine and Robert MacNeice were married quietly in Plymouth in the summer of 1947. Henry Lynton, unlike his uncle, did not accept his invitation to the wedding.

It was now generally acknowledged that Stephen would leave his controlling shares in Lynton's Chemicals to his nephew, and that when he retired Henry would take over as head of the firm. During the past nine months the young American had worked his way up through the various departments, and was now proving himself as a salesman. He had made himself popular by never trading on his name and by showing that he could be trusted as a colleague. No matter what indiscretions were uttered in his presence, nothing ever got back to his uncle. He had found himself a comfortable little flat near Marble Arch – no mean feat in a city with an acute shortage of accommodation – where he frequently entertained. And if further proof were needed of Stephen Lynton's intention to name his nephew as his successor, Henry had recently entered an application for British citizenship. There was no one now, throughout the whole of Lynton's, who failed to treat him as the Heir Apparent.

Stephen was not quite sure how it had come about. He was no fonder of his nephew than he had been at the beginning, finding Henry's extrovert personality and restless energy as exhausting as ever.

But blood was certainly thicker than water and the thought of future generations of Lyntons being in charge of the company which he and his father had slaved so hard to create made the outcome more or less inevitable. Furthermore, Stephen had to admit in his heart of hearts that Henry would be good for the company. In the two years since the end of the war, Stephen was conscious of a change in the commercial climate. The influence of America – her go-getting ways and vigorous marketing techniques – was beginning to affect the more gentlemanly British methods. It was too soon, as yet, to guess what impact the restored German and Japanese economies would have on world trading; but Stephen was no fool and saw further ahead than most people, particularly his nephew, gave him credit for doing. He was, in any case, sixty-six years of age, and, in the not too distant future, would be thinking, if not actually of retiring, then at least of slackening his hold on the reins of power. That apart, he knew himself well enough to accept that he was not the man to take Lynton's successfully into the cut and thrust of the post-war world. Neither would Ralph have been.

Stephen's grief for his son's death went deep – one reason why he never mentioned it to anyone. Displays of emotion were un-British and to be frowned upon. Stephen believed devoutly in the stiff upper lip. He had always had doubts about leaving the company to Ralph, although he had been loath to admit it. But Ralph had been such a gentle boy; so ready and able to make allowances for people, so quiet and academic that he would have made a very poor businessman. He was as unlike his cousin Henry as it was possible to be. Henry would be the making of Lynton's.

By the time he travelled to Plymouth for Katherine Grey's wedding, Stephen had made up his mind. He would see his solicitor the moment he

49

returned to London and make the necessary dispositions. But there was no need to say anything to Henry just yet. He needed a few more years as salesman and then some hard slog on the factory floor in order to understand the basic workings of the industry. He would have to contend with men academically cleverer than himself if he were to run Lynton's Chemicals successfully and win.

Paris in August was hot, noisy and overcrowded. Katherine, standing at the hotel window, desperately trying to get some air, found it hard to believe that it was a mere three years since the departure of the Germans. There were shortages and signs of hardship, but the Parisians were bouncing back with their traditional resilience. Late last night – all night, it seemed to Katherine – a gang of workmen had been digging up the road outside the hotel, to the accompaniment of two pneumatic drills. She wondered bitterly if the French ever slept. The way she felt at the moment, there was a great deal to be said for the British habit of downing tools at half-past five.

Robert came through from the bathroom, wrapped in an enormous white towel.

'The water was cold again,' he complained irritably. 'Its's a damned inefficient heating system.'

'Give them a chance,' Katherine protested mildly. 'They're coping with all sorts of difficulties and managing extremely well. You still can't get hot running water in a British hotel. And you must admit they do wonders with the food. I'm looking forward to my dinner.'

Robert grunted and shed the towel, sitting on the edge of the bed. He was tall and muscular, trained during his years in the army to the peak of physical fitness. He had the black hair and piercing blue eyes of the true Celt, with nothing of the red-headed Pictish strain found in many Lowland Scots. He was a very handsome man, as Katherine was well aware. She noticed the way women looked at him in the street and in restaurants, and the envious glances they gave her. She ought to be telling herself how lucky she was, instead of feeling strained and nervous.

There had been something not quite right between them ever since Robert's return from Germany; and most of the difficulties, Katherine suspected, had been of her own making. She had been on a brief visit to Edinburgh to meet his parents. They had made her welcome in their undemonstrative fashion, and her future mother-in-law had conducted her over the old Victorian house, situated on the outskirts of the city. Katherine had been shown the rooms which she and Robert would occupy when they were married.

'You, see, they're quite separate from ours. We'll not be interfering.'

The rooms were pleasant, newly decorated, and Katherine had found Edinburgh a beautiful city. Nevertheless, she had returned to London in a state of profound depression. That it had anything to do with Henry Lynton, she had resolutely refused to acknowledge. She had seen very little of him since he went on the road, although he had taken her to see Olivier's film of *Henry V* and Alec Guinness in *Oliver Twist*. On both occasions he had behaved impeccably, and there had been no repetition of the incident at Chapel Rock. He seemed to have lost interest in her except as a friend; someone to take out now and then, when he remembered her existence.

What more could she want when she was engaged to another man; one, moreover, whom she had made it perfectly plain that she intended to marry? It did occur to her that she might be less determined to become Robert's wife had her father been less forthrightly opposed to the marriage. But she dismissed the idea as an insult to her intelligence. Surely she was mature enough to know her own mind! She loved Robert, Katherine told herself with unnecessary firmness. Things would be fine once they were married and settled together, instead of being subjected to constant separations. But she did not define what she meant by 'things'.

She went over now and sat beside him, putting her arms around him, smoothing his back, still damp from his bath. His response was immediate, pulling her down to lie flat on the bed and kissing her violently. One hand was already groping under her skirt.

'Hey! Wait a minute! I didn't mean . . . Robert! I'm dressed for dinner!' She fought him off, struggling into an upright position. He tried to pull her down again, but she got to her feet, smoothing her dress and fussing with her hair. 'I'm sorry. I . . . I wasn't . . . I didn't intend it the way you thought I did. It was . . . just a gesture of affection.'

'For God's sake!' She couldn't blame him for being angry. She had acted impulsively in response to a guilty conscience, without stopping to think of the implications. 'This is my honeymoon! I don't want gestures of affection. I want you. In bed! You're my wife now. I can do as I damn well like!''

Her feeling of contrition evaporated.

'Why should it be what you want? Why don't you simply say that we're married, instead of that I'm your wife? And it's *our* honeymoon! I'm involved in this, as well. Remember?'

The expression on his face was so ludicrous as he sat there staring at her, open-mouthed, his naked body glistening with sweat, that she stopped being angry and was tempted to laugh. The trouble was, Robert had no sense of humour, at least not where he himself was concerned. He would at once assume that she was laughing at him. Which, in a way,

Katherine supposed that she was. She sat down beside him once more, stifling her amusement.

'I'm sorry,' she said. 'It's just that I'm all ready for dinner, and if you don't hurry and dress we'll be late. You know Madame likes her guests to be in the dining-room at eight o'clock sharp, and it's a quarter to, now. Look, we won't go out this evening. We'll have a drink in the hotel bar and an early night.'

His good humour restored by her apology, Robert kissed her and began to dress.

'OK,' he answered, grinning. 'Don't expect to get too much sleep. And not just because of those bloody drills, either!' he added viciously as, outside in the street, the night shift took over.

Henry sat up in bed, looking with distaste at the woman beside him. She lay flat on her back, her legs still spread, her mouth slack. She was snoring. Henry slid from under the bedclothes, pulled on his dressing-gown and padded across the little hallway to the kitchen. He lit a burner on the gas-stove and started to percolate coffee.

The dim light of a February morning was rimming the windows, faint and ghostly in the still darkened room. He flung back the curtains with an impatient gesture and looked out on the grey deserted streets of a London Sunday. He switched on two bars of an electric fire, wondering how long it would be before the English woke up to the benefits of central heating. He warmed his cold hands, continuing to stare out of the window, seeing nothing.

There was an emptiness in his life. He needed a woman of his own: one who would be a companion to him and the mother of his children. This procession of one-night stands – girls he'd taken out for the evening from the office, even prostitutes, like the one in his bed at present, picked up, on the spur of the moment, in Piccadilly – was all very well. He had been having that sort of casual sex since he was an adolescent, and it had taught him how to be an expert lover. But he was twenty-seven years of age now. He wanted to settle down.

Then, why didn't he? He had met several eligible girls at the various parties to which he had been invited; one in particular had been eminently suitable, her father being on the board of Lynton's. A pretty, nubile girl. What was wrong with him that he hadn't been able to fancy her?

The coffee was bubbling under its glass dome. Henry poured a cup and carried it into the bedroom. The girl was awake and sitting up, her round red face still crumpled with sleep, a trickle of saliva staining her chin. Henry looked at her in disgust, but it was a disgust directed more at himself than at her. Many men would have yelled at her to get out, but he refused to lower himself to that level. He put the cup of coffee on the bedside table, beside the money which he had already placed there. The girl's tearful gratitude washed over him and made him feel sick. It was with difficulty that he restrained himself from ordering her out there and then.

'The bathroom's the second door on the left, on the other side of the hall,' he said. 'Don't leave until you're ready.' He returned to the kitchen and sat down at the table to drink his coffee.

He knew perfectly well what was wrong with him; had, in fact, known for some time, ever since the day, a year ago last October, when he had kissed Katherine Grey in the musty-smelling chapel of St Hyacinth. He was in love with her, but she didn't want him. She loved her Scotsman; well enough, at least, to marry him.

Henry heard the front door of the apartment – flat, he supposed he had better learn to call it, now that he was going to become a naturalized Englishman – open and shut, and knew that the woman had gone.

He went back to the bedroom and stripped the bed, tossing the soiled sheets and pillowcases into a corner. Later he would parcel them up to take to the seven-day-a-week cleaners and laundry in the next street.

God! This was a backward country! There were hardly any washing-machines and very few refrigerators. And they were certainly not provided as part of the standard equipment in a furnished apartment. In the shops, where wartime austerity still reigned, they were almost impossible to buy. Luxury goods, the assistants called them, as they regretfully shook their heads. In the States they had been regarded as essentials for decades.

Henry wondered sometimes if he weren't a fool to stay.

'You're going out again?'

Robert's mother was standing in the hall as Katherine came downstairs. Her voice was reproachful.

Katherine tried to keep her voice level. 'I'm going to town to do some shopping.'

It was remarkable how many times during the week Mrs MacNeice was either passing through the hall or standing in her sitting-room doorway as Katherine left or returned to the house. Katherine was sure it was just coincidence: her mother-in-law was much too kind a woman to spy on her intentionally. She simply had an instinct for the comings and goings of other people.

The MacNeices had kept their promise not to interfere. They never visited Robert and Katherine's rooms except by invitation, but it was inevitable, none the less, that they should see a great deal of one another. Katherine was expected to have lunch every Sunday with Robert's parents, downstairs in the family dining room. Robert's sister, Alison, her husband and two children came over from Murray-field to join them for tea. It was equally inevitable that Katherine's childless state, after a whole year of marriage, should be the subject of constant specula-tion. She knew, by the hints Mrs MacNeice dropped and by the whispered conversations conducted by Alison and her mother in the kitchen.

Mrs MacNeice said now, 'Do you think you ought to be going out? Ye're looking a mite peaky. Ye're not, by any chance ... well ... expecting?'

'No,' Katherine answered, holding her temper on a tight rein. 'And I'm feeling perfectly well, thank you, Mother.'

'Oh. I just wondered.' Isabel MacNeice turned to go back into her sitting-room, then hesitated. 'I thought ... I thought I heard you and Rob having a bit of an argument last night. Father and I couldn't help overhearing when we came up to bed. We weren't eavesdropping, you understand.'

'Of course not.' Katherine's tone was neutral. 'It wasn't anything. Just a minor disagreement.'

'Oh? If you say so.' Mrs MacNeice drummed her fingers against the door jamb. 'It sounded a wee bit serious to your father and me.'

The habit she had of referring to her husband as 'your father' set Katherine's teeth on edge. She answered shortly, 'You and Mr MacNeice were mis-taken. It was only a tiff. Is there anything you want me to bring you from town?'

'No, thank you. I get my order delivered every week from MacDougall's. I don't need to keep pop-ping out to the shops. And, anyway, the town will be so crowded with this Festival and all.' Mrs MacNeice snorted disgustedly. 'A daft idea! I give it a few more years and it will die a natural death.'

Katherine smiled, but made no comment. She left the house and walked to the bus stop a few yards along the road. She was well aware that the city centre would be crowded. Last September, when the first Edinburgh Festival had been held, had proved bad enough, with the enormous influx of foreign visitors. This year, now that the event had been better-publicized, it would be even worse. But Katherine could not stay indoors on such a lovely afternoon. She would go mad with boredom. She must do something.

She wanted to work: it had been the subject under discussion the previous evening, when Robert's parents had overheard them quarrelling.

'I've told you a million times,' Robert had shouted, 'I won't have my wife working. Your job's home here, looking after me! Now, will you shut up? I want to listen to the wireless. It's "Take It from Here".'

As the voices of Jimmy Edwards, Joy Nichols and Dick Bentley filled the room, Katherine had deliberately walked over to the radio and turned the switch to 'off'. Then she swung round and faced her irate husband.

'We have to discuss this, Rob. It's important. Important for me. I'm bored to death here at home. Two rooms and a small kitchen don't take much cleaning. And I'm not going to sit with your mother all day. Your father has two bakery shops and he's opening another in Glasgow next month. I'm a fully qualified secretary who's had experience with a large company. I can speak and write passable French and Spanish. Do you seriously expect me to believe that there isn't some work he could find for me? That I wouldn't be an asset? It's a family firm, for heaven's sake! And I'm family!'

'You're not working, and that's that!' Robert's voice, from being raised and angry, had sunk to a sulky monotone. 'My mother's never been near the business, not even during the war, when labour was so scarce. What you need, my girl, is to start a family of your own.'

'And I've told you a million times that I'm not having children while we're living with your parents. Not until we have a proper home of our own.'

She remembered how furious Robert had been when he discovered that she had been fitted with a Dutch cap. But he hadn't been able either to bully or persuade her into making love without it. He had not dared tell his mother the real reason why he and Katherine had no children, because he knew exactly what she'd say.

'You should have married a decent Scots lassie, not some hard-boiled English girl from London. These wartime romances seldom work out. I warned you, when you first wrote to say you were engaged.'

Katherine had not mentioned it, either, but only because she felt it was no one's business but their own.

The bus arrived and she got in, finding herself a seat by the window. Poor Robert! She confused him. He couldn't understand her at all. Looking back, it seemed as if these past thirteen months had been nothing but arguments and rows, starting with the tiff they had had in the hotel bedroom on their honeymoon. That had been the moment when she realized that she had made a mistake in marrying Robert, although she hadn't admitted it to herself at the time. In trying to prove her independence to her father, she had sacrificed it to another man; and to a man with whom she was not in love.

Had she ever been in love with Robert? Katherine doubted it now. There had been so much marrying and getting engaged during the war that people had been swept along on the tide. There had been a lot of promiscuity, too, during those six years, but the sexual freedom it had brought for women had proved illusory. It had ended with the VE-Day celebrations. And, indeed, women themselves had been tired of it, and a little shocked by it all. They had flocked home to their domestic duties to such good effect that the previous summer, the summer of 1947, the Ministry of Labour and National Service had been forced to mount a Get-Women-Back-to-Work campaign, with special campaign huts up and down the country. But it hadn't produced any startling results, especially not here, in Scotland.

By the time Katherine got off the bus it had turned warm, and she wished she had worn sandals instead of high-heeled shoes. She walked the length of Princes Street, looking in shop windows at the displays of goods which were being offered to overseas visitors, not only without coupons, but also free of purchase tax. Deciding that everything was too expensive, she crossed the road and wandered along by the railings, idly watching the people in the Princes Street Gardens. She paused by the Scott Monument, trying to decide what to do. She could have a snack at the Brown Derby and go to a film. Both *The Red Shoes* and Olivier's *Hamlet* were showing, and drawing in the Festival crowds. Or she could buy rolls and butter and have a picnic, making the most of the weather. Tomorrow would probably be wet and cold.

A hand gripped her shoulder.

'Katherine? I thought it was you. It's good to see you again.'

She turned, startled, recognizing the voice with its softly accentuated American burr.

'Mr Lynton!' She held out her hand. 'What are you doing in Edinburgh? And it's very good to see *you* again.'

She stumbled over the trite phrases, her heart racing, desperately trying to mask her pleasure. He looked just the same; a little less American, perhaps, in the dark English business suit and conservative tie. But nothing could disguise his energy, his sparkle and totally un-British zest for life. The square face, beneath its thatch of red hair, beamed at her, while the grey eyes, with their fringe of sandy lashes, paid her unspoken compliments. Nevertheless, Katherine was reminded of her first impression of Henry Lynton, almost two years ago. Fire and ice. Instinct warned her that there was a cool brain ticking over inside that fiery head. He was both introvert and extrovert; calculating as well as impulsive. He would know how to build and to destroy.

'What's with this "Mr Lynton"?' he demanded, raising sandy eyebrows. 'I told you before, admittedly without much success, that the name is Hank.'

Katherine laughed. 'I can't call you that. It conjures up visions of skeins of wool.'

'OK. Think of something else. Only I warn you, I can't stand "Henry". It's so terribly formal and dull.'

'I think "Henry" is a lovely name. Or what about "Hal"?'

'"Hal" is a bit medieval, don't you think? "Henry" is fine.' He regarded her, smiling. 'I was hoping we might meet. I remembered, you see, where you lived. I came up yesterday on business, but we finished early, and now I'm on my way to get some lunch. Can you join me, or are you meeting someone?' And without waiting for a reply, he drew her hand through his arm and shepherded her across the road.

5

He took her to the Waverley Hotel and regaled her, very amusingly, with the current office gossip. He also gave her details of last November's Royal Wedding, the King and Queen's Silver Wedding celebrations in April and the first Olympic Games held since the end of the war, which had been staged at Wembley. He made Katherine realize how desperately she missed London.

'It seems to be all play and no work,' she observed tartly, chewing on a leathery piece of steak and wishing she had chosen the haggis.

Henry grinned. 'Do I detect the whiff of sour grapes? You need not have exiled yourself up here, you know. Your father and I both asked you not to. And, anyway, it's not like that at all. I'm rushed off my feet. Uncle Steve is making sure I earn the rather meagre salary that he pays me – this lunch, incidentally, is on expenses – and that I know the industry inside out before he makes me his heir.'

Katherine raised her eyebrows. 'Isn't it settled? I had a letter from one of the girls at Lynton's the other day, saying that everyone knew for certain that your uncle was leaving you his shares; that you'd hold the controlling interest in the firm when he dies.'

Henry put his knife and fork together on his empty plate and shrugged.

'Everyone else may know for certain, but I don't. Uncle Steve has said nothing definite to me.' He considered Katherine from the other side of the small table they were sharing and thought that she looked different. She was plainer than he remembered her, and he was acute enough to attribute the fact to her lack of animation. She was a woman who only blossomed into true prettiness when she was happy. But it was an interesting face, a little like her father's in its strong character and variable expression. She had finished her steak, and he leaned across, covering one of her hands with his. 'You're miserable,' he said. 'The marriage hasn't worked out.' It was not even a question, just a bald statement of fact, and it irritated Katherine.

She jerked her hand from beneath his and snapped, 'Don't do that. Someone who knows Robert and me might be watching. Of course I'm not unhappy. Whatever makes you say that?'

He did not answer her question but turned instead to a passing waitress and ordered two ice creams.

'And brandy with the coffee,' he added. It would help wash away the taste of the meal.

'Are you free this afternoon?' he asked her. 'I don't have to go back until tomorrow. I was given two days to negotiate the new factory site at Musselburgh and I did it in one. And at a lower price than I was instructed to offer. That's the old Yankee charm for you, although I shan't be able to say that much longer. In two months' time I shall be as British as you are, with a nice blue passport signed by Ernest Bevin.' He covered her hand again with his. 'I had intended returning to London this afternoon. I'm booked into a family hotel – I believe that's its description – in Calton Terrace, but it isn't exactly home from home. Now that I've met you, though, I'd like to see something of Edinburgh. The castle, maybe, and Holyrood Palace.'

Katherine hesitated, but this time she didn't withdraw her hand until the waitress brought the ice creams. There was nothing to go home for, after all. There would only be her mother-in-law and a couple of her friends to afternoon tea. Moreover, Robert and his father would not be back until very late. This was the week when they did their autumn stocktaking. There was no radio programme she wanted to hear, except the new daily serial, 'Mrs Dale's Diary'; and she couldn't pretend that it held an instant's allure for her compared with the company of Henry Lynton.

'Very well,' she agreed. She glanced up and suddenly smiled. Her whole appearance changed, lit with an inner radiance. He hadn't been wrong, Henry decided: she was a very attractive woman.

They walked up The Mound and Bank Street to the Royal Mile, a little breeze ruffling the grassy spaces into a vista of silver and green. It was still warm for September, but one or two clouds shuttled busily across the face of the sun. Arthur's Seat shimmered in the afternoon haze.

The castle was packed with visitors, the Americans immediately recognizable by the cameras slung around their necks and the excitement they generated, finding expression in staccato bursts of high-pitched nasal slang. Henry took hold of her hand and Katherine forgot that she was twenty-five years of age – old enough to know better, as Aunt Margery would doubtless have informed her – and wandered through the ancient rooms like any goggle-eyed tourist. It no longer worried her that she might be seen by one of Robert's acquaintances. She had ceased to think about it, happy in a way she had not been for over a year. They looked at the banqueting hall, where the Scottish Parliament had once met, and the ancient regalia of the Scottish kings. Then they strolled through the Lawn Market and the Canongate to Holyrood Palace, stopping at John Knox's house on the way, where Henry bought her Buchan's *Montrose*. It had gold lettering on a dark green binding, but the text was printed on wartime economy paper, and the edges were rough and untrimmed.

'I've always wanted it,' Katherine said, hugging the book to her as if it were some precious manuscript. 'Thank you. I have his *Cromwell*, and I enjoyed it, even though I don't find Buchan easy to read.' She felt like a child who had woken up on Christmas morning to find her stocking overflowing with presents. It was a ridiculous sensation, she told herself firmly. She didn't know what had got into her today.

By the time they had finished with Holyrood, the bright afternoon was slackening towards a cloudier evening. The sky above Salisbury Crags was streaked with mulberry, rose and orange.

'"Crystal tresses in the sky,"' Henry quoted softly. 'Why is it that Shakespeare always has a phrase for everything? And no one has ever managed to say it better.' He took her arm. 'How would you like to come to the movies with me? I want to see *The Red Shoes*.'

'You enjoy ballet?'

'Sure. Why not? Some men do like to watch dancing, you know.'

'Robert wouldn't agree with you. Nor, come to that, would my father.' Again she hesitated, feeling guilty, wondering if her mother-in-law would be worried by her continued absence. She could telephone. She hunted in her bag for two pennies.

'I've met an old friend from London,' Katherine said when, finally, they had discovered an unoccupied phone box and she had dialled the MacNeices' number. 'We're going to the pictures. I shan't be late.'

She hung up before her mother-in-law could raise objections, and reflected virtuously that she had not lied.

The cinema was crowded and stuffy. Katherine

sat beside Henry in the second row of the balcony, their knees touching, but no longer holding hands. She kept hers firmly in her lap, fingering the rough edges of the book. This was madness. She had been married for little more than a year and here she was at the pictures with another man. And it was useless to pretend any more that her feelings for Henry Lynton were platonic; that he was simply a business acquaintance, Stephen Lynton's nephew. She kept remembering the feel of his lips on hers, that day at Chapel Rock, and wanting him to kiss her again. She had never known a man for whom she felt such a sexual attraction, and yet who could also be the perfect friend. They had so many tastes in common that it was a pleasure to be with him. There were no boring silences; nor, even worse, was she made the recipient of tedious anecdotes concerning a way of life in which, shamefully, she had no interest. Shamefully, because it was Robert's way of life: sport and the bakery business. It irritated her, however, that she should feel guilt. Robert had no interest in her pursuits: why, then, should she be expected to involve herself with his? Because she was his wife. It was perfectly simple.

Then she lost herself in the film. The story she dismissed as trite, a little stagey. But the dancing was superb. She had watched Helpmann many times at Covent Garden, partnering Fonteyn and the beautiful red-headed Moira Shearer. But she had never seen Massine on stage.

'It would be marvellous to see him in person,' she said, as she and Henry emerged into the darkness of late evening. She shivered, cold suddenly, after the warmth of the cinema.

'We'll get something to eat.' Henry put his arm around her, pressing her close to his side.

Katherine glanced nervously at her watch. It was half-past nine.

'I really ought to go,' she said, but it was a half-hearted protest.

Henry's embrace tightened. 'Come on. Let's have supper.'

They went to the Brown Derby and had Welsh rarebit and coffee. It was a quiet meal. Both of them seemed subdued. But when they at last found themselves in Princes Street once more, Henry's mood changed. Crowds were gathering on the castle parade for the nightly Tattoo, one of the Festival's most popular features.

'You can't desert me now,' Henry pleaded. 'You can always pick up a taxi at the station. Watch the display with me. I'll keep you warm.'

Katherine was swept along on the tide of his enthusiasm, which had renewed itself at the prospect of prolonging their treat. He was like a little boy, she thought; then recollected the analogy she had made about herself. Perhaps that was the secret of their mutual attraction. They were both children at heart.

There were a few unreserved seats left, and they found places at the end of a row. The castle crouched above them on its rock, its lighted windows embroidering the darkness. Floodlights illuminated the parade and the arch of the ancient gateway. The Tattoo was not the impressive military display which it was to become in later years, but there was Highland dancing and marching to the skirl of the bagpipes. When it was over the people drifted away slowly, as though reluctant to leave the magic behind them.

'Let's walk through the gardens,' Henry suggested, and they moved off along one of the paths.

'I don't suppose I shall see you again,' Katherine remarked after a moment's silence. 'You'll be catching an early train tomorrow morning.'

'Yes.' He said nothing for several seconds, before adding abruptly: 'Why don't you come with me?'

She stopped, trying to see his expression in the darkness. 'You're not serious!'

'Why not? You're not in love with your husband. You're in love with me.'

Katherine knew that it was true. She was in love with Henry Lynton.

"All the more reason why I shouldn't leave Robert. The mistake was mine. I can't let him suffer because I was stupid.'

Henry faced her, gripping her shoulders. From Princes Street came the voices of a man and a woman, laughing and calling goodnight. They sounded happy.

'You mean it would be better to ruin three people's lives rather than risk unpleasantness?' Henry was angry.

'You don't understand. People don't get divorced so easily in this country. The procedure's long and messy. There's a social stigma attached to it. Your uncle wouldn't be pleased. He might even change his mind about making you his heir.'

'Let him!'

But she heard the quaver of uncertainty in his voice and noted his momentary hesitation. Was Henry as much in love with her as she was with him? Or was he one of those who only wanted what they couldn't have? She twisted out of his clasp and ran, stumbling a little on the high-heeled shoes, as fast as she could along the path. The air rasped in her lungs and there was a pain in her side. The next thing she knew, she was outside Waverley station. A solitary taxi was cruising, looking for a fare. She got in and gave the driver her address.

She heard her name shouted as Henry appeared on the forecourt, hot and dishevelled in the glare from the overhead lamps.

'Katherine! Katherine!'

The driver made a move towards the brakes, half-glancing over his shoulder.

'Take no notice,' Katherine ordered; then, as the man still seemed irresolute, snapped: 'Drive on, please! At once! Do you hear me?'

'OK. If ye say so. But yon fellow seems awful insistent.'

The taxi gathered speed. Her last glimpse of Henry was as the car turned into Waterloo Place. He was standing still, looking after her. He seemed forlorn and oddly, for so assured a personality, lost.

'And who was the friend you bumped into?'

Robert was seated on the bed, taking off his socks. His method of undressing, leaving his socks until last, had lately begun to irritate Katherine; but she was well aware that the irritation was symptomatic of a deeper emotion: a compound of guilt and dislike . . . Dislike? Surely that was too strong a word! She was tired and her mind was playing tricks. She was fond of Robert.

'Oh . . . No one you know. I don't think you've ever met him.'

The pronoun slipped out without her being conscious of it. Fortunately, Robert did not appear to notice.

'Someone from London?' He stood up, stretching and yawning.

So far, Robert had uttered no word of reproach for her late return home, nor had he permitted his parents to do so, although Isabel MacNeice had obviously been itching to condemn the extravagance of a taxi. Katherine suddenly felt that she owed her husband the truth and, with as much assumed indifference as she could muster, said, 'Yes. Stephen Lynton's nephew, Henry.'

Robert paused in the act of pulling on his pyjama trousers. 'So it was a man. I thought just now you said "him", but I hoped I was mistaken. Do you mean to say you've been wi' a man all day? Until this late in the evening?'

Katherine went on brushing her hair, now released from its combs and pins and tumbling about her shoulders. The copper strands in it gleamed under the electric light, giving it an almost metallic sheen.

'There's no harm in that, surely?' She laid her brush down gently on the old-fashioned dressing-table, taking care not to damage the plate-glass top. Even the furniture was not their own: their wedding presents were still stored in a Plymouth warehouse. 'It's not as if there's anything between us.' One kiss, that was all, but was that nothing? She recalled its intensity and passion. 'He is Mr Lynton's nephew. I could hardly refuse when he asked me to show him round the city.'

'Of course you could have refused! If you'd wanted to! You don't work for Stephen Lynton any more. You don't have to oblige him.'

Robert finished putting on his pyjamas and came to stand behind her, staring over her shoulder into the mirror. She could see a vein pulsating in his throat.

'Henry Lynton was alone in Edinburgh and wanted to see the sights. He wanted company.' She spoked slowly, patiently, like someone explaining to a fractious child . . . How that comparison with children kept cropping up today. It made her uneasy.

'I don't hold wi' you gallivantin' around wi' another man!' Robert's handsome face was sulky. Katherine accepted wearily that there was going to be a row. There needn't be, if she were willing to be contrite and submissive and say that it would never happen again. But she could not bring herself to do any of those things, and prepared for battle. She had a right to a life of her own.

Then she noticed how exhausted Robert was looking. There were dark circles beneath his eyes and his skin had an unhealthy pallor. He had been working hard for fourteen hours, while she had been enjoying herself. She was trapped, as so often before, by her sense of guilt.

'Rob!' she exclaimed desperately, swivelling round on the stool to face him. 'Find me a job in the firm. Please! If you insist, your father will agree. There's the opening of the Glasgow shop next week. Let me do something to help.'

'No. I've told you, I won't have my wife soiling her hands with the business. Your job is to have children. A couple o' bairns and you won't have time to think of anything else.'

'If that's what you want,' Katherine answered tightly, 'then let's get a place of our own. I'll find it. You won't have to lift a finger. I'll make all the arrangements. I'll go round and do the viewing. I'll get our stuff brought up from Plymouth. Robert? Please!'

He spoke with a chilling finality. 'We can't afford it. My father isn't paying me much – every penny is going to build up the business – but we are living here rent-free. That was part of the agreement when I was demobbed. MacNeice's is going to be big.'

'Then, let me be a part of it!' Katherine cried again, in one last desperate appeal.

'No! No! No! Good God, woman, can't you understand your own language?' He bent forward and very gently encircled her throat with one hand, pushing back her head. 'And no more days out wi' strange men, right? I'll not be made a laughing-stock. Ever! Now come away to bed.'

They made love; or, rather, he made love to her. Katherine was too angry to do more than submit. When it was over, she felt used, without really understanding why. She lay beside Robert staring into the darkness long after he had fallen asleep, and thought of Henry Lynton. She didn't suppose she would ever set eyes on him again.

She saw him ten months later, in the middle of Oxford Street. Someone called her name, and when she turned round there he was, red-haired, oozing strength and vitality. But, as always, she was struck by the contrast of his eyes, those cool grey depths which seemed to weigh her up along with the rest of the world; calculating, knowing, wary.

The past ten months had produced an uneasy truce between her and Robert. It was as though they had tacitly agreed to make no further demands of one another. Robert would let the vexed subject of children alone – temporarily, at least – if she did not mention working. The new shop in Glasgow had opened on time and now another was being planned in Kilmarnock. It meant a lot of hard work for both Robert and his father, and they were away from home until late every evening. Recently there had been overnight trips as well. Katherine had done her best to be patient and to help her mother-in-law around the house. She had spent hours learning how to bottle fruit, make haggis, turn shirt collars and even cuffs; or had simply sat and listened to the gossip of Isabel MacNeice and her cronies. She started knitting, complicated Fair Isle patterns, to stop herself going crazy with boredom.

So when Robert announced that he was going to London for the last two days of July, Katherine insisted on accompanying him.

'I haven't had a holiday since our honeymoon, Rob. I need a change.'

'It's a business trip,' he argued. 'I shall be tied up the whole weekend. An old friend of Father's is thinking of putting a considerable amount of money into the firm, if I can convince him it's a sound investment. You'll hardly see me. You'll be lonely in a strange hotel.'

'Rob,' she answered, dangerously calm, 'London is

71

my second home. I shall be far less lonely there than I am here, in Edinburgh. I'm coming with you.'

After a great deal of further argument, in which his mother took his part, Robert, at the very last minute, relented.

'But don't blame me if you're bored and lonely.'

Words failing her, Katherine went upstairs to pack. As she transferred stockings from the dressing-table drawer to her case, she saw a corner of her passport protruding from beneath a pile of hand-kerchiefs. Idly she picked it up, turning it over in her hands, thinking of holidays spent abroad before she married Robert. On a totally inexplicable impulse she dropped the passport into her case, tucking it between two dresses. On the overnight journey south, jolted awake in her sleeping-berth, she recol-lected her senseless action and wondered what on earth had prompted her to do it. But by the time the train reached King's Cross the following morning she had forgotten all about it.

Robert left her to settle in at the small, eminently respectable hotel just off Bedford Square, and set out at once for Fulham.

'I shan't be back until late,' he said. 'Mr MacFar-lane will probably ask me to stay to dinner. I did warn you that you'd be on your own. Don't wait up.'

Katherine had coffee in the hotel lounge before going out to look at the shops. Clothes rationing had ended the previous January, and she hoped to find an inexpensive version of the military-style travelling coat shown by Pierre Balmain in his spring collection. She wondered if there might be something in Marks & Spencer . . .

'Katherine.' Henry Lynton stood, holding her hand, smiling into her eyes. 'What the hell are you doing in London?'

She stammered, 'Rob-Robert's here on business. I . . . I came with him.' She explained the circumstances as briefly as she could. She did not want to talk about her husband. She just wanted to remain holding Henry Lynton's hand. She realized that, subconsciously, this meeting was what she'd been hoping for, praying for; the real reason why she had been so insistent about coming to London.

Henry released her and consulted his watch. 'Have lunch with me.' He grinned. 'I think we've been here before. I get a sense of *déjà vu.*' He regarded her thoughtfully, no longer smiling. 'This time, I promise you, you won't have a chance to run away from me.'

'I don't want to,' Katherine answered breathlessly. 'I don't want to run away from you ever again.' What was she saying? The words seemed to have a life of their own.

'Good. And I have a couple of tickets for Covent Garden tonight. The Ballets Russes de Monte Carlo. Will you come? Hightower, Riabouchinska, Eglevsky – Massine. You told me you always wanted to see Massine in person. Now's your chance. The friend who was coming with me', he added hastily, 'has been taken ill.' A quick telephone call, announcing his own indisposition, would solve that problem. He didn't even like the girl he had asked to go with him. 'It's the last performance tonight. It will be an occasion. End of the season. What do you say? Will you come?'

This time, Katherine did not even have to think twice.

'Of course I'll come,' she told him.

6

After the ninth curtain call, the Covent Garden orchestra packed up and went home. The audience stayed on, standing and clapping, apparently tireless. Londoners, starved of visiting companies for the six years of the war, were now insatiable for everything that came their way. Tonight's ballet programme, which had ended with *Le Beau Danube*, had held them enthralled from start to finish. Katherine turned to smile at Henry, who was stamping his feet with complete abandon. He returned her smile and started to cheer. The people around them joined in.

At last the curtains parted yet again and Massine and Riabouchinska came on stage, half-dressed for the street. Massine wore grey trousers and an open-necked shirt, Riabouchinska a grey flannel suit and white blouse, her fair hair tumbling in profusion over her shoulders. With tears in their eyes, they thanked the audience for the very last time and begged them to go home and empty the theatre. The manager appeared to endorse their pleas. Finally, laughing, grumbling good-naturedly, the audience complied. People streamed out into Covent Garden market where a few stall-holders were just beginning to set up for their night's work.

Henry took Katherine's elbow and steered her in the direction of a café which stayed open until two in the morning. Light spilled from the door and windows, slabbing the paving stones with gold. He ordered tea and found them a corner table, where they had a view of the still slowly dispersing Opera House crowd.

'Thank you,' Katherine said, sipping the scalding hot liquid from a chipped white china mug. 'That was an evening I shall remember as long as I live.' She lowered her eyes, concentrating on the swirl of milk floating greasily on the top of her tea. 'I'm only sorry it had to end.'

'So am I,' Henry answered. There was silence for a minute or two; then he added, 'I'm going to Switzerland tomorrow. I'm seeing some clients on Tuesday, in Lucerne. An agricultural consortium, interested in our new chemical fertilizer. Romantic, isn't it?'

'It's not a romantic business,' Katherine answered, but absently. Her thoughts were racing, going round in circles, forcing her into a decision. She remembered the passport in her case; and the impulse which had made her bring it no longer seemed irrational, but invested with significance. Until this moment, she had never believed in Fate: the divinity which, according to Shakespeare, shaped men's ends. Now, suddenly, she wasn't so sure. She clenched the mug handle until her knuckles showed white. She made up her mind.

'Would you take me with you?' she asked. 'I've decided. I'm leaving Rob. I'm not going back to Scotland with him tomorrow.'

Henry glanced up, startled. 'You mean that? Truly?'

'Yes. I shall leave him, anyway. But I'd like to go with you, to Switzerland. I realize it won't be for very long, but it would make the gesture more final, somehow. Make him accept that I'm in earnest. That is, if you want me.'

'You know I do.' He reached out and took her hand, raising it to his lips. It seemed, at the moment, the appropriate romantic behaviour. 'But what about Robert?'

'I'll go back to the hotel – I have to collect my

things – and tell him either tonight or tomorrow morning.'

'I'd better come with you,' Henry suggested, but was relieved when Katherine shook her head.

'He might be asleep when I get in. And it's something I have to do myself. It's my problem. There's no reason why you should be involved.'

'There's every reason. I love you. I asked you to leave him once before, remember?'

'Yes. I ran away from you. I told you I wouldn't do that again, and I'm keeping my promise. This time I'm running away *with* you, instead.' Katherine finished her tea and stood up, pulling on a fur jacket over her pale blue dress. 'What time does the boat train leave tomorrow?'

'Four o'clock from Victoria station, travelling overnight. Newhaven – Dieppe. It's cheaper that way.' Henry gave a mirthless grin. 'Uncle Steve doesn't believe in wasting his shekels.'

'That's why he's rich.'

'Not as rich as he could be. He practises false economies which don't impress his customers.' Henry got to his feet. 'Let's find you a taxi.'

They walked hand in hand as far as St Martin's Lane, the magic of the evening still hanging about them like an invisible cloak. Katherine's decision and Henry's unprotesting acceptance of it were part of the unreality. They picked up a taxi outside the Coliseum and Henry got in with her.

'I'll come as far as your hotel.'

He kissed her and they clung together, murmuring endearments. Henry asked, 'You're sure of this? You're sure you know what you're doing?'

Katherine nodded. 'I'm positive. I should never have married Robert, not after I'd met you. I was just trying to prove something to my father: that I knew my own mind, I suppose. In the end, all I've done is show him that I'm just a silly vacillating woman. He

76

won't like that. He always thought that I was somehow different.'

But after he had seen her safely into her hotel and
the taxi had moved off again in the direction of
Marble Arch, Henry, leaning back in his seat, watching the dazzle of neon lights beyond the window,
realized that Katherine was different. She was a
woman who, having made a mistake, was not only
prepared to admit it, but was also willing to remedy
the situation. It argued a strong personality and a lack
of regard for convention, which might be expected in
her father's daughter.

Henry knew a moment's deep unease. Did he
want a wife with a personality as strong as his own?
Might it not lead to trouble and complications later
on? But he suppressed the thought as he let himself
into his empty flat, going through to his lonely
bedroom and the half-packed travelling case on the
floor. What was certain was his desire for Katherine
Grey: he had been attracted to her from their very
first meeting. Furthermore, she had reserves of confidence and strength upon which he could draw in the
continuing tussle with his uncle over his claim to the
Lynton inheritance. And Stephen was fond of his ex-
secretary, whom he had known even as a child. The
families were linked for two generations, even if it
were only on the basis of employer and employee.

Henry got into bed and switched off the light,
imagining how it would be to have Katherine lying
beside him. He thought of her long elegant legs, her
full breasts and soft skin. Desire overwhelmed him.
He stretched luxuriously in the darkness.

Katherine switched on the light, sensing that the
room was empty. Robert had not yet returned. She
glanced at her watch and saw that it was a quarter to
twelve. Unless Robert came in soon, she would have
to postpone telling him of her decision until the

morning. Perhaps it was just as well, as they had to share a bed for the night.

It was too late to bath and, in any case, the hotel rules informed her that there was no hot water after eleven o'clock. Many wartime economies were still in practice. The water, however, remained tepid, and Katherine ran some into the basin, then stripped and washed. That, too, was a legacy from the war years: an ability to use the minimum of everything to the maximum effect. As she came through from the bathroom, wearing only the Chinese silk kimono which had belonged to her mother, the door opened and Robert appeared.

It was at once obvious that he was drunk. He moved noisily, bumping into the furniture. His eyes were glazed, his speech slurred. He sat down abruptly on the bed.

'Clin . . . Clinshed deal . . . Mac . . . Mac . . .'

'Mr MacFarlane?' she suggested coldly, and Robert nodded.

'Him . . . Very hosh . . . pitable fellow.' He took a deep breath and with a superhuman effort brought his straying senses a little more under control. He managed to focus his eyes, taking in the fact that Katherine was naked beneath the Chinese silk. The realization seemed to sober him even further. He got up and began weaving his way around the bed.

Katherine slipped off the kimono and reached hurriedly for her pyjamas.

'Stay away, Rob! I'm not in the mood. There's something I have to tell you.'

Her words didn't register. Robert grabbed for her, pushing her down on the bed. His breath reeked of whisky and she twisted her face away from his, as she tried to fight him off.

'No, Robert! No, I tell you! Stop it!'

Her resistance only inflamed him further and his weight pinioned her beneath him. No matter how hard she struggled, Katherine was unable to free herself.

'You're ... my wife. You do ... ash ... you're told.'

Katherine began to panic. The last thing she had envisaged was Robert making love to her tonight. For one thing, she wasn't prepared, and for another – a far more important reason – she was leaving him in the morning for another man. It was a horrible situation. She should never have come back tonight. She should have returned with Henry to his flat and waited to tell Robert until the morning. Her one hope was that he was too drunk to manage it, but she soon discovered that she had underestimated her husband. After a while she ceased struggling and lay still, realizing that she had no option but to submit. The less fuss she made, the sooner it would be over. Robert had never before forced her to make love against her will, and the experience frightened her. After it was over, it made her feel dirty, despoiled and slightly sick ...

She managed to crawl from beneath Robert's now slack body and make her way to the bathroom. This time she ran the bath full of cold water and plunged in, regardless of the shock to her system and chattering teeth. There was something healing, as well as cleansing, in the icy ripples which lapped against her shrinking flesh. Then she got out, dried herself, put on her pyjamas and the silk kimono and went back into the bedroom.

Robert was still lying across the bed where she had left him, his mouth open, snoring loudly. Katherine was shivering uncontrollably, but not from the effects of her bath. The cold water and rough towelling had left her skin glowing with warmth. It was the feeling that she had been powerless to prevent what had happened that jangled her nerves. Perhaps her father was right. Perhaps she wasn't the marrying sort. Perhaps she shouldn't be running away with Henry Lynton tomorrow. But women needed men: it was a fact of life. They couldn't really cope on their own. From her earliest years, Katherine had heard what people said about women, like Aunt Margery, who did not marry: a dried-up old maid, a desiccated spinster; 'poor old thing, she'll never know what it's all about'. The prospect of remaining unmarried, of being the object of such pity, worried most women. That was what her father had never properly understood.

Besides, she was in love with Henry Lynton, Katherine reminded herself sharply. She should never have married Robert. She went over and took hold of her husband's legs, managing, after a while, to pull him on to his side of the bed. He muttered a little under his breath, but did not open his eyes. She crawled between the sheets, pushing one of her pillows down beside her.

She hadn't expected to sleep at all, but it was light when she next opened her eyes, and her watch showed that it was half-past six. Robert was still snoring, dead to the world. Katherine dressed, made up her face and packed her case. She wrote a brief note to Robert on a sheet of hotel notepaper, leaving it on the bedside table, where he would see it as soon as he woke. She told him that she was going away with Henry Lynton, but gave no details, other than that their destination was Switzerland. She would write him a longer letter as soon as she returned, telling him where to send the rest of her clothes. She added that her decision had nothing to do with last night, if, that was, he was capable of remembering what had happened. But when she re-read that last remark it sounded too wifely; and already, in her mind, she was distancing herself from Robert. She no longer felt that she had any connection with him. So she tore up the letter and rewrote it, using just the first two paragraphs. Then she put on her jacket, picked up her case and went downstairs.

She asked the girl on the reception desk to get her a taxi, and informed her that Mr MacNeice would be settling the bill later on. At Victoria station, Katherine put her case in the left-luggage office and went to get some breakfast. It was going to be a long day until Henry arrived at four o'clock.

'You're mad,' Henry said with conviction. 'Why, in hell's name, didn't you look me up in the telephone directory and come round to the flat? Why hang around all day, on the station?'

'Because I wanted the beginning of our relationship to coincide with the beginning of this journey.' Katherine indicated the fields and hedges of the English countryside which were flying past the carriage window as the train sped south, on its way to Newhaven.

Henry laughed. 'You're a romantic idiot!' He put his arm around her, ignoring the disapproving glances from the compartment's two other occupants. 'Leaving Robert a note like that, as well! You've been reading too many novels.'

Katherine made no reply, except to snuggle closer to him. For some reason she could not quite fathom, she had decided not to tell Henry all the events of the previous evening. Instinct warned her that he might not believe her account of what had happened. She remembered a boyfriend once saying to her: 'There's no such thing as rape. You can't force a woman who's unwilling.' It was a sentiment she had heard expressed on more than one occasion over the years; and she had been half inclined to believe it herself until last night. So she simply said that Robert had been drunk, and was still too fuddled that morning to understand her.

'I thought it best to get out and away.'

Once more, Henry felt the faintest stirring of unease. He sensed a ruthlessness in Katherine which matched his own. She wouldn't be easy to handle. There could be a titanic clash of wills . . .

Oh, to hell with it! To hell with his doubts and worries! He was crossing bridges long before he came to them. Katherine Grey – he still refused to think of her as Katherine MacNeice – excited him as no other woman had ever done. They had the same tastes, the same interests; they laughed at the same sort of things. He could not envisage a time when he would find her boring. Her decision to come away, and leave Robert, had delighted him. He had beaten her husband in the end, and it gave him a sense of power. Henry Lynton liked to win. He knew how failure and indecision could corrode the soul. He had seen it in his father. Geoffrey Lynton had made up his mind and acted upon it once in his life, when he decided to leave England for the United States; and he had spent the rest of his life looking over his shoulder, wondering if he had done the right thing. Regrets had sapped his will, as no doubt they would have done had he remained at home, debating whether or not he should have emigrated to America. Henry had determined from a very early age to get what he wanted. And what he had wanted since his arrival in London had been Katherine Grey and Lynton's . . .

The Channel crossing was calm and they spent the daylight hours on deck, arriving in Dieppe in the small hours of the morning as fresh as when they boarded the steamer at Newhaven. Katherine had been unable to book a wagon-lit for the train journey, so Henry sat up with her, and they hired two of the pillows brought round by an attendant. They dozed in a corner of the carriage, arms entwined. By the time they reached Basle for breakfast and a change of train, it was August the first and Switzerland's National Day. Already, so early in the morning, children were out singing in the streets, and all the houses were draped with flags and flowers.

They were in Lucerne by lunchtime.

'I'll register you as Mrs Lynton,' Henry said, 'and ask them to change my reservation for a double room.' His eyes glinted at her from beneath his sandy lashes. 'Is that OK?'

Katherine returned his look coolly. 'I shouldn't have come if I hadn't intended going to bed with you.'

Yet again, her directness jarred slightly.

'That's settled, then. After we've eaten I'll change some of my traveller's cheques and your English money. Not more than fifty pounds, remember? That's all we poor English can take abroad. Sometimes I think I'd have done better to have stayed an American.'

'Where would I get fifty pounds?' Katherine demanded, laughing. 'I think I have ten, the month's housekeeping money. And I haven't thanked you yet for paying my fare. This whole adventure is crazy! I've hardly any clothes with me. Just enough for a weekend in London. And what am I going to do when I get back?'

'We'll decide all that later. Meantime, I'll telephone Uncle Steve on Wednesday evening, after dinner, and tell him I'm staying on for a short vacation. He'll be so pleased with the result of my deal with the consortium that he won't raise any objections.'

'You're very sure of yourself,' Katherine objected, as they approached the reception desk. 'Suppose you don't make this deal?'

Henry did not bother to answer, so confident was he of his own capabilities and powers of persuasion.

They were given a room with a large double bed and a balcony overlooking the lake. Katherine went outside and leaned against the iron railing.

It was a brilliant day, as clear and transparent as

a bubble. Sunlight filtered through the trees in the hotel garden, turning each leaf into a quivering pendant of gold. The flowers in the beds had a crystalline quality, and the distant mountains looked as brittle and fragile as blown glass. Knowing how awful summer weather could be in Switzerland, Katherine felt, with unaccustomed superstition, that it was a good augury for the future.

Henry came up behind her and put his arms around her waist. They stood for a moment or two, locked together, looking out over the sun-dappled expanse of water; then he whispered, 'Let's skip lunch. Let's go to bed.'

She knew at once that Henry was a much more effective lover than Robert could ever hope to be. Her husband, in spite of his years in the army, was inexperienced, his sole aim being to gratify his own desire before falling asleep. Latterly, she had not even bothered to fake an orgasm. Robert had never been interested in what she wanted: Henry, on the other hand, needed to satisfy her. She suspected that it reflected adversely on his own image of himself if he failed to please. Before they got into bed she had been scared of disappointing him, but she soon realized that, as with Robert, Henry took the initiative. All he expected of her was for her to submit and allow him to demonstrate his skill.

Afterwards they lay side by side, while Henry smoked one of his American cigarettes, Lucky Strike or Camels, which he preferred to the English varieties.

'Happy?' he asked. 'You're not regretting coming with me, after all?'

'No, of course not.' She rolled on to her stomach and glanced up at him where he sat, propped against the banked-up pillows. 'I've burned my boats, crossed my Rubicon, forded my Delaware. I took a conscious decision to leave Robert. I knew there would be no going back. Robert's not the forgiving type. His ego will be badly bruised by my desertion.'

'Will that be all?'

'Yes,' Katherine asserted confidently. 'If I'd thought for one moment that I should be injuring him in any other way, I should never have come. I suppose the truth is that Robert and I never cared very deeply for one another. We were thrown together by the circumstances of war, and believed that we could maintain the same relationship in peacetime. I think we both knew it wasn't going to work from the beginning. But in Britain it's generally considered better to go on patching up a marriage, however unhappy, rather than cut the knot. As I told you before, divorce is still a dirty word, especially in Scotland.'

Henry nodded, blowing a smoke ring. 'Britain's a backward country, all right. It's about time people realized that it's the twentieth century.'

The remark annoyed Katherine, but her sense of humour forced her to acknowledge that she was hardly in a position to defend the desirability of old-fashioned moral values.

Henry stubbed out his cigarette in the ashtray by the bed and asked,'What do you want to do for the rest of the afternoon?'

Katherine slid her hand along the inside of his thigh and grinned at him provocatively.

'How about what we're doing already?'

Henry clinched his deal with the Swiss consortium and telephoned St John's Wood, as he had promised, on Wednesday evening. Stephen raised no objection to his nephew remaining in Switzerland for a few more days, provided he was back in London the following Tuesday morning.

'You see?' Henry demanded, resuming his seat in the hotel lounge. 'I'm indispensable. I can't be spared beyond next Monday. I thought we'd go up to Engelberg for the rest of the week. I rang the Hotel Titlis early this morning.'

Katherine raised her eyebrows. 'You were very sure of both Mr Lynton and myself. I'm not certain I like that.'

Henry was offended. 'I reckoned you'd be pleased. Most women prefer men to make the arrangements.'

'Do they? Or is that just what men like to think, I wonder?' She realized with horror that she was pushing them to the brink of a quarrel – a tiff, at least – and drew back hurriedly. 'Darling, I was only joking. Honestly!' Of course she had only been joking! Hadn't she? 'Engelberg's in the mountains, isn't it? I'm just sorry it will be for only two or three days.'

Henry was mollified. 'We'll come back again,' he promised, 'on our honeymoon. Meanwhile, let's make the most of the time we have.'

Looking back on those three days in after years, Katherine remembered them as the happiest of her life. She and Henry seemed in perfect accord from the moment they boarded the little train which took them high up in the mountains. They had a room which looked out on to the snow-capped distances of Mount Titlis, and were awakened each morning by the tinkling of cow-bells. They spent their days walking, swimming in the open-air *schwimmbad* or going by ski-lift and cable-car to the mountain lake, the Trübsee. In the evenings, they spent some of their Swiss francs at the local Kursaal, before going back to the hotel and bed.

And for those three nights spent under the roof of the Hotel Titlis, enclosed in one another's arms and the all-embracing silence of the mountains, they achieved a union of mind and body which was almost perfection; a love which flowed from one to the other and back again, full circle. Katherine, packing to leave on Sunday morning, casting a last, lingering glance around the sunfilled room, was shaken by the realization that such moments in life were rare, and would probably never happen again.

PART TWO
1953–1957

A time to be born and a time to die

Ibid.

7

'You can't go on staying here alone,' Katherine complained impatiently. 'I've been worried to death now, for almost ten months. Every time the telephone rings, I think something has happened to you. You could die here in the middle of the night, and no one would be any wiser until Mrs Lake came in, in the morning.'

'If I were dead,' Victor Grey pointed out with asperity, 'it wouldn't matter. Not to me, at any rate.'

'Well, it would matter to me and to Henry! So we're having no more nonsense! This place has to be sold and you're going out to Chapel Rock, where there are people who can look after you. Mr Lynton insists that I move you as soon as possible.'

'I'm not leaving my home!' Victor shouted. He began to gasp for breath, but still managed, somehow, to keep talking. As Katherine hurriedly found one of his tablets and splashed some water into a tumbler, she caught a mumble of: 'Bloated capitalists! Bloody great barn of a place!'

'Reconcile yourself to the idea,' she snapped back, 'because that's where you're going. Unless, of course, you want to spend the rest of your life in the geriatric ward of a hospital?'

Katherine slammed out of her father's bedroom and went to cool off in the garden. For early summer, it was chilly and wet. Queen Elizabeth's coronation, which had taken place three days earlier, on June the second, had been plagued by cold and damp. More rain threatened now from a thunderous sky, looming grey and heavy over the fringe of Dartmoor, and a gleam of pallid sunlight lit the underbelly of a single cloud. Katherine's bad temper, however, did not stem from the poor weather, but from the fact that she was eight months pregnant. Irritability had been the hallmark of her first pregnancy, three years previously when her daughter was born; but at the time, Katherine had attributed it to the awkward circumstances which surrounded the conception and birth. Her divorce from Robert had not been made final until the September of 1950, when Charlotte was already four months old.

That had been a bad time, Katherine reflected, pausing to smell the honeysuckle which ran riot against the back wall of the bungalow. She and Henry, on their return from Switzerland, had found themselves virtual outcasts, condemned by friends and family alike. Stephen Lynton had been outraged by his nephew's behaviour, and for a while Henry had even been in danger of losing his job. His uncle had eventually relented, more for his own sake and the sake of the firm, than for Henry's; a tacit admission that his nephew had become an important factor in his vision of the future of the company. But Stephen had postponed informing Henry of the new will he had made; and even now, after almost three years of exemplary married life, Henry was still in ignorance of his uncle's ultimate intentions.

'The old man's keeping me on probation,' he would snarl at Katherine when he was in one of his despondent moods. 'The carrot and the donkey. We'll probably find, when he dies, that he's left everything to Battersea Dogs' Home.'

Katherine did her best to console her husband, but she had problems of her own. Aunt Margery had refused point-blank to speak to her when she had first visited Plymouth after the divorce, relenting only to say, her eyes brimming with tears, 'How could you, Kate? How could you act in such a way, when your poor dear mother and I always brought you up to behave like a lady? What will all the neighbours think?'

And although Victor Grey had begged his sister not to talk 'like a bloody bourgeoise', he had, nevertheless, made it plain to Katherine that he was far from approving of her conduct.

'You should have stuck it out, my girl,' he had told her grimly. 'You'd made your bed, against all my advice, and you should have made more of an effort to lie in it.'

From Robert and his family there had been a deafening silence. All correspondence between them and her had been carried on by solicitors. One day Katherine had returned home to Henry's flat to find her big travelling case awaiting her in the entrance lobby of the building. All her clothes and belongings were packed neatly inside, but there was no communication of any kind. Not that she had really expected one, or indeed deserved one; but it would have been consoling to have received some word of forgiveness; to know that she had not caused too much havoc. Wryly, she had accused herself of wanting to have her cake and eat it.

She and Henry had been married very quietly at Caxton Hall Register Office just before Christmas of the same year. Apart from two acquaintances of Henry, who had been witnesses, there was no one present but themselves. Charlotte had been left at The Lodge, in the care of a disapproving Mrs Symonds. There had been no honeymoon, and Katherine had settled down to a life of domesticity, looking after Henry and her daughter.

Eighteen months later, however, she was once again growing restless. The urge to do more than simply take care of Charlotte, shop, cook and have the occasional meal with a friend once more possessed her. It occurred to her every now and then that she had merely exchanged one dependency for another. Sunday lunch, downstairs, with Robert's family had become Sunday lunch with Stephen at The Lodge. Evenings spent alone, waiting for Robert to come home from the bakery, had turned into evenings spent with Charlotte, waiting for Henry to return from Lynton House. And when he travelled, he would often be away for nights on end. Katherine had once again proposed that she be allowed to work.

'We could employ a girl to live in, for Charlie. She's nearly two now, Henry, and potty-trained. I don't expect anything as grand as my old job as Stephen's secretary; of course I don't. But there must be something for someone of my experience. Will you ask him?'

'As soon as I get a spare moment,' Henry had agreed with apparent enthusiasm. But the spare moment had never arrived.

'I'm working on it. Leave it to me!' he would protest, whenever Katherine reminded him of his promise.

In February 1952, King George VI died and the country was plunged into mourning. Six months later, Katherine had been devastated by a much more personal loss.

'Your aunt's going to stay for a couple of days with that friend of hers, in Lynmouth,' Victor had informed his daughter over the telephone. 'Do her good. She needs a break. I shall be all right. Mrs Lake from next door will look in each day to see that I'm surviving. It's only for two nights, and Marge is leaving me plenty of food. In fact, the bloody larder looks as if we're already under siege. God knows when she thinks I'm going to eat it all. Most of it will still be here when she gets back.'

But Margery Grey never returned to the bungalow which, for so many years, had been her home. During the night of August the fifteenth, after drenching rain, the West Lyn burst its banks and flooded down the steep hillside on which the town and harbour of Lynton and Lynmouth were built. Everything which stood in its path was swept away by the torrent. Among the many lives lost that night were those of Margery Grey and her friend.

Victor had stubbornly refused to move from the bungalow, and Katherine, realizing the depth of his grief, had tried for a long while not to insist.

'He won't leave Devon,' she had said in answer to Stephen's solicitous enquiries. 'But he ought not to be there on his own, having to rely on a neighbour.'

'He won't come to London,' Henry had put in, lighting one of his uncle's excellent cigars. 'We've all but gone on our knees and begged him.'

Stephen, who had been dining at the flat that evening, shrugged.

'Then, there's no problem. Heaven knows, there's enough room at Chapel Rock for him and half a dozen more. Mrs Hislop will be delighted to have someone other than her husband to look after. And it's only just over the Tamar, after all. As the crow flies, not more than nine or ten miles from Plymouth.'

Katherine had demurred. 'It's very kind of you, but I'm not sure if my father would agree.'

'But surely it's the only answer,' Stephen had argued reasonably. 'He can't, as you say, remain on his own. And you cannot be constantly travelling to and from the West Country in your condition.'

So Henry had already informed his uncle that she was once more pregnant. As she had only told Henry the previous evening, he had not, she reflected, wasted much time. But it was understandable. The one thing which had done most to reconcile Stephen to their marriage had been the prospect of another generation of Lyntons. And this time, both he and Henry would be hoping for a boy.

She had visited her father just after Christmas. It had not been possible to spend the holiday with him, because Stephen had expected them to stay in London, and Henry had been anxious to please his uncle.

'Honey, even if he has left me a controlling interest in the firm, wills can still be changed.' He had kissed her gently. 'I'm only thinking of you and the children. We don't dare risk offending Uncle Steve more than we've done already.'

As Katherine had anticipated, her father had been adamant in his refusal to move to Chapel Rock.

'What the bloody hell would I do in a place like that? I've never been used to it, and neither have you, my girl. You'd have done better to have stuck to someone of your own class. At least that Jock of yours was a common or garden working man.'

'And what do you think Henry is?' she had flared at him. 'Sometimes you make me so angry I could scream. I thought you were all for the classless state. You won't get that by refusing to break through the barriers.'

For once, Victor had been silenced, finding his own arguments turned against him. But it had only made him more intractable about moving.

Katherine had returned to London, defeated.

'We can't force him to sell the bungalow,' she had reported wearily to Henry.

Then, two days ago, Mrs Lake had telephoned to say that Victor was unwell.

'I called the doctor, Mrs Lynton, and he says your father shouldn't be living on his own. I won't shoulder the burden any more, my dear, I won't really! My husband says to tell you I can't do it.'

Katherine had caught the first available train, taking Charlotte with her.

'And don't take no for an answer this time,' Henry

had warned her, as he saw her off at Paddington station.

Katherine had no intention of doing so. Much as it broke her heart to go against her father's wishes, she would get medical authority to back her decision if necessary. She swung on her heel and went back into the house.

Victor flicked his eyes sideways as she entered the room. He was propped up against his pillows, his left arm around Charlotte, who had climbed on to the bed to sit beside him. They were looking at one of her picture books, and Victor was concocting improbable stories, totally at variance with the illustrations' innocuous captions.

'And that little boy there,' he continued, ignoring his daughter's presence, after that single, half-apologetic glance, 'is going to run away to sea, when he's finished that slice of bread and jam he's eating. He's really a changeling, left by fairies, the son of a merman and a princess . . .'

Katherine leaned over and closed the book, provoking a chorus of indignant protests. She picked up Charlotte and carried her to the bedroom across the hall, putting her down in a cot kindly lent by Mrs Lake's daughter.

'It's time for your afternoon rest,' Katherine said firmly, hardening her heart against the tear-stained face lifted so piteously to hers. 'Here's Teddy. Now go to sleep, like a good girl.' She went out, ignoring the furious wails, and returned to her father's bedroom.

'Poor little devil,' Victor commiserated, listening to the crescendo of sound. 'There we both were, minding our own business, keeping one another entertained, when in you sweep like an avenging Fury, and break up our peace. I don't see much of my granddaughter as it is. I should have thought I was entitled to a bit of her company. Entitled to some of her time. I should have thought . . .'

94

Katherine drew up a chair and sat facing him patiently waiting for him to run out of steam. Eventually his voice tailed off and he glared at her, as belligerent as a sulky schoolboy.

'Now,' she said, 'let's discuss your future, shall we? Sensibly and calmly. Try to use that intelligence of yours. Or, at least, some common sense. Mrs Lake isn't willing to continue looking after you, and I can't say that I blame her. You're not her responsibility: you're mine. Chapel Rock is beautiful. It's not grand. It's in too dilapidated a state for that. All right, I know it's quiet, but you'll have more company than you have here. You'll have Mrs Hislop to boss around. And you have Aunt Margery's car.' She saw the quick blink of his eyes at the mention of his sister's name, and went on hastily: 'Knowing Mr Hislop, he'll be only too delighted to drop anything he's doing to take you for a drive. It isn't as though you get out much now. It must be over a year since you saw the centre of Plymouth, or the Hoe. Come on, Dad! Be reasonable. If you won't come to London, there's no alternative.'

He said nothing for a moment, lowering his eyes to contemplate the veined and mottled hands clasped together in his lap. Outside the window an early-flowering rose tossed its fiery head, the petals flying upwards, like sparks on the wind. It was one of those days when everything had an edge to it; neighbouring trees and roof-tops were two-dimensional, paper shapes against a dun-coloured sky.

Victor's answer, when it came, was unexpected. 'Of course,' he murmured, without raising his eyes, 'I could try blackmail.'

'What?' Katherine was bemused. 'What did you say?'

'Blackmail,' Victor replied cheerfully. 'Let me alone, or I'll tell Henry that Charlotte isn't his child.'

There was a long silence. At last Katherine asked

slowly: 'Now, how did you discover that? Everyone says she looks like me.'

'Everyone who didn't know Robert. And that includes your husband. I don't believe they ever met.'

'No, they didn't. But a lot of people, including Stephen Lynton, did meet Rob at some time or another. Many of them came to the wedding.'

Victor wriggled his toes beneath the bedclothes, regarding the agitated counterpane with a detached, unblinking interest. After a while, he transferred his gaze to his daughter.

'Most people only see what they expect to see, and there's no doubt that the child is like you. She has your colour hair, hazel eyes, your mouth. But there's a lot of her father in her, too, if you look for it. That long Scots face, for one thing. And there are fleeting expressions when, just for a second or two, she's the spitting image of Robert. Haven't you ever noticed?'

'Oh, yes, I've noticed.' Katherine took a deep breath. 'That's how I first realized that she wasn't Henry's child. You see, she could have been fathered by either him or Rob. I won't go into the circumstances, mainly because it's none of your damn business.'

'Temper, temper!' admonished Victor. He assumed a falsely hearty American accent. 'Remember, kid, I've got you over a barrel!'

'Oh, shut up, Dad. I'm in no mood for your twists and tricks. Can I take it, then, that you're prepared to tell Henry the truth if I don't agree to let you stay in the bungalow?' She jerked herself clumsily to her feet. 'All right, have it your own way. Die here all alone, if that's what you want. See if I care!'

Victor reached out and grabbed her wrist, just as she was about to flounce out of the room.

'That's enough of that, my girl! You don't really believe I'd squeal to Henry, do you?'

Relief made her crosser than before. 'How do I know what you're capable of? And do stop using that theatrical gangster-movie slang!' Katherine sat down again, manoeuvring herself awkwardly into the least uncomfortable position. The unborn child felt enormous. 'So what do you propose to do?'

Victor sighed pathetically. 'I suppose I'll have to give in. There isn't anywhere else for me to go, except live with you in London, and that would kill me. Or an old people's home, and that would be the death of me, too. I should die of boredom. At least at Chapel Rock I presume I can have my own rooms; my own things. Or some of them. There will be a lot to clear out,' he added menacingly. He resumed his phoney American accent. 'OK, kid! Ya got me!' Their eyes met and he sniffed defiantly. 'All right, all right! But there's no point, is there, in looking like James Cagney if I can't talk like him every now and then? And now that I've agreed to be a good boy,' he went on meekly, 'can I have my granddaughter back?'

Katherine heaved herself cumbrously to her feet. 'I shouldn't really do it. Getting Charlie up again after I've put her down for her nap will undermine my authority for the next few days, at least. But as it's for you . . .' She moved towards the bedroom door.

Her father blew her a kiss. 'Don't worry about your secret. It's safe with me. Just pray the next one's a boy, so that he can carry on the capitalist tradition of Lynton's Chemicals. Come the revolution,' he shouted after her, as she disappeared through the doorway, 'everything will bloody well be state-owned!'

Nicholas Lynton was born at seven o'clock in the evening on the fourth of July, and his safe arrival was celebrated by both his father and his great-uncle in champagne.

'To the future of Lynton's,' Stephen said, raising, his glass.

'To Lynton's,' Henry echoed, doing the same.

He had telephoned his uncle as soon as he heard the news, and had been invited to The Lodge. His protestation that he was on his way to the hospital to see Katherine had been peremptorily dismissed.

'She won't be feeling much like visitors tonight,' Stephen had said. 'And now that you have a son, there's something I want to discuss.'

Henry had arrived within half an hour, driving himself in his Citroën. He had a lifelong passion for French cars.

Stephen motioned him to an armchair and took the one opposite, on the other side of the empty fireplace. The drawing-room was still exactly the same: nothing had been moved or replaced. The windows had recently been cleaned and showed rainbow-coloured smears. Henry glanced expectantly at his uncle.

Stephen placed his glass of barely tasted champagne on the little table beside him. He was as abstemious in his drinking habits as in everything else. It crossed Henry's mind to wonder if his uncle had ever been young. The older man placed his fingertips together in the way that he had, and gently tapped them one against the other.

'I shall come straight to the point,' he said, 'I don't want to waste your time or mine by beating about the bush. I didn't like the circumstances of your marriage, as you very well know, and I did think very long and seriously about my intentions concerning you and the future of the company. However, I have always been fond of Katherine, so I decided – against, I may say, my natural inclinations – to wait and see how the marriage prospered. I know that many people felt that I was condoning immorality; indeed, I felt it keenly myself.'

Prosy old bore, Henry thought savagely. Spare me

the lecture! Just get to the point. But he said nothing, and schooled his features to an appropriate mixture of contrition and humility.

'However, as things have turned out,' Stephen continued, picking up his glass of champagne, then putting it back on the table, untasted, 'you and Katherine have shown that you can behave like responsible adults. Two children in three years – even though Charlotte was born out of wedlock – demonstrates that you have settled down to a regularized and stable married life. I can see that you are both genuinely fond of one another. Your father-in-law is comfortable, I trust, at Chapel Rock? He is being well looked after by the Hislops?'

Henry could have yelled with frustration. Instead, he smiled politely and said, 'Very well. Kate had a letter yesterday morning. Hislop drove Victor all round Plymouth one evening last week to see the Coronation lights and decorations. I understand there's an impressive reproduction, several feet high, of the royal crown on the Hoe. Saint Edward's crown, is that right? You see how English I'm becoming.'

Stephen gave his customary thin smile, which never quite reached his eyes.

'Your knowledge does you credit. But I am sure you will always do everything thoroughly. You are a very ambitious young man. That's one of the reasons that I've decided to make you my heir. I feel the future of the company will be safe in your hands.'

For a moment, Henry was sure that his heart had stopped beating. At last! At last! Relief surged through him, almost making him gasp for air. He tried to appear indifferent, as though his uncle's information had no power to affect him; but his hand was shaking as he lifted his glass. Some of the champagne splashed on to his immaculate flannels. He did not even notice.

'I'm . . . I'm very grateful, sir,' he stammered. He cursed silently. He was behaving like an excited schoolboy who couldn't believe his luck.

Stephen went on, ignoring his nephew's gratitude, 'I should make it clear, however, that your ability is secondary to the fact that you are my own flesh and blood. You are a Lynton. Had Ralph lived, the company would of course have been his. Now it will be yours. Lynton's will be another industrial and commercial dynasty. The name will continue to have meaning and not be just an empty title, once I am dead. That is the most important thing, as far as I am concerned. I trust that it is of equal importance to you.'

8

Henry lay on his back, staring into the darkness. Faintly, through the half-open window, he could hear the late-night traffic as it circled Marble Arch, and the shouts of revellers as they hailed a taxi in nearby Bryanston Street.

Katherine returned, shedding her dressing-gown, and clambered into bed beside him.

'Everything OK?' he asked.

'It is now, I hope.' She pulled the bedclothes over her shoulders. 'I think Nick's teething, but I've got him off to sleep again. Of course Charlie woke up and wanted a drink of water.'

'They need separate rooms.' Henry turned on his side, to face her. 'We ought to think of moving from here.'

'Why?' Katherine was upset. 'I like this flat. It's so central, and we don't miss a garden, what with Hyde Park and Green Park and St James's all within walking distance. And there's the spare room, as soon as Charlie's ready to sleep on her own. I know it's very small, a boxroom, really, but surely we needn't consider moving from here for some years yet.' She propped herself on one elbow. 'Now that Nick's getting on for one and Charlie's four, I was thinking I should soon be able to get someone in to look after them during the day. Oh, not for another year, perhaps, but when Charlie's at school and Nick's a bit older. I should like to get back into the company. I'm not really cut out for Motherhood with a capital M.'

Henry made no reply for a moment or two, then he put out his hand and gently stroked her cheek.

'That's a pity,' he murmured, 'because I think we ought to have another child.'

'What? But ...' Katherine stopped, guiltily. She had so nearly said 'But we have two, already,' before she remembered that Charlotte was not Henry's daughter. He didn't know that, and most of the time nowadays she forgot it herself. The jolt to her conscience when she did recollect was therefore all the greater. Nevertheless, she did not want another child. She could see her life stretching ahead of her in an endless string of pregnancies, constantly trapped.

Guilt surged through her once again. Surely no woman worth the name should regard her children as some kind of prison from which she was seeking escape! Except in the industrial north, women never worked after marriage, but devoted themselves to their husbands and families. Men were the breadwinners; women stayed at home. It was the natural order of things. But it wasn't the way of life her father had brought her up to take for granted; even though, with Victor, Katherine had always recognized the yawning gulf between theory and practice.

'Why do you want another child?' she asked. 'Aren't two sufficient?'

Henry kissed her lightly between the eyes. 'Sure. For us. But I'm thinking of Uncle Steve. He'd like to know that the next generation of Lyntons was secure. He'd like another boy.'

'He'd like ...?' Katherine sat up, words, for the moment, failing her. At last she said more calmly: 'Darling, he's not some medieval dynast. The Lyntons aren't even an old-established family. Dad always maintains that your great-grandfather made his money in very dubious circumstances before he invested in the copper mines. Besides, if you hadn't

102

turned up, what would your uncle have done then? And it took him long enough to decide to make you his heir. If he'd been that keen on preserving the Lynton name, he could have married again and had more sons of his own.'

Damn, thought Henry. He had handled that badly. It had been a mistake using Stephen as an excuse. But he liked the life he had now; the life he had never experienced as a boy; the knowledge that Katherine was there, waiting for him, whenever he returned to the flat. He liked the security of a real home: his woman, his children, dinner in the oven, slippers on the hearth. He couldn't bear the thought of a return to that scrambling existence he had led with his father: empty rooms, cold meals, loneliness. He had known when he married Katherine that she was not the cosy, domesticated woman he needed to make his day-dreams come true, but he had thought, he still thought, that he could manage her; remould her ideas. It was just a matter of tact and low cunning.

He put out a hand and smoothed her hair, hoisting himself higher in the bed.

'I'd like to please the old boy,' he wheedled. 'He's done a heck of a lot for me. I've no claim on him, after all. He could have told me to get the hell out, particularly as he doesn't much care for me. He finds me too overpowering.'

Katherine's body relaxed slightly and her attitude became less hostile. She glanced round at him, her face an oval blur in the darkness. A street lamp sent wavering patterns of light across the carpet, but they did not reach as far as the bed. She wasn't fooled for a minute. She knew perfectly well that this desire for another child had nothing to do with Stephen's wishes. But it was flattering to be needed. Robert had never had need of her in any way but one. His closest relationship had been with his father, and then with his mother and sister. She told herself that she was selfish, ungrateful, a wretch. There were many women who would gladly change places with her if they could.

'All right,' she agreed finally. 'If it's what you want, we'll have another baby. But promise me that, should it be a boy, it'll be the last. Surely your uncle', she added ironically, 'must be satisfied with two male heirs.'

Henry drew her down into his arms, his mouth already seeking hers, his left hand cupping her right breast.

'Of course,' he muttered. 'Of course.' Her lips parted under his and he gave himself up to the pleasure of making love. She conceived easily, and another child would keep her occupied for at least three or four years more.

'Well, thank goodness everything's off rationing now, except coal,' Mrs Hislop said, rolling out pastry in a cloud of flour. She gave the sifter another shake, not because her rolling-pin needed it, but because it amused Nicholas, who was strapped in his high chair near the kitchen table, happily watching the proceedings. The housekeeper nodded at Katherine. 'Why ever don't you sit down and take the weight off your feet? You need all the rest you can get when you're pregnant.'

Katherine smiled. 'I'm not tired. And I must fetch Charlie before she wears Dad out. I hope he's not being too much of a burden to you, Mrs Hislop. I appreciate that he can be very awkward.'

Mrs Hislop lined a brown china pie-dish with some of the pastry.

'He's got some queer notions, I'll grant you that, but I don't let 'em bother me. No more does Hislop. Your dad's no trouble, otherwise. And he's got a rare few tales to tell about when he was at sea.' She poured in steak and gravy from the saucepan. 'He's lonely, though, in spite of that television set you gave him. I'm glad you've been able to get down for a bit with the children. A pity Mr Henry wasn't able to come with you, though.'

'He's in America, on business,' Katherine said. 'Mr Lynton keeps him at it.'

'Mmm.' The housekeeper's mouth set in a tight, repressive line, intimating that she could say a great deal if she chose. 'Leave the baby with me,' she suggested, 'if you want to find Miss Charlie. He's no problem. Good as gold, aren't you, my handsome?'

Nicholas smiled angelically, and Katherine, not for the first time, was reminded of her mother. He had the same fragile colouring and soft fine brown hair. His eyes, though, were grey, like Henry's, and he also had the makings of his father's chin. Other than that, however, he was a shy, gentle, trusting child, in love with all the world. It was Charlotte who should have been the boy.

As she pushed open the green baize door into the hall, Katherine could hear her daughter's voice.

'I can see you, Mummy! I can see you! But you can't see me.'

Katherine raised her eyes to the quatrefoil opening to the right of the minstrels' gallery.

'I may not be able to see you,' she retorted, ' but I know where you are and I'm coming to get you.'

As she moved towards the stairs, there was an ear-splitting shriek from above. She turned into the corridor where her father had his bedroom, just in time to see her daughter clamber on to the stone ledge of the chapel window, which someone, either herself or Mrs Hislop, had carelessly left open. Katherine stood still, her heart in her mouth.

'Don't be silly, Charlie. Come down at once.'

The child glanced over her shoulder, laughing, and swayed backwards and forwards on the balls of her feet. Katherine hardly dared to breathe.

'Charlie,' she pleaded, 'get down. Please.'

The response was an even stronger rocking motion. Charlotte seemed to have no concept of fear.

Victor appeared in the doorway of his room, leaning on a stick. The voice which had , in its time, put the terror of God into so many young ratings, spoke now with unmistakable authority.

'Do as your mother tells you, Charlotte, or you'll find yourself on a charge. On deck this moment, my girl!'

Charlotte grimaced, but obeyed immediately, performing a half pirouette on the narrow sill and stepping down into the corridor. Katherine moved like the wind to slam the leaded panes shut, fastening them securely. Then, her fright giving way to anger, she slapped her daughter's legs hard.

'Don't ever do that again! You could have been killed.'

Charlotte's mouth puckered and her eyes filled with tears, but she refused to shed them. She sniffed loudly instead and wiped her nose on the back of one hand, glaring defiance. Katherine stared at her helplessly.

'Don't smack her again,' Victor warned, noting the involuntary twitch of his daughter's right hand. 'She didn't realize she was doing wrong up there. But she was wrong to disobey when she was told to get down. You've punished her for that, so let be. Come to your old grandpa, sweetheart, and I'll read you a story before dinner.'

'Lunch,' Katherine corrected automatically.

'Lunch, then,' her father retorted irritably. 'What the hell does it matter?'

And what, indeed, did it matter? Katherine wondered. She stooped to kiss Charlotte's hot, flushed face. The child, sensing that she was no longer in disgrace, tucked her hand confidingly into her mother's and reverted to the topic which had occupied her waking thoughts for the past few days, to the exclusion of almost every other.

'Will Daddy bring me a present from America, Mummy? Will he? Will he?' She wrinkled her little nose consideringly. 'I hope it's not a doll. I hate dolls. They're so stupid.' The hazel eyes lit up suddenly, and the green flecks in them positively danced. 'P' raps he'll bring me a real machine-gun,' she suggested.

Atlantic City was much the same as Henry remembered it, when he had left for England eight years previously. The long rolling sweep of the Atlantic Ocean, the famous board-walk, the gambling houses, the piers, each offering a variety of entertainment unparalleled almost anywhere else in the world: nothing had changed. How well Henry recalled band concerts on Garden Pier or riding the rolling chairs along the promenade. And it was always warm, even in winter, protected as the city was by the New Jersey pine belt and washed by the Gulf Stream.

People were, perhaps, a little more prosperous, a little better-dressed in the post-war boom, which was already threatening to give way to a recession. Here and there, a nagging doubt, a little uneasiness was creeping in regarding Senator Joseph McCarthy's Communist witch-hunting methods. It was rumoured that the United States Senate was all set to pass a vote of censure on him. But in general, in Atlantic City, as elsewhere in America, there was a feeling that the Cold War was justified; that the Russians were an ever-growing menace to world peace, even more precarious since the end of the three-year Korean war.

'Hell! What did our boys fight and die for?' Jason Clifford demanded, as he and Henry sat over cigars and brandy after dinner. 'I repeat, what, if it wasn't to make the world safe for democracy? My only son' –

he waved his cigar in a brightly glowing arc towards a framed photograph on the polished oak sideboard – 'was killed on Omaha beach during the D-Day landings. If he hadn't been, I shouldn't be talking right now about selling out to your uncle's company. Junior'd have been here, ready to take over from me.' He sipped his brandy, letting the golden liquid roll slowly around his tongue. 'So I'm a hundred per cent behind McCarthy's efforts to rout out all the Commie bastards; sympathizers, fellow travellers, whatever they're called. Whatever they're damned well up to, it stinks, sir, and shouldn't be allowed. We thought 1945 was the end of the fighting, but was it? Hell! Six years later, Korea!' He swallowed more brandy and smiled apologetically. 'Guess I'm boring you. Maisie always says I talk too much.'

'Not at all,' Henry answered politely. 'As a matter of fact, I'm right behind you. I don't see how we could have done anything else but fight the Nazis, but it's a great pity that we had to strengthen Russia's role in world affairs by doing so.' He paused, staring into the flames of the table candelabrum, surprised to discover that he was not merely being diplomatic, but speaking the truth as he saw it. His political opinions were hardening: he was becoming what his father-in-law would stigmatize 'a right-wing Tory'. In the past, he had voted for the Democrats. If he were still an American citizen today, he would be a hard-line Republican.

He recharged his glass from the decanter and raised it in the direction of Jason Clifford.

'Here's to your and Mrs Clifford's happy retirement, and to the successful completion of our deal. I felt confident you'd accept our offer for the South Carolina plant.'

Jason laughed. 'Your uncle's an astute businessman. He won't regret the little extra it's cost him to beat off the other tenders. The name Clifford Chemical Corporation – CCC as it's known over here – is worth every penny for the standing and goodwill it'll bring him.'

Henry said nothing, but thought ruefully of the battle royal he had waged with Stephen and other members of Lynton's board to persuade them to raise the necessary capital. United States expansion was something they were all most reluctant to undertake. They liked to play safe. They were far too cautious, and he had argued with them for hours, returning each night to the flat beaten and exhausted, until finally, one day, by some miracle, he had managed to scrape together a majority vote of one and carry his point.

He had had no such problems persuading the banks to raise the money necessary to ensure the success of the deal. Cliffords was not among the very top rank of the world's chemical producing companies, but it was reputable enough to have attracted some fairly respectable bids. Henry, however, had never had any doubt that the Lynton's offer would secure it. It was the foothold in the States which he had always wanted.

It amused him to sit in Jason Clifford's dining-room, eating his food, smoking his cigars, treated with deference as an equal, and to recall the brief time he had spent as one of the Corporation's lowly and poorly paid salesmen, just before the outbreak of war. Jason Clifford had no idea of this, and Henry had no intention of enlightening him.

The dining-room door opened and Maisie Clifford and her daughter-in-law reappeared, bringing a child with them.

'Janey woke up,' the younger woman explained, 'and remembered she hadn't said goodnight to Grandpa. I'm sorry if we're interrupting an important discussion, but Mother' – she glanced anxiously at the senior Mrs Clifford – ' was sure you wouldn't mind.'

'Of course they won't mind!' Her mother-in-law was a woman of firm opinions. 'All this segregating of the sexes after dinner is ridiculous. And, anyway, they've had more than enough time. I understood there wasn't anything left to discuss in the way of business.'

'Quite right, my love.' Jason beamed at his wife and then at Henry. He held out his arms to the little girl. 'Come and kiss Grandpa goodnight, sweetheart.'

The child went to him at once, winding her thin arms about his neck and snuggling against his dinner jacket. After a moment, she whispered something to him.

Jason grinned. 'You minx!' He looked across the candle-lit table at Henry. 'She'd like to kiss the "nice gentleman" goodnight , as well.'

'I should be honoured,' Henry replied.

Jane Clifford slid off her grandfather's knee and came round the table to stand beside Henry's chair, her eyes on a level with his. She was, he judged, about ten years old, with long fair hair which streamed unbraided down her back, over the shoulders of her high-necked flounced and tucked white cotton nightdress. The effect was quaintly old-fashioned; and the bright light-blue eyes set in the smooth round face above a turned-up nose gave the impression of a china doll. Only the chin, with its hint of strength and underlying stubbornness of will, marred the illusion. Her young body was at present straight and arrow-thin, but there was a promise of latent development.

The arms which slid around Henry's neck were warm, the young lips moist and welcoming. Unprepared, he experienced a strong physical reaction. He was appalled and hastily forestalled her attempt to

110

climb into his lap by leaning forward and resting his elbows on the table.

'I have a little girl at home,' he burbled. 'Charlotte's four. I guess you're a bit older than that.'

'I shall be ten in September,' Jane Clifford answered gravely. 'That's my daddy over there.' She nodded at the photograph. 'I never saw him. He was killed before I was born.'

'I'm sorry.' Henry stared at the rainbow glimmer of light where the candleshine caught the decorative, ballooning side of the brandy glass. 'I didn't know your father, but I was there, as well. At the D-Day landings.'

Her eyes widened, the pupils huge and black, set in their rims of pale blue irises. 'You're a hero, too, then,' she breathed admiringly.

'Well . . .'

'Of course he is! Of course he is!' boomed Jason Clifford. 'Now, off to bed with you, sweetheart. You need your beauty sleep. And if you're ready, Henry, we'll join the ladies in the other room.'

As he spoke, somewhere in the house the telephone began its shrill insistent ring.

Katherine had spent the afternoon with her father and daughter down by the river. Mrs Hislop had readily agreed to look after Nicholas.

'I'll get him to sleep presently, my dear, so don't worry. And Hislop won't be here to keep the poor little mite awake with his chattering.'

Katherine had driven Victor and Charlotte in the Austin, going the long way round by the drive and the asphalted ramp, which led from inside the main gate down to the Tamar. Charlotte was disgusted; much as she loved riding in a car, she loved the delights of the valley garden more.

'Grandpa can't walk very far, you know that,' Katherine had admonished her, when she complained. 'And we don't want to leave him behind, now do we?'

To her surprise, the ready 'No!' which she had anticipated was not immediately forthcoming. Charlotte put her head on one side and weighed the proposition on its merits.

'I suppose he is fun,' she conceded at last.

Far from being offended, Victor roared with laughter.

'She has a very practical turn of mind, that child. Not an ounce of unnecessary sentimentality in her.' When Charlotte had moved out of earshot he added slyly: 'That's the Scot in her, of course. An unsentimental race, the Jocks, for all they're forever crying into their whisky and singing sad songs about their homeland.'

'Be quiet, Dad!' Katherine snapped, knowing from experience what very acute hearing her daughter possessed.

Later in the afternoon, Charlotte again demonstrated her pragmatic approach to life when Katherine described to her how, in the old days, vagrants used to get on top of the lime kilns at night, for warmth, often falling asleep and being overcome by the fumes. They were found in the morning, burned to death.

'Shouldn't have got up there,' Charlotte pronounced, after due consideration. 'Trespassing.' she added.

Her grandfather regarded her fondly. 'She's very intelligent for her age, Kate my girl. Speaks properly, too. None of that baby mush, like "moo-cow". Good vocabulary. She's a credit to us.'

Katherine did not quarrel with his use of the personal pronoun. Although Charlotte saw her grandfather far less often than she did Henry, there was no doubt in her own mind who had the greater influence on her. Charlotte frequently prefixed sentences with the words 'Grandpa says . . .'. She rarely quoted Henry.

They drove back to one of Mrs Hislop's Cornish teas: pasties, just out of the oven, scones, jam and thick, crusty cream. Nicholas welcomed them home with his radiant smile, not seeming to feel the least neglected. When, later, both children had been put to bed, Katherine sat with her father in his room, watching television. After a while, however, the flickering black and white images made her even sleepier than she was already. She kissed Victor goodnight and went to her own room, thankful to tumble into bed.

The ringing of the telephone woke her about three hours later. At first she was not sure what had roused her, but then she saw Mrs Hislop, in a plaid dressing-gown and pink furry slippers, standing in the bedroom doorway.

'It's for you, Mrs Lynton,' she whispered, over-awed. 'From London.'

Katherine went downstairs to the hall. She had not stopped to put anything on her feet and the marble tiles struck coldly. When, finally, she replaced the receiver, she found an anxious Mrs Hislop at her elbow.

'That was Mrs Symonds,' Katherine said slowly. 'The housekeeper in London. Mr Lynton had a heart attack late yesterday evening.'

9

As soon as she entered the bedroom, it was obvious to Katherine that Stephen would not recover. His thin body was wasted to a shadow, and his eyes had a yellow, liverish appearance. His skin, stretched tightly across the framework of fine bones, was almost transparent.

He said, with the ghost of a smile: 'I'm dying, my dear, at last.'

Katherine made no attempt to reassure him, because there was palpably no need. He was glad to be dying; to be joining, as he believed, his wife and Ralph. His happiness was apparent; mind and body were already merging. There had been so much violent death during the war, so much fear, that Katherine had never before realized that death could be either welcome or beautiful: the melting of the flesh into the spirit; the withering of the husk to release the flowering soul. For that reason alone, she thought, all violence was abhorrent: an affront to human dignity and the right to a peaceful death.

Henry would be unable to get home before his uncle died. Mrs Symonds reported that she had telephoned his hotel in Atlantic City just before she had contacted Katherine.

'He wasn't in. Of course, it was much earlier over there; still yesterday evening. But they got in touch with him and he phoned me back. I told him the doctor didn't hold out much hope, and he said he'd return as soon as possible. It's a long way, but thank God for the aeroplane. He wouldn't be here for weeks if he had to come by sea, like in the old days. Do you want some tea? I've made some for the girl and me. It's her day for helping out in the kitchen.'

Katherine was tired. She had hardly slept after the telephone call, and had taken a taxi into Plymouth at some ungodly hour in order to catch the earliest train. The housekeeper's monologue was beginning to irritate her, until she realized with surprise that Mrs Symonds was very upset, and talking was a means of staving off the tears. It had never struck Katherine, in the past, that the woman was fond of her employer; now it occurred to her that the brusque manner could have masked a deep affection. She refused the tea, patted Mrs Symonds's shoulder and went upstairs to see Stephen.

A nurse was with him, but it did not need her gently hopeless shake of the head to tell Katherine what she could so plainly see for herself. She pulled up a chair and sat down by the bed, taking one of the hot dry hands in hers.

Like all the rooms in The Lodge, Stephen's bedroom was oppressively furnished with heavy Victorian pieces, a dark red Axminster carpet with a worn and faded design, and long, thickly lined velvet curtains which shut out the light. After that first sentence, Stephen had lapsed into silence once more. Katherine glanced at her watch and raised her eyebrows at the nurse.

'Not long now,' the woman mouthed, her fingers on the failing pulse. She indicated Katherine's already expanding figure. 'Don't stay, dear, if you don't feel up to it.'

'I'm all right,' Katherine answered. 'I'm over morning sickness. Just increasing discomfort and indigestion now.' But she was aware of exhaustion. At least she hadn't had to cope with Charlotte and

115

Nicholas on the train. Her father and Mrs Hislop had insisted that she leave them both at Chapel Rock.

'Don't talk to me about indigestion!' the nurse was beginning. 'I remember my first . . .'

Stephen stirred suddenly, his hand fluttering under Katherine's like a dry leaf trembling in the wind. He opened his eyes, focusing them with difficulty on her face. He muttered something which she did not catch, so she leaned nearer to him.

'Happy . . .' The word was barely more than a whisper.

'Yes, I know you are.' She squeezed his hand.

He moved his head fretfully on the pillow. 'You . . . happy?'

This time she discerned the faint note of interrogation, and hastened to reassure him. 'Yes, of course. Very happy.'

But was she? Didn't she occasionally feel that the relationship between herself and Henry was beginning, for some unknown reason, to go wrong? Her father was not short of a theory, when she had accidentally let slip her fears to him.

'What can you expect? As far as I can gather, you never met before you married him except in some bloody stupid romantic situation! Chapel Rock, Edinburgh Festival, ballet at Covent Garden, idyllic holiday in Switzerland; it would have made a damn good novel by that woman your mother was forever reading. What was her name? Denise Robins? And there was that other one: Ethel M. Dell.'

She had ignored him at the time, but afterwards had been beset by worries that he could be right.

Stephen was speaking again, the effort beading his forehead with sweat.

'Henry . . .'

'Don't worry,' Katherine soothed. 'He'll be here as soon as he can. He's in America. Remember?'

Through the narrow gap between the curtains,

116

she could see the cedar trees tossing their branches in a sudden gust of wind. The July day had turned stormy, clouds, black and swollen, piled in great bastions beyond a ghostly ridge of light. The nurse got up quietly and switched on the bedside lamp, arranging the shade so that the dying man's eyes were shaded from the glare.

The hand in Katherine's jerked convulsively, and she became aware that Stephen's breathing was growing erratic, increasing and decreasing in volume. A phrase used by Aunt Margery many years ago, when her mother had been so very ill, flashed into Katherine's mind. The Cheyne-Stokes syndrome: she knew that it heralded death . . .

'He's gone,' the nurse said reverently, standing up. She noticed how pale Katherine was looking. 'You go downstairs, dear, and get Mrs Symonds to give you a nice cup of tea. I'll phone the doctor and see to everything here. Just leave it all to me.'

Katherine rose to her feet, staring down at the waxen face, where the familiar features were already melting into anonymity, the death's-head skull protruding through the transparent skin. Half an hour ago, this empty shell had been a man with thoughts, emotions, knowledge. Now nothing! She shivered and turned away.

The funeral was over, and John Morley had just finished reading the will. Apart from a number of personal bequests, Stephen's controlling interest in Lynton's, The Lodge, Chapel Rock and his private fortune were all bequeathed to his nephew with no strings or provisos attached.

'Well,' said Henry, getting up from his armchair and going across to a side table, where Mrs Symonds had placed the whisky and sherry decanters with their appropriate glasses, 'that's that. You'd like a drink, I dare say, John. Reading wills is a thirsty

117

business, especially on a warm day such as this. I trust Morley, Stafford and Browne will continue to act for me, as they did for my uncle.'

'We shall be delighted, of course,' John Morley answered, indicating his preference for whisky.

But Katherine had noticed the quick lift of the solicitor's eyebrows at her husband's use of his Christian name. At Stephen's insistence, Henry had previously avoided the easy first-name familiarity which came naturally to every American. As plainly as if he had uttered the thought aloud, Katherine could tell that John Morley considered Henry had wasted no time before stepping into the dead man's shoes.

She stretched her legs in front of her, slipping further down in her chair, relaxing for the first time in days. The revealing of the contents of the will had been delayed until the guests had departed, and now there were only themselves and John Morley left in the drawing-room. Mrs Symonds had slipped away to start the washing-up as soon as her share in the bequests had been made known to her. The Hislops had not been present, making Victor and the children an excuse to remain at Chapel Rock. They would receive news by post of the two thousand pounds which Stephen had left them.

John Morley sipped his whisky and glanced round the room.

'Will you be moving in here? It needs doing up, of course, but it's an ideal place for children: quiet and plenty of room.'

Katherine smiled sleepily at him. 'My sentiments exactly,' she agreed. 'There's a garden at the back with a tree which would take a swing. It will be splendid.'

'But what about Chapel Rock?' the solicitor went on, while Henry stayed silent. 'It would fetch a very good price, and it's a bit of a white elephant, I should have thought, as far as you two are concerned. The Hislops are retiring age, and now that they have their legacy they'll be able to buy a little bungalow somewhere. There shouldn't be any problems.'

Henry poured himself more whisky and sat down again. If he had felt any sorrow at his uncle's death he was concealing it admirably, thought Katherine. The grey eyes sparkled, and his stocky body, even in its present restful pose, pulsed with barely suppressed energy and life.

'I certainly shan't be getting rid of Chapel Rock,' he said. 'On the contrary, I shall be putting the place to rights as soon as possible. The Hislops, I agree, will eventually have to go, and I shall advertise for a much younger couple. I want it as a showplace: the ancestral home to impress my foreign visitors. Besides, Kate's father lives there now. I couldn't turn him out; and Kate'll want somewhere to take the kids in the summer. Oh, no! I'm certainly not selling Chapel Rock.'

'But . . . It's a bit off the beaten track, surely,' John Morley protested. 'I should have thought a somewhat smaller place in Hampshire or Surrey . . .'

Henry laughed. 'My dear John! What you don't seem to realize is that Lynton's is going to be big.' He repeated the word with a broad grin. 'Big!' His American accent grew more pronounced. 'I intend, eventually, to have my own aeroplane. There are a couple of fields above the house at Chapel Rock which could easily be turned into a landing strip. You see, I've thought it all out. No, it's this place I want to be shot of. I've always disliked it.'

'Henry, no!' Katherine sat up, staring at him in horror. 'Mr Morley's right. Redecorated, with new furniture, this would make a marvellous family home. I agree we can't stay where we are much longer.'

'I have no intention of remaining there. I've

already been to a realtor's, a firm near Piccadilly. And yesterday I went to see an apartment in Park Lane. Honey, you'll love it. A great view of the Serpentine, five bedrooms, two bathrooms; plenty of room for the kids and a maid. From now on, sweetheart, we shall be doing a lot of entertaining. Can you imagine inviting people here?'

Katherine was appalled. She felt the stirrings of resentment. Henry was making it perfectly plain that the money and properties were his; that he would be taking all the decisions; that what she wanted was subordinate to his wishes.

John Morley, sensing the sudden atmosphere, put down his glass and rose to go. He glanced around him.

'I shall be sorry not to be coming here any more. I've grown fond of the old place, over the years. I don't think your uncle would be very happy about your selling it, but of course the house is now yours and you must do what you like with it. Mrs Symonds will be upset.'

Henry saw him out, then returned to the drawing-room and Katherine's silent hostility. He sat down on the arm of her chair and put one arm around her rigid shoulders.

'Honey, I'm sorry I didn't have time to consult you, but the last few days since I've been back from the States have been hectic. I've hardly had a moment even to sleep.'

Katherine said, keeping her voice level, 'I don't want to live in some smart flat, three storeys up, and I'm not a lot of good at entertaining. We've been married for almost four years, so you must know my standard of cooking. Adequate, but far from brilliant. I want a family home, where the children can run wild when they feel like it. I want a garden.'

'A while ago, when I wanted to move, you didn't. You argued that a garden wasn't essential. You had the parks, you said. Well, you'll still have the parks, only nearer.'

'That was when I thought it meant moving out to the suburbs. But we have a house, now. In central London.'

Henry shrugged and got up. 'I'd hardly call St John's Wood central.'

'You're splitting hairs,' she accused him. 'So what do you intend to do with The Lodge? Sell it?'

It had been Henry's plan to do just that, but when he found himself face to face with the necessity of making a decision, he jibbed. It was that damned acquisitive streak again: he could not bring himself to part with the place now that it was finally his.

'I shall let it, as it stands,' he answered, coming to a sudden resolution. 'It should fetch a good rent; and if ever, in the future, we find ourselves in need of it, we can get rid of the tenants at a few weeks' notice.'

That was something, Katherine supposed. They wouldn't have lost the house for ever, and she might, one day, be able to persuade Henry to change his mind. In the mean time, she could foresee alterations in her life which she did not relish. Henry was planning to move into the sort of society of which she knew nothing. Being secretary to the head of Lynton's was not at all the same thing as being married to its boss. Nothing in her upbringing in suburban Plymouth had prepared her for this. Moreover, she could see her prospects of ever working again fading into the realms of the might-have-been. Her role would be played out on a different level: supportive; decorative. Could she have envisaged ever becoming the power behind the throne, she might have reconciled herself to the prospect, but she knew Henry too well to anticipate such an outcome, even for a moment.

She was still in love with him; and she now had two, soon to be three, other people dependent on her – their one sure rock in an increasingly confusing adult world. Freedom for women was a relative matter: there were always the children.

Henry had retired to one of the armchairs and was watching her closely from beneath his half-shut lids. When she did meet his eyes, finally, he began to smile, the puckish grin screwing up his features.

'"There's no art"', he quoted, '"to find the mind's construction in the face." I'm not sure, for once, that Shakespeare hit the nail squarely on the head. Sometimes, my love, your face is like an open book.' He patted his knees invitingly and she went across to sit on his lap. He kissed her. 'You'll be OK,' he reassured her. 'You must buy some new clothes. The bank will advance me as much as I need while I'm waiting for probate. Go to the best. Hartnell. Hardy Amies. Jewellery, too. But I'll help you choose that. Make sure it's a good investment.'

He was like a small child, she thought, as she had once thought about herself, opening a sackful of presents. And what woman could possibly resist such a sight? But she couldn't help recalling another quotation. *I have another duty . . . My duty to myself.* It was a little while before she remembered that it was from Ibsen's *A Doll's House.*

Katherine's second son, Guy, was born on the sixth of January 1955, and there was no doubt that this baby favoured his father. His head was covered with a mass of soft down which showed every sign of rapidly turning red, and his eyes were a pale enough blue to be taken for grey. He weighed almost nine pounds at birth and was immensely strong. All the nurses in the hospital said so.

'Look at the way he grips my finger, the little darling.'

'He has a fine pair of lungs, Mrs Lynton. There's nothing newborn about the way he screams.'

'A very good trencherman,' Sister remarked, adding her mite to the swelling chorus. 'You'd better supplement breast-feeding with plain boiled milk

122

and water, my dear, or that young man's going to wear you out.'

Henry, in spite of being desperately busy, made time to visit her with the other children. Charlotte and Nicholas, however, were less interested in their baby brother than in wandering around the room, investigating the various cupboards.

Henry had insisted on a private nursing home, which had not pleased Katherine, and brought down on her head outraged protests from Victor. It occurred to her now and then, particularly in the long still watches of a hospital night, when she lay wakeful, her eyes tracing patterns of light and shade on the whitewashed ceiling, that she was constantly being pulled two different ways: by her deep affection for her father and her love for her husband. She wondered, sometimes, what it was she wanted for herself.

She and Henry had been installed in the Park Lane flat by the end of the previous October, and the children's evident pleasure in the view of the Serpentine beyond the wide picture windows had gone a long way towards reconciling Katherine to the move. They also now had Magda, a German girl who lived in. Her company during the day compensated Katherine in some measure for the lack of Charlotte, who had started school: a private school, another bone of contention with Victor.

The afternoon before she was due to leave hospital, Katherine was sitting by the window in her room, trying to work up some interest in a newspaper article concerning the proposed Barbican redevelopment scheme, north-east of St Paul's, and failing miserably. The warmth of the radiator was making her as sleepy as her recently fed son, who lay in milky contentment in the cot beside her. The opening of the door made her jump.

'You have a visitor,' the young Irish probationer

announced, her round country face beaming at Katherine from beneath the starched white cap. 'A gentleman,' she added with a smirk.

She disappeared, and standing in her place, his face partially hidden by a large bunch of hothouse flowers, was Robert. He laughed when he saw Katherine's dismayed expression and, coming forward, deposited his bouquet in her lap, holding out his hand.

'I'm in London for the week, on business,' he explained, drawing up a chair and sitting opposite her. 'I saw the notice of your son's birth in *The Times*, so I thought I'd drop in and offer my congratulations, and also tell you that I've married again. I wanted you to know that I no longer bear any ill will.'

'That . . . that's very kind of you, Rob . . . considering everything.' Katherine, recovering from the shock of seeing him, managed to find her voice. She gave an embarrassed laugh. 'And of course congratulations to you, too, on your marriage. Is it . . . is it anyone I know?'

Robert shook his head. 'Sheila's from Aberdeen. I only met her myself seven months ago, when we opened a new shop in the city.'

'Ah! A Scots girl. Your mother must be pleased.'

'She is. And is this the wee laddie?' He got up and peered into the cot at the sleeping Guy. 'He's a fine child. You must be proud of him. You have two others, I believe.'

'Yes.' There was a moment's silence while Robert resumed his seat; then Katherine went on awkwardly, 'Rob, I'm very sorry about what happened. I know that, at the time, you must have hated me.' She paused for a second, but he did not deny it. 'I shouldn't have married you, I accept that now, feeling the way I did about Henry. I wasn't in love with you, and my one consolation – perhaps I should say self-justification – has been that I don't think you

124

were in love with me, either.' She regarded him straitly. 'Were you?'

'No. But I didn't realize it until I met Sheila. That was when I finally lost the bitterness I'd felt towards you; when I finally faced up to the truth that by running off the way you did, you'd done us both a favour. Besides,' he added cheerfully, 'I've been able to learn from my mistakes with you. There's never been any question of Sheila and me living with my parents. I made that clear to them from the outset. And Sheila's expecting a baby.' His grin broadened. 'In six months' time I'm going to be a father.'

Katherine thought guiltily of Charlotte, but it was too late now for confessions. Robert looked happy and prosperous: it would be cruel, as well as foolish, to disturb his peace of mind. As he rose to go, she smiled.

'Thank you for coming to see me, Rob. I'm very grateful and it's more than I deserve. But it's always good to know that one has been forgiven.'

'No point in harbouring animosity,' he answered gruffly.

His features had thickened, but he was still a very good-looking man. His wife no doubt considered herself a very lucky woman, and who was to say that she was wrong? But Katherine had no regrets. She knew for certain, in that moment, that she would never exchange Henry for Robert.

10

Katherine arranged the triple glass of her dressing-table so that she could see her back and observe the fall of the dress in the mirror. The new strapless evening gown, with its full three-quarter-length skirt of black taffeta, embroidered with jet bugle beads, was by Hartnell; the high-heeled black satin shoes by Raine. She still found it difficult to accept such clothes as normal wear, and to come to terms with the outlay of money which they represented.

Henry came up behind her and kissed her bare shoulder.

'You're looking beautiful,' he whispered. 'Mind you wear the diamond necklace.'

Katherine opened the small drawer in the centre of the dressing-table and took out a velvet-covered box. In it she kept her growing collection of jewellery. The narrow rivulet of small matched diamonds had been her coming-home gift after Guy was born. She clasped it round her throat, the late evening sunlight catching the facets.

This isn't really me, she thought. It's someone else pretending to be Katherine Lynton.

Henry, watching her reflection in the mirror, must have recognized some change in her expression, although she would have sworn that she had not moved a muscle.

He pulled her round to face him, exclaiming

impatiently, 'For Christ's sake, Kate! We're wealthy now! I'm a success. Stop feeling guilty and try to enjoy it.'

She laughed and kissed his cheek. 'Does it show that much? I'm sorry. It's just that people like the Claypoles make me nervous.'

'For Pete's sake, why? Beryl Claypole hasn't half your brains.'

Katherine grimaced. 'Maybe not. But her father is first cousin to an earl, and she has what's very important in this country – background! It gives the sort of confidence which has made the English upper classes a byword for rudeness.'

Henry swore. 'Hell's bells! Can't you forget this class thing just for one evening? Beryl and Leo don't frighten me, and God knows I don't have any of your precious background!'

'You have personality and power,' Katherine retorted. 'And whatever your passport says, you're still an American. The combination adds up to a very potent aphrodisiac.'

Henry laughed, pleased, and kissed her again. 'You're the only woman I want to attract,' he protested. 'Anyway, you'll like the Cliffords. Concentrate on them. Tell them what to see when they visit Scotland.'

Katherine went through the connecting door into Guy's room, where Magda was busy changing his nappy. As she entered, the German girl looked up and smiled.

'He's getting big boy.' Magda shook talcum powder with a liberal hand.

'He should be. He's eight months old.' Katherine smoothed the soft red hair. Guy made a grab for her finger.

'Mum-mum-mum,' he gurgled.

'He knows you!' Magda was delighted.

She was such a nice girl, Katherine thought: it was hard to believe that, ten years ago, she would have been the enemy.

Charlotte bounced in, in her nightdress, an unresisting Nicholas in tow. She was tall for her five years, shooting up straight and athletic, like her father. There was so much of Robert in her, if only one looked for it. But the face was almost a mirror image of Katherine's own.

'I want you to be good tonight.' Katherine said. 'There's to be no repetition of last time, mind, Charlie! If there is, you'll be in trouble.'

Charlotte giggled. Three weeks earlier, she had startled Katherine and Henry's guests by wandering into the dining-room stark naked, demanding a drink of water. Katherine, apologizing profusely, had dragged her daughter off to her bedroom.

'I'm warning you, Charlotte,' Katherine continued sternly, 'you're to go to bed and stay there. And don't irritate Nicky. You're tired, aren't you, my poppet?'

Her elder son raised his face trustingly to hers and smiled. Although he had celebrated his second birthday just over a month ago, he was still small and delicate for his age; a thin, fine-drawn child with large limpid eyes that looked upon the world with a kind of wondering detachment. Katherine bent and kissed him.

'Now, remember!' she admonished her daughter as she left the room. 'You're to do exactly as Magda says, and I don't want to hear a peep out of you after you go to bed.'

Katherine crossed the hall to the dining-room, where two white-coated caterers were putting the finishing touches to the table.

'It looks very nice,' she murmured in answer to their greeting. 'Thank you.'

On occasions Katherine would prepare the meal herself, but tonight, with those well-known gourmets, the Claypoles, present, she would not risk it.

The Claypoles and Henry's American business acquaintances, the Cliffords, who were now retired and on a tour of Europe, had been asked for eight o'clock, for eight-thirty dinner. There was still half an hour before they arrived and Katherine wandered over to the window, watching the summer evening crowds in Hyde Park. The August weather had turned hot, bringing the girls out in their colourful bell-skirted cotton dresses, with wide elastic belts that cinched in their waists. The men, for the most part, were in flannels and open-necked shirts, although some of the younger boys sported winkle-picker shoes and long jackets, echoes of the Edwardian look which had been so fashionable a few years earlier.

It was a beautiful apartment, Katherine admitted to herself, glancing around her. She had three splendid children, a husband whom she loved, money, clothes: she ought to be happier than she was. Perhaps she would feel differently when she had fully recovered from Guy's birth. The delivery itself had not been difficult; but, as with Charlotte and Nicholas, she had breast-fed the baby until he was five months old, a process she found extremely tiring. Her sex drive had reached a low ebb, and Henry's overtures met with little response. After a while, accepting the reason for her present indifference, he had ceased to make them and had moved, temporarily and at Katherine's suggestion, into the spare bedroom, so that he would be undisturbed by the night-time feeds. But it was three months now since she had finished breast-feeding, and Henry had made no move to return to her bed. Regaining her strength, Katherine had begun to miss him.

The front doorbell rang, recalling her to her surroundings. She moved into the hall to welcome the first arrivals.

Dinner was over and the three ladies had retired to the drawing-room, leaving the men to their cigars and port. The conversation during the meal had centred mainly on the Princess Margaret–Peter Townsend affair, which was making headlines in all the world's newspapers.

'I know what I'd do,' Beryl Claypole had said, glancing around the table. 'I'd tell the whole lot of them to go to hell! All this fuss because Townsend's divorced! My God! You'd think we were still living in the Stone Age! The Archbishop's an interfering old woman, and I shall tell him so, if ever I get the chance. It was bad enough when they wouldn't let poor old Teddy marry Wallis Simpson, but at least that was twenty years ago.' She had turned the full battery of her charm on Jason Clifford. 'You must think we're a nation of dinosaurs.'

At twenty-eight, Beryl Claypole was a very striking woman, tall, clear-skinned, with very dark hair and blue eyes. Leo Claypole, a pale cipher of a man, whose only claim to attention was his money, regarded his wife with fond indulgence, not seeming to mind her quite open flirtations with other men. Jason Clifford had succumbed early in the evening to Beryl's unashamed advances, and Henry, as usual, seemed to find her amusing. It was some comfort to Katherine to discover, halfway through dinner, that Mrs Clifford did not like her fellow guest any more than Katherine did herself.

In the drawing-room, separated from her admiring audience, Beryl grew restive. She sipped her coffee, eyeing her hostess over the rim of her cup.

'Darling, is that a Hartnell you're wearing? I thought so. He has such bourgeois taste. Those terrible clothes he designs for the Queen! I mean, I ask you! If you want flair, it has to be French. I aways go to the Paris collections.' She gave her high-pitched neigh of laughter, like a startled horse. 'Don't take

130

any notice of me, Katie! You look lovely, you really do. I can quite see that dear old Norman suits some people. A lot of people. You can find copies of his clothes in all the main stores.'

'I think Kate looks very nice indeed,' Mrs Clifford remarked in her slow, appraising way.

Beryl laughed again. 'Darling! That's just what I mean.'

Damn! thought Katherine. Why do I mind so much what this shallow stupid woman says? But she knew that, however much she strove to ignore the blatant rudeness, it left its mark, making her feel inadequate. She wished she had the gift of repartee, that she could give as good as she got, but she had no talent that way. Whenever she tried, she only managed to sound petulant and childish. It was some little consolation to recall that the monstrous Mrs Muspratt in *Brideshead Revisited* had also been called Beryl.

Henry came in, followed by Jason and Leo. Inevitably, after a while, and in spite of Clifford's presence, the conversation drifted to politics and the May general election, when the Conservatives had been returned with a majority of six.

'Never mind.' Beryl laid one hand on Henry's arm. 'They got in, that's the important thing. And now Winnie's resigned at last, we have adorable Anthony at Number Ten. Eden's always been my heart-throb. One of them, anyway.' She glanced provocatively at Henry. 'He's so handsome. Thank God people seem to have recovered from that shocking post-war madness when they voted the Labour party in. Now it's really going to be a new Elizabethan age!'

Katherine suddenly found her tongue, recalling a conversation with her father.

'I hope not,' she snapped. 'It's high time people were educated to regard the state of the economy as an act of government, not as an act of God. The connection between economics and politics is some-

131

thing which, in the past, we have signally failed to learn. That's why Marx and Engels could never get anywhere in this country, in spite of the fact that the conditions in the second half of the last century should have made us ripe for revolution.'

There was a moment's stunned silence, then Beryl raised her eyebrows and smiled.

'Henry darling,' she drawled, 'you didn't tell us that your wife is a Socialist. I do hope you don't catch the bug.'

Henry smiled nervously. 'Oh, Kate's not as red as she sounds, are you, honey? She just likes a good argument occasionally.'

'Sounded like one of those damned working-class Bolshies to me,' said Leo, while Beryl gave her maddening whinny of laughter.

'Perhaps that's because I am working-class,' Katherine rapped back, her colour flaring. 'And let's not forget', she added nastily, seeing the slightly shocked faces of the Cliffords, 'that Americans were the original revolutionaries, for all their recent support of McCarthy.'

She realized guiltily that she had now created the sort of atmosphere which every hostess worth her salt tried to avoid. Henry's face was suffused with blood, and she remembered too late that the bank of which Leo Claypole was president was one of Lynton's chief investors. Damn! she thought. Damn, damn, damn!

But she was unable to retract her words. To do so would be a betrayal of everything Victor had taught her to believe in. She simply had to brazen it out.

It was, oddly enough, Beryl Claypole who came to her rescue, turning the conversation by asking Jason Clifford how long he and his wife would be staying in London, and had they seen Gielgud's awful Japanese production of *King Lear*? It was not out of the goodness of her heart, but merely that she had grown bored with politics as a subject of conversation. The awkward moment passed, however, although it would most certainly not be forgotten. Katherine had only to look at Henry's face to know that.

She was undressing when he came into the bedroom just after midnight. She was sitting on a stool, combing her hair.

'I'm sorry,' she said, twisting round to smile at him. 'I shouldn't have upset your guests.'

'No.' His tone was icy and there was no answering smile. He leaned against the wall with its green and gold Regency striped paper, his arms folded across his chest.

'I've said I'm sorry,' Katherine urged a little desperately. 'I agree it wasn't very polite to put people's backs up, but Beryl Claypole isn't a very polite woman, either. She had been patronizing me and making snide remarks all evening. And surely I'm entitled to my opinions.'

'Not where my business dealings are concerned. Can't you get it through your head, Kate, that wives are supposed to support their husbands? That's very important in the commercial world. We shall be damned lucky if Leo doesn't recommend the bank to pull out of Lynton's.'

'Oh, surely not!' Katherine cried, dismayed. 'Why on earth should he?'

'Because he might think I'm tarred with the same brush as you. The word "Socialism" frightens people like him to death.'

'Rubbish!' she exclaimed stoutly. 'I've never heard such nonsense!'

'Haven't you?' Henry's wrath exploded, having been bottled up for so long. His hand whipped out and caught her across the face. 'Just thank your lucky stars we're not living in the States, or I could find myself before the Un-American Activities Committee.'

Katherine pressed her hand to her smarting cheek, anger welling up inside her.

'Don't ever hit me again,' she told him quietly, 'or I'll walk out of here and I won't come back.'

'Like you did with your first husband, I suppose.' Henry was too furious to consider his words. 'You're very good at walking out on people, aren't you, my dear? I've already been banished from your bedroom.'

Katherine gasped for breath, seizing on the one point she could answer without becoming incoherent.

'I suggested that you use the spare room so that you shouldn't be disturbed while I was feeding Guy. I haven't been feeding him now for three months.'

'And I'm supposed to come running as soon as you click your fingers, is that it? How do you see me, Katherine? As some kind of stud, ready to satisfy your needs as soon as you require me? Let me inform you that there is no shortage of women eager to console lonely men.'

There was a pause before Katherine said tonelessly, 'I see.'

Henry cursed himself silently for letting his temper run away with his tongue.

'Look, Kate,' he said, 'I'm sorry. I didn't mean to let you know. It's just that I can't live like a monk, that's all. I never have been able to. The women don't mean anything. Most were simply call-girls.' He saw her blank look and explained impatiently, 'High-class prostitutes.'

'Really?' Her eyes were like flint. 'Is that what Beryl Claypole does for a hobby?'

It was a complete shot in the dark. Katherine had nothing to go on. Perhaps it was the recollection of that proprietorial hand on Henry's sleeve.

'What . . . What are you implying?' he demanded, but his tone was defensive.

Intuition, instinct, crystallized into certainty.

'I'm saying', Katherine replied, 'that there haven't been any call-girls. Beryl Claypole is your mistress, isn't she?'

'I . . . Yes, all right, she was. But it's over. She soon gets tired of people. All the same, perhaps it's just as well that she's still fond of me and feels that she owes me something. Her influence with Leo might counteract the damage you've caused tonight.' And Henry swung abruptly on his heel, walking out of the room, slamming the door behind him.

The following morning Katherine packed, bundled Magda and the children into one of the cars and drove down to Chapel Rock.

'I told you you shouldn't have married,' Victor observed, with a certain amount of relish. 'But it's done now, and this time you have three children to consider. You'll have to swallow your pride, my girl, and go back to your husband.'

Katherine and her father were sitting in deck chairs on the lawn above the valley garden, with Guy gurgling contentedly in his carry-cot beside them. Magda had taken the two older children for a picnic and Mrs Hislop had gone along to lend a hand. She had been unwell recently, and Katherine had insisted that she take the day off.

'You shouldn't work so hard,' she had chided gently.

The housekeeper sniffed. 'I've worked hard all my life, and I'm not used to doing nothing. Though I suppose I'll have to get used to it after this month, when Hislop and me retire. The builders and decorators are moving in at the beginning of September, and Mr Henry's arranged for a resident nurse to come in and look after your father. Until, that is, the new people arrive.' She had glanced around the kitchen, tears in her faded blue eyes.

'I've always said it was a crying shame to let a

place like this go to rack and ruin, and it's lovely to think Mr Henry's going to have it restored to its former glory. But I'll miss it. A bungalow out at Crownhill won't be the same.'

'You must visit Chapel Rock as often as you like,' Katherine told her, kissing her wrinkled cheek. 'Dad will always be glad to see you. So will the children and I, during the school holidays. I shall instruct the new housekeeper that you and Mr Hislop are to be treated like VIPs.'

Pleased and reassured, Mrs Hislop had seemed almost cheerful when she climbed into the back of the Peugeot with Charlotte, Nicholas and an over-flowing picnic hamper. Her only remaining misgivings were immediate, concerning the advisability of allowing herself to be driven by a foreigner.

'I only hope that Magda knows which side of the road she's on,' she had muttered darkly, adding, 'I've left a cold lunch in the kitchen for you and Mr Grey. Don't worry about Hislop. He'll snatch a bite whenever he comes in.'

Katherine had loaded the washing-machine – installed some months ago, at Henry's insistence – with dirty nappies, then persuaded her father to sit with her out of doors. Victor was looking tired and his breathing was laboured. The small morning-room at the back of the house, on ground-floor level, had recently been converted into a bedroom for him. Even with the Hislops' assistance, he was no longer able to negotiate the stairs.

It was a heavy, windless day of glaring sun which made it imperative that they sit in the shade. Below the neat terraces, beyond the retaining wall, the valley garden was flooded with shadow. Meadow-sweet scented the air and the formal flower-beds blazed with light and colour: the dark, drenched blue of scabious, lilac-budded phlox, the scarlet gash of poppies and the sunset pink and blue of hydrangea bushes. Chapel Rock was going to miss Arthur Hislop, Katherine reflected, leaning back in her deck chair and enjoying the warmth of the day.

After a while, finding his daughter unresponsive, Victor began to doze. Katherine also closed her eyes, watching the bright circles of yellow and orange roll up under her lids. She had been at Chapel Rock now for three days and there had been neither letter nor telephone call from Henry. She wondered what he was doing by himself in London. Or was he by himself? Might he not, in spite of his assurances that his affair with Beryl Claypole was over, have turned to her for consolation? Victor had told Katherine that she was a fool to have left her husband alone at this juncture.

'He'll go back to this Beryl woman as sure as God made little apples, and I don't know that I bloody well blame him!'

Her father had, inevitably, dragged the whole story out of her within twenty-four hours of her arrival, and, as usual, his attitude had been ambivalent. While repeating his theory that she would have been happier as a single woman, he had, in almost the same breath, scolded her for banishing Henry to the spare room on some trumped-up excuse, just because, in his words, she 'wasn't feeling like it'. As long as she was married – and Victor, with unwonted piousness, hoped to God she wasn't going to disgrace the family name by going through the divorce court for a second time – Henry had every right to expect her to be a wife to him in every sense of the word.

'Man', Victor had pronounced sententiously and a little blasphemously, 'does not live by bread alone.'

And Katherine had wondered, not for the first time, about those women who had lined the quayside in New Zealand and about the dusky maidens of Tonga. She suspected that her father had been a less than faithful husband, and had justified his actions

137

by his protracted absences from home. But where had that left her mother? Where, even in 1955, did it leave women in general? Still, she supposed resentfully, bound by the strait-jacket of convention.

Katherine felt furiously angry and hurt by Henry's infidelity, but also responsible, as though she, and not he, were the guilty party. She was still in love with him and the children needed their father. It behoved her, therefore, to try to become more the wife he wanted. But he must get in touch with her; she owed herself at least that much. She would remain at Chapel Rock until he did so; then she remembered that in just over a fortnight's time, the new term would be starting at Charlotte's school . . .

Katherine had been so absorbed in her thoughts that she had heard neither the car's engine nor the crunch of feet on the gravel path which encircled the house. The first she knew of Henry's arrival was his hand pressing her shoulder and his voice softly murmuring her name.

Her eyes opened to see him leaning over the back of her chair.

When she would have spoken, he shook his head and whispered, 'Come for a walk. We don't want to disturb your father.'

Guy was also asleep, so they walked down towards the river, through the valley garden, maintaining silence until they reached the little chapel, set in its cluster of protecting trees. As though obeying some unspoken instruction, Katherine pushed open the door and they went inside.

It was still as musty-smelling and dank as when they had last stood there together, all those years ago. Its peace enveloped them: a benediction; an absolution.

'I'm sorry.' Henry said at last, holding out his hands. 'What I said was unforgivable. It won't happen again. I promise.'

Sensing that his promise referred to more than their quarrel, Katherine answered unsteadily, 'No, no! It was all my fault. I really will try harder to be the sort of wife that you need.'

She was in his arms, his mouth on hers. They clung to one another for a long moment before he picked her up and laid her gently on the ground; and it wasn't until much later that she noticed the hardness of the floor, the scurrying beetles and the drift of last autumn's dead leaves.

11

The following May, Katherine's fourth baby, another boy, was stillborn, and she was warned that she must have no more children.

Unlike the previous three, it had been a difficult pregnancy, and she had been ill with morning sickness until almost the end of the third month. The last few weeks, on her doctor's advice, she had spent in bed, while Magda had coped with the cooking and the children. Mrs Mossop, the daily cleaner, had proved to be worth her weight in gold, so that Katherine had had nothing to do but read and watch television, while growing increasingly bored.

'You'll be all right once you've got the new baby to look after,' Mrs Mossop had encouraged her. 'Just thank your lucky stars, dear, you've got 'elp. Well, I'm orf early today. Grace Kelly's wedding's on the telly and I wouldn't miss that for the world.'

But, a month later, there was no new baby to occupy Katherine's time. Henry insisted she go to Chapel Rock to recover.

'Leave the kids. They're quite capable of doing without you for a week or two. Even Guy. Magda can manage perfectly well.'

Katherine had no doubt of it. She had complete faith in the efficiency of the young German girl. Her only worry was leaving not the sixteen-month-old Guy, but the three-year-old Nicholas. Guy had already shown himself sturdily independent, quite

140

happy to exchange his mother for anyone who was willing to take care of him. He was almost as big as his brother, an early indication that he had inherited his father's physique. He would also be tall. He was going to be a very big man.

Nicholas, on the other hand, remained small and delicate, like Katherine's mother. 'A typical Crozier,' was how Victor described him.

The previous summer, before they returned to London, Henry and Katherine had taken all three children to Plymouth, to see the Sunset Ceremony at Stonehouse Barracks. Charlotte had loved it, hopping up and down in excitement, while Guy, still under eight months old, had sat in his push-chair smiling and beating his little fists up and down in time to the music. But the bugles and drums had terrified Nicholas, who had burst into noisy tears, hiding his face in his mother's skirt.

Katherine's proposal that she take Nicholas to Cornwall with her was scouted by Henry.

'Honey, it's time he learned to do without you. You mustn't namby-pamby him. He's the elder boy. One day he'll have to take over Lynton's.'

So Nicholas, sitting on his mother's bed, watching her pack her case and get ready to leave, hid his sense of loss and betrayal behind the blank mask of his face and did what he had learned to do at a very early age. In moments of stress, he retired into the bolt-hole of his mind.

It was usually pleasant in there, with no Charlotte to plague or make fun of him. He could conjure up the valley garden at Chapel Rock; the water-lily pond and the dovecot. He could scramble along the beloved and familiar paths with no one to scold him because he was getting his clothes torn and dirty. He always pictured sunlight, with the cooing of the doves and the humming of the bees hanging in the bright untroubled air . . .

'I shan't be away long, darling,' Katherine said, kissing him. 'Be a good boy while I'm gone.'

Nicholas flung his thin arms round her neck and clung to her in desperation.

I can't go, Katherine thought wildly. Or I'll have to take him with me.

But she knew how angry Henry would be and felt too weak to risk a scene. Besides, she really did need some time away from the children in order to recover fully.

Magda and the two boys stood at one of the dining-room windows overlooking the street, while Katherine got into the taxi which was to take her to Paddington station. Chapel Rock was too far for her to drive herself, in her present condition. Nicholas, prompted by the German girl, waved his hand and tried not to cry, saving his tears until he was in bed that night, and could stifle his sobs in his teddy bear. Although his sister now had her own room, and Nicholas shared with Guy, he knew from experience that Charlotte had ears like a hawk. If she heard him crying, she would tease him unmercifully in the morning.

Eventually he fell asleep, only to be roused towards dawn by a terrible thirst. The night-light on the bedside table had gone out, but there was a chink of daylight showing between the bedroom curtains. Nicholas wriggled out of bed, taking care not to disturb the sleeping Guy, and made his way to the bathroom. By dint of scrambling on to the lavatory seat, he could reach the cold tap and the tumbler which was kept on the glass shelf over the basin. When he had finished his drink, he toddled back across the darkened hallway. As he did so, the door of Magda's room opened and his father came out, going straight into his own room, next door. Nicholas supposed vaguely that, with Mummy away, Daddy had been lonely or frightened, and visited Magda for company. He had done it himself, often.

Nicholas climbed into bed and pulled up the covers. The little incident was pushed to the back of his mind.

It wouldn't have happened, Henry thought, if he had gone to the Claypoles' or accepted any one of the other half-dozen invitations he had received. There were plenty of people only too willing and eager to entertain him during the two weeks that Katherine was away. Instead, he had told his chauffeur to drive him straight home because he was feeling tired after a particularly protracted board meeting, and he wanted an early night. Magda was cooking herself some supper when he got in.

She had shared it with him, and afterwards they had sat side by side on the living-room couch, watching an American television series called 'I Was a Communist for the FBI'. Henry had fallen asleep in the middle of it, and it was an hour later when he woke to find Magda bending solicitously over him. On the television screen an announcer was previewing the first ever Eurovision Song Contest, to be held on May the twenty-fourth. Eurovision was the current technological miracle of the age.

'You are tired,' Magda said in her accented English.

Henry wondered idly why it was that a foreigner speaking broken English, however badly, was so much more attractive than the reverse. He had smiled sleepily and raised one hand to brush it lightly against Magda's breast. She hadn't flinched or drawn back in alarm and, after that, what followed seemed inevitable.

The truth was, Henry acknowledged, lying in his cold bed and watching the early-morning light sift through the curtains, he needed women. Some men had to have booze or tobacco to offset the pressures of

143

their daily lives: he had to have sex. He had mistakenly assumed that when he married and settled down, one woman would suffice, especially as he was so much in love with that woman. But the relationship of husband and wife, as he had quickly discovered, was far more complicated than straightforward copulation.

Beryl Claypole was not the only woman he had slept with since his marriage; and even while he was promising Katherine that there would be no one else, he had known, deep down, that he was bound to break his promise. He despised himself for making it, but he felt that a peaceful domestic life was worth a lie, just as Henry of Navarre had thought Paris worth a Mass. All the same, he must be careful. It would be better if Magda left. He did not want Katherine to find out.

His anger veered towards his wife. Why could women not be more understanding? Why did they all set such store by marital fidelity? They must know that these casual affairs meant nothing, yet they seemed to feel threatened by them. He supposed it was the maternal instinct: they had to protect the home they had made for their young.

The pendulum of emotion swung again and his annoyance and irritation with Katherine changed once more to self-disgust. He loved Katherine; had loved her since that first meeting ten years ago; went on loving her through all their quarrels and disagreements. And she loved him. Thank God she appeared to have dropped that silly notion of wanting a career: he must not jeopardize the present harmony of their marriage. He must not practise his infidelities so close to home.

Katherine switched off the television and sat staring at the blank screen, where a tiny pinprick of light gradually withered and died.

Harriet Blake, the young nursemaid who had replaced Magda, knocked and entered the living-room.

'The children are all in bed, Mrs Lynton. If it's all right, I'm just popping out to post a letter. I shan't be very long.'

'Yes ... Yes, of course, that's fine. Take the evening off if you want to. Mr Lynton and I have had to cancel our dinner engagement.'

Harriet's plain, homely face creased in concern.

'Is Mr Lynton working late again? It's this nasty Suez crisis, I suppose.' Her lips set in a thin vicious line. 'I hope the Prime Minister sends the troops in. That'd teach those wogs a lesson.'

Katherine blinked, startled. Such blind patriotism in one so young and uninformed had, she supposed, a certain appeal. It would, at all events, have appealed to Henry and every other British businessman who saw part of his livelihood threatened; and it was an undeniable fact that twenty-five per cent of all British exports and imports passed each year through the Suez Canal. When Egypt's Colonel Gamal Abdel Nasser had nationalized it in July, it had caused panic throughout the world, but particularly in France and Great Britain. Henry, certainly, seemed to have spent the last three months in one crisis meeting or another, while the board tried to work out an alternative route by which they could ship their chemical products to the Far East. But even Katherine was able to see, without being told, that such an alternative would be extremely costly as well as causing unacceptable delays.

She got up and crossed to the window, pulling back the curtain and peering out into the miserable October night. The trees in the park stood like wraiths in the mist; people hurried by, huddled into their mackintosh collars, protecting their faces from slanting arrows of rain which stung the flesh. The street lamps stared at their drowned reflections in the puddles, and the noise of cars driving along Park Lane was muted by the glistening wet surface of the road. Katherine shivered and dropped the curtain back into place, turning thankfully to the warmth and light of the living-room.

She curled up, one leg tucked beneath her, in a corner of the big four-seater settee. The room was very modern – Henry's choice – with walls patterned in different papers, the couch and armchairs up-holstered in red and black.

'Chapel Rock's the place for antiques,' he had said, when they had first discussed the furnishings for the Park Lane flat. 'This place has to be bright and up-to-date; a place where people don't feel intimi-dated; a place where they can relax and have fun.'

Katherine had not argued, but she did not share the present obsession for multi-coloured walls and the plain unadorned lines of modern furniture. She had grown up in the nineteen-thirties décor of the Plymouth bungalow, with its uniformity of wallpaper in every room, its picture-rails and dados, its much more ornate sideboards, tables and chairs. She accepted that the flat was smart, but she found it unhomely. Henry laughed at her and told her she was behind the times.

Katherine felt restless tonight, without quite knowing why. She picked up her book, a recently published biography of Richard III, then put it down again. The battle of Towton suddenly seemed irrel-evant. She heard the front door of the flat open and close, and knew that Harriet had come back from posting her letter. She had politely refused the extra night off.

On a sudden impulse Katherine went to look at the children, to see if they wanted a bedtime story, but all three were fast asleep. She wandered aim-lessly back to the living-room and switched on the television set once more. The newsreel commentator was dealing with the second big story of the night, the revolution in Hungary. There were pictures of people singing and dancing in the streets of Budapest. Cardinal Mindszenty had been freed from the prison where he had been held since 1949. Imre Nagy had declared the country a neutral state, like neighbouring Austria. But Russian tanks were massing along the eastern border.

The grainy black and white images faded from the screen, and a moment later viewers were taken over to Downing Street for yet another report on the latest Suez crisis meeting of the Cabinet. Katherine got up and switched off the set for the second time in half an hour. The telephone rang and, when she answered it, it was Henry's secretary, Polly Ogleby, to say not to wait up for him.

'He'll be very late, Mrs Lynton. It'll be coffee and sandwiches in the board-room, I'm afraid. A lot will depend on what the PM has to say in his next statement.'

Katherine hung up with a sense of uselessness and dissatisfaction; of being stranded on the fringe of events. She recalled past crises at Lynton's when, as Stephen's secretary, she had been at the hub of things, just as Polly Ogleby was now. She felt cheated and very, very bored.

Her thoughts veered to Harriet, who had been with them now for nearly four months. When Magda left rather suddenly, in June, Henry had said, 'No more foreigners. They're more trouble than they're worth. Contact one of the agencies for a proper nursemaid. And for God's sake don't choose a good-looking one, or she'll be leaving before we know it to get married.'

At the time, Katherine had merely laughed and thought nothing of it. The fact that Harriet Blake actually was a plain girl had been mere coincidence:

147

her credentials and references had been excellent, which was all that mattered. Now, however, recalling Henry's words, Katherine suddenly found herself wondering why Magda had left so abruptly. It was true that she had offered a perfectly valid reason for her departure – her mother was ill and she had to go home – but Katherine remembered that the German girl, when she said goodbye, had been wearing some very expensive jewellery. The fact, unremarkable until now, suddenly assumed an uneasy significance . . .

'Oh, stop it!' Katherine admonished herself aloud, the sound of her own voice in the otherwise quiet room providing her with a little comfort. 'You're being stupid.' Henry had promised that his affair with Beryl Claypole had been a single instance of self-indulgence; that it would never, ever happen again.

She would telephone Chapel Rock and speak to her father. Victor didn't get on with the new housekeeper, Mrs Godfrey, and her husband as well as he had done with the Hislops. But as there were now two women who came in daily from the village to help clean the house, and a gardener three times a week to give Mr Godfrey a hand, her father saw more people than before and had a larger audience for his stories. He also had a telephone extension in his newly restored and decorated sitting-room.

He was pleased to hear Katherine's voice, but barely did her the courtesy of returning her greeting before launching into a diatribe about Suez.

'Bloody Tories! What are they doing up there in London? Eden's going to involve us in another war, mark my words! Bloody Queen Mary's Gift! Nasser's got every right to nationalize the Suez Canal. All this talk is so much eyewash. Vested capitalist interests, that's what it is, my girl!'

Katherine eventually rang off feeling even more irritated than she had before making the call. Her own opinions were confused and she felt she was being pulled two ways. Being both a dutiful wife and daughter was tearing her apart.

She switched on the radio, but the normal programme had been interrupted with the news that Russian tanks were across the Hungarian border and converging on Budapest. With a sigh, Katherine went back to the battle of Towton and its driving snow. There was a kind of perverse comfort to be had from the knowledge that life had been no better five hundred years ago.

He was tired and hungry and felt as though he had been walking for ever. He sat down under a tree, on the wet, night-shrouded grass, in one corner of a field. The Austrian border could only be a few kilometres to the west, if his calculations were correct, and he would need all his wits about him if he were to get across safely.

Sandor Scott was thirty-six years of age; too old, he thought miserably, to be going into exile, to be leaving his parents, his home, his country; everything he held most dear.

'You must go,' his mother urged, tears running down her cheeks. 'Go to England. It's where your grandfather came from. You may even have relatives there. Papa will tell you. What a blessing you're no longer married. I thought it a tragedy when Agnes died, but God works in mysterious ways.'

His father had come into the room, looking very pale, but otherwise composed, holding a blotched and faded picture-postcard of the Danube in his hand. He passed it to Sandor.

'I found this years ago, after Grandfather died. It was in an old tin trunk in his bedroom. You see it's dated the seventeenth of August 1892, not long after he arrived here. For some reason or another, he never sent it. Perhaps he forgot or changed his mind. But it's addressed to a Miss Jean Lynton, somewhere in London.' János Scott had clasped his son in his arms. 'Your mother is right. You have to go. Like Imre Nagy, you'll be a marked man.' He had smiled through his unshed tears. 'You'll make a new and better life for yourself in the West. You're a qualified man and you speak almost perfect English. You won't find things too difficult. You won't starve.'

No, he wouldn't starve, Sandor thought, staring into the darkness. A research chemist, one quarter English and with a comprehensive command of the language, was a lot better off than thousands of his compatriots who were even now escaping into Austria.

After a while, when he was rested, Sandor eased himself to his feet and, by the dim ray of a small pocket torch, consulted his compass. Then he trudged forward into the next field. He had been walking for days now, with the occasional lift in a car or lorry. Last night he had very nearly run into a police patrol, but had managed to avoid it by plunging thigh-deep into an icy stream and wading along its sandy bed for half a kilometre. His wet clothes had dried on him and were rough and uncomfortable.

Bodily discomfort, however, was easy to bear compared with his anguish of mind. Three years earlier, when Imre Nagy had replaced the hated and feared Mátyás Rákosi as Premier, it had been hoped that the latter's economic policies, which had nearly ruined the country, would be halted. Unfortunately Rákosi had still been head of the Party, and had violently opposed Nagy's reforms, aimed at giving the people more freedom and improving living conditions. Last year, Rákosi had succeeded in forcing Nagy out of the government.

The discontent had steadily increased during the past twelve months until, on October the twenty-third, it had boiled over into open revolution. Imre Nagy had seized power, proclaiming Hungary a nation in her own right, owing loyalty to no other country. For a few days people had fooled themselves that the Kremlin would accept the *fait accompli*; that the impossible had happened. Even Sandor, who had persuaded his fellow laboratory workers to declare their support of the new government, had allowed himself, at first, to believe it. But not for long. In his heart of hearts, he had known that Khrushchev could not, and would not, let it happen.

Sandor wondered what had become of Cardinal Mindszenty. Someone had told him that the priest had taken refuge in the United States Legation, and he hoped to God it was true. There would be no mercy shown to the ringleaders and architects of the uprising. Imre Nagy was as good as dead.

The realization that, once across the border, he would be a refugee hit Sandor with all the force of a blow to the solar plexus. If he managed to get out of Hungary alive, he would be dependent on other people's charity and goodwill. He hesitated a moment, not sure that he could go on, and glanced back across his shoulder. But if he returned to Budapest he would be rounded up and shot, and he had never had that kind of physical courage. Moreover, it would kill his mother.

He set his face resolutely to the west and went on walking.

12

'Who's he bringing down here this time?' Victor asked morosely. 'There's always someone or other coming to stay.'

'You know that's not true,' Katherine protested, laughing, pausing in her arrangement of a vase of spring flowers. 'Henry hasn't used Chapel Rock nearly as much as he thought he was going to.'

Victor thrust out his lower lip like a sulky school-boy and eased himself deeper into his armchair.

'There was that American couple who were here last year. What's their name again? Clifford? They stayed here for two months last summer. The child was all right. Jane she was called. I got on quite well with her. Then Henry came down with a couple of business acquaintances in November, just after the Suez crisis ended.' Victor grew querulous. 'It's not the same as being in my own home, Kate.'

She put the last daffodil in place and went to sit beside him, perching on the arm of his chair.

'Darling, we've been through all this before. Surely living here is far better than being in a hospital or a nursing home?' She hugged his thin shoulders. 'Come on! Admit it! Most of the time it's just you and the Godfreys. This whole great house and beautiful garden! You have all the privacy you want. And in the school holidays, like now, the children and I can be with you all the time. Henry and Mr Scott will only be here for the Easter weekend.'

Victor frowned. 'Scott? I thought you said this chap was Hungarian!'

'He is, but his grandfather was English. Came from up north originally, I think Henry said. Somewhere near Berwick-on-Tweed. Anyway, at some point when he was working in London – the grandfather, that is – he met Jean Lynton, Stephen's aunt – Henry's great-aunt – fell in love with her and persuaded her to get engaged. Her brother, old Joshua Lynton, didn't think the young man was good enough for her and broke up the romance. Sandor's grandfather, who was an engineer, went off to do some work in Budapest, met a Hungarian girl, married her and stayed. Henry knew all the details because his father had told him the story at some time or another, to illustrate the sort of family attitudes he'd had to contend with.'

'That sounds like old Josh Lynton,' Victor agreed. 'I've heard your mother say many times that he was a stiff-necked narrow-minded old bastard. Couldn't ever forget, I suppose, that the Lyntons came from nothing and nowhere themselves. So what happened?'

'How did Sandor Scott come to get in touch with Henry, you mean? As far as I can gather, just before Sandor left Hungary, his father gave him a postcard which he'd found among the grandfather's things, after the old man died. It was addressed to Jean Lynton at The Lodge, but had never been sent. There was nothing apparently to indicate what the relationship had been; it just said that the grandfather had arrived safely in Budapest. However, it was a tenuous link with this country, so when Sandor finally arrived here from Austria he went to The Lodge, and the present tenants put him in touch with Henry. And, as I said, Henry knew the story and was able to fill in the background. And when he discovered that Sandor was a research chemist, of course he immediately offered him a job. Maybe that's simplifying matters in a firm the size of Lynton's, but the upshot is that Sandor Scott is now at the Southampton lab and fast becoming extremely important. But, more than that, he's also become Henry's friend.' Katherine smiled, watching the shadows of the flowers etch themselves on the pale yellow wallpaper. 'I don't think Henry's ever had a close friend before. And Sandor, although he speaks beautiful English, is homesick and lonely. Whenever time and distance permit, they're practically living in one another's pockets,' Katherine stood up, smoothing down her skirt. 'They're the same age. It was a foregone conclusion, as far as I was concerned, that Henry would ask Sandor here for the Easter weekend.' She crossed to the window. 'It looks as though this glorious weather's going to last. Do you feel like joining the children in the garden?'

She could hear Guy and Charlotte's excited voices as soon as they got outside. Guy, now over two years old, was toddling around the flowerbeds, followed by an anxious Harriet. Charlotte, at seven, was more coltish than ever, her thin wiry body clad in shorts and a T-shirt. She hated dresses and dressing up as cordially as she disliked dolls and doll's prams. At the moment she was halfway up a tree, investigating an abandoned bird's nest.

Nicholas, always the odd one out, was curled up on a garden seat reading Beatrix Potter. Not yet four, he was already capable of entertaining himself for hours at a stretch.

'It's not natural,' Victor would grunt, eyeing his elder grandson askance.

He glanced at him now, as Katherine helped him to sit beside Nicholas, but he forbore to comment. The child looked up and smiled seraphically, then buried his nose once more in his book.

It was very warm for the time of year. The grass was dotted with periwinkles, like a galaxy of pale blue stars. Hawthorn foamed along the retaining wall; and although the crocuses were now cold and ashen, in their place were carpets of primroses and buttercups, golden plunder for the delighted Guy to gather with his fat dimpled hands. A blackbird shouted from the branches of a nearby tree. Katherine lifted her face to the late April sun and stretched luxuriously.

'You can't pretend you'd rather be in the bungalow,' she remarked after a moment or two, eyeing her father severely.

He made no answer, which she took as acquiescence. But later, when she had gone indoors again to help Mrs Godfrey with the lunch, Victor muttered rebelliously beneath his breath, so that only the sharp ears of Nicholas heard, 'I'd rather be in Tonga or New Zealand. I'd rather be anywhere but here.'

'But, Mr Grey,' Sandor said patiently, laying down his knife and fork and spreading his beautiful hands for better emphasis, 'you cannot, surely, defend the precepts of Soviet Communism. Not after what has happened in my country.'

It was Good Friday evening and the children were in bed. Katherine, her father, Henry and Sandor Scott were having dinner in the newly redecorated dining-room. Henry was sparing no expense in the restoration of Chapel Rock, and had engaged the most reputable firm of interior decorators he could find in London. Their efforts were at last beginning to show results. The flocked Victorian wallpaper in the dining-room had been stripped away to reveal the original oak panelling underneath. The marble fireplace, of French design, had been cleaned of smoke and grime, so that its ornate swags of flowers and pale cornucopias of fruit were visible in all their profusion. The table and the chairs, with their delicate straw-coloured seats, had been acquired only after a painstaking search. Henry really was to be congratulated, Katherine thought, smiling at him down the length of the table.

During the last few months, for no reason that she could pinpoint, it was as if all their early love and affection for each other had been reawakened. Perhaps it was because she had grown more reconciled to being the kind of wife that he needed. Perhaps it was because Henry assured her, over and over again, that she was the only woman he had ever truly wanted. He had started bringing her unexpected presents: flowers, chocolates, items of jewellery.

Henry returned her smile and raised his glass, winking conspiratorially as her father and Sandor continued their argument.

'. . . no worse', Victor was saying, 'than British reprisals after the Indian Mutiny. Or take the Boer War, for example . . .'

Their voices hummed on, rising and falling, but for once Katherine took no notice. The saddle of lamb and redcurrant jelly had been superb. Mrs Godfrey was a treasure. They had been extremely lucky to find her and her husband in this era of almost full employment.

'. . . no different' – Victor was holding forth again – 'from Eden sending in the troops at Suez!'

'Ah!' Sandor stabbed a long, elegant finger at his opponent. 'But your Prime Minister resigned in January. He was wrong and he had to go. Khrushchev will not only remain, but he will be upheld by his countrymen for what he did to Hungary. He will only be unseated if he appears too weak.'

Katherine put her knife and fork together and leaned against the carved back of her chair, watching the play of light and shade across the faces of the men. She had long ago given up trying to make her father take life easily, in anything but the physical sense. His mind was too active, his political awareness too acute for him to accept quietly any views which did not correspond with his own. This year he would celebrate his seventieth birthday, and he displayed much of the malevolence of old age. His heart condition had not deteriorated over the past three years, and the local doctor who attended him saw no reason why Victor should not live to be a hundred.

'So it looks,' Victor had told his daughter, 'as though I'll be around for a while to upset you.'

As he was, at this moment, upsetting Sandor Scott with his deliberately exaggerated admiration for Marx and Lenin. Katherine transferred her attention to her guest.

She had only met the Hungarian twice before, and neither time for very long. The impression she had gained of him then was of a rather silent man, but whether his reticence was natural or induced by circumstances, she had no way of knowing. Listening to him now, arguing with her father, she surmised that he was not normally shy.

He was a very pleasant-looking man, with dark curling hair and sallow skin, saved from a classic profile by a slightly crooked nose, which at some time had obviously been broken. His mouth was on the thin side, with a downward slant to the corners; but his best feature was undoubtedly his eyes. They were large and well set, with a velvety quality to the dark brown irises. He was not tall – not, she supposed, much above five feet six or seven – but his slight build gave him an illusion of height.

Katherine liked him, and she rescued him now from her father's clutches as Mrs Godfrey appeared to collect the dirty plates.

'That will do, Dad,' she said, laughing, but with sufficient emphasis to let Victor know that she meant it. 'We've had enough politics for one evening. Mr Scott is here for a rest.'

'Sandor,' he corrected her quickly. 'Please call me by my Christian name.'

She was astounded by the sudden surge of physical attraction which she felt for him, so strong that, for a second or two, she found it difficult to speak.

'Yes. Yes, of course. Sandor,' she said at last, the banal words almost sticking in her throat.

To her relief, Mrs Godfrey reappeared and placed a shallow earthenware dish in front of her.

'Bread-and-butter pudding made with cream and rum,' the housekeeper announced dourly. 'Mr Grey's favourite.'

Victor gave her one of his glinting sidelong smiles, and Katherine once again had a fleeting glimpse of those New Zealand and Tongan women waiting to eat out of his hand. Her father intercepted her look and the smile slid into a grin.

'As you can see, I'm very well catered for,' he said. 'Mrs Godfrey's better than a Royal Marine.'

'A naval expression,' Katherine explained in answer to Sandor's puzzled glance.

The moment of sexual attraction had passed and she was inclined to think that she had imagined it. She had been separated from Henry for over a week and she wanted him. She had momentarily transferred that need to her guest. That was the simple explanation.

She picked up a serving spoon and cut into the thickly encrusted pudding.

Henry turned his head on the pillow and kissed the lobe of her ear. Katherine snuggled closer to him, entwining her legs with his, a strand of her hair tickling his chin.

'Have you missed me?' she asked.

His arm tightened around her. 'Of course I've missed you. I always miss you when you're away.'

She raised her eyes to his and laughed. 'But work

158

makes a pretty good substitute. I've never known any other man so addicted to his job.'

He looked away, watching the pale patterns of moonlight edge their way across the bedroom floor. Outside the uncurtained window, the moon itself seemed to be caught like some solitary exotic flower in the budding, lacy branches of the trees.

'I suppose I feel I have to be better than perfect,' he said. 'I can't forget that I'm standing in a dead man's shoes: my cousin Ralph's. Stephen trusted me to take his son's place and carry on the Lynton name. I intend to honour that trust and make it famous. I want Lynton's to be one of the biggest chemical companies in the world.'

'It's already twice as large as when your uncle died,' Katherine protested sleepily. 'Isn't that enough?'

'Not for me. I owe Stephen a debt.'

'You can't go on repaying all your life.' She stroked his chest, liking the feel of the coarse red hair. 'Besides, if you hadn't come along, Lynton's would already have been finished in any flesh-and-blood sense of the word. The name might have survived, but I doubt it. The firm would just have been swallowed up by some giant like ICI.'

He stroked her arm, but made no comment. He had grown thinner since the Suez crisis, and less American. He could not forgive his former compatriots for the part they had played in the withdrawal of British and French troops from Egypt. He spoke of President Eisenhower with concentrated loathing.

After a while Katherine drifted into sleep, but woke towards dawn to find Henry gone from her side. She knew a moment of panic before she saw him standing by the window, a lighted cigarette in one hand. The smoke rose in a faint blue spiral, stencilling itself on the chilly morning air.

She got out of bed and went across to him, taking

159

his dressing-gown which she draped round his shoulders. His skin was icy to the touch and he was shivering.

'For God's sake, come back to bed,' she urged. 'You'll catch pneumonia, or a cold at least. What's the matter? Are you feeling ill?'

He shook his head, but allowed her to lead him back to bed. She drew the bedclothes around them and cradled him in her arms. Gradually, the warmth from her body seeped into his and he stopped shaking.

'Are you all right now?' she whispered.

He nodded. 'I couldn't sleep, that was all. I do love you, Kate.' And he proceeded to put his words into action.

It was one of the warmest Easters anyone could remember; hot enough to take the children to the beach and let them paddle in the sea. They drove south to Tregantle, where the sweep of the sand below the towering cliffs stretched for endless miles. Charlotte loved it, racing down the steep declivity of the twisting stony path while the laden adults trudged behind, grumbling at the physical effort involved. But they all agreed it was worth it once they were at the bottom. The unspoilt beauty of Whitsand Bay was one of the loveliest places, Sandor declared, that he had ever seen.

'What a pity Mr Grey cannot be with us.'

'Yes.' Katherine looked around her, releasing Nicholas's hot sticky hand from her own. 'We used to come here for holidays when I was young. We rented one of those chalets on the cliff.'

Henry had spread a rug and was lying supine, soaking up the sun. He murmured, 'These temperatures must be some sort of record for April.'

He was wearing lightweight trousers and an open-necked shirt, but there was something ill-at-ease

about him, Katherine reflected. In spite of his related
posture, he did not give the impression of a man at
home in the open air. Sandor, on the other hand,
blended happily into his surroundings, as she did
herself. Harriet was another one who looked uncomfortable. She had shed her habitual brown and white
uniform for an ill-fitting floral dress and straw hat,
but looked as though the wearing of such fripperies
was somehow beyond her. She sat leaning against a
rock, holding Guy on her lap, the picnic hamper and
all the impedimenta of childhood – spare nappies,
towels, beach shoes and damp flannels – crammed
into a canvas bag beside her.

Charlotte was trying to initiate Sandor into the
mysteries of cricket, using driftwood for stumps, an
old tennis ball and the bat which she had insisted on
having as a Christmas present.

'Come on, Daddy!' she yelled, aiming the ball
none too gently at Henry's legs. 'Don't just lie there!'

'I'm worn out,' Henry complained, 'humping that
picnic basket down that hellish path. And I know
nothing whatsoever about that beastly game! If
Sandor takes my tip, he'll have nothing to do with it
either.'

Katherine laughed and opened her book.

By mid-afternoon, Charlotte had abandoned the
game and gone paddling, accompanied by the faithful
Harriet. Katherine could see them both, distant
figures, running in and out of the long curving line of
the sea. Guy was asleep on the rug in the shade of
some rocks, while Henry snored peacefully beside
him. Sandor, too, was dozing, lying face down in the
warm sand, his head pillowed on his folded arms.
Every so often his body would give a convulsive jerk
and he would mutter a few words in a language
Katherine could not understand. She wondered how
much it cost him in mental distress to live a life of
permanent exile.

Only Nicholas was restless, growing fretful at the prolonged inactivity. He hadn't wanted to go paddling with his sister and Harriet, and had soon tired of playing ball with his mother.

'What do you want to do?' Katherine asked, resignedly laying aside her book as he came whining and rubbing against her.

'Don't know. Have tea.'

'The others aren't ready yet,' Katherine pointed out gently. She got up and took his hand. 'Let's go and look at the rock pools.'

The suggestion appeared to satisfy him and he trotted docilely along the beach, pausing occasionally to stare reproachfully and a little indignantly at other people who were also out for a picnic. Katherine had noticed before this tendency to exclusivity in her elder son.

They found a number of pools, most of them empty except for fronds of palely coloured seaweed, which floated like strands of drowned hair in their sandy depths. Once Nicholas, plunging in his hand to lift a strangely shaped zebra-striped pebble, disturbed a small crab, which scuttled resentfully for the protection of another stone. For the most part, however, the marine fauna had gone out with the tide.

'We'd better go back,' Katherine said at last. 'It's nearly four o'clock. Time for tea. It's not really summer yet. It could easily turn cold.' Mother and son began retracing their steps. 'There you are,' she added, pointing, 'Charlie and Harriet are coming up from the water. I expect they're hungry, don't you? And tired. You'll sleep like tops tonight.'

Nicholas nodded, something in the conjunction of Harriet's name and the mention of sleep stirring a chord of memory. He asked, 'Does Daddy go in Harriet's bed, too?'

'What?' Katherine glanced down at her son's

innocent face, not sure that she had heard him right. 'What do you mean, darling, "too"?'

Nicholas frowned slightly, uncertain of the meaning of her question. His mother looked cross, and he wondered what it was that he had done.

Katherine stopped and knelt beside him, turning him so that they were face to face. Whenever she recalled that scene afterwards, she could always remember how warm the sand had been against her bare knees.

'Did . . . Did Daddy sleep in Magda's bed? Is that what you're saying?' All the latent suspicion, the faint, nagging doubts, crystallized into a horrible conviction that she was hearing the truth. She gave Nicholas a little shake, her hands gripping his shoulders to stop them from shaking. 'Is that what you're saying, Nicky?' He nodded again, sullenly, still afraid that he had done something wrong. 'Are you sure, darling? How do you know?'

That, at least, was easy. 'Saw Daddy,' he told her confidently. 'Saw him come out of Maggie's room.'

PART THREE
1962–1967

A time to love and a time to hate
Ibid.

13

Sandor lay on his back, hands linked behind his head, watching Katherine dress. They had been lovers for over three years.

He knew, of course, why it had happened; recognized the particular strands of loneliness and unhappiness in both their lives which had brought them together. He had been aware that something was amiss with Henry and Katherine's marriage long before that summer afternoon in 1959 when he and Katherine had first gone to bed together. Looking back, Sandor was able to trace the consciousness of something being wrong to the latter half of the first weekend he had ever spent at Chapel Rock; Easter, five years ago.

He could hardly, he reflected, have escaped the knowledge of Henry's infidelities as his intimacy with the Lyntons grew. This had happened so rapidly that, after a mere six years in a country where he had arrived as a penniless refugee, Sandor was now a partner in a successful and expanding company. More than that, Henry had offered the hand of friendship in a way that ensured Sandor a place in his family, as well as in the firm; a wholehearted affection which he accepted gratefully, but which he was unable as openly and unreservedly to return.

Katherine had finished dressing, and came to sit on the edge of the crumpled bed.

'I'll have to go,' she said. 'The boys will be home from school soon.'

'I thought Harriet fetched them.' There was still a faint trace of accent in Sandor's speech. He had discovered, to his amusement, that women considered it romantic.

'She does.' Katherine smiled. 'But Nicky isn't happy unless I'm there when he gets in.'

'Ah, Nicky! I think you love him more than you love me.'

'Darling, of course I don't.' She leaned forward and kissed him. She smelt expensive. 'In any case, it's a different kind of love, as you well know.'

'Your father and your elder son are the second and third most important beings in your life. Victor and Nicholas. They bring out the maternal tigress in you.'

Katherine laughed. 'What utter nonsense! Still, you accept, then, that I love you best.'

Sandor lowered his arms and took one of her hands in his.

'No, you don't. In fact, I don't think I mean much to you at all.'

Katherine was indignant. 'What are you saying? Why do you suppose I'm your mistress if I don't love you? Who can possibly be more important to me than you?'

'Do you truly want to know?' She nodded, and he said quietly, 'Henry.'

Katherine stared at him. 'Henry? Oh, I see. You're joking. Well, it's a joke in very poor taste.'

'I'm not joking.' Sandor smiled wryly. 'You go to bed with me because you want to be revenged on your husband. You wish to get your own back – is that the correct expression? – for all the times that he is unfaithful to you. And deceiving him with his friend, the person who owes him so much, lends it an added piquancy.'

Katherine was on her feet, white with temper. 'If that's what you think, I shan't come again. How dare you be so insulting!'

Sandor slipped out of bed and, in spite of her

frantic struggles, managed to take her in his arms.

'It's all right,' he soothed, kissing her. 'I didn't mean it. I'm sorry. I'm just upset when you have to go. I envy you your family and home.'

But of course he had meant it, because it was the truth. He had thought that a woman of Katherine's intelligence and innate honesty would have known it for herself; but he realized that he had underestimated her capacity for self-delusion. Perhaps it was true, what his mother had always said: that women needed to believe themselves in love before they could go to bed with any man. Convention, he conceded, imposed such restrictions on them. He had thought Katherine different, however, and was a little disappointed to find that she was not. He had no doubt that he was in love with her, as he had never been in love with anyone in his life before; certainly not with his dead wife, Agnes. Until he met Katherine Lynton, he had believed himself incapable of physical affection. Deep down, there was a powerful strain of the ascetic in him.

Katherine gave a nervous laugh, before freeing herself from his embrace.

'That's all right, then. Where, by the way, does Henry think you are this afternoon?'

Sandor began, in his turn, to get dressed, pulling his shirt over his head.

'He doesn't keep tabs on me as though I were a junior office boy, you know. I can come and go more or less as I please.'

Katherine laughed. 'Yes, of course. How silly of me.' She walked across the room and put her arms round his neck, planting a kiss on the tip of his nose. 'When can we meet again? Will you give me a ring?'

'We shall see one another tomorrow night, at the Claypoles'. Henry said you'd both be there. Had you forgotten? It's Beryl Claypole's birthday. We're invited to dinner.'

'Damn! I can't bear that woman, and she gets

bitchier as she gets older. And that's saying something! Never mind. As long as I can see you.' She kissed him again, on the mouth, then hesitated, puzzled. 'Darling? Is something wrong? You've been preoccupied all afternoon.'

'Have I? Then, I apologize. With such an attractive woman in my bed, I should not have had the time or the inclination to think of anything else.'

'Soft soap, but it won't wash. Is there a problem? Is it anything to do with me?'

'Yes and no. Yes, there is a problem. No, it has nothing to do with you.'

'With Henry, then? A business disagreement? Henry has the instincts of a freebooter, you know. He's a pirate at heart. You, on the other hand, have the self-destructive tendencies of the martyr. Eventually, you're bound to rub each other up the wrong way.' Katherine picked up her handbag and gloves. 'Bye, darling, I must dash. See you tomorrow.'

After she had gone Sandor stood for a moment or two, staring at the half-closed bedroom door. At times, Katherine was a most perceptive woman. It was all the more surprising, therefore, that she had so little insight into her own feelings and motives.

Katherine let herself into the Park Lane flat with quarter of an hour to spare. Harriet, as plain and efficient as ever, was just leaving to collect the boys from school. Her homely features registered disdain at the sight of Katherine's flushed face and subdued air of excitement. She knew perfectly well what was going on in the household, and did not scruple to make her employers aware of her disapproval. But she was devoted to the children, and her presence would have to be tolerated for a little while longer. In another two or three years the boys would be following Charlotte to boarding school, and then Harriet's services could be dispensed with.

Katherine went into her bedroom, dropping her

handbag and gloves on a chair. The August sun blazed through the windows, and she pulled the curtains. Then she stripped off her frock and lay down on the bed. In a moment or two, she would run herself a bath.

She had not shared a room with Henry since that Easter at Chapel Rock, when she had confronted him with the truth about him and Magda. She had expected – had, indeed, half-hoped – that he would deny it; protest that Nicholas had been mistaken. In her own mind, during the drive home from the beach, Katherine had actually composed phrases of denial on his behalf.

'Nicky was dreaming, honey! He's only a little boy. Of course I wasn't coming out of Magda's room. I'd woken up early and gone to the kitchen for something to eat.'

Or: 'He was imagining things, sweetheart! He was half-asleep! Good God, Kate! Didn't I promise that it would never happen again, after Beryl Claypole?'

But in reality, Henry had made no attempt to refute her accusations. He had merely laughed – a trifle shamefacedly, it was true – and said, 'Yes, I slept with Magda. I've slept with lots of women, but none of them meant anything to me. I don't see what you're making all this fuss about. It's you I love. You're the only woman I've ever asked to marry me.'

'And I suppose you think that excuses you!' she had shouted.

'It doesn't excuse my breaking my promise to you, and I freely admit that I shouldn't have given you my word in the first place. But, honey, there are lots of men like me; men who need more than one woman. It's in the nature of the male sex to be promiscuous. Everybody knows that. Ask your father.'

'And what about women?' she had demanded furiously. 'Would you be so complaisant if I were going to bed with another man?'

'It's not the same thing at all,' Henry had retorted impatiently. 'It's an accepted fact that women don't need sex on a casual basis, the way men do.'

'Accepted by whom? Apart from men, down the ages?' She had been almost hysterical with rage, she remembered; beyond caring that she might be overheard. She had slammed out of the room and moved into a spare one until Henry and Sandor had left for London.

Katherine slid off the bed and went to sit at the dressing-table, taking up one of the silver-backed brushes, a present from Henry, and starting to brush her hair. She stared at her reflection in the mirror.

She was thirty-nine years of age, but knew she did not look it. Childbearing had hardly altered her figure; she was nearly as slim as she had been at twenty-three. There were no flecks of grey, as yet, in the chestnut-brown hair, and the hazel eyes were as clear as amber. Sandor had often told her that she was beautiful; and although she knew better than to believe him, it would be hypocritical to deny that she was still attractive.

Sandor . . . What had he meant, she wondered, by implying that she was still in love with Henry? She despised, hated, loathed, detested Henry! Why, then, did she continue to live with him? The children were one answer; convention another. In spite of the growing prevalence of divorce, it was still expected that the vast majority of married couples would stay together 'till death us do part'. A lot of people still regarded her as rather fast because she had been divorced by her first husband.

Katherine continued to brush her hair with long, even strokes, but absent-mindedly, her thoughts reverting to Sandor, recalling the first time they had made love on an afternoon, three years ago, at Chapel Rock. She had been there on holiday, with the children, and he had been sent down by Henry to

171

recuperate after a very heavy summer cold. She had been showing him the little chapel at the bottom of the valley garden. They had been quite alone, the two boys and Charlotte having gone for a picnic with Harriet and Mrs Godfrey. Victor had not been well, and had been resting in his room. Mr Godfrey must have been around somewhere, she supposed, but she had evidently considered him to be no threat. Not that she had had the remotest idea of letting herself be seduced by Sandor when they had gone inside. But when it happened, it had somehow seemed appropriate that she should be unfaithful to Henry in the same place where he and she had once made love . . .

Katherine paused, the brush in mid-air, her eyes suddenly narrowed. Sandor had accused her of using him to revenge herself on Henry, even if it were only a secret satisfaction. Surely he couldn't be right! Surely she wasn't still in love with her husband?

The idea was absurd. Katherine replaced the hairbrush and went next door to run her bath. She was in love with Sandor. Of course she was!

Sandor stretched his legs in front of him and looked at Henry across the broad expanse of polished desk. His brown eyes were sombre.

'Have you discussed this with anyone else yet?' he enquired, after a moment's silence.

'Only you. I propose to raise the matter at the next full meeting of the board. But I have the experts working on our tender. Brendan Young's already come up with some figures which should put us well in the running. I told you because I want to be one hundred per cent sure of your backing. There are bound to be one or two tender consciences. You've had two days to think it over, as you asked.' Henry eyed his friend sharply. 'Don't tell me you've developed scruples.'

'Not "developed", no,' Sandor answered steadily. 'I've always had them. I'm afraid you won't be able to count on my support.'

After Stephen's death, Henry had transferred the managing director's office from the back to the front of the building, the windows facing on to Conventry Street. It was a much more imposing room than the old one, the entire typing pool having been dispossessed and dispersed to make way for Henry, enthroned like some ancient potentate behind the vast oak desk. Wall to wall, the floor was carpeted in Axminster; a traditional pattern on a deep-pile, dark red background. Green velvet curtains fell from ceiling to floor, their rich folds glowing in the light of a solid brass desk-lamp. A despot, thought Sandor; and like the despots of old, Henry had raised him from nothing, summoning him from the relative obscurity of the provinces to Lynton House, supervising his installation in the Mayfair flat, advancing his career in giant strides. And Henry could just as easily break him.

Sandor knew it, as he watched the well-marked eyebrows snap together over eyes which, a moment before, had been clear and smiling, but were now as hard and unfeeling as granite. He also knew that there was nothing he could do to soften the blow of his unexpected defection. This was a matter of conscience; and where his conscience was concerned, Sandor accepted that it would always win.

Katherine had told him, only yesterday, that he had the self-destructive tendencies of a martyr. She was a more astute judge of character than her husband, who was regarding Sandor in angry astonishment.

Then the flush of anger receded, leaving the heavily freckled skin as pale as before, and Henry flung back his head and laughed.

'You had me going there, for a minute! I really

thought you meant it. You're joking, of course. This government contract's too big for us to miss, if we can possibly get it.'

'I did mean it,' Sandor answered evenly. 'Chemical warfare is something I would never dirty my hands with.'

Henry's laughter died, and the ugly tide of red suffused his face once more.

'"Dirty your hands"! What sort of fucking crap is that? These weapons will be for use against the Commie bastards who overran your country! Besides, in all probability, they'll never be wanted.'

'That's no excuse for making them. Their consequences could be horrific, and I wouldn't wish them to be used even against my enemies.'

Henry leaned across the desk, thumping it with his fist, his face congested.

'For God's sake, man, don't be be so bloody naïve. Don't imagine the Russians aren't experimenting and stockpiling chemical weapons, because they fucking well are! And if this country doesn't keep upsides with them, we'll be at their mercy. Think about that!'

'I have thought about it.' Sandor met Henry's gaze as calmly as he could, although his pulse was racing. 'It's an argument which has been adduced for centuries as a reason for developing everything from the longbow, gunpowder and the first handheld guns down to the atomic, and now the hydrogen, bomb. And look where it's got us! To the brink of total destruction.'

'Balls!' Henry threw himself back in his chair with a violence which threatened to break the seat, but he had grown a little calmer. 'It was only because both sides eventually had the same weapons that any sort of political balance was kept in the world. I'm sincere in that belief, Sandy.'

Sandor smiled faintly, relieved at Henry's use of the affectionate diminutive. But he wasn't going to be won over by any appeal to his softer emotions.

'And I'm sincere in my beliefs. You must accept that.'

'But good God, man! Only one, possibly two, of our factories would be used in the production, and we'd be working to orders. There's no question of us being involved in the experimental side of things. All that sort of work is carried out at Porton Down.'

'Nevertheless, I couldn't back your decision to bid for this contract, in case we won it. My conscience won't let me.'

Sandor waited tensely for the next explosion of wrath, but nothing happened. Henry continued to stare at him for a moment or two, a baffled expression on his broad, handsome face; then he laughed, raising his hands and dropping them again.

'OK! OK! If that's how you feel, I have no option but to respect your opinion. I didn't foresee it, I must admit, but I don't have the right to try to change your mind. All the same, I warn you, I'll push the motion through in spite of you. I'll drum up all the support I need before next Tuesday.'

Sandor smiled and got to his feet. 'And I shall wish you luck in the best tradition of British sportsmanship. My naturalization papers have come through, did I tell you? I am now an Englishman, like yourself.'

Henry chuckled. '_Touché_. After the Americans, I think the English must be the most hybrid nation on earth. But it doesn't really matter. Being English is more a question of accent and attitudes than purity of blood.'

'That's a very comforting thought.' Sandor commented, moving towards the door. As he opened it, he paused, his fingers on the handle.

'Henry . . .'

'Yes?' Henry glanced up from the pile of correspondence awaiting his attention.

'Oh . . . Nothing. Just thank you.'

Henry grinned. 'Thought you were for the high jump, didn't you? You must learn to understand me better than that. I can put up with open opposition, provided it's sincere. It's secrecy and double dealing, people stabbing me in the back, that I can't and won't tolerate. Ask Polly to come in here, as you go through the outer office, will you? There are some letters I want to dictate.'

The talk at dinner had mainly consisted of Marilyn Monroe's suicide and the growing prevalence of rock and roll music, with passing reference to a new group called the Beatles. Beryl Claypole, at the head of the table, had managed to look sexy in spite of wearing one of the latest 'sack' dresses, the modern female equivalent of the shapeless gowns of the twenties.

Katherine no longer found her intimidating, and was able, nowadays, to give as good as she got.

I've grown used to this life, she thought, as she sipped her coffee with the other women in the drawing-room, waiting for the men to join them. I've become the sort of wife that Henry wants me to be.

A mood of discontent descended on her. What had happened to the young girl from suburban Plymouth, who had bought her clothes off-the-peg at Spooner's and John Yeo's and Dingles'? What, in short, had happened to Victor Grey's daughter?

Leaving her fellow guests to chatter on, she got up and wandered over to the window, looking down from the Claypoles' first-floor flat into the quiet summer-evening calm of Mayfair. Sandor had behaved oddly tonight, when they had been gathered in this room before dinner. She could almost have sworn that he was trying to avoid her, so assiduously had he paid attention to the young woman provided by Beryl as his partner. He had given Katherine the briefest of smiles as she entered the room on Henry's arm, keeping up appearances, as always. And afterwards, when she had manoeuvred her way to where he was standing, his answers to her remarks had been short, and he had avoided meeting her eyes. She thought back to their last meeting, yesterday, trying to recall anything she might have said or done to offend him.

She turned as the door opened and the men came in. Sandor was deep in conversation with their host; or rather, he was listening while Leo held forth, pompously, on the subject of last month's Cabinet reshuffle. It was Henry who detached himself from the group and came over to join her at the window.

'Kate,' he said quietly, resting one of his hands on her shoulder. 'Don't you think this nonsense has gone far enough? Five years is a long time to be sleeping in separate rooms. Can't we be friends again?'

The appeal was unexpected and took Katherine by surprise. She was amazed to find that her palms were sweating and that the old sensation of excitement was churning in her stomach. It was ridiculous!

She replied coolly, 'You mean you're turning over a new leaf? No more women?'

'I can't promise that.' His fingers pressed into her flesh. 'I'm not going to commit myself again to a bond I shall most probably break. But other women don't mean anything to me. I keep telling you that. Why can't you accept me as I am? Why do you have to try to change me?'

Katherine swung round to face him, forcing his hand from her shoulder.

'You could never accept me as I was, Henry. You couldn't accept that I needed a career. You re-moulded me into the wife and mother that you wanted.'

She moved away before he could reply and resumed her place on Beryl Claypole's sofa.

14

Decades later, Katherine was to look back on the year 1963 as a watershed, not only as it affected her own life, but also for the world at large.

It was a year which began with the defection of Kim Philby to Moscow; with President de Gaulle's vetoing Britain's entry into the Common Market; and with the death of the Labour party leader, Hugh Gaitskell. Towards the end of the year Harold Macmillan resigned as Prime Minister and, a month later, the world was shattered by the assassination of President Kennedy in Dallas. The intervening months saw the wedding of Princess Alexandra, the overthrow of the South Vietnam government by a military coup, the first woman, a Russian, Valentina Tereshkova, in space, and all the scandal of what became known as the Profumo affair.

And beneath this current of national and international events Katherine sensed a revolution quietly taking place: a revolution of dress and manners and culture. It was Victor who gleefully defined it one Saturday evening shortly before Christmas, when he and Katherine, Henry and Sandor were watching the satirical television programme 'That Was the Week That Was'.

'People are losing their deference,' he remarked suddenly, breaking off to laugh at some observation of the anchor man, David Frost. 'England has always been a deferential country,' he resumed after a moment. 'People have always known their place; respected the social order. At last all that's beginning to change.'

The family was spending the holiday at Chapel Rock, as it had done for the past two seasons. Two years ago Henry had suddenly decided that what Christmas needed to make it truly festive was the Dickensian atmosphere of an old country house: what he had defined as 'Pickwickian surroundings'. The children had been delighted: all three still adored Chapel Rock. And it could not be a completely family occasion, Henry had insisted, unless Sandor accompanied them.

Sandor had agreed with reluctance. His relationship with Henry had become strained again after Lynton's had gained the government contract; although Henry, with the easy magnanimity of the victor, had exerted all his considerable charm to restore their friendship to its old footing. The constraint was all on Sandor's side, and was not helped by the guilt he felt over his continuing affair with Katherine.

Henry's words to him on that August day last year had struck home, causing him pangs of conscience. These had been aggravated by his ever-deepening love for Katherine; his ever-increasing conviction that, whether she realized it or not, it was really Henry whom she cared for; and his own growing dislike for part of the work that the company was now engaged in. He would dearly have loved to refuse the invitation to spend Christmas in Cornwall, but at the last minute his courage had failed him. The prospect of being alone, or among comparative strangers, for this most nostalgic of seasons had forced him to accept against his better judgement.

Charlotte came into the room, her face crumpled with sleep.

'The boys are fighting,' she complained. 'They've

woken me up. They're making a hell of a noise. At least, Guy is. Nick's just whining, as usual.'

'You mean Guy's bullying him,' Katherine said, getting up from her armchair. 'And I've told you about swearing, Charlie. It's not ladylike.'

Charlotte groaned and raised her eyes to heaven.

'You're so old-fashioned, Mum. Everyone at school uses words like "hell" and "bloody" and "bugger"! No one looks on them as swearing.'

She was four months short of her fourteenth birthday, and like most of her contemporaries was shooting up to a height which would dwarf her parents' and grandparents' generations.

'All that free orange juice and cod-liver oil,' Victor often pointed out with pride; to which Henry would acidly retort, 'You mean the Welfare State is creating a race of giants. I hardly think that's a matter for congratulation when state education's shrinking their minds.'

Victor said now, 'Is that so, Charlie?' He turned triumphantly to Henry. 'That's what your private education does for you! You get the privilege of paying a king's ransom to have your daughter taught to swear like a trooper.'

Before her father could marshal his counter-arguments, Charlotte exclaimed affectionately, 'What an old hypocrite you are, Grandpa! You swear all the time.'

'Don't you be cheeky, my girl!' Victor roared back, 'I'm a man. It's different.'

Charlotte dropped a kiss on the top of his head, where the snow-white hair grew as thickly as ever.

'That's nonsense! Women aren't going to be fobbed off with that sort of argument any longer. In future what's sauce for the gander will also be sauce for the goose. We're all human beings,' she added impatiently. 'Just because half of us are physically different from the other half doesn't mean to say we have to abide by a different set of rules. My form mistress, Miss Matheson, was very hot on that point during our end-of-term discussion. The subject was The Subjection of Women Down Through the Ages. She was very enlightening.' Charlotte gave the outraged Victor a hug. 'You should be the last person to object. In the Soviet Union women have been regarded as the equals of men since the Revolution.'

'She's got you there, Victor,' Henry jibed. 'All the same, I don't approve of a teacher encouraging those sort of ideas. I can't really believe that Miss Matheson, who's a very charming lady, really said such things. You couldn't fully have understood what she said, Charlie. Knowing you, you probably weren't paying attention.'

Charlotte made no comment, but followed her mother out of the room. As they mounted the stairs Katherine asked, 'Did your form mistress really say those things?'

'And a lot more that I couldn't repeat in front of a couple of old reactionaries like Grandpa and Daddy.'

'Don't let your grandfather hear you call him a reactionary,' Katherine advised, amused. 'He'd never forgive you.'

Victor, who was now seventy-seven, looked extremely frail these days, although he clung to life with all the tenacity of the proverbially creaking door.

As they approached the boys' room the volume of noise, faintly heard until now, dramatically increased. As Katherine pushed open the door Harriet appeared from the direction of the back stairs, clutching a mug of cocoa. Her homely face registered concern.

'Oh, Mrs Lynton, I'm so sorry. I've been down sitting with Mrs Godfrey for an hour. I thought the boys were asleep.'

Katherine reassured her. 'It's all right, Harriet,

You don't have to apologize. I don't expect you to be on duty twenty-four hours a day.'

The bedroom was warm, Henry having had the central heating installed when Chapel Rock was renovated after Stephen's death. He had also had the electrical circuit extended so that for some years now there had been electric light in every part of the house. In spite of these improvements, however, many of the rooms still tended to be gloomy and forbidding, with their old dark furniture, leaded windowpanes and low ceilings. Nicholas flatly refused to sleep alone, and Guy, eighteen months his junior, was forced to share his room.

Guy, who in two weeks' time would celebrate his ninth birthday, objected strongly. Sturdy and unimaginative, he never failed to make his brother's life as miserable as possible. At the moment he was dancing round Nicholas's bed, shouting at the top of his voice and brandishing a pillow.

'Come on, then! Come on, you lily-livered landlubber! Come out from under those blankets and fight! You've got three seconds, then I'm coming aboard!'

Katherine recognized Victor's influence. He was always telling Guy stories, either real or imaginary, about the sea. As a result her younger son's conversation was liberally interspersed with naval jargon, both ancient and modern. The kitchen was always the galley; he dropped things on the deck, not the floor; and he never enquired what he was supposed to be doing. 'What's the drill for today, then?' he would ask.

When Katherine had sorted things out, sending Charlotte back to her own room and ordering Guy into bed with a threat of dire consequences if he did not go to sleep immediately, she sat beside Nicholas and put a consoling arm around his shoulders. Sandor had said that he aroused the maternal tigress in her. It was true; but sometimes she wished that

Nicholas would make more of an effort to fight his own battles. She couldn't go on protecting him for ever. She made him too much of a baby already, shielding him from Henry's impatience, Charlotte and Guy's teasing. She would have to teach him to stand up for himself instead.

'I shouldn't be here,' Sandor said, getting into bed beside her. 'Not under Henry's roof. In London, you can at least come to my apartment.'

Katherine stretched out a hand and gently stroked his face. He was so thin; thinner even than when he had first come from Hungary, more than seven years ago. And he was beginning to lose his hair. If she ran her fingers through it, she could feel a bald patch near the crown of his head.

'No one will see or hear you,' she assured him lightly. 'That's why I chose this room right away from all the rest. Henry isn't the least likely to come looking for me, if that's what's bothering you. We haven't slept together for years.'

She remembered, fleetingly, that evening at the Claypoles', when Henry had asked her to make up their quarrel. She had rebuffed him, and then lain awake in bed half the night hoping that he would come to her; force her to a reconciliation. Of course, he hadn't. And, of course, she hadn't really wanted him to. Had she?

Katherine found herself increasingly confused in a world where old concepts, familiar attitudes and prejudices, were being constantly undermined. As a woman, what did she really want? Charlotte's generation wouldn't have these problems. They seemed to know exactly where they were going and how to get there.

She snuggled close to Sandor and they made love. Afterwards he sat up in bed, smoking one of his strong-smelling Russian cigarettes.

He said abruptly, 'The Farmerson Corporation

183

have offered me a job at one of their chemical research plants, near New York.'

Katherine's head turned swiftly towards him. Outside a storm was brewing, heralded by the wind which was screaming up the Tamar from the sea. Beyond the half-drawn curtains and the latticed window, she had been watching the frenzied dancing of the trees. A stray shaft of moonlight pierced the gathering clouds.

'You're ... You're not considering the offer, surely?' she faltered. And when he did not reply, she dragged herself up in the bed to sit beside him. 'Sandor? I'm waiting for an answer.'

He drew on his cigarette and exhaled the smoke. She could see it, faintly blue, stencilled on the darkness.

'I ... Yes, I have thought about it. They are offering me a great deal of money.'

'For heaven's sake! You're Henry's partner! Does Henry know?' she added as an afterthought.

'Not yet. I haven't discussed it with him.'

There was silence before Katherine insisted desperately, 'I can't believe you're serious. What about me?' The first drops of rain spattered against the window.

'You're one of the reasons I am considering going. There's no future for us, Katherine. If I asked you, would you leave your children and come with me to the States?'

'I ... Oh, for God's sake! That's not a fair decision to ask any woman to make!'

For women, there were always the children. Always.

'That's what I mean,' he replied quietly. 'Until they grow up and no longer need you, there isn't a choice. And Guy is less than nine years old. It will be a long time before you're free. So what do we do in the meanwhile? Go on living a life of deceit?'

'You always make everything sound so melo-dramatic!' Panic was lending an edge to her voice. 'And if I'm only one of your reasons for going, what are the others?'

He stubbed out his cigarette, adding the butt to the others which she had to clear away so carefully in the early morning, after each of his visits. The rain was heavy now, drumming rhythmically against the panes.

'I'm a research chemist,' he said, 'not an adminis-trator. The idea of doing what I was trained to do appeals to me. I hate the conniving and backbiting and jockeying for position that goes on at board-room level. And I do not approve of some of the work now being undertaken by Lynton's.'

'What sort of work?' Katherine asked, puzzled.

Sandor hesitated a moment before saying tersely, 'For Porton Down.'

Katherine was aghast. 'You mean . . . chemical warfare?'

'Only two factories are involved. I can't tell you which ones. It's only a fraction of all Lynton's manufacturing plant, but I can't approve.'

'No.'

She could see that. He was not a man who would find it easy to placate his conscience. Henry, on the other hand, would have no difficulty. He saw every-thing in terms of what would be good for Lynton's. No other consideration would weigh with him.

A nagging doubt that perhaps she was being unfair to her husband, that perhaps he might genuinely hold opposing views to Sandor's, was brushed aside. All Katherine could think of just then was that Sandor might leave her. She needed him to fill the empty spaces in her life.

'But if you don't approve, that's all the more reason why you should stay. You must try to con-vince Henry, persuade him . . .' Her voice tailed away

185

as she realized that she was clutching at straws. 'How soon do you have to give Farmerson's an answer?'

'I have until the end of January.' He put his arms around her. 'I haven't yet made up my mind.'

She clung to him. 'Promise me you won't go! Promise!'

He shook his head. 'I can't. I owe Henry so much. I can't go on repaying his kindness with deception.'

'You owe him nothing!' Katherine assured him passionately. 'Anything Henry has done for you is because it's in the best interests of Lynton's.'

'No. That's not true. He gave me his friendship. That was out of generosity of spirit. It had nothing to do with the firm. And I have betrayed that friendship with you.'

Katherine pushed him away angrily. 'Good God! Can't you stop talking like Henry Irving in *The Bells*?' She could see, in the dim thread of light from the window, that the allusion was lost on Sandor. She said crudely, 'Henry's probably fucking some girl from the village right this minute. "Betrayed" indeed! It's the language of the theatre . . . Oh, hell! I'm sorry. I didn't mean to flare out at you like that. I'm upset, that's all. You've frightened me with all this talk of leaving.' She moved back into his arms, holding him tightly. 'You won't go to America, when it comes to the point. I know you won't. England's your home now. You couldn't leave it to start all over again in the States.'

He rocked her gently, but said nothing, letting her chatter on, staring over her shoulder into the darkness.

The next day Katherine drove into Plymouth to do some last-minute shopping. At least, that was the reason she gave. In reality, she needed to get away from Chapel Rock; to be by herself for a while.

The children's constant quarrels and noisy arguments, made worse by the advent of Christmas Eve, Sandor's silences, Henry's veiled sarcasm, her father's malevolence were all getting on her nerves, as was Harriet and Mrs Godfrey's air of smug efficiency. She parked near the Lockyer Hotel and walked down to Royal Parade.

Christmas lights and decorations were everywhere, giving the impersonal post-war streets an air of festive gaiety. All the main stores were advertising Christmas grottoes. She had brought the children in last week, before Henry and Sandor arrived from London, and even Charlotte had stopped protesting that she was too old for such childish entertainments once they entered the first shop.

Katherine wandered around Popham's, looking for something to buy Sandor for the tree. She had bought his main present before leaving town: a pair of engraved gold cuff-links. He was one of the few men she knew who still wore shirts with cuffs that did not button. Nothing on the laden counters appealed to her, however, and glancing at her watch she saw that it was half-past twelve, almost lunchtime.

A hand gripped her elbow and a half-forgotten voice said, 'Hello, Kate. I thought it was you.'

She turned and exclaimed incredulously, 'Robert? It can't be!'

He was smiling down at her, as large as life and twice as natural, as Aunt Margery would have said. He was older, of course, the black hair salted with grey, and two distinguished white wings at his temples. His eyes, though, were as brilliantly blue as ever, and although he had put on weight his tall frame was still well proportioned and muscular. He looked fit and tanned, as if he had recently returned from sunnier climes, and the vicuña overcoat he was wearing Katherine unerringly attributed to Savile

Row. He gave the impression of a prosperous man.

'What on earth are you doing this far south?' Katherine demanded.

He laughed, releasing her elbow and shaking her proffered hand.

'I didn't know I needed official permission to come past Hadrian's Wall.' The underlying Scots accent was overlaid now with a patina of ubiquitous Oxford English. The vowel sounds were a little rounder, the consonants a little less crisp. 'No, seriously,' he went on, 'I'm here on business. Mac-Neice's bakery chain is moving into Sassenach country. The first London store opens in the New Year, in the Haymarket, and we're anxious to get started in the provinces as well. I'm negotiating for premises here in Armada Way, and maybe another smaller site in Mayflower Street. As a matter of fact, in June we're moving our headquarters from Edinburgh to London.'

'You expect to do that well here?' Katherine was impressed. She said impulsively, 'I was just going to have some lunch. Would you like to join me? That is ... I mean ... Perhaps your wife is with you?'

'No. Sheila's at home with the children. We have two, you know. A boy, Iain – he's seven – and a girl, Clara, who's five. And thank you. I'd like to have lunch with you, very much.'

So he had another daughter! Katherine felt as though a burden of guilt had been lifted from her shoulders; as though she had ceased to cheat him. She knew that the feeling was unreasonable, but she could not help it.

He suggested a pub, and she took him to the Breton Arms in Breton Side. She covered the first embarrassing silence after they had ordered by explaining the origins of the name.

'In the Middle Ages, Breton pirates were always raiding the Devon coast. They sacked and burned

Plymouth a number of times. Of course, Plymouth wasn't much more than a village then; just a cluster of houses around Sutton Harbour and the Barbican ... Well! What a surprise. You're looking very well. Very brown.'

'Sheila and I have just come back from a fortnight in the Caribbean. Mother looked after the children.'

'How is your mother? And Mr MacNeice?'

'Mother's as fit as she ever was. A constitution of iron. Father's not so good, though. He caught pneumonia last spring and hasn't really recovered. He's retiring when we move to London, and high time too. He and Mother have bought a house near Linlithgow, overlooking the Forth.'

'You'll be in charge, then? Managing director?' They were both finding the conversation more of a strain than they had anticipated.

'I've been that in all but name for the past nine months. But, as you can imagine, the old man wouldn't let go of the reins without a struggle.'

'He was always a glutton for work.'

The food arrived, and was crowded on to the small round corner table where they had elected to sit. The pub was full now with a noisy chattering throng of local business people and Christmas shoppers.

Katherine said awkwardly, 'Robert, you did mean what you said that time you visited me in hospital? Just after Guy was born. You have forgiven me, haven't you?'

He glanced up from his ham and salad and smiled.

'Yes, I shouldn't have said it, otherwise.' He paused, considering her. 'But you looked happier then. I thought perhaps you'd really got what you wanted.'

'And now?'

'Now, I'm not so sure. You have that discontented look in your eyes again. Isn't ...? Look, I know it's none of my business, and you can tell me to go to hell

189

if you like, but isn't your marriage working out?'

'Yes, of course it is.' How could she admit anything else to the man she had left in order to find happiness with another?

Robert made no comment for a moment or two, devoting his attention to his food, while all around them the babel of noise continued unabated. Then he remarked casually, 'You didn't pursue a career, after all? Somehow I thought when you married Henry Lynton that you'd go back to your old job in the firm.'

'I had children, instead.'

'But after they were old enough for you to leave them, I imagined . . .'

'It was an ambition I grew out of, I suppose.' She heard the defensive note in her voice and gave a bright artificial smile. She wondered how well she was deceiving him.

When they had finished their meal, Robert said he had to go.

'I have another meeting this afternoon, and then I have to catch the train to London. And in two days' time it's back to Scotland.' He held out his hand, friendly and impersonal. 'It's been nice seeing you again, Kate. It was you who made me think of Plymouth for our first foray into the English provinces. I remembered how much I liked the place, on the various occasions you brought me here. How is your father, by the way? I should have asked after him earlier. Is he still waiting for the Revolution?'

She laughed. 'I'm beginning to think he's a fraud. He'd die of fright if he really thought the Russians were coming.'

They made their way outside and she watched him walk up the road. She noticed how a couple of girls turned to look after him. He was a handsome man; she had never appreciated quite how handsome when she was married to him. She had no regrets, however. He excited no passion in her; inspired no

190

emotion except the pleasure of seeing a very old friend. The only thing about him which disturbed her was his likeness to Charlotte. It was there in every expression of his face, and if he were going to be living in London . . .

She turned away and started to walk in the opposite direction, towards the maze of streets leading to the Hoe. She consoled herself with the thought that other people would not notice the likeness. They would not be looking for a resemblance and so would fail to see it.

15

'You were planning this all through Christmas?'
Henry's eyes were like flint. 'You accepted my
hospitality, and all the time you were planning to
resign? What is it you want, Sandor? More money?'
He sneered. 'I'm willing to match whatever princely
sum Farmerson's are offering.'

'It isn't the money,' Sandor returned levelly. 'It's
the work. I shall be head of their research department. I want to get back to what I was trained to do.
I'm a chemist, Henry, not a pen-pusher.'

Henry flushed resentfully, uncomfortably aware,
as he so often was, of his lack of academic qualifications.

'If that's what you want, you can take over as head
of the laboratories at Lynton's.'

The big office on the second floor of Lynton House
was very quiet in the waning afternoon light. The
January day was grey and forbidding, a fine rain
turning to sleet in the gathering dusk. Shop and office
lights studded the darkness; and, faintly, through the
partition wall, came the clatter of Polly Ogleby's
typewriter.

'Well?' Henry prompted impatiently, when Sandor did not reply.

'No.' The monosyllable was flat and uncompro-
mising.

'No! Just like that? No! Without any thought or
consideration?' Henry got up, leaning forward, sup-

192

ported by his arms, hands planted wide on the desk top. His voice rose. 'That's all the thanks I get, is it, for taking you on when you were a penniless refugee? For lifting you out of the ruck and advancing your career? That's your loyalty, is it? That's your return for all I've done for you? Running off to join Farmerson's, just because you're bored!' By now Henry had worked himself up to such a pitch of fury that he was beginning to spit, the saliva flecking his chin and lips. 'Furthermore, I've practically made you a member of my family. I felt I owed it to you in consideration of what old Joshua Lynton did to your grandfather. But you! You have no sense of gratitude or obligation. You're a traitor, Sandor! A bastard!'

Sandor maintained his silence, waiting for Henry's anger to abate. Finally, when the storm of fretful, nervous rage had passed, and Henry had resumed his seat, he said quietly, 'I'm perfectly well aware of what I owe you. But my conscience won't allow continued involvement in a company engaged in the work Lynton's is at present undertaking for the government. I have never made any secret of my abhorrence of chemical warfare.'

Henry's wrath erupted yet again.

'Conscience!' he jeered. 'You talk to me of conscience, when you've been regularly screwing my wife!'

Sandor's face drained of colour. For a moment he looked so pale that Henry thought he might be about to faint.

'You ... You know?' he stammered at last. 'How ... How long have you known? How did you find out?'

Henry gave a short bark of laughter.

'I didn't. But I'm not the fool that you and Katherine appear to take me for. I've had my suspicions for a long time. You've just confirmed them, that's all.'

You stupid idiot . . . stupid idiot . . . stupid idiot . . . The phrase went round and round inside Sandor's head until it was reduced by repetition to a meaningless jumble of words. At the same time, he felt an enormous sense of relief.

'Why haven't you said anything until now?' he asked. 'Don't you care?'

'Hell's teeth! What do you take me for? Of course I care! But I wasn't sure; and anyway, in the circumstances, I didn't feel I had a right to mind.' Henry's anger evaporated once again and he smiled ruefully. 'I guess that admission might surprise Kate, except that I don't want her told. I don't want our relationship complicated any more than it is already. Let her think she's deceived me. She's entitled to that.'

Polly Ogleby knocked and came in with an urgent letter for Henry to sign. He picked up his fountain pen and dug the nib into the page with such vehemence that ink spluttered across the white surface, leaving a comet's tail of blots. Polly, glancing from one man to the other, sensed the tension in the air and withdrew as speedily as possible.

Henry went on, 'I shouldn't have voiced my suspicions if I hadn't been goaded into it. But at least some good may result. Now that you know I'm in the secret, you must see that there's no need for you to run away. I put you on your honour to end the affair as quickly and as decently as you can. If you're in love with Kate, I'm genuinely sorry, but don't kid yourself for a minute that she's in love with you. I've seen her in love, and she doesn't act the way she does with you.'

'I had realized that for myself,' Sandor replied with dignity. 'I've never imagined for a moment that I was more than a means of revenging herself upon you. That hasn't made any difference to my feelings for her.' He met the other man's eyes squarely for the first time since Henry's revelation. 'But it isn't because of Katherine that I wish to leave. Not primarily. What I said just now still holds true. I can't continue to work for Lynton's while you maintain connections with Porton Down.'

Henry's anger flared again, hotter than ever. Staring at the man on the other side of the desk, he felt that he had never really known him. There was, he told himself, something devious about Sandor, which made him hard to fathom. Henry had few hatreds, but such as they were, they ran deep. And to that list was now added the name of Sandor Scott. How dare he set himself up as an arbiter of other people's morals, question Henry's judgements and repay all his generosity with betrayal?

Henry was not given to introspection, or it might have occurred to him that this furious anger had been provoked because Sandor's criticism echoed doubts of his own. What did hit him with all the force of a sledge-hammer was that he had really disliked his friend for a very long time; as long, probably, as he had suspected his involvement with Katherine. By ignoring his suspicions, telling himself that they could not be true, or that even if they were, he had no right to object, Henry had managed to persuade himself that his feelings for Sandor had not changed. His insistence that Sandor join them all at Chapel Rock for Christmas – insistence which had been tantamount to a royal command – had stemmed from his need to prove that everything was as it had been.

Now, Sandor had brutally destroyed that illusion. He was throwing Henry's friendship back in his teeth. He was going to the States to join a firm which was Lynton's main rival in Europe and the Middle East. Nor had he attempted to deny his affair with Katherine, when a good robust lie could have salvaged the situation. His precious conscience again! Henry thought contemptuously. God save him and everybody else from men of conscience!

He was suddenly aware of a splitting headache. Behind his eyes, the pain was jagging in flashes of red and gold. He stared across the desk at Sandor, recognizing that there was no point of similarity between them; not one feeling that they had in common except love of Katherine. All Henry wanted now was to be shot of the whole messy business.

'Your resignation is accepted,' he told Sandor bluntly. 'To take effect from the end of the month. If you apply for the leave that is due to you, I trust that we shall not have to meet again.'

Sandor nodded and got up. His lack of height never failed to surprise Henry. In the lamplight his broken nose looked more crooked than it really was; the thin lips dropped at the corners more than ever. Sandor must have been handsome in his youth, Henry conceded, with his black curly hair and classic profile. But those days were long gone, and he wondered angrily what Katherine could possibly see in him. The skin was sallow, the body thin almost to the point of emaciation. Henry felt deeply resentful that his wife had given herself to Sandor while denying him.

The door closed behind Sandor but, just before it did, Henry heard him greet Polly Ogleby in his usual careful way. No crisis would ever shake Sandor's beautiful manners. Henry suddenly felt more of an American than he had done for years. There was something terribly false about the impeccable politeness of Europeans: it masked their true feelings so that you could never tell what they were really thinking. Had Sandor ever liked him, as he had liked the Hungarian? Had he, all this time, resented Henry's patronage? Who could tell? The man was an enigma, as, to a greater or lesser extent, was everyone in this quarter of the globe.

An intense longing to see the States again swept over Henry. He needed the frankness, the ebullience, the open-heartedness of his fellow Americans. The Cliffords had been pressing him to visit them for some time past. As soon as he had dealt with the aftermath of Sandor's resignation, he would go. Meantime, there was work to do.

He pressed the intercom and summoned Polly Ogleby.

'You're going, then,' Katherine, said.

It was a statement not a question. The floor was littered with Sandor's cases in various stages of packing. Suits and ties hung over the backs of chairs; shirts, folded and unfolded, lay scattered across the bed.

She glanced round the bedroom where she had so often lain in Sandor's arms, and thought how un-lived-in it felt, just like the rest of the flat. It was as though Sandor had always known that he was a bird of passage. A few years, and he was moving on.

It was well over a month since he had told her that he had accepted Farmerson's offer.

'And what about me?' she had demanded, just as she had done at Chapel Rock. She had received the same answer.

'You don't need me, Katherine. You may think you do, but you don't. Go back to Henry. He loves you as much as you love him.'

She had protested, begged Sandor to reconsider, assured him he was mistaken, but he had remained unmoved.

'It's over, Kate,' he had said, trying to feel as positive as he sounded. 'It's time to go our separate ways.'

Katherine had been uncertain whether she was more hurt or irritated by these high-flown words, and had given vent to her overcharged feelings by requesting him to talk like a human being and not like some character from a Noël Coward play.

They had not seen one another since, until this afternoon. He was flying to the States the following morning and her visit was a surprise to both of them. Katherine had been shopping in Bond Street and had decided, on impulse, to call.

'I couldn't let you go,' she said, when he opened the door, 'without calling to say goodbye.'

He had invited her in, apologizing for the chaos like a well-mannered stranger. He wanted to kiss her, but dared not in case it led to their making love. Katherine was now over forty, but looked much younger. She had always been interested in fashion and kept up with the current trends. The shorter skirts, just above the knee, suited her, revealing more of her shapely legs, clad in nylons in one of the new pale shades. Her hair, too, was done in the latest style, with a heavy fringe, the rest backcombed high over the crown of her head. She wore eyeliner and mascara and an almost transparent lipstick, all of which had the effect of emphasizing her green-flecked hazel eyes.

She followed him into the bedroom and stared at the mess.

'Would you like me to help?' she volunteered.

Sandor laughed. 'I think I can manage, thank you. I'm not quite as unmethodical as I look.'

She sat down awkwardly in the basket chair, suspended by a chain from the ceiling.

'I never can master these things,' she apologized as the chair swung wildly. 'Charlie has one in her bedroom at the flat. Henry told her she could refurnish the room to her own taste, and now it's full of junk from the Fulham and Portobello Roads. She entertains her friends there in the holidays, on the evenings we're not at home. That's all the young seem to think about nowadays. Having a good time and going to parties.'

'You sound envious,' Sandor smiled, dropping a pile of shirts into one of the suitcases.

'Perhaps.' Katherine rotated a foot in its expensive crocodile shoe. 'The young seem so much less inhibited than we were at that age. All these Mods and Rockers – I never know which is which – and all these pop groups! And they all have such peculiar names. The Beatles, Manfred Mann, The Animals, The Kinks!' She stopped suddenly and gave a little laugh. 'Oh God! I'm talking like a middle-aged woman. I can remember my Aunt Margery complaining in just the same way about similar things. I'm getting old, Sandor.'

He had his back towards her, leaning over yet another suitcase, but he did not turn round.

'No, you're not,' he said bracingly. 'There is a sense of freedom today which previous generations have lacked. Women, particularly, are stretching their wings. Some of them have always had affairs, but very discreetly. Now, they don't care who knows.'

Katherine changed the subject abruptly. 'Henry is very bitter about what he regards as your defection. I can't recall him ever being so angry. It isn't just the job. He feels you've betrayed his friendship.'

'I know. He told me. He left me in no doubt of his sentiments.'

Katherine wriggled out of the chair and went across to Sandor, holding his arms and leaning her cheek against his back.

'Couldn't you reconsider? He'd have you back like a shot, even at this late date.'

Sandor shook his head. 'No, he wouldn't. I'm sorry Henry feels that way. I should have liked to have parted friends. But he does not wish it, and there is nothing I can do.'

'What about us, Sandor? Can we remain friends?'

He stood very still. She could feel his arm muscles tense under her hands.

At last he said, 'I think it will be best if we make a clean break, Katherine. No letters or telephone calls.'

'For heaven's sake, why not? Henry need never

know. He doesn't see my post. Harriet brings it straight into me each morning. I'm very fond of you, my dear. I'd like to stay in touch.'

'What would be the point?' he enquired brusquely, snapping shut the locks of a case. 'Our affair's over, Katherine. Let's leave it that way.'

She released his arms and stood frowning for a moment or two. Then she asked, 'Is there something you haven't told me? Your decision that we shouldn't see one another again was very sudden . . . ' With a flash of intuition, she demanded, 'Does Henry know? About us?'

Sandor was incapable of lying when confronted by such a direct question.

'Yes,' he acknowledged, and told her what had passed between Henry and himself. 'He loves you, Katherine.'

She moved away, looking slightly dazed. 'Henry admitted, actually admitted, that he had no right to object?'

'Yes . . . It doesn't mean that he isn't jealous.'

'No.' Katherine smiled to herself. 'No, it doesn't, does it? It must mean, too, that he realizes how he's hurt me with all his affairs.' She looked round for her coat, which she had thrown on the bed. When she had put it on and rescued her handbag from beneath a pile of socks, she reached up and kissed Sandor's cheek. 'I meant what I said, you know. I am extremely fond of you.'

He returned the kiss, just as chastely, on her forehead. 'But you don't love me and you never have. I was right, wasn't I? About Henry?'

She laughed guiltily. 'I suppose it always has been Henry, ever since I met him. It's just that I don't really trust him, and we seem to have the knack of rubbing each other up the wrong way.'

When she had gone Sandor went over to the window and watched her walk down the street. Until that moment, he had not quite realized how much he loved her. He felt as though he was losing a part of himself, and he turned back abruptly into the room. It had an even emptier and more forsaken appearance than it had worn for the past few days. He must not think of that. He had a lot to do before he went to bed. He forced himself to finish his packing.

Henry was late coming home. He had telephoned the flat at seven o'clock to say he had a meeting and would not be in for dinner. Katherine had eaten alone and settled down to wait.

She was dozing on the big settee in front of the television when she finally heard his key in the lock. The clock on the mantelpiece showed that it was nearly midnight. The television screen was blank and Katherine switched off the set. Harriet and the boys had long since gone to bed.

Katherine's first thought, when her husband came into the room, was that he looked tired. There were dark circles under his eyes, and she noticed with a sense of shock that the fiery red of his hair had begun to fade. There were grey threads amongst it, and one streak which was almost white. Henry was ageing, and she had been so wrapped up in her own affairs that she had failed to notice.

He paused in the doorway, blinking in the unexpected light. Then he saw her as she rose from the settee.

'Katherine? Are you still up?' Anxiety shadowed his face. 'You're not ill, are you? There's nothing wrong with the children?'

'No. I waited up for you.'

Henry crossed to a side table and poured himself a whisky. It seemed for a moment as though he had not heard her, but then he turned towards her, frowning.

'Waiting for me? Why? You haven't done that for years.'

'I know.' Katherine shivered, suddenly cold. The central heating had dropped to its night temperature, and the room was growing chill. 'Henry, some time ago, you asked me if we couldn't be friends again, and I refused. I was wrong, and I'm asking you to forgive me. I realize that after thirteen years of marriage it sounds rather silly, but . . . couldn't we start again?' Her heart was beating ridiculously fast as she waited for his reply.

Henry's answer, when it came, was not encouraging.

'What has made you change your mind?' He sipped his drink, watching her speculatively over the rim of the glass.

Katherine hesitated, before deciding that honesty was her only weapon.

'It's not because Sandor's going to America, if that's what you think.' She saw the anger kindle in his eyes, and added swiftly, 'Sandor didn't tell me you knew until I guessed. He respected your wish that I shouldn't be told, but he couldn't lie when I challenged him directly. You know Sandor.' She moved towards Henry, her hands outstretched. 'Oh darling, what a mess we've made of things, between us! Sandor never meant anything to me really. I just wanted to get my own back for all the pain you'd caused me. Sandor knew that. He told me, and I wouldn't believe him, but he knew me better than I knew myself. Henry? Can't we make a new beginning?'

He turned away from her, and for one awful moment she was afraid that her appeal had failed. But it was only to set his glass down on the table. Then he opened his arms and she went into them, an arrow homing into the gold.

'Come to bed,' he whispered urgently. 'Come to bed.'

They had never made love so passionately before.

It was as though they were compensating for all the lost years of estrangement. In between making love they constantly embraced, murmuring endearments. They could not have enough of one another.

Sated at last, they lay quietly side by side, holding hands, staring contentedly into the darkness. Katherine turned her head and glanced at the illuminated bedside clock.

'It's nearly four in the morning.' She giggled. 'I haven't even taken off my make-up. I must look a sight! I bet my mascara's smudged all over the pillow.' She wriggled on to her side, facing Henry. 'Darling, about Sandor . . .'

He put two fingers on her lips. 'Don't talk about him. I never want to hear his name mentioned again. He's a bastard. He ought to be fixed.'

'I just wanted to say that it won't happen again. With anyone. Darling, I promise.'

Henry put an arm around her, holding her tightly.

'It's all right, honey. Forget it.'

'I can't.' She was silent for a moment, stroking the inside of his thigh. She continued, 'I meant what I said. I want this to be a new beginning for us both. I want you to make a promise, too, that you're through with other women.'

He had seen the demand coming, and didn't know how to meet it. He also wanted a fresh start, but he understood his own nature too well. Why couldn't Katherine simply accept that other women meant nothing to him?

It was an old dilemma, and one to which there was no satisfactory solution. He was bitterly jealous of Katherine's affair with Sandor, and wanted her promise: he could not bear to think of her with any other man. At the same time, he did not want to give yet another promise on his own behalf, which would just as surely be broken.

It was, of course, different for women. Everyone

203

knew that. It was an accepted fact. Katherine wouldn't have gone to bed with just anyone: she had obviously been fond of Sandor . . . But he would not let himself think of that.

Henry's innate honesty asserted itself. The affair had happened because Katherine had been unhappy; because he had hurt her. The foundations of a successful marriage had to be laid by two people, not by one. His embrace tightened until Katherine laughingly protested that she was unable to breathe.

'I promise,' Henry said quickly, before his misgivings overcame him.

'You mean it? You swear you mean it?' He could see the intense expression on the face so close to his.

'Yes, I mean it,' he answered, and kissed her.

But inside his head, a voice mocked his good intentions. Oh, yes! Of course you mean it – now! But you just wait, old son. Just wait until some pretty face catches your eye. We'll see just how much your promise means then!

16

'Go and take it off!' Victor exclaimed irascibly. 'It's bloody indecent. Kate! Don't you care that your daughter looks like a tart?'

Charlotte crowed with laughter and crossed her shapely legs. The offending skirt of pale blue cotton inched a little higher.

'It's no good, Dad,' Katherine told him. 'Short skirts are the fashion, and they're getting shorter by the day. You'll just have to grin and bear it. Besides,' she added drily, 'I notice you don't complain about the two girls who come to help Mrs Godfrey in the morning. If Charlie weren't your granddaughter you'd be ogling her, as well.'

'But she is my granddaughter,' Victor objected, adding virtuously,' and I don't know what you mean by "as well".'

The three of them were sitting on the lawn at Chapel Rock, while below them the valley garden lay dreaming in the hot August sun. A tangle of loose-strife had pushed through a crack in the retaining wall and was nodding gently in the soft summer breeze. Although it was hidden from view by its belt of trees, in her mind's eye Katherine could visualize the broad expanse of flowing river, silent and glassy, with its fringe of rushes, drowsily quiet in the after-noon heat.

The boys were somewhere about, but not, she

guessed, together. Nicholas would be curled up with his nose in a book, Guy off with the local boys, fishing or climbing or playing a noisy game.

Katherine leaned back in her deck chair, raising her face to the sun and stretching her arms luxuriously above her head. The last eighteen months had been almost perfect, with only one or two storms to cloud her happiness. The biggest of these, as she had always foreseen, had been Nicholas's hatred of boarding school. In some ways, Katherine thought that it would have been better if he had protested openly, instead of silently enduring. It would at least have lent some substance to her case when she had argued it with Henry.

'If Nick really feels that way,' Henry had said, reasonably enough, 'let him tell me himself.'

But Nicholas would do nothing to antagonize his father, of whom he was secretly afraid. Henry was determined that his children should have the best education possible, and in England that meant a public school.

It was not to be expected that Victor would remain silent on the subject, particularly now that the country had a Labour government, which was committed to introducing a more comprehensive educational system: one far less selective. But as her father found it increasingly difficult to write letters, as the arthritis in his hands grew worse, and as Henry was rarely at home during the twice-weekly telephone calls between Park Lane and Chapel Rock, it was Katherine who was the main recipient of Victor's views, which she knew already and, to a large extent, shared. But in the present blissfully happy state of her marriage, she refused to rock the boat; and in some ways she felt that being cut loose from her apron strings might benefit her elder son.

There was no such problem with Guy. He was already looking forward to following his brother in less than a year. He had fulfilled all his early promise of being a big, handsome and athletic boy.

'The only thing he lacks', Charlotte would remark unkindly, 'is a bit of grey matter between the ears.'

This was an exaggeration, as Katherine would indignantly point out, but only just. Guy had scraped through the school's entrance examination in bottom place, after a great deal of extra tuition.

Charlotte herself was now ˌfifteen and working for her 'O' levels, which she would sit the following summer. Her teachers predicted a promising future for her, and quite possibly a place at either Oxford or Cambridge, should she want it. Charlotte was not sure that she did, but at present she was keeping an open mind.

She was a strong-willed girl, and very much part of the developing social scene, with its accent on youth and pleasure. But she also had a self-discipline notably absent in some of her contemporaries. Katherine had once complained bitterly to Henry that it was as though no one had ever been young before; as though the coming generation had suddenly discovered the secret of youth.

Which, in a way, she supposed they had. For centuries, in dress and manners, children had been smaller editions of their parents. Now, all at once, it was they who led the way and their mothers and fathers who followed. Quite middle-aged women were shortening their hemlines, backcombing their hair, and studying the 'pop' charts; while their equally middle-aged husbands were going less frequently to their barber, wearing jeans and leather jackets, and altogether trying to appear as dashing as that new cult hero, James Bond. Why this revolution had happened, no one seemed quite sure, nor could they pause to find out. Everyone was much too busy just keeping pace.

It was only the elderly, like Victor, now seventy-nine, who had the time and the inclination to protest; and the sight of Charlotte's mid-thigh-length skirt had earned her this afternoon's lecture. She did not, somewhat to her mother's surprise, lose her temper, but merely smiled good-naturedly at her grandfather from beneath the canopy of her garden chair.

'I've told you before, you're a fraud, Grandpa. All this talk about women being the equals of men! You don't really believe it. As soon as we make a bid for freedom, you're the first to want to clap us in irons.'

'Dressing like a whore isn't equality,' Victor retorted. 'In fact, it's putting the clock back. You're behaving like a twentieth-century equivalent of the courtesan.'

Charlotte chuckled. 'I doubt that very much. What's more, I think you know it isn't true. That's why you're getting so upset. And Mother's right. You were leering at those two girls from the village this morning. That's the trouble with men, they're not consistent. They want their women to be chaste, but other women to behave like whores. They even want their own women to behave like whores in the bedroom.'

'You'll be chased all right, in that skirt,' Victor snapped, while Katherine laughed and Charlotte groaned, raising her eyes to heaven. 'There's one blessing,' he went on, the fierce look dissolving into a smile, 'you've the legs for it. Some of the sights I see about nowadays make me shudder.'

Charlotte grinned saucily. 'You old rogue,' she said affectionately, which pleased him very much. 'Oh, this is lovely. What a pity Dad isn't with us.'

'What's he gone to America for this time?' Victor demanded. 'Buying up another company, is he?'

'He's gone to visit the Cliffords,' Katherine murmured sleepily. 'I think he felt the need to get back to his roots.'

Victor snorted, before saying petulantly, 'I'm going indoors. This sun's too hot. I'm not feeling very well today. Sometimes I don't think I'll last much longer.'

Charlotte hooted with mirth, then got up from her chair and hugged him. 'I never heard such nonsense! You're going to be here to plague us for ever!'

It was the second occasion on which his stay with the Cliffords had been interrupted by the news of sudden death, Henry reflected, replacing the telephone receiver on its cradle. Not that, in one respect, Victor Grey's death could be regarded as sudden; it had been possible, even likely, at any time during the nineteen years that Henry had known him. But now that it had finally happened, quietly in his sleep, at Chapel Rock, Henry felt a sense of desolation. He had seen comparatively little of his father-in-law since his marriage; but whenever he had paid one of his brief visits to Cornwall, Victor had always been there to make him laugh. Henry knew how much Katherine and the children would miss Victor; how deeply they would mourn his loss. They would need him. He would have to go home, and just at present that was the last thing he wanted to do.

The Cliffords had retired to California, to a house overlooking San Francisco Bay and the Golden Gate Bridge. Henry rejoined his hosts and their granddaughter by the side of the outdoor swimming pool.

'Not bad news, I hope?' Jason Clifford asked, looking up from the gaily cretonned lounger where he was stretched out, a glass of iced beer close to his hand. He studied Henry's face and came to his own conclusions. 'What's happened, Hank?'

At her husband's words Maisie Clifford glanced up from her magazine, and Jane, who was lying prone on an air-bed, floating on the pool, raised her head from her folded arms.

'My father-in-law has died. I'll have to fly home as

209

soon as possible.' Henry grimaced wryly. 'This is the second time something like this has happened.'

Jane slid off the air-bed and swam to the pool's edge, heaving herself out of the water in a shower of iridescent drops.

'I remember,' she said. 'Years ago, in Altantic City, when I was quite a little girl, someone died and you had to rush off and leave us.' She picked up a towel and began to dry her arms and legs.

'You were about nine or ten,' Henry said. 'I recollect the occasion perfectly. I learned the news of my uncle's death the same evening of our very first meeting.'

'Goodness! What a memory you have!' She raised her eyes to his, laughing.

Jane Clifford was now almost twenty years of age and had grown into a stunning beauty. Constant exposure to the Californian sun had tanned her long limbs to a pale golden brown, and bleached the fair hair nearly white. This striking contrast, together with the big china-blue eyes, made her outstanding even in a city – a state – of beautiful women. Until this present visit, Henry had last seen her some years previously when she had been touring Europe with her grandparents, following the death of her mother. Henry had dined with them at their London hotel. Jane had then been at the puppy-fat stage, a brace on her teeth and her hair pulled back into a pony-tail, which had not suited the chubby contours of her face. He had scarcely been able to believe his eyes when he saw her again, on his arrival in San Francisco.

The urge to return to his roots, as Katherine had described it to Victor, had been growing stronger over the past eighteen months, in spite of his domestic happiness. He had been aware for some time of an increasing restlessness, a sense of being trapped, which he knew stemmed from his rash promise to

Katherine. He loved Katherine; he would never love anyone else, but he was not a monogamous man. Nevertheless, he had given his word, and this time he had every intention of keeping it. But he persuaded himself that a short separation from Katherine would do him good: they had grown so close that they were in danger of stifling one another.

He became aware that Maisie Clifford was addressing him.

'Does that mean you have to leave immediately?'

Henry smiled regretfully. 'I'm afraid so. Perhaps you'll let me come again, later in the year.' As he spoke, he tried not to let his eyes dwell on Jane Clifford's shapely figure in its revealing black bikini.

'Of course you can visit us any time you like,' his hostess said gently. 'We are all so very sorry. You must be very upset.'

'More than I expected to be, considering the state of my father-in-law's health. I didn't realize that I was so fond of him. Well, if you'll excuse me, I'll telephone the airport, and then I'll go pack.'

Half an hour later, as Henry was locking his case, there was a knock on his bedroom door. He called, 'Come in,' expecting to see Jason, but it was Jane who entered. She had donned a short towelling robe over her swimsuit, held together by a loosely fastened silver chain belt. One slim brown wrist was encircled by a heavy gold bracelet and there were gold earrings dangling from the lobes of her ears. Henry took a deep breath and reminded himself that he was old enough to be her father.

'I hope you don't mind my coming to your room like this,' she said, 'but I wanted to speak to you before you left.' She perched on the edge of the bed, the robe opening to reveal even more of one sun-bronzed leg. 'Mr Lynton, do you think . . . ? What I mean is . . . If I come to London, will you give me a job?'

211

He stared at her. 'Come to London?' he repeated stupidly, trying to ignore the sudden increase in his pulse rate. 'Why on earth would you want to leave all this lovely Californian sunshine and come to London, where it nearly always rains?'

Her blue eyes opened wide in amazement. 'Haven't you heard the phrase "swinging London", Mr Lynton? Heavens above! London is where it's all at! England. The home of the Beatles and the Rolling Stones. King's Road, Carnaby Street, Chelsea. Biba and Mary Quant.' She regarded him pityingly and Henry felt a hundred years old. But, then, she and Charlotte were much of an age . . .

'Do your grandparents know of your intentions?' Damnation! He was beginning to sound pompous; and like a pompous Englishman, at that.

Jane returned his look demurely, but there was a jut of her determined chin.

'Not yet. But I can manage Grandma and Grandpa. Don't worry your head about that. I could manage them a deal easier, though, if they knew I had a job to go to, and that you'd be keeping me under your eye.'

Dear God! he thought, mocking himself. She didn't see him as a seducer, but as a guardian. *In loco parentis*. Let that be a lesson to you, Henry, my boy!

He hesitated for a moment, knowing that for his own peace of mind he should discourage her; but the temptation of seeing her every day was too great.

'We-ell,' he agreed cautiously, 'I'll see what I can do. I'll have a word with my personnel department. What can you do? Shorthand? Typing?'

'I can type,' she said; then laughed and confessed, 'With one finger. I could learn, though. Truth is, I'm fresh out of college. Grandma took me away. She thought I was wasting my time. I guess I was, at that. Grandpa says I ought to be a model or a movie star, but I don't know. That sort of career can chew a girl up and spit her out. Look at Marilyn Monroe.'

Jane Clifford might not be academically bright, Henry decided, but she had a lot of common sense. Personnel must be able to come up with a vacancy somewhere. There were plenty of clerks at Lynton House. One of them was always leaving to get married. And if there wasn't a job going, they could create one; and he would see that Jane took a secretarial course at night school. Polly Ogleby was engaged, and she and her future husband were going to be married next year. They would be emigrating to Australia after the wedding . . .

'If you're absolutely sure that's what you want,' Henry said slowly, 'I don't see why something can't be arranged.' He slipped his passport into the pocket of his leather hand-grip, where he could reach it easily, and felt in his jacket pocket for his gold propelling pencil. It was engraved: 'Henry from Katherine. 1955.'

Ignoring the inscription, he asked, 'Have you a piece of paper? I'll give you my private office number. Telephone me there in a few days' time. I might have something to tell you.'

Katherine couldn't believe that Victor was dead; not even now, as, in accordance with his wishes, she watched his ashes being scattered out to sea. Her father was the last link with the old days; the only person who had been able to share her memories of her mother and the bungalow, Aunt Margery and the corner shop; of the time before she had 'come up in the world'.

The phrase was so evocative of her father that she had to smile, even through her tears.

'Think you've come up in the world, my girl, don't you? Just you pause and remember who you really are. Plain Kate Grey from Higher Compton, that's who! And don't you ever forget it.'

It had been Charlotte who had found him, going in

to wake him with his breakfast tray. For days after, she had been inconsolable, blaming herself in a fit of irrational superstition.

'I shouldn't have told him that he'd be here to plague us for ever,' she sobbed. 'It was tempting fate.'

'Rubbish!' Katherine had declared stoutly, taking her daughter in her arms. 'And he had had a splendid day. He told me so, when I went in to kiss him goodnight. There was nothing he liked better than having you and the boys and me around him. And Mrs Godfrey had cooked his favourite roast beef and Yorkshire pudding, and he'd beaten us all at Monopoly after dinner. He'd gone to bed a happy and contented man.'

Henry had managed to get to Plymouth in time for the funeral, a simple service at Efford crematorium. Victor had little to leave except the thousand-odd pounds which had resulted from the sale of the bungalow. And over the years he had made inroads even into that. What remained went to Katherine; but in a recent codicil he had directed that all his navy papers be given to his grandson, Guy.

Katherine found them in the old battered tin trunk in which Victor had stored all his personal belongings and business correspondence for as long as she could remember, and which he had insisted on keeping in spite of Henry's repeated offers to buy him a desk.

'I'm used to this old girl,' he would say, patting the lid. 'We've been round the world together. I shouldn't know where to find anything in a desk.'

Katherine sat on the floor in the deserted room, leaning her head against the side of the empty bed. Around her were the last mementoes of her childhood: the bits and pieces which Victor had brought with him to Chapel Rock. Soon they would be thrown out and the room refurnished. Most of the furniture was old and ugly, some of it falling apart. But she would keep the patchwork quilt which Aunt Margery had made so lovingly from scraps of material begged from her friends. The square nearest to her Katherine recognized, with a pang of nostalgia, as a piece of her old school summer dress.

She opened the tin box and began sorting through the neatly tied bundles, each one labelled in Victor's careful hand. There was all the correspondence connected with her mother's and Aunt Margery's deaths, but that was too painful to look at for the moment. Katherine restored the bundle to the trunk. There was a stack of documents relating to the purchase of the bungalow, which, in 1923, had cost her parents six hundred and fifty-five pounds. Birth, death and marriage certificates, including her grandparents', were there as well.

The naval papers were at the bottom of the trunk in a thick green envelope. There was Victor's Certificate of Service, printed on material that was more like linen than paper; his Certificate of Wounds and Hurts; his Discharge; and his Writer's History Sheets. It was the last which fascinated Katherine most, as she skimmed through the columns devoted to the paymaster lieutenants' and captains' comments. She did not know what she had expected; but certainly not this long list of glowing compliments.

'An exceptionally good CPO Writer, hardworking and intelligent.'

'Thoroughly reliable.'

'A very hardworking and efficient Writer of exceptional ability. Has a thorough knowledge of Captain's office work and is recommended for the Training Service.'

'An exceptionally conscientious and hardworking CPO Writer. Displays initiative and tact to a marked degree.'

Tact? Her father? Red Vic, the scourge of the quarter-deck and the bane of his commanding officers' lives? Katherine tilted her face towards the ceiling, addressing him, wherever he was, laughing and crying at the same time.

'You old fraud! I bet you're up there, right this minute, spinning St Peter one of your yarns. Probably, knowing you, the one about the medical examination.'

Then she broke down completely, sobbing as though her heart would break, burying her face in the patchwork quilt.

'Kate! Kate, honey!' Henry was kneeling beside her, enfolding her in his arms. 'Hush,' he said, stroking her hair. 'Hush. Vic was in a lot of pain sometimes; you know he was. And he had grown extremely frail. In his condition, he could have died years ago. You had him for a lot longer than you might have expected.'

The harsh, racking sobs eased a little, and after a few moments Katherine sat quietly, her head on Henry's shoulder. She sniffed and groped in her skirt pocket for a handkerchief with which to dab her swollen eyes. The room was very still. Through the open french windows she could hear the chirping of the birds. The scent of summer roses, which her father had loved so much, was as thick as clotted cream.

17

'Sheila. Robert. I'm pleased you could come.' Katherine moved forward to greet her guests. Behind her, Henry murmured the usual platitudes.

It was not the first time the MacNeices had visited the Park Lane flat, but it was the first time that Katherine had asked them to dinner to celebrate a family occasion. February the second, 1967, was Henry's forty-fifth birthday. He had been a little taken aback by Katherine's suggestion that Robert and Sheila be included among the guests, but as he rather liked Sheila MacNeice he offered no real objection.

When the MacNeices had moved south from Edinburgh, three years previously, Katherine had made up her mind that it was pointless trying to avoid them. The rapid growth of the MacNeice bakery chain had made Robert a prominent figure in the City, and the chances of meeting him socially and frequently were high. With their two children, Robert and Sheila had moved into a large Victorian house near Belgrave Square, where Katherine had duly gone to call on them.

She had been prepared to dislike Sheila Mac-Neice, although she was unsure why. Instead, and perhaps surprisingly, the two women had become good friends, although a wariness persisted between their husbands.

Sheila was tall and leggy, some years younger

than Katherine, with reddish-gold hair and a wonderfully clear, almost transparent skin. At thirty-nine, she was a very striking woman. She and Robert had first visited the Park Lane flat in the spring before Victor died, during a half-term holiday when Charlotte was at home. Katherine had chosen the date deliberately, wishing to get the introduction over as soon as possible. As Robert had shaken his daughter's hand, she had found herself holding her breath, waiting for someone to comment on the likeness which, to her, was so apparent. But nobody had, and, later in the evening, Robert had even remarked that Charlotte looked like Henry.

'I can't see it, myself,' Henry had replied. 'I've always thought she favours her mother.'

Katherine had said nothing, glancing covertly at Sheila MacNeice, trying to guess what the other woman was thinking. Sheila, however, had been talking to Charlotte, and gave nothing away.

She said easily now in her still strong Scots accent, indicating Katherine's cream lace dress, 'I'm probably committing some social solecism by mentioning it, but I'm glad to see you haven't had the courage to go all the way, either.'

Katherine laughed. 'Heavens, no! I'm too old for the present skirt length. Just below the bottom is definitely for the youngsters.' She indicated an open door across the hallway. 'Leave your coats in there, then come into the drawing-room and meet the other guests.'

These included Beryl and Leo Claypole and a young girl, who was introduced by Katherine as 'the granddaughter of some American friends of Henry, Jane Clifford'.

Sheila MacNeice judged the girl to be about twenty-two or -three years old, very pretty in a fair-haired, blue-eyed, china doll sort of way. She had an air of innocence both unusual and intriguing in one

218

of her generation, which the shrewd Scotswoman decided was entirely spurious. Of all the women present, Jane Clifford was the only one wearing a full-length evening skirt.

After dinner Sheila found herself seated next to Jane on the long drawing-room settee.

'Are you living in England?' she asked. 'Or are you just here on a visit?'

'I'm Mr Lynton's private secretary,' Jane answered primly, sipping her coffee.

'Really?' The one word spoke volumes, and Sheila's glance wavered momentarily towards Katherine, who was discussing the television serialization of *The Forsyte Saga* with Beryl Claypole and a couple of her other guests. She wondered if Katherine was aware of her husband's reputation as a womanizer.

Much later, when Katherine accompanied her into the bedroom to collect her wrap, preparatory to leaving, Sheila said casually, 'That American girl's a very attractive creature. She's Henry's secretary, she tells me.'

'Yes.' Katherine spoke with an unconcern and confidence which made Sheila ashamed of her suspicions. 'Henry's known her since she was a child, and her grandparents are close friends of his. Jane badly wanted to come to London, so Henry arranged for a work permit and found her a job in the firm. He also persuaded her to do a secretarial course at night school; and when Polly Ogleby left to get married, he wangled the job for Jane. I gather there was some bad feeling over it amongst the other typists at Lynton's but, as he said, what's the point of being boss if now and then you can't pull a few strings?' Katherine continued easily, as Sheila moved over to the dressing-table to apply a fresh coat of lipstick, 'Jane's an orphan, and I think Henry regards himself as a surrogate father. Her real father was killed on Omaha beach, on D-Day, and as Henry was there too, and survived, it gives him an added feeling of responsibility.'

Sheila sucked her lips, evening out the application of colour. Then she replaced the cap of her lipstick and slipped it inside her bag.

'I suppose she has her own flat?' she asked, turning away from the mirror and picking up her sable wrap from the bed. 'Most young girls seem to nowadays.'

'Yes.' Katherine assisted her with the fur. 'Jane has a place somewhere in Holland Park, not very far from where I used to live before I married Rob . . . ' Her voice tailed into an awkward silence.

'Before you married Robert,' Sheila MacNeice finished for her, smiling.

She followed Katherine into the hall, where Robert was waiting. Henry was with him, and Jane Clifford. Henry turned towards his wife.

'I'm driving Jane home, honey, is that OK?'

'Yes, of course. I'm only sorry you're all leaving so early.'

'We are the last to go,' Sheila pointed out, 'and we've had a wonderful time.'

Robert nodded. 'It is half-past twelve. Look, why don't we take Miss Clifford home, Henry? I can drop Sheila off first and then go on to Holland Park. It would save you turning out at this hour of the morning.'

Jane glanced quickly, almost furtively, Sheila thought, at Henry, who said smoothly, 'I shouldn't dream of putting you to so much trouble. Besides, I could do with a breath of fresh air, after all that booze.'

Robert laughed, relieved. 'You'll have to watch it, Henry. In fact, we'll all have to watch it once they bring in this new Road Safety Act. The police will be able to test your breath to see how much you've been drinking. They'll never wear it in Scotland. There'll be riots. You won't be able to call your soul your own.'

Henry glanced anxiously at his watch, groaned and rolled out of bed. Jane lay looking at him, her naked body curled up amongst the rumpled sheets and blankets.

'Two o'clock,' Henry muttered. 'What the hell can I say has kept me?'

Jane sat up, the light from the bedside lamp slithering across her young unblemished skin.

'You'll think of something,' she predicted. 'You always do.'

'I'm not usually here this late at night. I'm only supposed to be taking you home.'

'You should have thought of that sooner,' Jane told him pertly. 'I didn't force you to stay.'

Henry came back to the bed, leaning over to kiss her.

'You witch! You looked so lovely tonight, I couldn't wait to get you alone. None of the other men could keep their eyes off you, either, including my wife's former husband, that long-faced pious Scot.'

'I think he's rather handsome,' Jane answered provocatively. 'And I certainly don't think he's pious. I don't know what makes you say that.'

Henry paused in the act of pulling on his socks, glancing sharply over his shoulder.

'Why? Did he try anything on?'

'No, of course not!' Jane sounded cross. 'But he kept on looking at me during dinner.'

'I told you, they all did. I suppose you did it on purpose?'

'Did what? What did I do on purpose?'

'Wore a long skirt and a high-necked blouse, demure as a nun. All the men were naturally consumed with curiosity to know what was underneath. Especially as all the older women were

221

slavishly following the present fashion which leaves absolutely nothing whatsoever to the imagination. In their case they revealed what would have been better concealed.'

Jane lowered her eyelids. 'I don't think that's true about Katherine. She looked very charming.'

'Kate always looks well, whatever she wears,' Henry replied abruptly.

Jane noted, as she had so often done in the past, his curious reluctance to discuss his wife. It created the one barrier, the single bone of contention, between them.

'What will you tell Katherine?' she asked resentfully. 'You'll have to tell me so that I can corroborate your story.'

'Oh . . . I'll say there was a power cut and I didn't like to leave you alone in the dark. Electricity failures aren't that uncommon under this Socialist government. Kate doesn't know anyone now in this part of London. She won't trouble to confirm it.'

'What about the telephone?' Jane indicated the receiver, which had been taken off its hook. 'She may have been ringing.'

'Hell! I'll cross that bridge when I come to it. If I do.' He leaned over the bed again, kissing Jane on the lips, but this time more roughly. 'I'll see you tomorrow. Don't be late at the office.'

When he had gone, Jane got up and had a bath, put on her nightdress, tidied the bed and went into the kitchen to heat some milk. When it was ready, she carried it into the sitting-room and sat beside the electric fire.

She was not, she thought bitterly, getting anywhere at all: Henry was still in love with his wife. This was something she hadn't bargained for when she had embarked on the affair. She had been certain that she could break up the marriage as soon as she wished; but all she had to show for two years of

222

scheming was her position as Henry's secretary. And even that was problematical, depending on whether or not her work permit was renewed. She needn't go home, of course; she could remain in England, living on her grandparents' money. But she preferred to be self-supporting.

Jane drank some of her milk. She was unable to recall when she had made up her mind to marry Henry Lynton; probably the first time she had ever met him, when she was a child. And nothing in the intervening years had caused her to change her mind, not even those agonizing visits to London with her grandparents when she was in her early teens, and Henry had had no glance to spare for the chubby young girl with braces on her teeth and the unbecoming strained-back hair.

Living with Jason and Maisie Clifford from an early age, Jane had developed a preference for older men. The lack of a father had left a void in her life which she had desperately needed to fill. Being around her grandfather had given her a taste for authority and power. Henry exuded both qualities in full measure, more than any other man she had known.

Jane put the empty cup on its saucer and went through to the bedroom, climbing into the now cold bed. Damn Henry! Why hadn't he told her that he was in love with Katherine? Why, more importantly, hadn't she been able to see it for herself? She turned out the bedside lamp and snuggled down amongst the welter of pillows and blankets. Well, it wouldn't make any difference. She wanted Henry and she was going to have him, one way or another. She would have to think about it; consider tactics. It had occurred to her tonight that Katherine was jealous of her husband's attentions to other women, and this made sense of office gossip that there had at one time been a very serious rift between them. But if

Katherine were to find out about Henry and Jane, it would have to appear accidental . . .

Under Jane's soft, doll-like exterior lurked a spoiled and pampered child who, from birth, had been used to getting her own way. Her doting grandparents had denied her nothing, and her mother had died too early on in Jane's life ever to have exerted any real authority. Jane rolled on to her back and gazed at the ceiling, unable to sleep. She had been invited to spend the Easter weekend in Cornwall with the Lyntons. Perhaps an opportunity would occur to advance her plans then.

'You must have been late last night,' Katherine remarked at breakfast the next morning. 'I didn't even hear you come in.'

'There was a power failure in Holland Park,' Henry lied glibly. 'I don't know how widespread it was, but I didn't like to leave Jane on her own. It went on until two o'clock. I had to wait until then.'

As he drank his orange juice and buttered his toast, Henry reflected that he was becoming an expert liar. He didn't admire himself for it, but he had done it so often during the past two years that his conscience was growing blunted. He salved it by persuading himself that it was really Katherine's fault. She should never have wrung that promise from him. She ought to have been more understanding.

Since the departure of Harriet, after Guy had gone to boarding school, Katherine had made breakfast herself. The invaluable Mrs Mossop still came in during the day, and prepared lunch whenever it was needed. In the evenings, if it were only the two of them, plus the children in the holidays, Katherine cooked dinner; but more often than not, Henry was out and she had a snack, sitting in front of the television. If they were entertaining, either Mrs Mossop would lend a hand, or, if it were a big affair,

Katherine would hire a reliable firm of West End caterers. Sometimes, if she stopped to think about it, she was appalled by the useless, sybaritic life she was leading. Aunt Margery would not have approved.

Henry said, 'Shit!' and put down the letter he was reading.

'Bad news?' Katherine looked up anxiously from her own pile of correspondence consisting largely of invitations and bills. She feared it was some communication from the school about Nicholas, who was, or so his headmaster informed them, proving to be a disruptive influence. As he approached his fourteenth birthday the once shy little boy was growing into an unusually politically motivated and orientated young man for his age. Katherine was constantly having to stand between him and his father's anger.

This morning, however, Henry's annoyance had nothing to do with his elder son.

'It's from the estate agents,' he said, indicating the letter with a flick of his thumb. 'The present tenants at The Lodge have just given notice to quit.'

'What, again?' Katherine sighed. 'That's the third lot in less than four years.'

'I ought to get rid of it,' Henry said, knowing full well that Katherine would protest. 'We shan't ever live there now.'

'One of the children might want it. It would make a marvellous family home.'

'It would make at least three very good apartments,' Henry retorted. 'I'd get an excellent price for it if I were to sell it. There's a real shortage of accommodation in London.'

'There always has been. Don't put it on the market just yet. Wait a few more years. See what happens.'

'You mean wait and see if Charlie brings home some long-haired weirdo from university. I warn you, Kate, I'm having none of these hippies or flower-

225

power people, or whatever they call themselves – some damn fool name – on my property. OK! OK! I promise I won't get rid of it just yet. But I'm not going to be in a hurry to instruct the agents to relet it. It won't hurt to let it stand empty just for a month or two, while I consider the matter.' He picked up his next letter and slit it open. After reading it, he sat very still.

'What's the matter now?' Katherine asked, becoming aware of his sudden tension. This time it must be Nicholas. 'Henry? Say something, do, instead of sitting there like a stuffed owl.'

'It's from Leo,' he said quietly.

'Leo? Leo Claypole? What on earth's he writing to you about? He was here last night!'

'He probably didn't want to say anything with other people around,' Henry answered slowly. 'He must have written this yesterday morning.'

'Well?' Katherine demanded impatiently. 'What does he say, for heaven's sake?'

'It's to let me know that he's heard a rumour that my name's been put forward for a knighthood. The Queen's Birthday Honours List, in June.'

'Henry!' Katherine breathed, awed. 'But why you?'

'I don't know. Well ... The government have renewed their contract, and the lab at Southampton is currently working on a very important piece of research. Mind, you're not to mention it to anyone. Nothing is settled until I hear officially. Leo's rumour could be wrong.'

'I can't believe it!' Katherine exclaimed. 'Sir Henry Lynton. It sounds so strange.'

'I tell you, nothing's certain. All the same, how would you fancy being Lady Lynton? Or doesn't the idea appeal to Victor Grey's daughter?'

'I'm not quite sure.' Katherine laughed shakily. 'Yes, I am. Of course I'd be thrilled. It's a shock, that's all, to discover that I'm such a snob.'

'Most people are,' Henry said practically. He finished his coffee and shuffled the remaining letters together. 'I must go. I told them to send the car early for me this morning. I have an important meeting with Sir Wilfred Eshley at ten.'

He came round the table and kissed her goodbye. A few moments later, Katherine heard the front door slam and then the whine of the lift as Henry descended to the ground floor. Guiltily, she turned back to her own post and extracted the letter with the American stamp from where she had hidden it, in the middle of the pile.

She had recognized Sandor's writing as soon as she had seen the letters lying on the mat. Usually she went downstairs to collect their mail, but on occasions, if she were late, the manager of the shop which occupied the ground-floor premises would send up one of his assistants with it. She had overslept this morning, and had barely had time to scoop the post from the mat before Henry had emerged from the bedroom, groaning and demanding coffee, complaining that he had drunk too much the previous evening.

As she picked up her unused knife and slit open the envelope, Katherine wondered what had happened to make Sandor break his self-imposed rule that they should not communicate with one another.

It was not a long letter. 'But I find I cannot go on', Sandor wrote, 'without feeling that we are, at least, in touch; so that if you ever need me, you will know where I am. I shall not expect an answer. I know that you would not wish to break your promise to your husband.'

Katherine stared at the words, feeling guilty. She had treated Sandor badly, and he was obviously lonely in America. His parents had both died within six months of one another during his second year in England, and she was all he had. Had he really made no close friends during his self-inflicted exile from the country he had come to regard as his second home?

The rest of the letter was prosaic to the point of formality. There was nothing there that Henry could not see, if only he could be persuaded to overcome his bitter hatred of Sandor. But he would not allow even the Hungarian's name to be mentioned if he could prevent it, so deep was his sense of betrayal. Not, Katherine thought with a wry smile, on account of her, but because Sandor had defected to a business rival. And to make matters worse, shortly after Sandor had arrived in New York, Farmerson's had stolen a lucrative Middle East contract which Henry had considered as good as his. He was convinced, against all reason, that Sandor was at the bottom of the affair.

Katherine sighed and rose from the table. She would finish reading her letters later in the morning. Meantime, she must clear the breakfast things away.

18

'What was that?' Jane asked. 'I'm sure I saw something move. A butterfly or something, up there, on that wall.'

She and Charlotte were crossing the main hall at Chapel Rock. Good Friday had been a miserable day, cold and wet, confining everyone within doors. Today, Saturday, was a little better, and Charlotte, finding to her annoyance that her mother expected her to entertain Jane Clifford, had grudgingly suggested a walk.

'At least it isn't raining. We could go as far as the quay.'

She did not like the invasion of Chapel Rock by strangers; but if she were feeling peevish, Jane was more so. Since their arrival on Thursday evening, Henry had almost ignored her. She had spent two nights lying awake until well into the early hours of the morning, waiting in vain for him to come to her room. Instead, he had preferred to sleep with his wife.

When she thought about it, Henry's attentions had been less marked since that night in February, when he had driven her home after his birthday celebration. His visits to Holland Park had not ceased, and on two or three occasions he had driven her out into the country for dinner: nevertheless, she did not see him as frequently as she had once done. At work, too, he was inclined to adopt a more peremptory manner towards her, as though trying to discourage any office gossip or speculation about their relationship. It was, therefore, with an added anticipation that Jane had looked forward to this weekend. While they were at Chapel Rock, she would be able to see more of him. Everything would be all right, she told herself, when they were together at Easter.

Katherine, Charlotte and the boys had gone on ahead as soon as the school holidays started, and Jane had looked forward to the two-hundred-mile car trip, alone with Henry. But he had been quiet, almost at times morose, responding off-handedly to her chatter and inaugurating no topic of conversation. Her resentment had been further fanned, after their arrival, by discovering that she was expected to make friends with the reluctant Charlotte, who was six years her junior, besides being a great deal more bookish. Charlotte had won a place at Newnham College and would be going up to Cambridge at the start of the Michaelmas term.

The two girls had, in fact, little in common, apart from an interest in clothes. Yesterday had been hard going and today was no easier. In desperation, Charlotte had suggested that, after lunch, they take one of the cars and drive into Plymouth, by way of the Tamar Bridge; but in the mean time there was the quay and a walk through the valley garden.

'Up there,' Jane insisted, pointing. 'I'm sure something moved. Perhaps a bird has got in.'

'No.' Charlotte smiled. 'Someone's up there. Mother or one of the boys. You see that quatrefoil carving, to the right of the little gallery? That's a spyhole. If you stand in the corridor upstairs, you can look straight down into the hall. Come on, I'll show you.'

She led the way up the main staircase and turned left, then left again, into the corridor which led to the indoor chapel, and which ran parallel with the hallway's eastern wall. Katherine was coming out of the bedroom she shared with Henry.

'I thought you two were going out,' she said.

'We are in a minute, but I'm showing Jane the spyhole,' Charlotte answered. 'She hasn't seen it before. Were you standing there, just now, watching us?'

Katherine laughed and blushed faintly. 'I'm afraid I always look through, when I pass it. A sneaky habit, really, but no one's likely to be doing anything private in the hall. Its original purpose, of course, was to see if your visitors were welcome or not. If it was someone you didn't like, you just decamped down the back stairs and disappeared into the garden so that you couldn't be found.' She smiled at Jane. 'You must have extremely sharp eyes. The person up here is usually invisible.'

'It was just a flicker of movement,' Jane explained. 'I happened to be looking up and I saw it. I thought it was a butterfly or a small bird that got in through one of the windows.' She went across and peered through the opening, which was just on a level with her eyes. 'Hey! This is quaint! These old English houses are certainly full of surprises. Funny, but I never noticed it before, when I was staying here that time with Grandpa and Grandma.'

Katherine nodded. 'It is intriguing. I remember how it fascinated me when I first came to Chapel Rock. That was long before I married Henry. Now, alas, I take everything for granted. Nothing has any magic any more. Well, if you two girls are going for that walk, I'd go now, before it starts to rain again.'

The two girls moved away, Charlotte leading, Jane following, looking extremely thoughtful.

On Sunday the weather changed, the almost continuous wind and rain of the past two days roaring away northwards, leaving behind a quiet morning of muted greens and mud browns. Hazel shrubs dangled their catkins in a shimmer of yellow tassels, and a patch of early primroses gleamed, pale gold, under the still-dripping trees. The distant hills were etched sharply black and white against the fragile eggshell blue of the sky. A cold spring was suddenly hinting at the promise of summer.

Katherine was upstairs helping Mrs Godfrey to make the beds, as neither of the girls from the village came at weekends. Charlotte and Nicholas were both in their rooms, working on holiday projects set by their respective schools; and Guy had announced his intention at breakfast of accompanying Mr Godfrey to Long Meadow, above the house, the field which Henry had once earmarked as a private air-strip. Thank goodness that idea had come to nothing, Katherine thought, as she went into their room and began stripping the bed. Where Henry and Jane Clifford were, she had no idea: she was just thankful, for the moment, to be alone.

She opened the window and took a few deep breaths, looking out over the driveway which vanished in a sweep of gravel among the trees. Henry and Jane were just disappearing along its length, obviously taking the long way round to the quay.

The housekeeper put her head round the door. 'Need any help, Mrs Lynton? Not changing sheets this morning, are you?'

'No, thanks, Mrs Godfrey. I can manage here. We'll change the bedding tomorrow. You carry on with the lunch. I thought something easy today. Your French onion soup, that's always delicious, and a cheese soufflé. Nice and light. And there's the beef for dinner.'

Mrs Godfrey nodded and disappeared. Katherine stripped and remade the bed, smiling to herself as she did so. Henry had been very loving the past few months. As she moved from one side of the bed to the other, she caught sight of her reflection in the dressing-table mirror. She paused, staring at herself in the glass.

Not bad, she thought, for forty-four. Her figure was as trim and neat as it had ever been: she could still wear a size twelve dress. The chestnut-brown hair was as lustrous as ever, a fact which, nowadays, she laughingly but frankly attributed to her hairdresser's art.

'I'm not going grey until I'm well over sixty,' she would say, at the same time hearing in her imagination Aunt Margery's and her father's strictures.

'Only fast women dye their hair! Mutton dressed as lamb is what I call it.'

'Nothing wrong with a few grey hairs, my girl. It adds dignity to a woman.'

At the thought of Victor, however, Katherine turned abruptly away from the mirror, her eyes brimming with tears. She missed him every day, but particularly when she was here, at Chapel Rock, where he had lived for so many years. Whenever she went into his suite of rooms on the ground floor, she still expected to see him. She picked up the silver-framed photograph which he had brought from the bungalow, and which she had rescued from the clutter in his sitting-room after his death. The face of the young petty officer – it had been taken in the days before he had been promoted to chief – looked back at her from beneath the peaked naval cap, the likeness to James Cagney more marked even than when he grew older, and age had begun to smudge the sharpness of his features.

She could see the likeness coming out again in Guy, although he also resembled Henry: a big, square-faced, red-haired boy. But all he wanted to do was join the Royal Navy, like his grandfather. He had no other ambition.

Katherine replaced the photograph on the bedside table and finished making the bed. As she passed the window, she was surprised to see Henry and Jane Clifford returning along the drive. What was still more surprising was that they seemed to be arguing. A few moments later, as she stepped into the corridor, she heard the front door slam and the sound of raised voices. Instinctively, and without any conscious intention of eavesdropping, she moved across to the spy-hole.

The only person she could see at first was Jane, looking extremely smart and pretty in fawn trousers and a huge floppy Aran knit sweater. Her fair hair was held back from her face by a wide blue band which, Katherine was sure, just matched the colour of her eyes. A silver pendant, set with aquamarine stones, hung around her neck, and a jangle of thin silver bracelets encircled one wrist. Her voice, clear and carrying even at the best of times, and now definitely raised, reached Katherine's ears without difficulty.

'You've been avoiding me ever since we arrived. Please, Henry, tell me what I've done wrong.'

Henry moved into view to stand close to her, gripping her arm. 'For God's sake, lower your voice! Do you want the whole household to know?' His voice, too, was raised in order to make itself heard above hers.

'I don't care who knows! Henry, I thought you loved me! But you haven't been near me these past three nights.' Jane broke free of his restraining hand, ignoring his efforts to silence her. 'Don't I please you any more in bed?'

Katherine was rooted to the spot where she stood, the blood drumming in her ears. For a moment or two, she refused to believe what she was hearing.

Henry was saying something now, but too low for her to catch. Jane's next words, however, were clearly audible, in spite of the fact that she had begun to cry. Even at that distance, Katherine was able to see the tears glistening on her cheeks.

'I always understood you were planning to divorce Katherine and marry me. It's no good trying to deny it! You gave me that impression. If you didn't mean it, it was cruel. Cruel!'

'For Christ's sake!' Henry was shouting now, oblivious of who might overhear him. 'I never said anything about divorce. If I did give you that impression, then I'm sorry, but I'm certain that I didn't. Anyway, I as sure as hell didn't intend to!'

'But you do love me.' Jane moved towards him, entwining her arms around his neck, pressing her young body close to his. 'You must love me. You couldn't have gone to bed with me all those times, else. Please, Henry! At least admit you love me.'

'Yes, yes, of course I love you.' Henry put his arms round the sobbing girl, patting her perfunctorily on the shoulder. At that moment, he would have agreed to any proposition to quieten her.

Katherine moved away from the spy-hole as stiffly and blindly as if she were an automaton. She went back into the bedroom and closed the door. It seemed odd that everything should look exactly the same as it had ten, fifteen minutes ago, when she had been so happy. Nothing had changed: the same bird was singing outside the window, in its tree. The thin spring sunlight still caught the edge of the silver photograph-frame. Henry's discarded dressing-gown still lay across the back of a chair. Yet, in those few moments, her life had once more broken apart, and this time she doubted if she would be able to pick up the pieces.

Her knees felt weak and she sat down on the edge of the bed. A spasm of intense anger shook her, making her feel hot and physically sick. Then it receded and she began to tremble.

Practical considerations rose to the surface of her mind, mercifully suppressing her sense of hurt. One way or another, she would have to get through the rest of today and tomorrow morning without betraying her feelings. After Henry and his now unwelcome guest had departed for London the following afternoon, she would stick out the rest of the school holiday for the sake of the children. She dared not risk saying anything to Henry: she would somehow manage to avoid his attentions tonight. This was no quarrel to be fought over in the privacy of their bedroom: the sort of fight which ended with them making love. This time it was different. This time she was going to leave Henry, for good.

'You can't!' he exclaimed, his face as white as his shirt. Angry and scared of losing her, he said the wrong thing. 'You can't leave me now. It could ruin my chances of a knighthood.'

The children had returned to school two days ago, and Katherine had driven herself from Cornwall, starting out very early that morning. She had let herself into the empty flat and waited impatiently for Henry's return from the office. When he had telephoned to say he would be out that evening for dinner, she had informed him brusquely that unless he came home immediately, she would not be there when he returned. Something in her tone of voice had convinced him that she was serious, and when she had hung up Henry telephoned Jane to cancel their dinner engagement.

'What's wrong?' she had demanded eagerly. 'You sound upset.'

Henry had been evasive, and Jane had replaced the receiver looking thoughtful.

When Katherine had said nothing at Easter, continuing to behave like her normal self, Jane had been convinced that her plot had failed. She had had so little time to plan, and picking the right moment had always been a chancy business. There had been no guarantee that Katherine would be in the upstairs corridor at the precise instant that Jane staged her little scene. But perhaps Katherine had overheard, after all. Henry sounded worried. Jane went into the kitchen to make herself some coffee and await developments.

Katherine had wasted no time. Henry, tired and hungry, had found himself confronted as soon as he set foot inside the door. All the way up in the lift, his sense of unease had been growing. The name of Jane Clifford was hurled at him and his uneasiness changed to fear.

'This is the second occasion on which you've broken your promise to me,' Katherine said viciously, following Henry into the living-room as he pushed angrily past her. 'Well, this time I'm going! I'm leaving you. I've had enough. I want a divorce.'

And then his temper had betrayed him into making his big mistake. He had made the remark about his knighthood.

Something akin to contempt flickered at the back of Katherine's eyes.

'Oh, your knighthood! I'm sorry,' she answered with heavy sarcasm. 'How very remiss of me. How could I have forgotten?'

Henry tried to retrieve the situation. 'Balls to the fucking knighthood,' he said explosively, trying to take her in his arms. 'I don't care a damn about it compared with the prospect of losing you.'

She fought him off, retreating to the other side of the settee.

'Don't give me that crap!' she spat at him. 'You've never been able to keep your hands off other women.'

'It doesn't mean anything!' He was beginning to shout. 'How many more times? It doesn't mean a blasted thing!'

'Not to you, perhaps.' Her voice was shaking with rage. 'But it does to me! But my feelings don't seem to enter into it, as far as you're concerned. How do you think I like it, being the laughing-stock of all our friends?'

'You aren't! Can't you get it through your thick, stupid skull that lots of men sleep around? It means sod all, these days. Ask Charlie. Ask Nick or even Guy. This new generation believes in spreading itself around.'

'But we're not the new generation! It's not the same for us. And you didn't like it one little scrap when you discovered that I was Sandor's mistress.' She added in a quieter voice, 'It's the same old story: one law for men and another for us.'

Henry slammed with his fist on the back of the settee.

'Christ! Not the women's liberation bit again! Why don't you go and burn your bra, or whatever it is the silly cows do?' He saw the expression on her face and sought to get a grip on his temper. In his terror that she really meant what she said, he was driving her even further away from him. He held out a hand which was shaking. 'Let's start this conversation again. I love you. Whatever I say, whatever I do, hold on to that fact, because it's true. I can't change the way I am, Kate. God knows, I've tried. But I like women. I can't see a pretty girl without wanting to lay her. But you are the only woman I have ever wanted to spend my life with.'

'You promised—' she began accusingly, but he did not wait for her to finish.

'I know I promised. And I promised before. And each time I've broken my promise.' He walked round to the front of the settee and sat down, looking up at her pleadingly. 'Kate, honey, I shouldn't have given you my word. I am what I am. Please say you forgive me.'

Her face was set in rigid lines of disdain. 'I kept *my* promise. I haven't even written to Sandor, although he's written to me.' Katherine was silent for a moment, then burst out again, 'Jane Clifford! How could you? A girl young enough to be your daughter!'

'She's twenty-four. A woman.' Henry tried to speak reasonably.

'And you're forty-seven.' Katherine breathed deeply. 'Well, I'm sure she'll make you an excellent wife. I shall, of course, name her as co-respondent.' She went towards the door, forcing herself to remain unmoved by his agonized look of appeal. 'For the time being, I'm moving into The Lodge, as it's still empty. I'll inform the agents in the morning.'

'And after that?' Henry's tone was more hopeful. Let her go for now, he thought. St John's Wood wasn't far. He could still persuade her to change her mind.

'After that,' Katherine said, preparing to leave the room, 'when everything's arranged, I shall go to America. To Sandor.'

'Of course you're going to change your mind, Mother!' Charlotte, home for the Whitsun half-term holiday, leaned back in her chair and crossed her nylon-clad legs. 'Dad's sorry, and you know what he is. At least, *I've* always had a pretty good idea.'

Katherine regarded her daughter resentfully. Charlotte had developed the irritating habit of reversing their roles. The young were much too self-assured these days.

'I don't think she should forgive him,' Nicholas put in with quiet violence. 'I don't think Mummy ever ought to go back.'

Mother and sister looked at him in surprise. He normally said so little that they were apt to forget that he was there.

'Who asked for your opinion?' Charlotte demanded indignantly. 'What do you know? You're

239

only fourteen.' She added, with a magnificent disregard for relevance, 'And your voice has only just broken.'

'I do know,' Nicholas shot at her, his eyes flashing. 'I hate my father.'

The three children were staying for the week with Katherine, at The Lodge, having been put in possession of most of the facts by letter. Not all; Katherine had merely revealed that she and their father were separating and that they intended to divorce. She had given no reasons. It was all the more of a shock, therefore, to discover that Charlotte apparently needed no telling. How long had she known about Henry? Katherine wondered. How had she guessed? By a process of osmosis, she could only suppose. Children unconsciously absorbed what they saw and overheard. She was shocked, too, to find how deeply Nicholas disliked his father.

Charlotte was saying, in the condescending adult tone that so infuriated her brother, 'What you don't seem to grasp, my dear Nick, is that Mother intends to live in America. She wants to marry Sandor Scott. It won't affect me, of course. I shall be going up to Cambridge in September. I'm old enough now to lead my own life. But what about you and Guy? You'll either have to stay with Daddy or go to the States. I should think carefully about that, if I were you, before you encourage Mother in this folly.'

Nicholas cast his mother an agonized glance, which she tried to ignore. This time, she wasn't going to let herself be trapped by the children. They could make up their minds either to go with her, or to stay behind with Henry.

But in the wakeful nights that followed she knew it wasn't going to be that easy. It never was where children were concerned. Sandor was more than willing to have all three of them, although Katherine had warned him from the beginning that Charlotte

240

would not be coming. Ironically, it was Charlotte who had most sympathy for Henry, setting herself up in opposition to Nicholas's active hatred and Guy's indifference to anything but his own concerns.

But in spite of her resolution Katherine could not bear to think of Nicholas being unhappy, which he would be in a strange country, separated from his beloved Chapel Rock. She spent sleepless nights and miserable days trying to steel herself to be resolute. She had neither seen nor heard from Henry since the night she left the flat. He seemed to have resigned himself to the situation ...

The letter from the deputy head of Farmerson's New York laboratories reached her at the beginning of September. Sandor had been killed in a road accident four weeks earlier. The car he was driving had veered off the highway, crashing into a tree. Sandor had died instantly. Among his personal papers was a note instructing that, in the event of his death, Katherine was the person to be informed.

PART FOUR
1970–1975

A time to mourn and a time to dance
Ibid.

19

'You ought to regularize your domestic position, Henry,' Leo Claypole said with unusual bluntness. 'It's the reason you didn't get that knighthood.'

'Leo's quite right, my dear,' Beryl added seriously. 'And it's pointless assuming that mind-your-own-business expression. We shouldn't dream of treading on such delicate ground if it weren't for your own good.'

Henry speared a small piece of excellent Stilton from the side of his plate and balanced it on the edge of a water biscuit before replying.

'I was wondering why I'd been press-ganged for supper. I had a feeling it wasn't solely for the pleasure of my company.'

Beryl Claypole peeled an orange with a small silver knife, then separated it carefully into segments.

'You must blame me, Henry. Leo was against the idea to begin with. But we are two of your oldest friends.' She flashed him a smile, lowering lashes heavy with mascara to veil the sardonic amusement in her eyes. 'Someone has to be frank with you. I feel it should be us.'

'Really?' Henry's tone was polite, but the anger was already pulsating in a tiny vein in his neck. 'I'm sure', he added suavely, 'you won't enjoy it. Plain speaking is so disagreeable.'

Leo looked uncomfortable but his wife laughed, a full-throated, appreciative chuckle.

'Don't be sarcastic, Henry. It doesn't cut any ice with me.' She ate a slice of the fruit, dabbing with her napkin as the juice ran down her chin. 'All right! I admit everyone loves giving advice and telling other people how to run their lives. But just because it's enjoyable doesn't mean it's not sometimes necessary. Would you stand by and say nothing if you saw a friend making a mess of things?'

'I should hardly call an annual profit of almost a million pounds and one of the highest share dividends on the Stock Exchange making a mess of things,' Henry retorted coldly. The blood in the little vein pulsed faster, becoming noticeable, like a nervous tic.

'Oh, business-wise, you're sound enough!' Beryl was dismissive, as only someone with a lifelong disregard for money could be. Henry doubted if she had ever known a second's financial worry in all the years of her existence. Her father had been a merchant banker, she had married another. What mattered to Beryl Claypole and her kind, even in 1970, were the social niceties and distinctions. 'I'm talking about the fact that, although you and Katherine are now divorced, you still haven't married Jane Clifford.'

It was a warm evening, the long windows of the Claypoles' first-floor flat standing wide open. The sound of traffic in Piccadilly was faint, borne to their ears on a light summer breeze. The June evening was beginning to draw to a close, shadows inching across the floor and coagulating in little pools of darkness. Beryl got up from her chair and switched on the lights. The shadows slunk back into their corners.

Henry suspended his annoyance at her intrusion into his affairs long enough to eye Beryl dispassionately. But she was looking very elegant now that the mini-dresses of the past few years had given way to full- and mid-calf-length skirts. The older, fashion-conscious woman had suddenly come into her own again, able to dress with dignity and decorum instead of being forced to wear clothes well above the knees. Tonight Beryl had on a long royal blue skirt of very fine wool and a softly pleated white silk blouse. Sapphire and diamond earrings winked in her ears, their sparkle echoed in a matching clip and bracelet. When she moved, Henry could smell the distinctive scent of Chanel No. 5; not a perfume he was fond of, but right, somehow, for Beryl. It brought certain memories of her sharply into focus; memories which had not been evoked for years.

She resumed her place at the table, the overhead light falling directly on her face and dispelling Henry's mood of nostalgia. The features, sharpened now by the contrast of light and shade, reminded him of a bird of prey. He found it difficult to believe that they had ever been lovers.

He deeply resented that she had tricked him into coming here this evening. When Leo had telephoned him at Lynton House during the course of the afternoon, he had managed to convey that it would be a small supper party for a few close friends, invited on the spur of the moment. He had not suggested that Henry bring Jane, but that in itself was unsurprising. Henry knew that Beryl Claypole disliked the younger woman as much as she, herself, bored Jane.

'That old trout!' Jane would exclaim disparagingly whenever Beryl's name was mentioned.

When Henry arrived, however, he found he was the only guest. He had been puzzled, but unsuspicious, conceding that he must have misinterpreted his brief telephone conversation with Leo. Throughout the main part of the meal they had discussed Edward Heath's recent election victory; England's catastrophic and humiliating defeat by West Germany in the World Cup in Mexico – a subject dear to Leo's heart, and a loss all the more keenly felt because, since 1966, England had been the Cup holders; and whether it had been either necessary or wise to ban South Africa from the International Olympic Committee. It was not until cheese, fruit and coffee had been set on the table that Leo, with a little prodding from his wife, had broached the topic which explained the real reason behind the invitation.

Henry said now, as evenly as possible, 'My private life is my affair. And I can't believe that in this day and age anyone cares who is shacking up with whom, or why. Last summer, during the long vacation, Charlie was living in some hippie commune, in carefully cultivated undergraduate squalor, somewhere off the Old Kent Road.'

'Charlotte's young,' Beryl answered tartly, pushing aside the uneaten remains of her orange. 'What is she? Nineteen? Twenty? Not yet down from university. The young have enormous licence to shock these days. It's expected of them. In two or three years' time Charlotte will be a pillar of the Establishment; the acme of respectability. I've seen it happen too often not to know what I'm talking about. But a man of your standing, both socially and financially, is not expected to outrage public opinion by "shacking up", as you term it, with his ex-secretary in quite so flagrant a manner. If Jane Clifford is your idea of a soul mate, then for God's sake marry her!'

'I'm perfectly happy as I am,' Henry answered stiffly.

'No doubt,' was the acid retort, 'but is Jane?'

'That is my business!' Henry exploded, bringing his fist crashing down on the table and making the wine glasses jump. His coffee, in one of the tiny cups which he so despised, spilled over into the saucer. He added sullenly, 'I never wanted a divorce in the first place.'

'But what on earth did you expect?' Beryl Claypole snorted. 'A discreet affair or two is one

247

thing; but a girl young enough to be your daughter, flaunted right under Katherine's nose, quite another. No woman worth her salt could be expected to put up with that sort of behaviour.'

Leo put in, 'All the same, Katherine hasn't married again. If you're serious about not wanting to marry Jane Clifford, isn't there something you can do to put matters right?'

Henry smiled crookedly. 'Get back with Kate, you mean? Don't think I haven't tried. But she won't have anything to do with me. She'll never agree to see me when I phone The Lodge.'

'Surprise her, then,' Beryl recommended. 'Call when she's not expecting you. Find out if you can't change her mind.'

'And what about Jane?' Henry asked. 'Do I just abandon her? She's still expecting me to marry her one day.'

'She's young. She'll get over it,' Beryl answered callously. 'Once you make it plain that the affair is finished, I doubt if she'll shed any tears. You're no Don Juan, Henry. You're forty-eight. The poor girl might even be glad of her freedom.'

'If you'll excuse me.' Henry rose to his feet with what dignity he could muster, leaving his coffee untasted. 'I really must be going. Thank you for your supper, Beryl, but please, if you ever feel the urge to meddle in my life again, let me warn you – don't! I'm perfectly capable of managing my own concerns and I don't take kindly to interference. Good night, Leo.' Henry nodded towards his host. 'You want to set your own house in order before you try doing the same for other people. Don't bother to see me out.'

Walking home along Piccadilly in the summer twilight cooled Henry's head as well as his temper. He was inclined, upon reflection, to give Beryl Claypole the benefit of the doubt and believe that she had meant well. But pride had forbidden him to tell her the whole truth: that he was heartily sick of Jane Clifford and longed to be rid of her. The trouble was, he did not know how, without lowering himself still further in his own estimation. And, in any case, what would be the point? Katherine had made it plain that she wanted nothing more to do with him.

He had been so sure that she would eventually come back to him that her petition for divorce had come as a terrible blow. He had tried to see her then, to reason with her, but he could not get near her. She had barred his entry to The Lodge and refused to answer his calls.

His bafflement had turned to rage, and he had allowed the divorce to go through uncontested. Jane had moved into the Park Lane flat and started to talk about marriage. She had not been pleased that, under the terms of the settlement, Henry had permitted Katherine to keep The Lodge and set aside three months in the summer when she could visit Chapel Rock undisturbed.

That had been two and a half years ago and nothing had changed, not even Jane's optimism that she and Henry would one day be married. He was running out of excuses for postponing the event, one of which had been the death, the previous year, of Jason Clifford. He was beginning to feel trapped, wanting to end an affair which, for him, had long ago grown stale. But Jane made it clear that she was emotionally dependent on him, and would not answer for the consequences if he left her. He was not quite sure that he believed in her threats of suicide, but he dared not take the risk. Yet neither could he bring himself to take the irrevocable step of marriage, which would cut him off from Katherine for ever. It was stalemate.

Across the road, in Green Park, the trees stood like black paper cut-outs, flat against the cooling sky.

The steady stream of cars, flowing past him from Hyde Park Corner, pierced the gloom with their headlights; distant, luminous buds which flowered for a moment like bronze chrysanthemums and then were gone, as the traffic pressed on towards Piccadilly Circus.

Henry turned into Old Park Lane, behind Hamilton Place, but then changed his mind. He wasn't ready yet to go home to Jane, to her incessant demands for love and reassurance, her querulous reproaches and the flat which held so many memories of happier times. He retraced his steps to Piccadilly and found a cruising taxi. He would take Beryl Claypole's advice.

'St John's Wood,' he told the driver. 'I'll give you details when we get there.'

He had no idea what he hoped to achieve, even if he did manage to take Katherine by surprise, but he would cross that bridge when he came to it.

Twenty minutes later he was standing on the gravel sweep in front of The Lodge, the clump of cedars towering above him, black and menacing. As he lifted the brass ring of the knocker, the face behind it seemed to leer at him, as though it knew that he had come on a fruitless errand. Henry glanced at his watch. Ten o'clock: Katherine would still be up.

The years fell away, and he remembered his second visit to the house. Katherine had answered the door to him. He had thought her attractive and wondered what she would be like in bed. He had not expected to fall in love with her.

But on this occasion the door was opened not by Katherine but by Nicholas, who stood in the open doorway, his thin wrists protruding from the sleeves of a towelling dressing-gown, his grey eyes blinking owlishly in the waning light. As always, the sight of his elder son acted on Henry like a spray of itching powder.

'What are you doing home?' he barked. 'Where's your mother?'

'We ... We broke up a month early. School, I mean. Measles.' The unexpected appearance of his father threw Nicholas into a fit of nervous confusion. 'I ... I'm in bed. I ... I'm studying.' He seemed to feel that this called for further elucidation. 'I'm studying in bed.'

Henry raised his eyebrows. 'Queer place to study. I want to see your mother.'

'She's not here. She's gone to Cambridge. Visiting Charlie.' Nicholas added defiantly, 'She won't be back until the day after tomorrow.'

Henry was conscious of acute disappointment. He felt cheated and needed to vent his spleen on someone. As so often in the past, Nicholas was handy and seemed fair game.

'Well?' he demanded. 'Aren't you going to ask me in? Your mother and I may be divorced, but I'm still your father.'

'Oh ... Yes. If you want to come in ... ' Nicholas stood aside and Henry stepped into the hall. 'Guy home as well, I suppose. Where is he? Not got the measles?'

'No. We both had it as children. He's gone out. Some girl or other.' Nicholas did not add that, with Guy, there invariably was some adoring female in the offing; usually, he told himself with uncharacteristic venom, as good-looking and as vacuous as Guy himself.

The hall was exactly as Henry remembered it; the dark mahogany furniture, the heavy carved balustrade of the staircase, the leaded windows with their panels of coloured glass. Everything was a little shabbier, a little more lived-in, which, he supposed, was only to be expected after years of tenants, who had treated the place even more casually than if it had been their own.

Henry walked into the drawing-room and switched on the light, thankful to note that Katherine kept a decanter and whisky glasses on the marquetry table. The decanter was more than half full and he poured himself a drink, swallowing the spirit neat before turning towards Nicholas, who had reluctantly followed him.

'Are you going to join me?' He lifted the decanter invitingly, but Nicholas shook his head.

'No. I don't drink.'

The bald statement, untempered by any deprecatory excuse or apology, infuriated Henry.

'You don't, don't you? Taken the pledge? I thought all the young abused their bodies these days. Alcohol, drugs . . . You'll have to get used to a drink or two when you take my place as head of Lynton's.'

'I'm not taking your place, ever!' Nicholas's hands were trembling as he thrust them into his dressing-gown pockets, but he stood his ground. 'I don't want anything to do with Lynton's, or anything it stands for. People like you are leeches, feeding off the backs of the poor.'

'Jesus Christ!' breathed Henry. 'Give me strength. If you must spout crap, at least spout original crap, not a load of jargon and worn-out clichés!'

Nicholas's fair skin flushed a dull red. His chin – Henry's chin – jutted forward.

'We don't all have your gift for words,' he said, ponderously sarcastic. 'But at least my friends and I have standards. Principles. We don't make chemical weapons for the government. I'm ashamed to tell people that my name is Lynton.'

For some reason, this admission did not provoke the anger in his father that his previous remarks had done. Henry merely shrugged and finished his whisky.

'Your great-uncle Stephen would have been disappointed at your decision. But there's still your brother.'

'Guy?' Nicholas laughed in genuine amusement. 'You can't be serious, surely? Guy wants to join the navy. He isn't interested in your precious company, either.'

'The navy?' Henry paused in the act of pouring himself a second drink. 'Where did he get that crazy idea from?'

'From Grandfather, of course!' Nicholas was impatient. 'He left Guy his naval papers in his will. But Guy wanted to join the service long before that; and if you hadn't been so wrapped up in the business and having affairs with other women, if you'd paid just a little bit more attention to us, your family, you would have known.'

The accusation was unanswerable, and all the more galling for that. Henry replaced the decanter on the table and raised his glass to his lips with a hand which was not quite steady.

'We'll leave my private affairs out of this conversation,' he said thickly. 'That's between your mother and me, and nobody else. I don't have to take any lip from you on the subject.'

'Private affairs! Don't make me laugh!' Nicholas had forgotten his nervousness in a sudden blaze of temper. 'Your affairs have been too numerous to be private property. You've never once thought about Mother and how she feels. You make me sick!'

'The feeling is mutual.' Henry's eyes were blazing. Nicholas had the oddest impression that they were no longer a cool remote grey, but tawny, like an animal's with little red flecks in their depths. 'You were a miserable, whining baby, and you've grown into a self-righteous, ineffectual prig! I haven't forgotten that it was pictures of you at that anti-Vietnam demonstration two years ago in Grosvenor Square that got my face, as well as yours, plastered all over the front pages of the gutter press. They had a field day with that one, didn't they?' Henry's gaze sharpened. 'I'd give a great deal to know who leaked the information about the Southampton and Bolton plants to the newspapers in the first place.' He gulped down the whisky and put the empty glass back on the table. 'And what are you going to do with your life, then? Eh? Answer me that. Don't come crying to me when you find yourself without a feather to fly with. I've lavished enough money on a failure like you. You don't even come to see me, like Charlie and Guy. But don't think I care. From now on, you're on your own. You can do as you damned well want!'

'I intend to,' Nicholas answered as steadily as he could. He hated violence of any kind, one reason why he had forced himself to take part in the demonstration outside the United States Embassy, and others since. He knew that he was a coward, who would prefer a quiet academic life, encouraging militancy in others without endangering himself. 'An armchair revolutionary', one of the masters at school had once called him contemptuously, and the jibe had found its mark. From then on he realized that if he were to have any self-respect, he must take a more active part in shaping the brave new world which he and so many of his contemporaries envisaged.

Henry's anger evaporated, as it always did when anyone refused to be intimidated by him. He recognized a courage in his elder son which had nothing to do with heroics; the sort of rash, unthinkingly brave gesture which came so naturally to Guy.

He said quietly. 'I didn't mean any of that, you know. I just lost my temper. I do from time to time. You're going up to Oxford next year, aren't you? What are you reading?'

'Medieval French.' Nicholas· blinked, more unnerved by Henry's rapid change of mood than by his anger. He recalled that, as a child, he had always been totally confused by his father's mercurial temperament. He added defensively, 'I suppose you think that's an utter waste of time.'

Henry shrugged. 'I think it's pretty irrelevant for the second half of the twentieth century. On the other hand, I guess someone has to be able to read old manuscripts. Though what the hell it matters what William the Conqueror said to King Harold in 1066, God alone knows!'

'History is important.' Nicholas's features were suddenly animated. Henry could see, to his surprise, that when he lost his habitual defensive expression Nicholas was every bit as good-looking as Guy. It was a different kind of handsomeness, but it radiated its own appeal.

'If you say so.' He began moving towards the door. 'Me, I've always agreed with Henry Ford. History is bunk.'

'But it teaches you what mistakes people have made in the past,' Nicholas said, excitedly waving his arms.

'But does it prevent their descendants falling into the same errors over and over again? You know damn well it doesn't. Folks learn lessons from their own mistakes, never from other people's. Still, if it's what you want to do...' Henry paused, his hand on the door knob, then he released it and came back into the room. 'I repeat, I didn't mean any of the things I said just now. If you're ever in any kind of trouble – legal, financial, anything – and you need help, I'll always be there.' He laid a tentative hand on his son's dressing-gown sleeve. 'You can count on me.'

'Yes. Right. Thank you.' The awkward response was accompanied, after a moment's hesitation, by a fleeting smile.

Encouraged, Henry asked, 'How...How's your mother? We don't see a lot of each other these days.'

'Oh...She's OK. She's fine.' Nicholas seemed puzzled, as though he didn't know what to say. His mother was just someone who was always there. He rarely paused to consider her as a person.

'Does she . . . does she ever speak about me?' Henry wanted to know.

'Sometimes. Yes, I suppose she does. Of course, I'm not here during term-time.'

'What does she say?'

'Say? I don't understand.'

'What does she say about me?' Henry made a conscious effort to keep his voice level; to stop it rising on a tide of impatience.

Nicholas looked blank. 'I honestly can't remember. The usual sort of things, I imagine. Like, she'll have to ask you to do something about the attic roof because it's leaking; or you'll have to get a man in to look at the plumbing.'

'I see.' Henry gave a mirthless laugh. 'Romantic stuff.' He squeezed his son's arm, then let it go. 'I must be off. Jane will be wondering where I've got to.' He saw Nicholas stiffen at the mention of Jane's name, but he felt too tired to pander to his son's sensibilities. 'Don't forget what I said. If you ever need me, you know where I am.'

After he had gone Nicholas stood for a moment or two, staring thoughtfully at the empty whisky glass. For the first time in his life, he found himself wishing that he and his father were better friends. Then he shrugged. It wouldn't work: they were too different. He went upstairs to his books.

20

'I never thought I'd be doing this,' Katherine said, smiling. 'It's one of those things you read about, or see in films, or on TV. But it's not something you imagine yourself ever doing.'

Charlotte returned the smile, her strong arms and hands wielding the long pole with ease and dexterity.

'A punt on the river is much the best way of seeing Cambridge,' she told her mother, as they rocked out from under Silver Street bridge. 'It was worth waiting until today. The weather is just that much better.'

It was, indeed, a beautiful day. The light had a crystalline quality, the showery June clouds having suddenly given way to a blaze of heat. The sunbeams were full of dancing motes, and along the bank yellow spears of iris thrust between fading cuckoo flowers and kingcups. Katherine trailed her hands in the cool flowing water, watching the endless, busy traffic of the river. It seemed that all Cambridge was out on the Cam today, the occupants of the various canoes and punts shouting to, and greeting, one another. On the grass people were sunbathing, their half-naked bodies greedily exposed to the all too infrequent warmth of an English summer sun.

Higher up the river, just past Clare bridge, Charlotte steered into the bank and moored the punt, dragging out the canvas hold-all which held their picnic.

'That's St John's,' she said, nodding her head

vaguely in the direction of Margaret Beaufort's magnificent foundation. 'You said you'd watched "The Six Wives of Henry VIII" on TV. John's and Christ's were founded by Henry's paternal grandmother.' She added, 'I hope you've enjoyed yourself, and that these two days haven't been a bore.'

'With so much to see? You must be joking. King's College chapel alone would be worth the visit. Thank you for asking me.'

Charlotte rummaged in the hold-all, producing the filled bread rolls, fruit and wine which they had bought together earlier in the morning, spreading the food on paper plates on the grass and adding two plastic cups.

'We're not drinking out of those, are we?' Katherine asked, horrified, but Charlotte only laughed.

'For God's sake, Mother, it's only cheap plonk, not one of Dad's rare vintages. As a matter of fact,' she went on, a little uncomfortably, 'my invitation wasn't entirely disinterested. I want to talk to you.'

Katherine raised her eyebrows. 'I'm flattered, of course, but can't you talk to me at home?'

'I suppose so, but the boys always seem to be around when I'm there. Anyway, I thought you'd like to see more of Cambridge.'

Katherine bit into a cheese and tomato roll and asked thickly, 'Well? What do you want to talk about?'

'You and Dad.' Charlotte uncorked the wine bottle, splashing the contents into the two plastic cups. The liquid cascaded in a dark red, sun-drenched stream.

'Yes?' Katherine said politely, but her tone was discouraging. Charlotte, however, was not to be deterred.

'I know you think I ought not to poke my nose in, but it's no good saying it's not my business, because it is . You're my parents. I'm fond of you both, and the

258

way things are at present, your lives are just a mess. You're still in love with one another, so why don't you forgive him and have him back?'

Katherine made no reply for a moment, staring out over the sparkling water. A punt went by, a sun-bronzed young Adonis wielding the pole, two girls in thin cotton dresses lying on cushions, one in the stern, the other in the bows. They all waved and yelled at Charlotte, who gestured in return.

'Your father's still living quite openly with Jane Clifford,' Katherine said at last. 'That hardly suggests he's still in love with me.'

'Jane Clifford bores him stiff,' Charlotte retorted. 'My guess is that he was growing tired of the affair long before you even found out about it. She doesn't mean anything to him, and I'm ready to swear that he doesn't mean very much to her. Any wealthy older man would do just as well. She's emotionally immature. She needs a father figure.'

'Quite the psychologist!' Katherine exclaimed, more viciously than she had intended. She added quickly, 'Sorry. I didn't mean to snap. I dare say you're right. You've seen them more recently than I have.'

She took another roll from the paper plate lying between them on the grass, but made no attempt to eat it.

'Well, he hasn't married her, has he?' Charlotte argued reasonably. She embraced her knees in their faded denim jeans. 'That should tell you something. But if you don't watch out, it'll be too late. If you don't offer the olive branch soon, Daddy'll marry her out of sheer frustration. Her or somebody else. Don't tell me you're remaining faithful to Sandor's memory, because I shan't believe you. You weren't in love with him.'

'You know a lot.' Katherine began tearing the bread roll and its contents to pieces, without seeming aware of what she was doing. After a moment, she glanced up at her daughter's accusing face. 'All right. You win. I wasn't in love with Sandor. But I was very, very fond of him, nevertheless.'

'Being fond's not the same thing. So what on earth is stopping you and Dad getting back together? You're the one who's putting obstacles in the way. I do know that.'

Charlotte was totally unprepared for the vehemence of her mother's reply.

'I'll never go back to Henry! Never!'

She started to expostulate, but the expression on Katherine's face silenced her. She thought she had never seen her mother look so grim. After a decent interval, she enquired gently, 'Can I ask why not?'

Katherine hurriedly blinked away tears which had welled up and threatened to overflow.

'Look,' she said, 'I've had a wonderful two days, so don't let's spoil them. Darling, I realize your intentions are good, but I can't continue with this conversation. My reasons are my own affair. I know that sounds as though I'm snubbing you, and I'm sorry. But please can we drop the subject?'

Charlotte hunched offended shoulders.

'OK. If that's what you want,' she answered huffily. 'I apologize for raising it in the first place. If you're determined to ruin your life, I can't prevent you. Let's finish our picnic, shall we? It would be a pity to waste the food.'

'Dad called while you were away,' Nicholas said, wandering into his mother's bedroom, where she was unpacking after returning from Cambridge. She had not taken many clothes, and had almost finished putting them away by the time Nicholas appeared. 'The night before last, about ten o'clock. I was in bed. I had to get up.'

Katherine glanced at him, startled. 'What did he

want?' She was annoyed to discover that her pulse was racing.

Nicholas shrugged. 'He wanted to see you. He was in a foul mood to begin with, and took it out on me.'

The note of self-pity grated on Katherine's nerves and she asked sharply, 'What did you do to upset him?'

'Nothing!' Nicholas was hurt. 'You know he's never liked me. He sneers at everything I do. He even raked up that business of the Grosvenor Square demo. That shows you the sort of temper he was in.' He added fair-mindedly, 'He'd calmed down a bit by the time he left. Sort of apologized and told me he didn't mean half he said.'

'No.' Katherine's face was bleak. 'He never does. That's Henry's trouble. He can't control his tongue when he's angry. But why did he want to see me? You haven't said.'

'He didn't tell me.' Nicholas wandered over to the window overlooking the garden at the back of the house. It was wet again, and a few delphiniums and lupins fretted against the most distant wall, their bright blooms weighted down with the rain. 'He asked how you were. If you ever spoke about him. The sort of things you said. Questions like that.'

'I see.' Katherine hung up the last item from her case, a pale beige linen dress, and shut the wardrobe door. 'Where was Guy while this was happening?'

'He wasn't here,' Nicholas said resentfully. 'He was out with that Mallory girl who's so potty about him. He didn't come home until nearly midnight.'

'Nick! You promised faithfully you'd keep your eye on him while I was away! He's only fifteen.' Katherine was angry, but whether with herself, Nicholas or Guy, she wasn't quite sure. 'I suppose I shouldn't have left you two alone, but the visit to Cambridge was arranged months ago. I didn't know school was going to break up a month early because of measles.'

'That's right! Pick on me!' her elder son exclaimed furiously, flinging away from the window. 'Everyone else does! Why do I always get the blame for everything? I'm not Guy's keeper. He won't listen to anything I say. You know damn well he won't!'

'All right,' Katherine said. 'I admit it's unfair to expect Guy to take notice of someone who's only two years older than he is.' She sighed. 'He doesn't even attend to me. I expressly forbade him to stay out after half-past ten, but that doesn't appear to have stopped him. What he needs is a man to keep him in order.'

Nicholas looked alarmed. 'You're not thinking of going back to Dad, are you? I'll bet Charlie's been getting at you while you were in Cambridge. She was always Dad's favourite. He used to say it was a pity she wasn't the eldest son.'

Katherine patted his arm, noting how bony it felt through the thin cotton of his shirt sleeve.

'It's OK. Don't worry. You're right: Charlie did read me a little lecture, but I told her there was absolutely no chance of my getting back together with your father. Now, go along downstairs. I'll join you in a minute. I think Mrs Mossop has tea ready.'

The invaluable Mrs Mossop had loyally followed Katherine from the Park Lane flat to The Lodge, declaring that she 'wasn't going to do for that hussy, especially not now she's moved in there, bold as brass!'

When Nicholas had gone Katherine sank into a chair by the window, staring sightlessly before her. The chair, like everything else in the room, had belonged to Stephen, and to old Joshua Lynton before him. It was ugly and over-stuffed, upholstered in bright pink velvet. It was also extremely uncomfortable, but this afternoon Katherine did not even notice.

Charlotte was right: her life was a mess. She was forty-seven years old and drifting aimlessly, supinely living off Henry's bounty. He made her a more than generous allowance, let her live at The Lodge rent free, and permitted her the run of Chapel Rock each summer. She filled up her days with voluntary work and social engagements. She supposed she had seen every major theatre production and film showing in London over the past three years. Katherine Lynton. The ex-Mrs Lynton. Whatever had become of Katherine Grey?

She sat up straighter in her chair suddenly, squaring her shoulders. The children were almost off her hands now. In another three years Guy, her baby, would officially come of age. So wasn't it time she took herself in hand and went in pursuit of that career she had once so badly wanted? She had gradually lost sight of that goal during the twenty years of her marriage to Henry . . .

The thought of Henry brought Katherine up short, an unbearable longing for him washing through her. Even now, she could have forgotten about Jane Clifford; forgiven and forgotten, just as she had been persuaded to do once before. But it was not Jane Clifford who stood between her and her desire to be reconciled with Henry: she considered that Charlotte was probably right in her assumption that he had long ago tired of the younger woman. It was a much more compelling reason which held Katherine aloof; a suspicion, which was tantamount to a certainty, that Henry had taken a hand in Sandor's death.

She had only the haziest notion how these things could be arranged, largely culled from American films and television. But she knew there were such people as contract killers, who could be bought for a price. A car accident, someone tampering with the engine, would be one of the most obvious and least suspect ways to bring about a death. Katherine was unsure when she had first made the connection in her mind between Sandor's fatal accident and her

263

husband's involvement; probably, she reflected, almost as soon she had recollected a certain remark Henry had once made.

'He's a bastard. He ought to be fixed.'

He ought to be fixed . . . Had Henry fixed it? Had he arranged for Sandor to be killed?

Katherine got up from her chair and began pacing around the room. Henry could be ruthless. She, herself, had once said that he had the instincts of a pirate. He hated to be crossed. But, at the same time, had she not just told Nicholas that Henry never meant half he said? Why, then, did this particular chance remark hold such significance for her?

Katherine knew that she could never impart her suspicions to her children. If she were wrong – and she had no proof that she was right – it would be grossly unfair to Henry; but there was more to her reluctance than that. She was perfectly well aware that Charlotte would not only laugh her to scorn, but would also despise her for entertaining the idea, even for a second. She would be diminished in her daughter's eyes. Nicholas, on the other hand, would be only too willing and eager to believe the slander. No future representations that she had, after all, been wrong would convince him that she had been truly in error. Only on Guy would the impact of any such revelation be neglible. He simply would not care what his father had or had not done, provided Henry did not interfere with his own ambitions. Katherine had long since accepted that her youngest child was completely amoral.

Katherine was jerked out of her unquiet thoughts by the banging of the brass gong, which stood on a table at the foot of the stairs. Tea was ready and Mrs Mossop was growing impatient. It was her day for being paid, and she wanted to get her money and be off home. Katherine picked up her handbag and went downstairs.

Robert MacNeice slammed down the receiver in a burst of irritation which he knew to be quite unjustified. Delia Ferguson, who had been his private secretary for more years now than he cared to remember, and who had moved from Edinburgh to London in order to stay with him, was an unusually reliable woman. If she said her cold was severe enough to keep her in bed, then it was probably bordering on pneumonia. Nevertheless, her absence at this juncture was very unfortunate. Robert was up to his eyes in work, occasioned by the prospect of a merger with the giant multi-national Rosewall Foods.

He picked up the telephone receiver again and spoke to the switchboard.

'Typing pool, please,' he requested; and a few seconds later he was listening to the crisp efficient tones of the supervisor. 'Oh, Mrs Antrobus,' he said, 'Miss Ferguson's sick. I'll want a replacement at least for today and most likely for tomorrow as well. Maybe the rest of the week. Send me the best girl you've got.'

'Of course, Mr MacNeice. Right away.'

The line went dead. Robert sat back in his chair and waited. He loathed February. The month had always depressed him, even as a boy, with its leaden skies and sunless days. But ever since the death of his son two years earlier, on a cheerless February morning of biting wind and flurries of bitter sleet, he had hated it even more. Iain had been two months short of his thirteenth birthday when he had complained one evening of a blinding headache and a very stiff neck. A fortnight later he had died in hospital of meningitis.

It had almost destroyed Sheila and pushed their relationship close to destruction. Mutual grief, in their case, had not brought them closer together but torn the marriage apart, as they had both sought someone to blame other than a God in whom neither of them believed. For Clara's sake they had weathered the agonizing twelve months which followed, and were now happier than they had been for some time past. But periods of depression were common to them both. Robert knew that more than his son's life had been lost on the miserably cold day, two years previously.

This particular February of 1971 was producing its own crop of problems, none of them as devastating as those experienced after Iain's death, but sufficient to exercise Robert's mind and make him more than usually snappy, both at home and in the office. His resolution to accept Rosewall's offer and merge the MacNeice bakery chain into their vast and far-reaching organisation had not been taken lightly nor without a good deal of opposition from Sheila and his parents, all three of whom regarded his decision as a betrayal. But he was no longer interested in struggling to maintain MacNeice's as a private company, and he was assured of a place on the Rosewall board.

'And with a damn sight bigger screw than I'm paying myself now, and with only a fraction of the responsibility,' he had told Sheila.

'What do you think I care about the bloody money?' she had blazed back at him. 'Can't you see you're killing your father?'

But his father was dying anyway, Robert consoled himself, and had been for a good many years. There was no room for sentiment in business.

The merger, however, was not his immediate worry. On the fifteenth of February, in one week's time, Britain was converting to decimal currency after centuries of pounds, shillings and pence. The repricing of items in shops throughout the country was a major headache, repercussions being felt at the very highest levels. And it was at this moment, Robert reflected bitterly, that Delia Ferguson had elected to go sick.

He dismissed the thought at once as unworthy, and turned his attention to the papers on his desk. There was a knock on the door, it opened and Katherine walked in.

Robert's jaw dropped ludicrously, and made her smile. She was looking smart and efficient in a navy-blue suit with a midi-length pleated skirt and a tailored white blouse. She sat down in the chair on the opposite side of the desk, her pencil poised above her notepad, her face turned enquiringly towards him.

'Good morning, Mr MacNeice. I'm ready if you are.'

'What . . . What on earth are you doing here?' Robert demanded.

'I work here, sir. I've been employed in the typing pool for the past three months.'

'But . . . But why? And, for God's sake, don't call me "sir".'

'I wanted a job,' she answered simply.

'But surely, Henry . . . ' Robert stared at her, lost for words.

'I said I wanted a job, sir, not needed. Henry was more than generous with the divorce settlement. But I was tired of the useless life I was leading, so I took a crash course to brush up on my shorthand and typing, then registered with a secretarial agency for a full-time job. Just before Christmas, I landed this. I hope you don't mind.'

'No, of course not . . . I was just surprised to see you. I naturally had no idea . . . We haven't seen much of one another since you and Henry were divorced.'

'No.' Katherine gave a tight-lipped smile. 'I've rather let our old friends drop. It could be awkward, meeting Henry. We're not exactly the best of friends. It was not an amicable divorce.'

'No.' Robert picked up a pencil from the tray on

his desk and began fiddling with it. 'So I gathered. I mean . . . One hears things.'

'I imagine one does.' Her eyes twinkled, then grew serious again. 'I've never had the chance to say how very, very sorry I was to learn of your son's death. I did write at the time; a short letter, because there's really nothing anyone can say at such a moment. You may not have read it . . .'

'Yes. I remember it. Thank you.' He cut her short, unable even now to discuss Iain's death with equanimity. He changed the subject abruptly. 'I shouldn't have thought it necessary for you to take a job in a typing pool, not with your experience and qualifications.'

'I took the first opening that came along,' Katherine said. 'And you forget. It's nearly twenty-seven years since I gave up working.'

'August 1947,' he murmured. 'That's when we were married.'

'I hadn't forgotten,' she answered warily.

He laughed, sensing her alarm. 'It's all right, Kate. Honestly. I don't regret a thing.' His accent broadened as he relaxed. 'We were never really suited. And I've been extremely happy with Sheila. We've been going through a sticky patch these last two years, but I think we're nearly over it. Iain's death hit Sheila hard. It hit us both hard, if it comes to that, but it always seems worse for a woman. However, things can only improve.' He laid down the pencil he had been rolling between his fingers, as though suddenly conscious of his unquiet hands. 'Well now, let's get to work.'

Two hours later, with a five-minute break for a hastily swallowed cup of lukewarm coffee, Katherine closed her notebook and retracted her ball-point pen. She had enough dictation to keep her chained to her typewriter for the rest of the day, and retired to Delia Ferguson's office next to Robert's which had been put at her disposal.

It was seven o'clock before the last letter had been typed and was ready for signature. Katherine added it to the pile already done, which she then carried through to Robert. He took the letters from her and began reading.

'You know,' he said, when he had finished signing, 'you really are much too good to be wasted in the typing pool. I'll have a word with Mrs Antrobus in the morning. One of my directors has just lost his secretary. I think you'd suit him very well.'

'Thank you,' Katherine answered quietly.

Robert laid down his pen with a sigh. 'How about some dinner? Sheila isn't home tonight. She's taken Clara to the theatre, so I'm a free agent. There's an Italian restaurant just round the corner. Do you like Italian food? I don't remember.'

'I don't think the question ever arose,' Katherine answered, gathering up the pile of signed letters. 'But the answer is yes. Very much. I'll just put these in their envelopes and leave them ready for special delivery in the morning. Goodness knows how long this postal strike is going to last. Ron Thomas and the government seem to have reached stalemate.'

When she rejoined him, fifteen minutes later, she was wearing a dark red wool coat with a big fur collar. Robert ushered her towards the lift. Cleaners were already at work in the corridors. Many of the office doors stood open, giving a view of chairs and waste-paper baskets piled on tables. Katherine hadn't realized that it was quite so late.

But she had nothing to go home for. At the moment, during term-time, she was alone in that big, empty, echoing house. She was shaken by a spasm of longing for Henry, but once more suppressed it. She was a working woman now. This was the life she had always wanted.

She stepped into the lift after Robert and pressed the ground floor button.

21

'If this is Vienna,' Jane Clifford said, 'I don't think much of it. If I'd known it was like this, I wouldn't have come.' She stared grumpily out of the taxi window at a giant oil refinery, as the airport was left behind.

'Wait,' Henry answered briefly, and lapsed into the silence which he had maintained for most of the time since quitting London. He had not wanted Jane to accompany him on what was mainly a business trip, and had spent a week regretting his rash promise to bring her with him.

'I've never been to Vienna,' she had remarked wistfully, when he had mentioned his visit to the Austrian capital.

It had been the evening of a particularly protracted row between them, and Henry had been anticipating tantrums and sulks for the next few days. Agreeing to let her go with him had, at the time, seemed an easy way out of the dilemma.

'You'll have to entertain yourself while I'm busy,' he had warned her, but Jane had assured him that she did not mind.

As the visit drew nearer, however, Henry wished he had never made the promise. The three-day trip would have given him a breathing space: time to be by himself. He resented Jane's determination to hold him to his word. Right up until the last minute he had hoped to persuade her to change her mind, but she had remained adamant.

'What a God-awful dump,' Jane muttered again as the road cut a swath through a cemetery. 'I thought Vienna was the city of romance. Or am I thinking of Paris?'

Henry did not deign to reply, hunching his shoulders and burying his face in The Times. Some of the news was good. After last month's fall in the bank rate from seven to six per cent, it had been reduced yet again to five. It meant that he would be a little less pressed for money. In America, at present, things were not going well. Last month an estimated two hundred thousand demonstrators had marched on the Capitol in protest against the Vietnam war, following the conviction of a United States army officer for the massacre of twenty-two Vietnamese civilians at My Lai. That sort of thing unsettled people and investments fell. The Clifford Chemical Corporation was already experiencing difficulties; and the situation was not much better here, in Europe, in spite of the fact that Britain, under the premiership of Edward Heath, seemed poised to join the Common Market.

It was because of the falling sales of Lynton's Chemicals that Henry had arranged this visit to see Hans Rothermeyer of Rothermeyer & Pusswold, the firm which handled much of his Continental advertising. And it was these same falling sales which should be occupying the major part of his attention, Henry told himself angrily, as the taxi swerved on to the central ring road, not the complications of his private life.

Not a day passed that he did not think of Katherine and devise a dozen ways of luring her back. But all his carefully laid schemes were only pipe dreams as long as he and Jane remained together. But how could he throw Jane off? His conscience told him that he should have married her as soon as his divorce from Katherine had been made absolute; and only that streak of ruthlessness in him, that fundamental sense of self-preservation, had stopped him from doing what Leo and Beryl Claypole would term 'the decent thing'. He was under no illusion that Jane was in love with him, but she did want to marry him, and to have the status and importance of being Mrs Lynton. The one thing she did not need was his money: the death, first of her grandfather and then, last month, of her grandmother, had left her a very wealthy young woman.

Nevertheless, Henry owed her something. If it hadn't been for her affair with him Jane would have returned to the States years ago, after her work permit expired. Instead, she had continued to live in London, losing touch with all her friends, and eventually moving in with him after Katherine had left the Park Lane flat for The Lodge. And the ironic thing was, Henry reflected, letting the newspaper fall into his lap, he had been faithful to Jane with a consistency he had never shown to Katherine. So much for guilty conscience!

Vienna's magnificent panorama of buildings was now unfolding before them; the museums, the university, the opera house, the theatres, the restaurants and coffee-shops. It wasn't, Henry thought, as the ribbons of early-evening lights flashed by, that he hadn't wanted to sleep with other women. His nature had not changed. It was simply that he felt his present domestic situation to be sufficiently unorthodox not to wish to complicate it further. Beryl Claypole had been right. Even today, in the wake of the Swinging Sixties, there was still a world of difference between the licence permitted to the young and the behaviour expected of a man of his age and position. It was nearly four years since Katherine had left him, almost three since they had been divorced. If something did not happen soon to resolve the situation, he would be forced to marry Jane Clifford. The hairs rose on the nape of his neck. He could feel the steel-toothed jaw of the trap slowly closing . . .

The taxi turned into Philharmonikerstrasse and pulled up outside the Sacher Hotel. Henry's original plan had been to stay at the Vienna Hilton, but on reflection he had decided that the plush Sacher, known world-wide for its chocolate cake, and a favourite haunt of the rich and famous, would afford Jane greater amusement. He paid off the taxi while the doorman summoned assistance for the luggage.

'Remember,' Henry instructed her briefly, 'you're Mrs Lynton.' Then he took Jane's arm and they went inside.

He had taken part in several anti-Vietnam war rallies in the past, but he had never been frightened before. In comparison with this surging mass of humanity milling in front of the American Embassy, they had been tame, almost gentlemanly affairs.

Nicholas and some of his friends had travelled down from Oxford earlier in the day, snatching a sandwich and a cup of tepid coffee in the buffet on Paddington station before making their way by Tube to Grosvenor Square. Here they had met up with other students from universities and colleges all over the country, and gathered in an orderly mass in front of the United States Embassy which occupied the entire west side of the square. Designed by the Finnish-American architect Eero Saarinen, the building had only been completed in 1960, and was dominated by a massive stone eagle whose thirty-five-foot wing-span stretched protectively – and provocatively in many eyes – across the roof.

The day was warm and sunny for early May, and the buds on the London trees were opening to the light. Little white clouds, like wisps of incense, stained the pale blue sky. Opposite the embassy the statue of Franklin Delano Roosevelt towered above William Kent's eighteenth-century garden, which formed the nucleus of the square.

To begin with, everything was quiet, following the accepted pattern of these events. A couple of Cambridge undergraduates knocked on the embassy door and, when it was opened, presented a petition. This called on the Americans to withdraw from South Vietnam, and boasted over three thousand signatures. The embassy official took it reluctantly, then returned inside, shutting the door firmly. By this time the police were making their presence felt, linking hands and cordoning off the approach to the embassy, holding back the demonstrators now packing all four sides of the square.

But the crowd was still reasonably good-humoured, trading friendly insults with the law, both sides laughing at one another's sallies. Nicholas, who had somehow managed to get separated from his friends, joined in the rhythmic chanting of: 'Yanks go home! America out of South Vietnam!' After about half an hour, when his voice was growing hoarse, he accepted the offer of a throat sweet from his neighbour.

'It makes you dry, all this shouting,' she said. 'My name's Annabel Hardwicke. What's yours?'

'Nicholas Lynton.'

He turned his head to get a good look at her and saw a round face under a helmet of dark brown hair, cut in a heavy fringe across the broad forehead. The eyes were brown, the mouth full with an upward tilt which made its owner seem to be perpetually smiling. The girl was not very tall, the top of her head only just above Nicholas's shoulder.

'I'm a drama student,' she volunteered. 'RADA. How about you?'

'Oxford. Trinity,' he answered, equally succinct. 'Medieval French.'

She laughed, a clear, joyous sound that pealed out above the chanting. What she was laughing at Nicholas had no idea, and doubted if she had, either; but he joined in, infected by her sheer high spirits and pleasure in living.

On a sudden impulse he asked, 'Can I see you again? I live in London, and I shall be home soon for the long vacation. At least I shall be here for part of the time, when I'm not in Cornwall. Oh, and then I'm hitch-hiking round Europe for a couple of weeks with some friends.'

The girl screwed up her eyes in amusement. 'When are you planning to fit me in, then? Sounds as though I shall need an appointment.'

It was at this moment that Nicholas realized that the mood of the crowd was turning ugly. The chanting had degenerated into bad-tempered abuse, and people were beginning to push in a concerted mass towards the embassy. One policeman had been knocked to the ground , and his colleagues had only just managed to haul him to safety before he was trampled underfoot. Another policeman was radioing for assistance.

Nicholas felt himself borne bodily forward in the press, his feet no longer touching the ground. There was nothing he could do to prevent it, and he remembered in a sweat of panic the terrible disaster earlier in the year at Glasgow's Ibrox Park, when sixty football spectators had been crushed to death in a similar situation. He glanced round desperately for the girl, but she had been carried away from him by the surge of bodies being forced between them. He just had time to see her scared face before she disappeared from view, hidden by the heads and shoulders of the surrounding people.

Lines from a poem by Chastellain, which he had been reading only yesterday, flashed into Nicholas's head, terrifying in their immediacy.

Le cœur qui veult crevier au corps
Haulce et soulième la poitrine
Qui se veult joindre à son eschine . . .

The heart which wishes to burst into the body raises and lifts the chest, which nearly joins the spine. It described exactly how Nicholas felt at that moment. And Chastellain's poem was called 'Le Pas de la Mort' . . .

People were screaming. One girl, near Nicholas, was unconscious, her face turning blue, her eyes starting from her head. Someone else was flailing his arms helplessly, unable to lower them to protect his ribcage. Nicholas himself was finding it increasingly difficult to breathe. The blood was drumming in his ears, there was a terrible piercing pain in his chest, consciousness came and went. Then, just as the agony became too great to bear a second longer, the whole world seemed to disintegrate in a burst of stars.

By the second full day of their visit, Jane Clifford was growing bored with Vienna. Museums and art galleries did not interest her, although, taking Henry's advice, she had visited the Kunsthistorisches museum, where even she had to admit to being overawed by the magnificently baroque interior. But, generally speaking, she preferred the shops, except that everything in Vienna was so expensive. There was very little that could not be bought more cheaply elsewhere. She did buy a fur hat and a long-fringed cashmere scarf in a subtle blend of blues and greens, but these were extravagances she did not repeat. She visited several coffee-shops, but too many of the delicious cream cakes and pastries played havoc with her self-imposed diet.

'For God's sake!' Henry exclaimed impatiently, when she had complained to him of boredom the previous evening. 'You're in Vienna! One of the most beautiful and historic cities in the world. Go and look at Schönbrunn Palace. Mozart played there for Maria Theresa when he was six! Go to the Hofburg and see the Lipizzaner stallions in the Spanish Riding School. There are more things to do than stuff your face with cakes.'

She had pouted. 'It wouldn't be so bad if you could come with me and explain things. Haven't you finished your stupid business yet?'

Henry shook his head. 'I'm afraid not, my dear. You'll just have to entertain yourself.'

He did not add, 'As Katherine would have done,' but the words were implicit in the scornful look he gave her. Jane had gone to bed in a huff, refusing him when, later, he wanted to make love. As a result he had left the hotel this morning without even waking her, and there was no message from him concerning lunch.

Jane shrugged to herself as she ran a bath. If that was how he was going to behave, Henry would just have to learn that she didn't care. By the time she descended to the foyer it was almost lunchtime, and she decided it would be easier if she ate in the hotel. The prospect daunted her. Contrary to Henry's expectations she found Sacher's, with its scarlet and gold décor, heavy Turkish carpets, mahogany furniture and gilt-framed oil paintings, rather depressing. Used to the slick glass and chrome of modern establishments, she would much have preferred the Vienna Hilton.

As she was about to enter the dining-room a hand seized her elbow, and a voice she did not immediately recognize asked, 'It is Miss Clifford, isn't it? Jane?'

She turned curiously and came face to face with Robert MacNeice.

'Gracious!' she exclaimed. 'This is a surprise. We haven't seen one another for ages.'

'No. Not since before Katherine and Henry were

divorced.' His tone was deliberately casual, breaking the ice on what otherwise might have been an awkwardly prohibitive subject. 'I'm lunching here. Are you alone? Would you do me the honour of joining me?'

A hovering waiter found them a table for two and brought the menus. Jane asked, 'What are you doing in Vienna?'

'I'm here on business,' Robert answered, smiling. 'I fly home tonight. What about you?'

'Oh, the same. At least, Henry's here on business and I just came along for the ride. We're going home tomorrow. I shall be pleased. To tell you the truth, I'm finding it all rather boring. Does that shock you, the same way it does Henry?'

Robert laughed, shaking his head. 'Not really. I'm not a sightseer either. And I hate opera and ballet and all the rest of that stuff. I never did have much time for the arts. Sport's my chief recreation. That's really why Katherine and I didn't hit it off. Our interests were so dissimilar. She and Henry were much more compatible.'

Jane grimaced, and Robert wondered why he had never before realized quite how pretty she was. Jane Clifford was a most attractive young woman.

'What about your wife?' she was asking, apparently unaware of his intensified gaze. Or perhaps she was used to it from men. She must excite a lot of attention.

'Sheila? Oh, she's like me, I suppose. We're not culture vultures. We know what we like and like what we know.' Robert wondered angrily what had happened to his powers of conversation that he should be reduced to such banalities.

But Jane was uncritical. 'That's what I always say,' she told him, laying aside the menu. 'I can't choose, I'm afraid. I'll leave it to you to order for me.'

She fluttered her eyelashes appealingly, and all

278

Robert's chivalrous instincts were aroused, as they had not been aroused for years. He was nearly fifty, but this girl, young enough to be his daughter, made him feel twenty-five again. It was a very long while since any woman had looked at him with such open admiration in her eyes.

Katherine had never needed him. Robert doubted that she had ever needed any man but Henry Lynton. Her independence, their widely differing tastes had doomed the marriage from the start; something which she, not he, had had the wits to recognize. Then he thought that he had found the ideal woman in Sheila, and it was true that, for a time, they had been happy. But Iain's death had driven a wedge between them, and Robert's hope that things were mending had proved to be ill-founded. Since that February evening, three months ago, when he had taken Katherine to dinner, he and Sheila had drifted even further apart. Each blamed the other for not doing more, when in fact both knew perfectly well that there was nothing to be done.

Jane, listening to Robert order in his Scots-accented but nevertheless apparently comprehensive German, noting the waiter's deference at his choice of wine, thought how competent he was. Good-looking, too; distinguished, his once dark hair now almost iron-grey. His age did not worry her: she had never liked younger men. Her male contemporaries bored her. She found them brash and immature, their heads full of impossible ideals. None of them could offer the protection and sophistication of an older man.

When they had finished their meal Robert glanced at his watch.

'My plane doesn't leave until six o'clock,' he said. 'That gives me four hours. Is there anything you'd like to do, or see, until then?'

'I'll have to check first at the desk, to see if Henry's

left any message for me.' Jane smiled. 'If not, perhaps we could go to the cinema. There's sure to be an American or British film showing somewhere.'

Henry had not telephoned the hotel, and Jane suddenly felt relieved. She turned to Robert.

'Come up with me to my room while I get a jacket. This May weather is so uncertain.'

She had no idea why she had invited him upstairs with her: he could just as easily have waited in the foyer. Whatever the reason, the invitation was certainly innocent, as was Robert's acceptance. Nothing was further from either of their minds than making love.

Yet, once the bedroom door had closed behind them, there seemed an inevitability about it, as though it had been foreordained. Inside the room Jane made no move to fetch her coat, and when Robert put his hands on her shoulders she turned and went into his arms as if it were the most natural thing in the world for her to do. After that, it was only a short step to getting into bed. It was only later, after Robert had gone, that Jane realized she had given no thought at all to the possibility of Henry's return. Quite simply, she had not thought about him at all, and neither had Robert.

Robert . . . Jane stretched luxuriously in the disordered bed, loving the sensuous feel of the cool sheets on her naked skin. Adding to her pleasure was the thought that she had now managed to seduce both of Katherine's former husbands. It gave her a feeling of power: the centuries-old triumph of youth over age. And it served Henry right! He had been less than attentive just lately. Moreover, there was his continued refusal to set a date for their wedding, pleading first one excuse and then another. Sometimes she had the absurd suspicion that he did not want to marry her.

She got up, dressed and made the bed, humming

to herself as she did so. She was just putting some of her clothes into her case, ready for their departure the following day, when the bedroom door opened and Henry came in.

'Keep packing,' he said, seeing what she was doing. 'We're leaving tonight instead of tomorrow. There was a message for me at the desk. Nick's been badly injured in some damn fool demonstration or other.'

Katherine was waiting for him at the hospital.

'It's not as bad as we thought at first,' she told him, almost crying with relief. 'Just a couple of broken ribs and extensive bruising. But he was lucky. They were all lucky. Someone could easily have been killed.'

'How did it happen?' Henry asked grimly, following her along the white-painted corridor and smelling the all-pervasive antiseptic smell. It always made him want to retch.

'There was a big anti-Vietnam war demonstration in Grosvenor Square. Apparently everything was going all right at first, but then the police believe some trouble-makers infiltrated the crowd with orders to stir things up. National Front members. People like that. Whether that's really what happened or not, the result was the same. People at the back began pushing and shoving towards the embassy. The ones at the front were crushed.'

Katherine pushed open the door of a ward and led the way between two neat rows of beds. Nicholas was in the last but one on the right-hand side, looking very pale and fragile. He was asleep.

'They've sedated him,' Katherine explained.

A large bruise disfigured one of his cheeks, and to his father's eyes he seemed a little boy again, small and vulnerable beneath the carefully smoothed and mitred sheets. But, as always, Henry's concern expressed itself in anger.

'What the hell's he doing taking part in all these senseless demonstrations anyway? That's Victor's subversive influence. You should have kept the boys away from him when they were younger.'

Katherine rounded on him, her face closed and set.

'That's right! Blame anyone but yourself! And lower your voice. People are staring.'

'Let them!' Henry retorted. 'And that's another thing! Why isn't my son in a private room?'

'He wouldn't be put in one!' Katherine hissed. 'He said he'd get up and walk out of the hospital if I arranged it. And if that's all you have to say, Henry, I'm sorry I got in touch. I hoped, just for once, you'd act like a loving and concerned father, but that appears impossible. You're running true to form. You've never liked Nick.'

'That's not true. He's my son. OK, we've never seen eye to eye. We've had our disagreements and I think he's a fool. But that doesn't mean to say I don't love him. Kate!' Henry gripped her arm. 'I have to speak to you alone. For God's sake let's go somewhere where we can talk. When you leave here, let me come back with you to The Lodge.'

Katherine hesitated, her eyes softening as she stared into his troubled face. Then, clearly, from further along the ward came the voice of a woman, visiting her husband, reprimanding her three-year-old son.

'Sandy! Don't touch that! D'you hear me? Sandy!' The voice rose. 'I'll kill you if you don't do as you're told!'

Katherine made a little noise between a gasp and a sob, half put out her hand to Henry, then swung on her heel and ran out of the ward. When Henry followed her, a moment later, she was nowhere to be seen.

22

The London streets were lined with good-natured crowds four or five deep, everyone eager to share in the royal Silver Wedding. The lowering November skies in no way dampened the onlookers' enthusiasm; and the truth was, Katherine decided, taking up a position on the pavement near Westminster Abbey, the year 1972 had, in many areas, been so disastrous that any celebration made a welcome change.

It had opened badly with the number of unemployed topping the million mark; and just over a week later, on the thirtieth of January, trouble had escalated in Northern Ireland, with thirteen civilians killed in Londonderry. The day had come to be known as Bloody Sunday. The following month the IRA had retaliated by bombing a public house in Aldershot, resulting in seven more deaths. Also in February, the miners had called a national strike culminating in a power crisis. A state of emergency had been declared by the government.

In May a work to rule by railwaymen had brought total shut-down of all rail services at weekends; and in July there had been no national newspapers for a week because the print unions had come out in sympathy with five dockers gaoled for contempt of court. In Ulster things went from bad to worse, and Iceland extended her fishing limits from twelve to fifty miles. Newspaper pundits predicted trouble and had already coined the phrase 'Cod War'. In August,

Prince William of Gloucester died in a plane crash.

In America President Nixon, who had just been re-elected for a further term of office, had stepped up the Vietnam offensive, ignoring a growing storm of criticism from both home and abroad; while in Washington burglars had been caught in the Watergate building, apparently raiding the headquarters of the Democratic party election campaign. All in all, Katherine reflected, not a year to be recalled with much affection.

Privately, however, she was as happy and contented as she was ever likely to be now that Henry and Jane were married. It was pointless to speculate what might have happened had she allowed Henry to escort her home that night, eighteen months ago, from the hospital. She remembered that she had very nearly agreed. She knew that she had desperately wanted to do so. If only the woman hadn't called out at that precise moment, it was probable that she would have said yes. But the child's name, Sandy – short, she guessed, for Alexander – had brought back memories; and suspicions had come flooding in their wake.

So she had run away from Henry as she had already done twice before, but the third time had proved to be once too often. Three weeks later she had seen the announcement of his engagement to Jane Clifford in *The Times*, and in September 1971 they had been married.

So far there was no sign of a child, and Charlotte, who visited her father and stepmother regularly, reported that all was not well with the marriage.

'If you ask me,' she had said only last week, lolling inelegantly in a corner of the drawing-room sofa, one denim-clad leg hooked over the brocaded arm, 'Jane's as disillusioned with Dad as he is with her. Now that she's got what she wanted, she finds it isn't, if you follow me. They fight like cat and dog, and I'd swear

Dad's at his old tricks again. Jane complains that he works late most evenings, but the way she says it makes me think she suspects what he's really up to. Moreover, I don't think she cares. I think' – and Charlotte had pursed her lips significantly – 'that she'd be only too happy to have it off with someone else, too.'

Katherine had felt bound to remonstrate with her daughter's choice of phrase, but without much conviction. She told herself firmly that she had no interest in Henry's marital affairs, and had her own busy life to lead.

The latter was certainly true. Once the MacNeice bakery chain had been taken over by Rosewall Foods, her rise in the company had been swift. At the time of the merger she had already been a director's secretary, and had eventually been assigned to Jonathan Anthony, the newly appointed chairman of the board. Over the past six months he had come to regard her so highly that he had accepted her recommendation and transferred the Rosewall advertising acount to the firm for whom Charlotte now worked.

'Nepotism! I love it!' Charlotte had crowed delightedly. 'My stock has risen at Royle and Chandos by at least two hundred per cent.'

'I recommended Royle and Chandos because I think it an excellent firm,' Katherine had replied starchily,'and because Rosewall's are very dissatisfied with their current advertising campaign. I just hope my confidence hasn't been misplaced.'

Charlotte was living at home, having decided that there was room and enough to spare at The Lodge for her and her mother to exist amicably together without either getting on one another's nerves or under each other's feet. It was also cheaper, as Katherine had drily pointed out. Nicholas, still at Oxford, and Guy, in his last year at school, came home for the holidays, although these no longer included visits to

Chapel Rock. Henry had made it plain that they were all welcome there at any time, including Katherine, but the situation had changed. The Lodge was hers by virtue of the divorce settlement, but Jane was now legally mistress of Chapel Rock, and Katherine could not bring herself to visit it in the altered circumstances.

The royal party was just arriving at the Abbey – the Queen in a fur-trimmed coat, the twenty-year-old Princess Anne in bright fuchsia – when Charlotte pushed her way through the crowd to her mother's side, ignoring the resentful murmurs of the people she had displaced.

'I thought it was you,' she said with some satisfaction. 'You'll never guess who I've just seen!' Her hazel eyes sparkled with malice. 'About half an hour ago, in the Strand, dawdling along near Australia House and holding hands like a couple of lovers.' She paused for dramatic effect, while all around them people cheered and waved, and the girls tried to catch Prince Charles's eye. Even Prince Philip, immaculate in morning dress, came in for his share of female adulation.

'Well, who?' Katherine demanded, irritated at having her attention distracted at such a moment.

Charlotte grimaced, her eyes following the royal party as it disappeared inside Westminster Abbey.

'Guess,' she urged, but added swiftly, 'No, don't bother, because you never would in a hundred years.' She turned her head and grinned at Katherine, who was at last looking intrigued. 'What do you say to your first ex-husband and your second ex-husband's wife?'

Robert and Jane had met by chance outside the Savoy Hotel, where Jane had been having a late breakfast with a friend. But the friend had a hair appointment and had been obliged to hurry away, leaving Jane

286

feeling flat and dispirited, and with the prospect of filling in time for the rest of the morning. Henry was abroad, at a conference in Bonn, and although he had grudgingly suggested that Jane might like to accompany him on this occasion, she had refused. Increasingly disenchanted with the marriage she had worked so hard to bring about, she had been glad of the rest from Henry's company and the cat-and-dog existence they were leading.

She was feeling miserable and cross with herself for not remembering that today, November the twentieth, the Queen's Silver Wedding celebrations were taking place. Unlike most Americans, Jane was not an ardent follower of royalty and their doings, and had not only forgotten that the streets would be packed with people, but also that many of them would be cordoned off for the various processions. At least, this morning, the crowds were largely congregated around Westminster Abbey.

'Jane! Mrs Lynton!'

Robert MacNeice was standing in front of her, tentatively holding out his hand. He looked unsure of his reception, and Jane to her annoyance, began to blush. They had not seen one another since Vienna, and memories of that last encounter were uppermost in both their minds. Jane and Henry had become engaged so soon after their return from Austria that Robert had intentionally avoided them, making sure in advance that any invitations accepted by himself and Sheila did not include the Lyntons. Now, here they were, face to face outside the Savoy; but the only surprising thing about their meeting was that it had not happened sooner. The few square miles of central London which they both inhabited were not much larger than a good-sized village.

'I . . . I read about your marriage to Henry,' Robert said hesitantly, still retaining possession of her hand.

'Yes.' Jane's eyes filled with tears. 'I – I'm sorry,'

she gasped, 'but I'm afraid it hasn't worked out. It was a terrible mistake. Please forgive me.' She released her hand and hunted in her bag for her handkerchief.

Robert looked uncomfortable. He made no attempt, however, to move away. 'I have a meeting at eleven o'clock,' he said, 'with Royle and Chandos, in Farringdon Street, but I should be free by half-past twelve. Let me take you to lunch. What about Simpson's?'

Jane smiled at him mistily, dabbing at her eyes with a wisp of lace and cotton.

'That would be lovely,' she said, 'Are you walking to Farringdon Street?' Robert nodded and she went on eagerly. 'Could I walk with you part of the way? I'm sick of window-shopping and there's nothing I need to buy. I hate just aimlessly wandering.'

'Of course.' He seemed genuinely delighted and, emboldened, she held his hand as they crossed the street. Neither of them noticed, as they passed Australia House, Charlotte going in the opposite direction, on the outside edge of the pavement.

Robert moved with long swinging strides: still the walk of a young man, Jane thought admiringly. It was difficult to believe he was over fifty. But, then, so was Henry, and he was equally vigorous. Why, then, was she so much less conscious of the age gap with Robert MacNeice? He inspired in her all the confidence, the feeling of being protected, which she needed and experienced with older men, but at the same time he made her feel sophisticated and intelligent, not like some ignorant and recalcitrant child. Henry never failed to mock the fact that she preferred the cinema to the theatre, magazines to books, pop to classical music.

Later, lingering over their lunch at Simpson's, where the waiters served slices of meat from the huge roasts on their heated carving trolleys, or ladled out portions of Lancashire hot-pot, tripe and onions, or boiled chicken, Jane felt suddenly relaxed.

'I love listening to you talk,' she said, leaning her elbows on the table and supporting her chin on her clasped hands. She lowered her lashes, so heavy and thick they could almost have been false. 'How ... how is your wife?'

'Sheila's gone back to Scotland,' he answered, thinking how beautiful Jane looked in the tight-fitting blue woollen dress which stressed the contours of her shapely figure. The blue and beige silk scarf draped negligently around her shoulders emphasized the colour of her eyes. The fair hair had grown since he had seen her last, and was gathered in an old-fashioned chignon at the back of her neck; an attempt, he guessed, to make her appear older than her twenty-seven years.

'Have you split up?' Jane's eyes opened up in astonishment. 'I haven't heard anyone mention it.'

'It only happened last month. Clara's at boarding school near Edinburgh, and most of her friends are up there now. She was very lonely in London during the school holidays, and it had got so that she didn't want to come home. So Sheila and I decided to give up the house in Wilton Crescent and buy one in Edinburgh instead. I have a flat now, in Albany.' He grinned. 'The Prime Minister's one of my neighbours.'

'Oh. I see.' The lashes were lowered again, but the gesture this time was consciously coy. Jane removed her elbows from the table and began playing with a fork. 'You must find it very lonely, all on your own.'

'Yes,' he answered, and added, 'Would you do me the honour of visiting me there sometimes?' Even as he spoke, he reflected how crazy was this formal approach to a woman he had already made love to. But there was something about Jane Lynton which aroused his latent chivalrous instincts.

There was nothing either shrinking or missish, however, in Jane's response. Her inbred American assertiveness was suddenly uppermost. Raising her eyes and looking straight into his, she asked bluntly, 'How about tonight?'

'You're very quiet today,' Annabel Hardwicke accused Nicholas. 'Anyway, do you mind telling me what we're doing here at all? I thought you had no time for royalty.'

Nicholas glanced down at her. 'You have to know your enemies,' he answered loftily. 'Besides,' he added, bringing the conversation down to nursery level, 'you can talk! You came when I asked you. You made absolutely no demur. And I thought you despised them more than I do.'

'I don't despise them exactly,' Annabel said, 'but I can think of things more worthwhile to be doing. I should be learning my lines for Rose Eyre. We're dong scenes from *The Shoemaker's Holiday* and I'm playing the shoemaker's daughter.' She wrinkled her nose disgustedly. 'Why do I always get given the ingénue roles?'

'Because you're small,' Nicholas answered promptly, putting his arm around her and giving her an affectionate squeeze. 'Also you have a nice, clean, honest, shining countenance to match your nice, clean, honest, shining soul.'

The smile was wiped from Annabel's face as she raised it to look anxiously into his.

'Is that how you see me?' she asked, after a moment's silence. She shook her head slowly. 'Darling Nick, you really don't know me at all.'

They were two of many hundreds of people cramming the Barbican that afternoon, patiently waiting for the Queen and members of the royal family to emerge from Guildhall, where they had been entertained to lunch by the Lord Mayor. Nicholas was not at all sure why he had come, except that nowadays he seized on any excuse for a trip to London while Annabel was there. During the holidays she went home to her widowed mother in Durham, and it was then that Nicholas realized what a big, lonely and empty place the capital could seem. He had been born in London, lived there all his life; but it was only after he met Annabel that the city took on meaning for him and became an entity in its own right. Annabel drew him out of himself; forced him, through her own interest and vitality, to look around him; to leave behind that secret inner world he had inhabited for so long. She took him to theatres, museums, art galleries. Together, they indulged her passion for London churches.

Today she had met him at Paddington, where they had bought cheese rolls and fruit before travelling by Tube to Moorgate station. For a while they had wandered about the Barbican, watching crash barriers being erected to hold back the crowds, then eaten their picnic lunch sitting in one of the pews of St Giles Cripplegate. The sixteenth-century church where Oliver Cromwell and Elizabeth Bourchier had been married also housed Milton's tomb. Nicholas, an arm about Annabel, his lips nuzzling her hair, had quoted softly:

'And looks commercing with the skies,
    Thy rapt soul sitting in thine eyes . . .'

She had looked at him then just as she was looking at him now, warily and a little apprehensively. She said, after a moment's pause, 'You mustn't put me on a pedestal, Nick. I . . . I'm not really a very nice person. I have lots of faults. You're not the first man I've been to bed with.'

'I didn't imagine I was,' Nicholas replied confidently. 'But I don't care as long as I'm the last. You love me as much as I love you. You told me so.'

'And I meant it. I do love you, Nick. I shall

291

probably never love anyone else. But that doesn't mean you own me. I belong to myself. No one else.'

'Of course,' he answered easily.'Everyone belongs to himself or herself. That's natural.'

'Not for women it isn't.'

He grinned, tightening his grip. The crowds were growing restless, waiting for their first sight of the Queen.

Nicholas went on, 'I shan't object to you carrying on acting, after we're married.'

'There you are! That's what I mean!' Annabel shrugged herself out of his embrace, her dark eyes stormy. 'You take it for granted we're going to be married. And you haven't even asked me yet.'

Damn! she thought to herself. Damn, damn! It wasn't what she had meant to say.

'Oh, well, if that's all that's bothering you,' Nicholas grinned, 'I'm asking you now. Will you marry me? I'd like to be engaged.'

'I shouldn't,' Annabel snapped; but the hurt expression on his face made her go on, 'Nick darling, I've admitted I love you. We sleep together when we can. Isn't that enough? I'm too young to be tied down, and so are you. There's absolutely no reason why we shouldn't go on as we are. For the time being, at least.'

'But you will marry me one day?' he persisted, again putting his arm about her now unresisting shoulders.

'Nick, I don't know. I honestly don't know.'

'But surely, if you love me . . .'

'Oh, stop it!' Annabel exclaimed crossly. 'You're spoiling the day. This is a silly conversation.'

Nicholas was upset by her attitude, but not seriously disturbed. He was as certain that she loved him as that he loved her, and for him that simply meant two things: total loyalty and eventual marriage. Marriage was an intrinsic part of the world in which he had been brought up, where even divorce led to a retying of matrimonial bonds. It was also of paramount importance in that medieval world which he inhabited in his studies.

> *Du chastel d' Amours vous demant:*
> *Dites le premier fondement!*
> — *Amer loyaument.*

For him, to love loyally was indeed the first foundation stone of the Castle of Love; although he chose to forget the second and more cynical stanza of the poem which suggested that to conceal wisely was the principal wall which made the building fine and strong and sure. Nicholas would never be able to conceal wisely where Annabel was concerned. Since falling in love, he wore his heart on his sleeve.

After he had been discharged from hospital after the demonstration in Grosvenor Square, he could not get her out of his mind. He had been nearly crazy with worry, wondering what had happened to her in that terrifying crush and subsequent panic. All he knew about her was her name and the fact that she was a student at RADA. So he had gone there as soon as he was able, to make enquiries, and discovered that she had escaped unhurt, apart from some bruising. He had taken her out once or twice during his period of convalescence, and she promised to write to him when he returned to Oxford. It had not occurred to Nicholas that they might become lovers until they had known one another for over six months; and then it was Annabel who proposed it.

'You're so old-fashioned,' she had said impatiently. 'This is the twentieth century, not the fourteenth. Men don't idolize women any more. They screw them.'

Nicholas had been shocked by her forthrightness, but not unwilling. After their first night together in the flat which Annabel shared with two other drama students, he knew that his love for her had become the most important thing in his life. Until then his mother was the only woman for whom he had felt any real affection, although he was fond of Charlotte in a vague kind of way. Now, suddenly he understood what love was: the complete commitment of heart and mind and body to another human being. He had not dared to hope that Annabel could feel the same way about him until one afternoon, lying in his arms when she should have been in class, she had declared passionately, 'Oh, Nick! I do love you. So very, very much!'

After that, dazed with happiness, he had taken it for granted that it was only a matter of time before they were married. He had been surprised, but not worried, by her refusal to meet his family; nor did it strike him as odd that her life at home, in Durham, was something he was never invited to share. That part of her existence was separate and did not concern him. If he thought about it at all, he decided that his introduction to her family and friends in the north would take place in due course. That Annabel was deliberately holding him at arm's length in some areas of her life, simply never entered Nicholas's head.

Before he could say anything more, someone in front of them called out, 'Here they are!' And there, indeed, were the Queen and Prince Philip and their two elder children, strolling through the cheering crowds, pausing every now and then to chat to people with an informality which would have been unthinkable before the watershed of the sixties, when so many barriers had crumbled, along with so many other shibboleths and taboos.

But the royal family also represented a continuity of those values which had existed before instant sex and women's demands for equal rights and liberation. Nicholas, fervent anti-royalist though he was, suddenly found himself regarding them in a more favourable light. At that moment the monarchy represented everything he most wanted for himself and Annabel: marriage and a stable family life.

23

'This is Annabel,' Nicholas said. 'Annie, this is my mother.'

The two women regarded one another warily; very much, Katherine thought, like two dogs guarding the same bone. 'Bitches' was obviously the more appropriate word, except that there was nothing bitchy about Annabel Hardwicke's broadcheeked face, in the wide-eyed candid gaze or in the firm, almost manly, handshake.

The girl looked ill at ease, patently wishing she had not come, and feeling uncomfortable in a pale green linen dress when she would have been happier in old jeans and a T-shirt. But when she spoke she betrayed no self-consciousness, nor did she make any attempt to disguise the North Country accent which Katherine could not immediately place.

'How do you do, Mrs Lynton? Nick talks about you a lot.' Was there a faintly ironic note to her voice? Katherine could not be sure.

'Does he?' Katherine was flattered, but did her best to conceal it.

'Yes,' the girl answered. 'I don't suppose you can say the same about me.'

'N ... No,' Katherine stammered, thrown into confusion, and irritated by her inability to conceal the fact. She gestured towards the drawing-room door. 'Please, come in. We were going to have tea in the garden, but it's turned so cloudy.'

This was awful. It was Nicholas's fault, of course, never mentioning that he had a girlfriend until, two days ago, he had announced that he would be bringing her home for Sunday tea. And why Sunday tea? Katherine wondered peevishly. It was such a cliché; such a conventional, anyone-for-tennis, hackneyed meal! Sometimes she despaired of ever understanding the modern generation, veering erratically, as they did, from nonconformity to respectability with unnerving speed.

She led the way into the drawing-room where tea, in the shape of sandwiches, scones and cakes, with strawberries and cream as an added bonus, was already laid out, scattered across a series of small side tables. Charlotte, who had also graced the occasion by putting on a frock, and a rather sulky Guy were waiting for them. Nicholas made the necessary introductions, keeping a guarded eye on his brother as he noted Guy's immediate response to Annabel's trim and extremely shapely figure. She was not at all what Guy had expected.

'Oh God, no!' he had protested, when Katherine had intimated that she needed his support for the coming ordeal. 'If Nick's managed to find himself a girlfriend, she's bound to look like the back of a bus. What other sort would have him? You can't honestly expect me to give up a Sunday afternoon for that!'

But Katherine had been immovable, and now Guy was quite pleased that she had made him stay. Annabel Hardwicke was not to be compared with the girls who queued up in their droves for the privilege of his company, but she wasn't bad-looking and she had very respectable tits! It never occurred to Guy to look at her face, or contrast its vivacity with the bland, carefully made-up features of his own escorts. He straightened up on the big settee and prepared to dazzle.

It was soon apparent, however, that he could cut

no ice with Annabel. She was impervious to his practised charm and returned the briefest of unsmiling answers to all his sallies. Guy soon lapsed into his former sulky mood: he was not used to being treated like a precocious schoolboy.

'You're at RADA, Nick tells us,' Charlotte remarked, filling an awkward silence.

'Yes.' Annabel accepted a cup of tea from Katherine and sat, balancing it awkwardly in one hand. 'In September I shall be starting my final year.'

'Acting's a very overcrowded profession,' Katherine said. 'Do you expect to be able to make a living?'

Annabel shrugged. 'Obviously I hope to. Whether I shall or not is in the lap of the gods. My mother made me take a secretarial course when I left school, as a kind of insurance.' She grinned suddenly, and the heavy, brooding expression lifted. She really was, Katherine reflected, a very pretty girl. Annabel continued, 'So I can always become a shorthand-typist and help Nick in his political career.'

Three pairs of eyes swivelled in silent astonishment to Nicholas, who stuttered defensively, 'It . . . It w-was only an idea.'

'I shouldn't have thought a degree in medieval French was much of a qualification for a seat at Westminster,' Charlotte objected. 'May one ask which party is to have the honour of returning you?'

'Nick's a fully paid-up member of the Labour party, as I am,' Annabel said quietly. She shot a glance at Nicholas in which affection was mingled with reproach for his lack of nerve.

Guy hooted with laughter. 'I'll buy you a cloth cap for Christmas,' he offered.

'Shut up, Guy!' Charlotte exclaimed witheringly. 'All the same,' she added, turning to Nicholas, 'the Labour party? With your background?'

'What do you mean by that?' Katherine demanded

fiercely, before either Nicholas or Annabel could reply. 'Your father and I are both from working-class stock, my girl, and don't you forget it! Just because people make money, it doesn't cut them off from their roots.'

'I should have thought that's just what it did do,' Annabel said contentiously, and Katherine realized that she had made the wrong move. Her intervention had been seen as patronizing: the hostess pouring oil on troubled water; the mother defending the weakest of her young. Annabel was feeling much as Katherine used to do in the early years of her marriage to Henry: aggressive, beleaguered; needing to scandalize and shock. Annabel wanted opposition: someone or something she could fight.

Well, she would have to go on wanting, Katherine decided, steering the conversation on to less controversial ground with a remark about the National Theatre and Laurence Olivier's resignation as director. She was too tired to have her sabbath peace disrupted. She looked forward now to Sundays as never before. Her weekdays as Jonathan Anthony's secretary were extremely taxing, as Rosewall Foods went from strength to strength. The Corporation's interests now extended far beyond the grocery and bakery chains which it had originally controlled, and life for all its employees was lived at a hectic pace. Katherine, although working on the same floor, rarely saw Robert from one week's end to another, and preferred it that way. Since Charlotte's revelation of nine months earlier, Katherine found it difficult to talk to him without wanting to pry. Her anger on Henry's behalf was totally irrational; ludicrous under the circumstances. Robert would have every right to resent it.

The front doorbell rang, followed, a second later, by someone banging with the knocker. The doorbell was a comparatively recent installation by Katherine, because it was easier to hear, but the present caller, after the first ring, preferred to ignore it. The hammering grew louder, and Katherine and Charlotte exchanged startled and enquiring glances, but waited for Mrs Mossop to answer the summons. Mrs Mossop, who agreed to work the occasional Sunday, partly because she needed the money to offset rapidly rising inflation and partly because she got bored at home with no one but her husband for company, could be heard trudging in her deliberate way across the hall. This was followed by a murmur of voices which rose heatedly in argument and ended in an explosion of anger. The next moment, the drawing-room door opened and Henry stalked into the room.

'I'm sorry, Mrs Lynton, but I couldn't stop 'im.' Mrs Mossop appeared, red-faced and agitated, in the open doorway. 'Pushed right past me, 'e did. You know what 'e's like.'

'Yes. Thank you, Mrs Mossop,' Katherine said hurriedly, rising to her feet. It was so long since Henry had called at The Lodge, and even longer since she had been subjected to one of his tantrums, that she felt aggrieved. Why today of all days?

Before she could introduce Annabel, or make Henry aware of the girl's presence, he had plunged straight in.

'What's all this nonsense?' he demanded, glaring at Guy. 'Why wasn't I told you'd applied to join the Royal Navy? I thought you were going on to university, then coming into the business with me.'

Guy glared back at his father and said the one word, 'Crap!' Turning to his mother, he added belligerently, 'I thought he knew.'

'I shouldn't think he needed telling!' Charlotte chipped in. She rounded on her father. 'Come off it,

Dad! You know damn well that Guy's never had any ambition except to join the Navy. Don't pretend. You've been aware of it for years!'

'Of course he has!' Katherine exclaimed furiously. 'He's just using the knowledge as a pretext to come here and make a scene. I don't know what your game is, Henry, but it won't work.'

Henry slammed his open palm down on the back of the settee, making Annabel jump and spill her tea. A brown stain marred the pale green skirt.

'I think I might have been consulted before the die was cast!' he shouted. 'I shouldn't have to learn things about my own children second-hand. Until John Morley mentioned it when Jane and I were dining there last night, I had no idea that Guy had actually enlisted, let alone been accepted. I don't like being made to feel a fool.'

'You have no right bursting in here like this and upsetting everyone,' Katherine said in a voice tight with anger. 'If you really want to discuss Guy's future we'll arrange a time and place, but there honestly isn't much point. He's over eighteen and can decide his own life. He left school four weeks ago, in case you're interested. I don't recall seeing you at the Parents' Day.'

'No right?' Henry demanded, ignoring the rest of her speech. His hands were clenched into fists and she could see the red glint at the back of his eyes. 'I have every right! I've worked myself into the ground to make Lynton's what it is today, so that one of my sons could take over from me and perpetuate the name! I've resisted every inducement, every pressure, to go public, so that it could remain a family firm. And that's been no mean feat, believe me. I've laboured and cajoled and persuaded and used every trick in the book to keep the company not just afloat, but thriving! And for what? To see some stranger eventually take over from me? Some outsider, who'll profit from everything I've done? My God! What a couple of sons you've raised, Kate. And I say "you" deliberately, because the influence has been mainly yours. Yours and Victor's!'

'What's wrong with our sons?' she asked, refusing to shout in return, but shaking, none the less, with uncontrollable rage.

Henry gave a bark of laughter.

'What's wrong with them? Look at them! One can't wait to join the armed forces, so that he can have someone do his thinking for him. The other . . . The other's so shit-scared of the real world that he takes refuge in the Middle Ages.'

There was an unexpected interruption from an unlikely source. Annabel rose from her seat on the settee like a small avenging Fury, and turned on Henry.

'We've never met before, Mr Lynton, and I hope to heaven we never meet again, but I'll tell you something. Guy's right. I've never heard so much crap in all my life! Either of your sons is worth ten of you. Why should they want to succeed to this business empire of yours? A business, moreover, that breeds death and destruction.'

'Who the hell are you?' Henry demanded, taken aback.

'I'm Nick's girlfriend and we're going to be married.' Katherine was the only one to notice the look of mute but pleasurable astonishment on Nicholas's face, and realized that this was a split-second decision on Annabel's part. The girl had succumbed to the impulse to score off Henry and might well regret it later. Annabel continued, 'And if you're interested, my name is Annabel Hardwicke. The Hardwicke has a final "e".'

Henry glowered at her from beneath his sandy eyebrows. 'Then, let me tell you this, Miss Annabel Hardwicke with a final "e"! Lynton's has done more good in the world than you and your like have had hot dinners. My chemical fertilizers are helping to produce food for the world's population. Without them, many of the Third World countries would be starving.'

'And if there's another war,' she spat at him, 'what good will all their crops do them? They'll be dead, along with the rest of us. And what you're doing is dirtier even than the nuclear arms race. That way, a lot of us at least stand the chance of being killed outright. Chemical warfare could turn us into walking zombies.'

'But it will never happen, you stupid child, as long as we keep pace with the other side. Your way, we'd be at the mercy of the Eastern bloc!'

'Better red than dead!' Annabel flung back at him, quoting from a source she had forgotten. 'I don't agree with your son's choice to go into the navy, but at least he'll be taking orders to kill other people, not helping to make the actual weapons that might one day destroy them.'

'I shan't be killing anyone,' Guy remonstrated indignantly. 'We don't send gun-boats any more. More's the pity.'

Annabel transferred her anger and scorn to her prospective brother-in-law.

'You'd be killing people all right if you were a soldier in Northern Ireland,' she told him.

Guy looked confused. 'But I'm going in the Royal Navy.'

'If you join any one of the services you have to be prepared to kill and to be killed, in defence of Queen and country. I'd think about that if I were you, before you sign the final papers.'

Guy addressed the room at large. 'She's crackers! Nutty as a fruit cake!'

'She has spirit, though.' said Henry, laughing. 'I like that.'

His anger had drained away and he was grinning

at Annabel like a fellow conspirator. It was a grin which robbed his words of any offence or patronage. The stinging retort which Annabel was just preparing to throw at him died stillborn on her lips. A moment later, however, Henry tossed away his advantage.

'What in God's name does a girl like you see in my elder son?'

Even as he spoke, he regretted the urge which always made him want to injure Nicholas. There was something about the boy, about the soft, fragile colouring, the delicate appearance, which seemed to flick him on the raw. Did he hope to goad him into some display of temper, in order to prove that he was his father's son?

Charlotte rose to her feet before Annabel could reply, and slid one arm about Henry's shoulders.

'That'll do, Dad. No need to get personal, so we'll change the subject.' She moved round to face him, looking directly into his eyes. 'You want a Lynton to follow you into the company, and neither of the boys is interested. On the other hand, I'm heartily sick of the advertising business. It really isn't my scene. So how about it? How about offering me a job? If it can't be Lynton and Son, why shouldn't it be Lynton and Daughter?'

The afternoon was cold and overcast. At four o'clock Katherine went through from her own office to Jonathan Anthony's, carrying a battery-powered lamp and two candles stuck on saucers.

'We're due for another power cut in exactly ten minutes,' she said, arranging them on his desk. 'And it has just been announced on the radio that Mr Heath has called a general election. February the twenty-eighth. That's two weeks' time.'

Jonathan Anthony sighed. 'He won't get back, you know. I'm willing to bet that Labour will win by a slender majority.'

Katherine shook her head, removing the tape from the dictating machine.

'I don't think you'll find any takers.'

It had been a bad winter, the solitary bright spot being the wedding of Princess Anne and Captain Mark Phillips in November. The Middle East oil crisis, following the Arab–Israeli war, had panicked the government into taking draconian measures. December had been the beginning of the four-day working week, a cutting back on the use of electricity supplies and the closing down of all three television channels at ten o'clock each evening. Shops and offices were instructed to use the minimum amount of light, with the result that Christmas shopping had been carried on in Stygian gloom, while in many places work came almost to a standstill. Petrol coupons were issued for the first time since the end of wartime rationing. And then, at the beginning of February, the miners had called an all-out strike.

In order to conserve coal, power cuts had been hastily arranged on a rota basis, local newspapers carrying lists of times and districts. Although this extremity of the general crisis had lasted only a couple of weeks, it was the last straw for an already sorely tried population. The Prime Minister, Edward Heath, had therefore decided to seek a mandate from the country. The general election campaign would be fought on the slogan: Who Governs Britain?

Back in her own office, Katherine put fresh typing paper and carbon into her machine and started to play the tape. There was a knock on the door and she cursed silently, flicking the recorder switch to off. Jonathan Anthony's mellifluous voice was silenced.

'Come in,' she called, making little effort to suppress the impatience in her tone.

As the door opened, the electricity was cut. Katherine turned up the wick of the hurricane lamp, standing ready lit on her desk, and saw Sheila

MacNeice's face hovering, seemingly disembodied, in the golden aureole of light.

'Good heavens!' she exclaimed weakly. 'What are you doing in London? Robert told me you were living in Edinburgh now.'

Sheila drew up a chair and sat down on the other side of the desk.

'I've come to find out what's been going on,' she said. 'I thought perhaps you'd tell me. It's no good asking Robert.'

Katherine hedged. 'Going on? Sheila, I'm awfully busy. Robert and I hardly ever see each other nowadays.'

'I expect you know, all the same. No matter how big a company is, there's always an efficient grapevine. And the rumour which reached my ears, even in Scotland, is that Robert is having an affair with Jane.'

'I wouldn't know,' Katherine answered shortly. 'What Henry and Jane do is not my business.'

Sheila regarded her directly from beneath a smart fur hat. 'You're sorry for Henry,' she accused her.

'Rubbish!' Katherine retorted, stung. 'I just don't want him to be made a fool of, that's all.'

'So it is true!' Sheila MacNeice gave a little spurt of laughter. 'You're the fool, Katherine, to worry about the man. He hardly played fair by you over the years.'

'He played fair according to his lights,' Katherine answered hotly, then lapsed into defensive silence before the expression on the other woman's face.

'If you feel like that about him, why don't you get back together?' Sheila enquired after a pause. 'Jane is obviously tired of the marriage.'

'No. No, I shan't do that.' Katherine stared unseeingly at the blank paper in her typewriter, then raised her eyes again. 'Sheila, I'm busy. If you want to see Robert – his office is just along the corridor. His name is on the door. You can't miss it. I can find out if he's in, if you like.'

'No, don't bother.' Sheila MacNeice shifted her hands awkwardly on the crocodile handbag. Even in the limited glow of the hurricane lamp, Katherine could see that she looked pale. 'I haven't come to see Robert – at least, not this afternoon. I'm calling at his rooms tonight. It's you I've come to see. There's something I want to ask you.'

'Well?' Katherine prompted, after a moment.

'Charlotte . . . ,' Sheila MacNeice began. 'I hear, by the way, from Robert, that Henry's taken her into the company. Is he grooming her to take his place? Eventually, I mean.'

'Perhaps. The boys aren't interested, at any rate.' There was a shade of reserve in Katherine's voice which made Sheila MacNeice glance at her sharply. 'But I really don't see—' Katherine was continuing, when the younger woman interrupted her.

'She's not Henry's daughter, is she? She's Robert's.'

There was a silence which seemed to stretch endlessly into the quiet, lamp-lit room. From far away came the rattle of a typewriter keyboard and the shrill, insistent ringing of a telephone.

'How long have you known?' Katherine asked at last. 'Have you told Robert of your suspicions?'

'No, of course not.' Sheila was offended. 'I wasn't a hundred per cent certain myself, but I thought it likely. I think I guessed it from the moment I first saw Charlotte. There was always something about her that reminded me of Robert's mother. Then I decided that it must be my imagination, because he didn't seem to see it. But every time I met her, I became more convinced that I was right. I worked out the dates as best as I could, and came to the conclusion that Charlotte could well have been conceived before you left Robert.'

306

Katherine nodded, recalling that half-forgotten long-ago night in the Bedford Square hotel, before she had finally run away to be with Henry. She admitted, 'I wasn't sure, at first, whose child she was, but as soon as she grew older I could see the resemblance to Robert. But no one else noticed, except my father. He was on to it from the beginning, but he was very observant.' Katherine took a deep breath. 'So what are you going to do with your knowledge?'

'Oh, don't worry, I shall keep it to myself. But knowing that Robert has another child will help to salve my conscience.' She stood up, still holding tightly to her handbag. 'You see, I've made up my mind to leave him, and I'm taking Clara with me. I intend going out to some cousins of mine in Australia.'

'Australia!' Katherine was horrified. 'Does Robert know?'

'Not yet. I shall tell him tonight. Also that I intend to divorce him. What he does then is up to him. And, of course, to Henry. It's rather like Musical Chairs, don't you think? One row of seats, but we all keep sitting down in different places.'

A reluctant laugh was forced from Katherine, but she sobered almost immediately.

'You do promise not to say anything about Charlie?'

'Cross my heart and hope to die.' Sheila spoke flippantly, but her eyes were serious. 'What you decide to do about it, either now or in the future, is a different matter. As I say, the knowledge is just a sop to my conscience for taking Clara so far away. And now I really must go. I've taken enough of your time already.' She stepped out of the circle of light, hesitated, and came back again. 'You know,' she went on quietly, 'a long time ago, Robert and I had something truly worthwhile going for us. Iain's death destroyed it. Don't ask me why; but I'm assured by

307

the experts that the loss of a child does sometimes cause that reaction. What I'm trying to say is that the thing which came between Robert and me was irreversible. There was nothing either of us could do to bring Iain back.' She paused once more, while Katherine waited silently, before going on, 'Forgive me, but it seems to me that there's also an invisible barrier between you and Henry. I don't know what it is and I naturally don't expect you to tell me. All I'm saying is, if it's surmountable, for God's sake do something about it before it's too late. Love is hard to come by. Try not to lose it.'

24

The final curtain descended and the first-night audience rose stiffly to its feet, clutching programmes and pulling on coats against the November cold. Seats were pushed up to reveal the usual litter of empty ice-cream cartons and chocolate wrappers. Henry, regarding them with distaste, made his way out of the nearest exit and walked briskly round the building to the stage door. The porter glanced up as Henry entered, leaning forward in his cubicle.

'Can I help you, sir?'

'I want to see Miss Annabel Hardwicke,' Henry announced, as though Annabel were the star of the rather uninspiring piece he had just sat through, instead of having one line in the final act.

The porter nodded. 'She'll be down in a minute, sir, if you'd like to wait. Can't send you up. There's three young ladies sharing a dressing-room, and it could be awkward. Good house, was it?'

'Not bad,' Henry conceded, propping himself against the cubicle ledge, prepared to be sociable. 'A few empty seats, but not as many as I'd expected. People have got jumpy since Birmingham. They don't feel safe in public places any more.'

The porter grunted. 'Terrible business. Terrible! Specially after what happened in the summer. I'd bring back hanging, drawing and quartering, that's what I'd do.'

Henry, used by now to this sort of comment, made

no answer. Just at present people were not in a rational mood, and it was pointless arguing with them. In July a bomb planted by the IRA had exploded at the Tower of London, killing one person and injuring forty-one others. A week ago, on the twenty-first of November, bombs had gone off in two Birmingham pubs, and this time the death toll had been higher. At the end of the night twenty-one people had been dead, a hundred and twenty maimed and injured, some of them horribly. Nothing like it had been seen in mainland Britain since the Blitz.

Henry glanced about him. This was the first occasion he had ever been backstage, and the bleakness of his surroundings surprised him. A stone-flagged corridor, starkly lit by an unshaded bulb, showed up walls of peeling paint and patches of creeping damp. At the end of the passage a flight of stone steps rose and twisted out of sight. A dim red glow, from a source of illumination higher up, revealed several posters advertising past productions, now tattered and yellow with age.

A young man – Henry recognized him as having played one of the servants in the first and third acts – ran lightly down the stairs, glancing incuriously at him, and waving a hand to the porter.

''Night, Bert. See you tomorrow. There's an extra rehearsal called for half-past twelve. Something dear Maurice isn't terribly happy about in the opening scene.'

The stage door swung to behind him as he vanished into the lighted Haymarket beyond.

Five minutes lagged by. More visitors came in, clutching bottles or flowers, and were directed upstairs to the single dressing-rooms. Henry wished he had thought of bringing a first-night gift for Annabel, but he had only decided to visit the theatre on a last-minute impulse, suddenly remembering that it was her professional début on any stage. He could not even remember how he had come by the information. Probably from Charlotte.

It was over a year since he had first met Annabel at The Lodge, and in the intervening months they had encountered each other on one or two occasions. But it had only been by chance, and this was the first time he had ever consciously sought her out. He knew that Nicholas would not be present at the theatre that evening, Charlotte having told him that her brother was going up north for a couple of days. Nicholas was working as constituency manager for a backbench Labour MP: a job which Henry regarded as a futile waste of an Oxford degree. As his elder son had not consulted him, however, he had been unable to make his opinions known, and was suffering from what Charlotte irreverently dubbed 'terminal frustration'.

Henry did his best to discourage too much intimacy between himself and his daughter during office hours, but it was not easy. She was his only link these days with Katherine and the boys, although Guy wrote from Plymouth, where he was training, when-ever he remembered. But he found any sort of correspondence a chore and his time was fully occupied. Henry therefore had to rely on Charlotte for news.

Charlotte, herself, was proving an asset to the firm; and although Henry still had reservations about her capacity to run the business in the future, he had to admit that she was rapidly changing his mind. If anyone could reconcile him to the idea of a woman in eventual charge of Lynton's, it would be his daughter. He looked in vain for any sign of serious emotional commitment in her life. She had plenty of men friends, but continued to live with her mother.

'I don't think', she had once said to Henry, 'that I have any maternal instincts. And if I don't want children, there's no point in marrying. I shall leave that sort of thing to the boys.'

There was a clatter of feet and the sound of female voices. Annabel and two other girls came into view round the bend in the stairs.

'Someone here to see you, Miss Hardwicke,' the porter called out, and Annabel slowed down in astonishment at the sight of Henry.

She was wearing an old duffel coat over the inevitable faded jeans, a knitted scarf in garish stripes of red and yellow, and extremely dirty white sneakers. Her jewellery consisted of a pair of thin gold hoops on the lobes of her ears and the engagement ring which Nicholas had given her. This contained a small flawed sapphire flanked by two tiny diamond chips, and riveted Henry's attention.

'Is that the best Nick could do?' he demanded.

Annabel stiffened, a martial light in her eyes. She turned to nod goodnight to her two companions, then faced Henry squarely.

'It's all he could afford and more than I wanted: I only agreed to wear it so as not to hurt Nick's feelings. We don't all judge affection by the amount of money spent on us, Mr Lynton.'

Henry grinned, and in spite of the antagonism he aroused in her whenever they met, Annabel found herself thinking how attractive he was. Of course, he was old; he must be over fifty. All the same, she couldn't help wondering what he was like in bed.

'A proper little spitfire, aren't you?' Henry chided. 'But I didn't come here to quarrel with you. I hope you'll let me take you to supper.'

'Like this?' Annabel was horrified. 'And it's too late to go all the way back to the flat to change.'

Henry recollected that she was living with Nicholas now, in a couple of rooms in one of the seedier roads close to Paddington station. He was amused to discover that she was as vain as the next person, in spite of the Bohemian attitudes she was at pains to convey.

He said, 'I've no objection to being seen with you just as you are, but if it would embarrass you, come

312

home with me. I make a passable omelette, and I'm even better at buttered eggs.'

'Why?' Annabel asked bluntly. 'Why go home with you, I mean?'

Henry had been ready to make some excuse about wanting to talk about Nicholas, but there was something in the fierce, direct gaze which made him ashamed to lie. He shrugged and said, 'My wife has left me. I'm lonely.'

'So why me?' Annabel's heavy brows drew together in a frown. 'You could always call Katherine.'

'She flew to the States yesterday on holiday. Charlie told me. And, anyway, what would be the point? You must know by now how she feels about me.' Henry smiled disarmingly. 'Won't you please take pity on a man old enough to be your father? After all, when you marry Nick we shall be related.'

Katherine rang the doorbell and waited, her sense of unreality growing stronger by the minute. What was she doing here, in this New York apartment block, when she should be at home planning for Christmas? Why had she suddenly decided to cross the Atlantic and seek out the man who had been Sandor's friend?

She supposed the answer lay in Sheila MacNeice's advice to her nearly ten months ago; advice which had lain like a weight at the back of her mind all summer. 'Love is hard to come by. Try not to lose it.' It was wrong to continue harbouring suspicions of Henry without doing something either to confirm or disprove them. And the only person who might be able to help her was the deputy head of Farmerson's New York laboratories, Alex Hoyos, who had written to her after Sandor was killed. Four weeks ago, at the beginning of November, she had told Jonathan Anthony that she must have a fortnight's leave. She had to go to the States on private business. It was urgent.

If Jonathan Anthony was displeased at the peremptory tone of the request, he did not show it. Secretaries as efficient as Katherine Lynton were hard to come by, and were entitled to the occasional display of temperament. He did his best to make things easy for her, and sped her on her way with his blessing. He arranged for a company car to drive her to the airport, and for her to stay in New York with one of Rosewall's top American executives.

'If you don't know the Big Apple,' he had commented drily, 'it's not a place to be floundering around in on your own.'

Katherine had appreciated both his gestures and his concern, particularly as there was a lot to worry him at the moment. Mrs Anthony, she knew, was far from well; cancer had been mentioned. And because of the political uncertainty which had prevailed throughout the year, Rosewall shares, like so many others, had plummeted. Things were a little better now that a second general election had been held in October, increasing the Labour government's majority of five over the Conservatives to a lead of forty-two. But this was only a majority of three over all other parties, and the Stock Exchange was still extremely jumpy . . .

The man who answered Katherine's summons was younger than she had expected, but with the same high cheekbones which had distinguished Sandor, and which proclaimed his Slavic origins.

'Mr Hoyos?' she asked. 'I'm Katherine Lynton. We talked on the phone this morning.'

'Yes. Hi. Won't you come in?' He held out his hand and took hers in a punishing grip. A tall elegant woman, in her early forties, came forward to join them. 'This is my wife, Sharon.'

Drinks and a dish of pretzels were laid out on a glass and chrome table. Otherwise, the apartment seemed to be furnished largely in stripped pine. A huge sofa and two armchairs were upholstered in a vivid pink that dazzled the eyes and drew the attention like a magnet.

The formalities over, Katherine found herself sinking deeply into a corner of the sofa, a glass of ice-cold lager in her hand.

'Now, what can I do for you, Mrs Lynton?' Alex Hoyos enquired. 'It sounded kinda urgent on the phone.'

'Did it?' Katherine was disconcerted. 'I didn't mean to make it sound like that. As you've probably guessed, Mr Hoyos, it's about Sandor.'

'Call me Alex. What can I tell you about him? It was all a long time ago.'

'Seven years,' Katherine murmured. 'Yes, I suppose it is. It seems like yesterday to me.'

To herself, she thought: I'm fifty-two. Fifty-two! In eight years' time, I'll be sixty. She knew she did not look her age, but it was poor consolation. She had taken her fortieth birthday in her stride, but fifty had been traumatic. It was the onset of the menopause, the realization that physical changes were taking place which would irrevocably curtail her capacities as a woman, which had proved to be so shattering. Perhaps it was why it had suddenly become so vital to get her life in order. In the last couple of years Katherine had begun to understand that old age, when it finally arrived, would not simply be a matter of rheumatic joints, defective eyesight and impaired hearing, but of waking up one morning and realizing that there was no tomorrow . . .

She became aware that Alex Hoyos had asked her a question and was patiently waiting for an answer.

'I . . . I'm sorry,' she apologized. 'You said . . .?'

'What is it you want to know about Sandor?'

Of course! He and his wife must think her mad, or, worse still, impolite. As a result, she asked more abruptly than she had intended, 'Was there anything funny about his death? I mean, was it truly an

315

accident, or was Sandor murdered? Could anyone have fixed the car he was driving?'

Alex Hoyos stared at her for a moment, then shook his head slowly. 'Hell, no! Whatever gave you that crazy idea?'

'I ... I don't know. I ... I just thought ... perhaps ... he might have had enemies. You know, a contract killing ... ' Her tongue seemed to be tying itself in knots and her voice died away, lost in a riot of barely audible half-sentences.

Alex put his glass down on the table and leaned forward, his long bony hands dangling between his knees.

'Katherine,' he said earnestly, 'if you'll pardon my saying so, you've been watching too much TV. I was in the car with Sandor when the accident happened. We'd been on a three-day trip to one of our South Carolina plants and were driving home. We'd been on the road since early that morning, and I guess Sandor was tired. It had been a pretty gruelling few days. He must have dozed off for a moment at the wheel, and the car careered out of control. It mounted the verge and hit a tree. Just before it did so, I was thrown clear. I escaped with nothing worse than a broken right arm.'

Katherine felt the relief surge through her, but she must make sure.

'You're absolutely certain that that's what happened? That Sandor fell asleep?'

'I'm positive.' Alex Hoyos reached out and took one of her hands between his, holding it tightly for greater emphasis. 'In the split second before the accident occurred, I saw him nod and noticed that his eyes were closed. I yelled, but it was too late. After that everything happened so fast, it was like a dream.'

Katherine breathed deeply several times. She felt purged, as though her system had been cleansed of some insidious poison. But she felt guilty, too, that

316

she had let suspicion fester for all these years. In the end, proving Henry's innocence had been so simple. It made her desperately ashamed that she had not tried to do it before.

Alex Hoyos was saying, 'I'm sorry. I should have told you all this when I wrote. Or, rather, when Sharon wrote. I couldn't with my busted arm. But I was pretty shaken up at the time, and the details of the accident seemed irrelevant. And it never occurred to me that you might . . .' He shrugged, at a loss for words.

'Let my imagination run riot?'

He grinned wryly. 'Well, since you put it that way, yes. But I trust I've now put your mind at rest?'

'Yes,' Katherine said. 'Yes, you have. Thank you.'

Sharon Hoyos opened another three cans of lager.

'In that case,' she smiled, 'let's celebrate. Katherine, you must stay for the evening.'

'I'm sorry,' the unknown woman's voice said at the other end of the telephone, 'Mr Lynton's away. He's in Paris.'

'When will he be back?' Katherine asked, and was told briskly not until after the New Year.

She replaced the receiver.

'You might have told me Henry was away,' she reproached her daughter, returning to the kitchen.

Charlotte paused in the middle of wiping up the supper things.

'Mother dear, I didn't know. Dad is the boss. The big cheese. Himself. As yet, I'm a very small cog in the machine. He doesn't tell me every time he goes away. His secretary, the terrifying Mrs Parsons, is the only person who is in his confidence.'

Katherine laughed and, pulling on her rubber gloves, began to scrub a dirty saucepan.

'It must be a protracted business trip, if that's what it is,' she objected. 'He's away until after the begin-

317

ning of January, and today is only the twenty-ninth of December.'

'Perhaps he's combining business with pleasure. Anyway, why this unprecedented rush to contact him? You haven't wanted to know him for over seven years.'

'No.' Katherine looked stolidly at the gleaming saucepan, refusing to turn her head and meet Charlotte's accusing gaze. 'But, then, for most of the time, he was married.'

'He still is, if it comes to that.' Charlotte wiped the saucepan and placed it on its shelf. 'Although, I admit, not for much longer. He's let Jane file for divorce, and presumably she'll marry Robert MacNeice as soon as she's free. His decree absolute came through a while ago, Dad told me.'

'Yes.' Katherine let out the washing-up water and performed the ritual wiping round the sink. She missed Mrs Mossop during the holiday periods. 'I know. You forget Robert and I work in the same building. Do you dislike him? Robert, that is. You sounded just now as if you might.'

'Did I?' Charlotte sounded surprised as she led the way back to the drawing-room. 'He's not a man I've ever given much thought to.' She glanced round at the holly and tinsel decorations. 'They always look so sad, don't they, once Christmas is over?' she went on, dismissing Robert easily from the conversation. 'I can't wait to get them down.'

'They're staying up until after the New Year,' Katherine retorted. She sat down and poured herself a whisky and water. 'It was a good Christmas, wasn't it? Both the boys at home. Pity, though, that Annabel couldn't be here to join us.'

'Mmm.' Charlotte stretched out in an armchair opposite her mother's. 'Some sudden engagement, Nick was telling me, up north. Understudy in some tin-pot pantomime in a place no one's ever heard of.

You can hardly say she's made the big time, can you? That play she was in folded after less than six months.'

'That wasn't her fault,' Katherine protested. 'She only had one line.'

Charlotte regarded her mother straitly and once again changed the direction of the conversation.

'You still haven't said why you're so eager to get in touch with Dad. It has something to do with that holiday you spent in America, hasn't it? You've felt differently towards him ever since you got back. America ... Does it have any connection with Sandor?'

Katherine coloured faintly, but shook her head. Charlotte was the last person to whom she could admit the terrible suspicions she had entertained about Henry. And, in any case, it was none of her daughter's business. It was up to her now to put matters right and to make amends.

She leaned back against the cushions and closed her eyes, feeling pleasantly tired. It was a nuisance, Henry being in Paris, but it didn't really matter. He would be returning in early January, and there was a slim chance that she might see him even before then. She was accompanying Jonathan Anthony on a trip to Brussels during the first week of the New Year, and they were stopping overnight for a business dinner in Paris. She would not have to be present at the meal, and would be free to take herself out for the evening ... She would telephone Henry's secretary in the morning, and find out where he was staying. She would surprise him at his hotel and he could treat her to dinner.

It would be like old times. She felt excited at the prospect and smiled to herself. This, surely, was one occasion when nothing could possibly go wrong.

The woman behind the desk said in broken English

that she was sorry, but Monsieur and Madame were out. She regretted, with a Gallic spreading of hands, that she had no idea when they would be returning.

Madame ... Katherine cursed herself for a fool. For some reason beyond her comprehension, it had not occurred to her that Henry might not be alone, not even when she discovered that he wasn't staying as usual at the Grillon, but at L'Hôtel, the exclusive and tiny hotel in the Rue des Beaux Arts on the Left Bank, where Oscar Wilde had died in 1900. She recalled now how reluctant the redoubtable Mrs Parsons had been to part with the information, only giving way in the end because Katherine had intimated that her need to get in touch with Henry had something to do with one of the children.

She left the hotel and walked to the nearest café, finding herself a place on one of the upholstered banquettes near the window. She ordered coffee. She had had no dinner, but suddenly she was not hungry.

After a while, however, common sense took over. Henry was no longer her husband. If he wanted to combine business with pleasure, as Charlotte had hinted, it was nothing to do with her. He was a free agent and could do as he pleased.

Katherine had no doubt that this was just another of his casual affairs; another in that long procession of philanderings which he had never been able to do without. This woman would mean as little to him as all her predecessors, and Katherine was at last beginning to believe Henry's assurances that he had never truly loved anyone but her. Not even Jane, she was now certain, had ever had any real hold on his affections. Henry had married her simply because of Katherine's own folly and her determination to think the worst of him.

It would be simplest, she decided, to leave their meeting until they were both safely back in London. She realized that she was, after all, hungry and ordered a mushroom omelette, together with a bottle of *vin ordinaire*. Many years ago she had acquired a taste for the rough red wine.

She was halfway through her meal when she happened to glance up and saw Henry just seating himself at a table near the door. His companion's coat was thrown over the other chair, the lady obviously having gone straight to the cloakroom. Henry was deep in discussion with a waiter and had not noticed Katherine. She instinctively drew back into the little alcove made by another banquette placed at right angles to her own. She did not wish to embarrass him now by revealing her presence.

A young girl came out of the ladies' cloakroom, her dark hair swinging about her face. She looked unhappy, but there was also a desperate, excited defiance about her as though she were at odds with the world; daring it to say she was in the wrong. The engagement ring still winked on her left hand as she put it up to smooth back a strand of hair.

It was Annabel Hardwicke.

PART FIVE
1978–1982

A time to keep silence and a time to speak

Ibid.

25

Katherine put aside the *Evening News*, which carried banner headlines about Princess Margaret's divorce from Lord Snowdon, and went into the kitchen to prepare supper. Charlotte would be home, as usual, and Nicholas had promised to look in.

'It won't be anything special,' Katherine had warned him. 'Ham and salad and cold apple tart. I'm too tired to do much cooking when I get home nowadays.'

She missed the tender ministrations of the faithful Mrs Mossop, who had retired the previous year. Katherine hadn't bothered to replace her, taking over the cooking herself, and thanking God for the advent of the freezer. As for the rest of the housework, she had solved that problem by shutting up many of the rooms in The Lodge, shrouding the furniture in dust covers. She and Charlotte shared what remained of the cleaning between them.

In the kitchen, Katherine took the ham from the refrigerator and began to wash and shred the lettuce. It was warm for early May, and the window was open. Faintly, from the other side of the high garden wall, came the sound of an electric lawn-mower. A bed of wallflowers and tulips made a gaudy patch of colour in line with Katherine's vision, and a lilac tree, thick with blossoms, nodded and dipped in the evening breeze, its heavy scent filling the air.

Katherine put the lettuce in a plastic basket and

started to shake it dry. Her actions were automatic, while her busy mind went back over the events of the day.

It had been something of a shock to come face to face with Annabel in the food hall at Harrods. Katherine had gone there during her lunch hour, to buy the ham. She had just paid for it when a voice, now as familiar to her as her own, sounded almost in her ear, asking for a whole cooked chicken. Katherine turned her head quickly and there was Annabel, looking much smaller and more vulnerable than she did on television.

It was nearly two years since Annabel's big break in a long-running television family saga. She had left after eighteen months, amidst newspaper predictions that she would find it difficult to get another job, so identified had she become with the North Country character she had been playing. But she had confounded all the pundits by working steadily ever since, making a film and appearing in innumerable television plays and advertisements. In fact, as Charlotte had remarked to her mother only the previous evening, Annabel was rarely off their screens these days.

'Poor old Nick,' she had commiserated lightly, 'it must be rotten, every time he switches on the telly, to be confronted by the girl who jilted him and married his father instead. Very damaging to the ego.'

'I don't suppose Nick has the opportunity to watch much television,' Katherine had retorted sharply. 'His work in the constituency keeps him pretty busy. Did you know that he's planning to stand at the next election?'

And the conversation had switched to politics without much effort, Katherine and Charlotte being in a state of constant disagreement on the subject. For with the election of Margaret Thatcher as Leader of the Tories, Charlotte had given her wholehearted

support to the Conservative party; whereas the olde
Katherine got, the more she returned to her roots. Sh
was becoming active in the Socialist ranks, egged o
by Nicholas. In the ensuing argument about the riva
merits of Callaghan and Thatcher, the subject o
Annabel had thankfully been buried.

And then, this morning, there Katherine was
looking straight into Annabel's large dark eyes, won
dering what on earth to do. Should she simply wal
away, without saying a word, or should she at leas
utter a conventional greeting?

Annabel took the decision out of her hands an
said in her clear decisive way, 'Hullo, Katherine.
haven't seen you for ages. You're looking very wel
How's Nick?'

'Do you really want to know?' Katherine asked
'Or are you merely being polite? Or are you asking o
behalf of Henry?'

Before Annabel could reply, a young woma
rushed up to ask her, in breathless accents, for he
autograph, and Katherine had taken the opportunit
to walk away. But all through the afternoon sh
had been haunted by the look of pain on Annabel'
face. Was it possible that she was still in love wit
Nicholas, even though she had married his father?

Katherine had been prepared for the broken en
gagement. Annabel had seen her as she left the café
that evening in Paris, but Henry had been sitting wit
his back to the door and had been blissfully unawar
of her presence. Had Annabel ever told him? Whe
she returned Nicholas's ring, she had given no reaso
other than saying baldly that she had changed he
mind. At the time she had been working as an assist
ant stage manager with a repertory theatre in Scot
land, and had sent back the ring by registered post
together with a very brief letter. Nicholas had let hi
mother and sister read it because it said, in fact, ver
little, and certainly nothing of a private nature.

'What will you do?' Katherine had asked.

And Nicholas had replied tightly, 'I shall go to Scotland.'

But before he had been able to get leave from his job, they had all been stunned into disbelief by the news that Annabel had married Henry. The gossip columnists had made much of the announcement, particularly of the fact that this was Henry's third marriage, and his second to a girl years younger than himself: young enough, they all kept stressing, to be his daughter.

'Mr Lynton,' one of them wrote, 'has a positive penchant for cradle-snatching.'

Nicholas had been very silent and grown very thin, once more turning in on himself, depending on his own resources. Katherine was unable to break through his shell of reticence, and after the first, unavailing attempt, ceased to try. There was no comfort she could offer. Even Charlotte had been too hurt and shocked to offer any excuse for Henry's behaviour. She was not a woman to sit in judgement on other people's actions, and once she had recovered from her initial repulsion, she and Henry had remained on speaking terms. But she refused to continue visiting him at home, and all her contact was maintained through the office. However tolerant Charlotte might be, and whatever allowances she made for her father in her own mind, their relationship was, for the time being at least, irreparably damaged.

Katherine chopped tomatoes, taking pleasure, as she always did, in the globes of bright colour, and their tangible proof that summer was at last on its way. She began to mix the salad dressing.

Her own reaction to Henry's marriage to Annabel Hardwicke had been to put her emotions into cold storage. She dared not let herself think too closely about it, nor to dwell on the enormity of what Henry had done. Besides, if she probed deeply enough, she could not find herself entirely blameless. It was her foolishness, her criminal stupidity and suspicion, which had driven the final wedge between them. So for the past three years she had thrown herself into her work, accompanying Jonathan Anthony on his trips abroad, oiling the wheels of his very busy life, and even standing in for his wife on semi-social occasions, as Muriel Anthony's health deteriorated. And since Mrs Anthony's death, nine months ago, Katherine had acted as Jonathan's hostess on a permanent basis . . .

His proposal of marriage this afternoon had, nevertheless, taken her completely by surprise.

He had said, in his quiet, prosaic way, 'I hope you'll give my offer serious consideration, my dear. I'm not in love with you. People of our age are, I think, past that sort of romantic nonsense.'

Katherine had wanted to shout, 'I'm only fifty-six, for heaven's sake!' but she had sat, hands primly folded in her lap, while he had continued, 'But I am, it goes without saying, extremely fond of you. You know my ways, my idiosyncrasies, and you already have experience of my social commitments and requirements. Above all, you know my job here, as well as I do. Sometimes, I think, even better. Naturally you would not remain my secretary, but I should be able to talk things over with you, at home. It would be an admirable arrangement. I do not expect an answer straight away, or even within the next few days. Take time to think the proposition over.'

An admirable arrangement . . . Katherine's heart contracted at the memory. It was all so clinical, so cold. It was not what she either expected or wanted from a marriage. Yet there was a great deal to be said in its favour. There seemed no possibility now that she would ever get back together with Henry. What he had done to Nicholas was unforgivable. She refused to let herself think about him for more than a few seconds. Her thoughts, these days, like her emotions, were carefully regulated. It was the only way she could keep her longings and her regrets in check. To do otherwise would be to betray not only herself but also her son.

She supposed, mixing the salad ingredients in a bowl and tossing them in the dressing, that marriage to Jonathan Anthony would solve the problem of loneliness in old age. But was she really afraid of being on her own? And did any one action ever solve anything? Who could tell what was around the corner? What would happen next week? She had been married twice already. Surely that was enough for any prudent woman.

The crux of the matter was that she couldn't really imagine herself in bed with Jonathan, or even overseeing the washing of his shirts and socks. He belonged in her life, but in his own compartment of the office. Their relationship was strictly a business one. She didn't mind playing hostess for him when the need arose, but that was as far as it went. She carried the bowl of salad into the dining-room and set it on the table, ignoring the voice in the back of her mind which told her that she was still, as she had always been, in love with Henry.

The front doorbell rang, and Katherine glanced at her watch. It was too early for Charlotte; and in any case, she had her own key. It was probably Nicholas.

Her first impulse, when she saw Annabel standing on the doorstep, was to slam the door in her face; but Aunt Margery's early training in good manners prevailed. Her attitude, however, was discouraging.

'What do you want? I'm busy.'

'Can I come in?' Annabel looked nervous, but she stood her ground. Her car, a blue Renault, was parked on the gravel sweep of the drive.

'Why?' Katherine's tone, she was happy to find,

was cool and remote, with no hint of her seething anger.

'I want to talk to you. Please.' The younger woman's gaze was as direct as ever.

'I wouldn't have thought we had anything to say to one another. Why now, suddenly, after all these years?'

'I suppose it was seeing you again today, in Harrods. I felt I owed you an explanation.'

'I should have thought it was Nick to whom you owed the explanation.' Katherine glanced at her watch again. 'I'm expecting him in half an hour. He's coming to supper.' She stepped back and held the door open a little wider. 'As long as you're gone by the time he arrives ...' She led the way into the kitchen and indicated a stool. 'I hope you don't mind, but I must finish preparing the meal.'

It was odd, seeing a face at once so familiar and yet so strange, in its absence of theatrical make-up and assumed characterization, at close quarters. In real life Annabel wore only a dash of lipstick, rather badly applied, and a coating of mascara on those wonderful lashes. Her taste in clothes, however, had altered drastically; and her white silk suit and expensive black accessories spoke of money and the ability to spend it. In the old days Katherine had never considered Annabel to be interested in her appearance, but now, she supposed, she had no option.

'Well?' Katherine said after a few moments, unable to bear the silence. She spread the slices of ham with French mustard and rolled them up. 'What is it you want to say?'

Annabel moistened her lips, concentrating on a blue china mug full of wild flowers which Charlotte had gathered the previous evening. The latest in a long line of boyfriends – menfriends, Katherine supposed they ought to be called nowadays – had taken her for a drive into the country. And this

330

morning Katherine had found the flowers wilting on the draining-board. She had put them in the water with no great hopes of their survival; but now they had perked up and were looking healthier: white campion in a tall ragged clump, guarding its lesser brethren, heart's-ease and daisy.

'Well?' Katherine repeated in growing impatience. 'Nick will be here soon. I don't want him to find you here.'

Annabel gave a lop-sided smile. 'No, I don't suppose you do. I know what you – and he – must think of me.'

Katherine abandoned the pretence of being busy and turned to face her. 'How could you have hurt Nick like that?' she demanded. 'Why on earth did you do it?'

Annabel sighed. 'I don't know. I mean I don't know why I let Henry make love to me in the first place. He came to the theatre, my very first opening night, and asked me out to supper. Jane had just left him. He said he was lonely, and I'm sure he was. Henry is a very lonely person. Because I wasn't dressed for a restaurant, he suggested I went home with him, and I agreed. I think I wanted to prove something to myself: that I was still my own woman.' She raised her eyes and met Katherine's. 'Nick's a very possessive person. He didn't mind what I'd done before I met him, but he expected absolute fidelity once we were engaged. I couldn't take it. I loved him. I wanted to marry him. But I also needed to be free.'

'So you let Henry seduce you as a kind of silent protest.' Katherine pushed a strand of hair away from her face with the back of a greasy hand. She laughed. 'Yours wasn't a new dilemma, you know. It's as old as the history of men and women.'

'Yes, but I was living in a new age. I was one of the new generation who thought – still think – that, as a woman, I ought to be able to have my cake and eat it, too. Men always have done. Why shouldn't we? Anyway,' she went on after a pause, when Katherine didn't answer, 'yes, Henry and I went to bed together. And I continued seeing him. I liked him and I felt sorry for him. He's much more vulnerable, whatever people might think, than Nick.'

She looked challengingly at the older woman, expecting her to dispute the statement, but Katherine only nodded.

'Yes,' she agreed slowly. 'I've always known that. Nick's easily hurt, but he has an inner core of strength. An inner world, where no one else can reach him. I think it's the one thing about him that Henry could never quite fathom – that remoteness. It always baffled and infuriated him because he felt excluded.'

'You do understand,' Annabel said. 'At least, in part. Well, there you have it. What would have happened if you hadn't seen us in Paris that evening, I've no idea. I probably wouldn't ever have told Nick about his father and me, because I loved him and really wanted to marry him. But I shouldn't have liked myself for it; and in some perverse way, I was glad when I looked up and saw you. I realized it would force my hand.'

'I didn't intend saying anything to Nick,' Katherine put in quickly, but Annabel merely shook her head.

'You knew, though. That was the spur I needed to make me break the engagement. Nick would never have forgiven me if I'd admitted the truth, so there didn't seem much point in confession. You see, at that time, I had absolutely no intention of marrying Henry.'

'What made you change your mind?'

'He asked me. So simple, really, it's laughable.'

'But you didn't have to accept him. In fact, it's the last thing I should have expected you to do.'

'I know. I felt exactly the same way, even while I was saying yes.'

'Then, why did you?' Katherine was pardonably bewildered.

Annabel slid off the stool and wandered restlessly around the kitchen. At the sink she paused, staring out of the window into the garden.

'I suppose the reason was what I said just now. I was fond of him. I was also very sorry for him. He seemed so alone. He had two failed marriages behind him, and I thought I could make him happy. And he didn't want very much from me. Sex and companionship was all it amounted to, really. He didn't want to possess me, and he didn't mind me continuing with my career.'

Katherine raised her eyebrows. 'He's changed, then. It was always a bone of contention between us, right from the beginning.'

Annabel went on staring out of the window. 'He's not in love with me,' she said. When Katherine made no reply, she turned her head, glancing over her shoulder. Katherine recognized the pose from her best-remembered television commercial for a famous brand of soap. Yet the gesture was completely natural. 'You can't forgive him, can you?'

'I can't forgive either of you,' Katherine answered briskly. 'Does that surprise you?'

Annabel shrugged and moved back to pick up the handbag which she had left lying on the stool.

'No, I suppose not,' she admitted.

The front door slammed and there was the sound of voices in the hall. Charlotte and Nicholas had arrived together. They came into the kitchen, Charlotte laughing and chatting on about some man who had made a pass at her on the Tube as she was coming home; Nicholas smiling and attentive, behind her.

'Oh, you put the flowers in water. Good!' Charlotte

exclaimed, her eyes going to the blue china mug. 'I meant to do it myself last night, but I was too tired. And then in the rush to get off early this morning, I forgot them . . .' Her voice tailed away as she became aware of Annabel. 'What the hell are you doing here?' she demanded.

Annabel's face flushed a dull unbecoming red, but otherwise she appeared in no way disconcerted.

'I came to see your mother,' she answered evenly. 'There was something I wanted to say to her. Hello, Nick.'

He nodded, unable to trust his voice. Katherine noticed that he was unobtrusively leaning against the wall, as though his legs were refusing to support him.

Annabel glanced from one to the other of the silent group and tucked her handbag under her arm.

'Well, I must be going,' she said, with a spurious brightness. 'It's been nice seeing you all again. Especially you, Nick. I hear you're going to stand as a Parliamentary candidate at the next general election.'

'Yes. My nomination has been accepted for Bristol Eastwood.' The final word caught in his throat and he turned it into a cough. His lips felt stiff, as though they were frozen.

Annabel brushed past him to the kitchen door, where she paused.

Reluctant, Charlotte thought nastily, to make a hasty and unimpressive exit.

But she was doing Annabel an injustice. The sight of Nicholas, so close, after all these years, had upset the younger woman. She had been unprepared for the surge of love which she had experienced on seeing him again. How could she have been such a fool as to let him go, even at the price of independence? She stretched out her hand, catching hold of the sleeve of his jacket.

'I'm sorry. I truly am sorry.'

He shook her off with an abrupt movement of his arm.

'Keep your pity to yourself,' he answered roughly. 'Not that I really blame you. I blame my father. You were too young and too weak-willed to resist him.'

'Nick, that's not fair!' Katherine was surprised how angry she felt; how she still sprang instinctively to Henry's defence. 'You can't put all the onus on just one person.'

'Can't I?' Nicholas turned to her, his face thin and pinched with anger, deep lines, which she had never noticed before, grooving the corners of his mouth. 'He never liked me. He always ridiculed me, even when I was a child. He never tried to understand me. I haven't forgotten what he said that day I brought Annabel here to tea. He called in, do you remember? He said, "What in God's name does a girl like you see in my elder son?" He'd made up his mind then to take her away from me. He couldn't bear to be proved wrong about me! Couldn't stand it that I, despised little Nick, could attract a girl like Annabel! So he set out to prove to everyone that I couldn't.'

'Nick, it wasn't like that,' Annabel pleaded, tears running down her face, leaving her cheeks streaked with mascara. 'Henry has never despised you. He doesn't find you easy to get on with, I agree. But from what he says, you've never gone even halfway to meet him.'

'She's right, Nick,' Katherine put in quietly. 'You always shut him out. You were the one who did the despising. Your father had such a different kind of upbringing from yours; and in spite of his British citizenship, he's still an American. They're extroverts, and taught to be so from the day that they're born.'

'That's right! You stick up for him as well!' Nicholas's tone was bitter. 'Jesus Christ! What is it about my father? After all he did to you, all those women, all the pain he caused you, you still defend him. Well, I'll tell you this! I hate my father. Hate him, d'you hear me? Anyone who is his friend is no friend of mine. And now I'm going. Oddly enough, I find I'm not very hungry!'

The kitchen was silent after his departure. Charlotte said at last, 'He's been bottling that up for a very long time.'

Annabel wiped her face with the back of her hand, unconcerned for her appearance. There was a smudge of mascara across both cheeks, and the application of lipstick had vanished altogether.

'I'm sorry,' she muttered. 'If I'd known this was going to happen, I wouldn't have come. You must believe me.'

Katherine sighed. She felt drained of energy; emotionally numb.

'It doesn't matter,' she said. 'It hasn't altered anything. All that hatred was there already. You just brought it out into the open.'

'Perhaps Nick will find somebody else, some day.' Annabel turned to go. She added to herself: Someone who will make him forget me.

She felt desolate, as though, at twenty-four, her life had already come to an end.

26

'The chaps don't believe me when I tell 'em you're my stepmother,' Guy said, grinning at Annabel across the table. 'Well, some of them do, I suppose. The ones that read the gossip columns and the Sunday papers.'

Annabel returned his glance coolly, thinking how good-looking he was in his naval lieutenant's uniform. Not that he appealed to her now any more than he had ever done. She had never liked big, athletic, over-handsome men; but she was glad to see him at Chapel Rock for Henry's sake. It was so long since any of his children had been there.

She had met Guy by chance that morning, while shopping in Plymouth. His ship had put into Devonport the day before for refitting, and he was on a twenty-four-hour shore-leave pass.

'Come and spend the rest of the day with us,' she had urged without expecting much success, aware, out of the corner of her eye, of Guy's companions, another naval lieutenant and a very pretty girl who was with him. 'Your father's at Chapel Rock. He was ordered down for a month's rest by his doctor. He's been rather overdoing things lately.' She had read the retort hovering on her stepson's lips, and her eyes had dared him to make it. 'He had a mild heart attack three weeks ago. Just a warning, but for once in his life he's heeding it.'

Somewhat to her surprise, Guy had accepted the invitation and made his excuses to his friend, promising to join him again in the evening. Annabel had driven him to Chapel Rock in her Renault.

Henry had been touchingly delighted to see his younger son, and had even shed a few surreptitious tears. He was still weak, he excused himself, after a fortnight in bed.

'Who's running the mighty empire, then?' Guy asked flippantly, over lunch.

Henry smiled benignly, refusing to be irritated. 'Charlie's there to keep an eye on my interests.'

Guy swallowed his wine in one gulp, making his father wince and reflect that neither of his sons had ever displayed any sign of discernment for a rare vintage.

'Good old Charlie!' Guy said. 'Always the man of the family.' He grinned with the good-natured confidence of someone who could denigrate himself without any fear of being taken seriously. 'You know, of course, that Nick is now a Member of Parliament.' He let rip with one of his loud insensitive guffaws, although Annabel gave him credit for not knowing about that scene at The Lodge twelve months ago. 'Bloody difficult, having a brother who's Labour MP. Don't boast about it, I can tell you!'

'Why not?' Annabel asked tartly. 'With the Socialists being thrown out of office all over the country, it was quite an achievement for a brand-new one to be elected.'

'God, yes! The Labour party really took a beating this time!' Guy exclaimed delightedly. 'Good old Maggie! She'll get things done. Time this country had someone in charge who knows what she's doing. Look at last winter. Nothing but strikes. Well, I was abroad. Didn't affect me. But the foreign newspapers were full of it. Made me ashamed to be British, I can tell you!'

Annabel was beginning to regret her decision to ask her stepson back to Chapel Rock for lunch. Then she caught sight of Henry's face, happy at having Guy there, his expression a little ironic, but agreeing with him in the main. She sighed to herself. She and Henry were poles apart politically, so she kept off the subject.

She was unfeignedly glad, however, to see him looking so much better. She had grown even more fond of him during the years of their marriage, but it was in much the same way that a niece might be fond of a favourite uncle. When he made love to her there always seemed something faintly incestuous about the act, and she no longer enjoyed it. Nevertheless, his recent illness had come as a shock to her. At fifty-seven, he still gave the impression of a much younger man. She had been at the BBC Television Centre, rehearsing for a play, when Mrs Parsons had telephoned her with the news.

'Mr Lynton has suffered a slight heart attack. Nothing very serious, the doctor says. He must stay in hospital for a couple of days, and then he can be allowed home.'

But Henry's own doctor and the ones at the hospital had all insisted that he must rest for at least two months.

'Get him down to Chapel Rock,' Dr Barnes had said to Annabel. 'Don't take no for an answer, or I won't be responsible for the consequences.'

So she had cajoled and bullied Henry into coming down to Cornwall. Fortunately her own commitments had permitted her to accompany him and stay for the first four weeks. But in a month's time she was due to fly to Los Angeles for her very first part in a Hollywood film. It was too good a chance to pass up, and she hoped that Henry would be almost recovered by then. But even if he were not, her affection for him, although strong, was not sufficient to make her miss the opportunity of a lifetime.

After lunch she and Guy went for a walk down

through the valley garden to the quay. White clusters of heavy-scented may brushed their shoulders as they passed, and the delicate petals of stitchwort starred the darkness under the trees. Dust powdered the round pink faces of the campion and the ragged white-and-pink of an early rose. Along the path which led past the chapel, primrose and celandine, trefoil and buttercup spread themselves in golden profusion.

'My mother paid us a visit here, last summer,' Annabel said, to break what had become an awkward silence. 'She hated it. She said she'd never come again.'

'Why not?' Guy asked indignantly. If he had a fondness for anything, other than himself and his own concerns, it was for this place, where he had spent so many carefree childhood days.

Annabel shrugged. 'She's a miner's daughter, from Durham. She married a miner. I think she couldn't really accept that houses and gardens like this still exist as family homes; lived-in, barred from public access. She couldn't cope with the luxury and the lushness. It was an affront, an insult, to people she had known all her life and grown up with. Sometimes I feel the same. I understand her.'

Guy was staring at her as though she had taken leave of her senses, and she supposed that such sentiments were impossible for him to comprehend, because he had grown up with Chapel Rock. It was an integral part of his life. But Nicholas would have understood: he had never taken anything for granted. He had always been able to put himself in someone else's shoes. Nick ... Nick ... Nick ... The name seemed to echo all around her, escaping from her head and flying upwards, mocking her from the gently budding trees ...

'Shall we go back?' she asked abruptly. 'There's a

breeze coming off the river. It's not as warm as I thought.'

Henry, watching their return from his bedroom, where he was resting in an armchair by the open window, had a sudden vision of Katherine, laughing and chasing the children along the paths, as she had done so often, or playing at hide-and-seek with them amongst the bushes and trees. He remembered her coming home, filthy dirty and generously plastered with mud, after taking Charlotte and the boys on a fishing expedition. There had been a solitary eel in a jam-jar, whose ownership was hotly contested by Charlotte and Guy, while Nicholas trudged silently alongside, clutching his mother's hand . . .

But at the thought of his elder son Henry's mind balked, as it so often did. He longed to tell Nicholas how sorry he was about what had happened; that he had never intended things to turn out the way they had. He liked Annabel, that was all; thought her attractive. And when he had found her willing, it had been the most natural action in the world to make love to her. Only he hadn't been able to leave it at that, had he? Bad as that was, he had then persuaded her to spend a week in Paris with him; to lie to Nick; deliberately to deceive him.

Henry wanted to tell his son how proud he was of him for having achieved what was virtually a little miracle in this month's general election. May the third, 1979, had sounded the death knell of so many Socialist hopes; but Nicholas, standing as a Labour candidate for the first time, had made it. It didn't matter that all his life Henry had voted first Republican and then Conservative; he was still delighted to talk about 'my son, the MP'. The sad thing was, Nicholas would never know. Henry accepted that he had forfeited all right to Nick's forgiveness, not only because of Annabel, but also because he had so often been unkind to him when he was younger. Katherine had warned Henry that he might one day regret his impatience, and she had been right. But, then, she had been right about so many things. Maudlin tears of weakness coursed down his face. He needed her; now more than ever. Annabel did her best, but, like Jane, she was far too young to share his memories; and memories were important as he grew older. It was vital to have someone who had grown up in the same period of time; someone to whom he could say, 'Do you remember . . .?'

'Kate,' he murmured, his head dropping forward on his chest, as sleep overtook him.

He woke an hour later, feeling unrefreshed, and went downstairs to tea. Guy and Annabel were waiting for him. They had almost finished the meal when Guy said thickly, through a mouthful of Mrs Godfrey's saffron cake, 'Oh, I meant to tell you! Or perhaps you both already know. Mother's getting married again.'

'What made you change your mind?' Jane MacNeice asked comfortably, passing a plate of sandwiches. 'The last time I saw you, you had no intention of marrying Jonathan.'

Katherine refused another sandwich and helped herself instead to a slice of chocolate sponge. She had been reluctant to accept Jane's invitation to tea, this warm Bank Holiday August afternoon, but Jonathan had more or less insisted.

'Darling, Robert MacNeice is a very important man in Rosewall's; too important for me to snub. And although he's your ex-husband, I thought you liked him.'

'I do,' Katherine said. 'We've got on very well in recent years. It's Jane I can't stand.'

'Then, you must overcome your prejudice,' he had answered firmly.

Katherine had resented both his tone and his rather censorious attitude: the implication that if she were to become his wife, she must learn to adapt herself to whatever social pressures might occur. So what did she say in answer to Jane's question? What had made her change her mind? She had been so sure of her own wishes in the matter, that evening last year when Jonathan Anthony had first proposed to her.

Partly, she supposed, it was his relentless persistence during the past fifteen months. Hardly a day had gone by when he had not repeated his offer, pointing out the mutual benefits of such a marriage. It also had something to do with her growing sense of isolation after Charlotte moved out of The Lodge, earlier in the year.

'I need a flat of my own, where I can bring my friends home for the night if I feel so inclined,' she had said in her usual forthright fashion. 'I'm nearly twenty-nine and I'm tired of having sex in the back of cars or in seedy hotel bedrooms.'

Katherine had made no effort to prevent her; on the contrary, she had positively encouraged Charlotte. She had never felt that a woman of her daughter's age should still be living at home. But Charlotte's departure had left her extremely lonely, rattling around in a house as big as a barn. She had thought of selling The Lodge, but her resolution always faltered at the final moment. Somehow she could never regard the place as hers to dispose of: she could never think of it as belonging to anyone but Henry.

All three children called to see her whenever they had the time, but they were increasingly busy about their own concerns. Guy was at sea a great deal, and Nicholas was either in the House, bolstering the dramatically thinned Labour ranks, or at his constituency headquarters. The last two times he had dropped by, he had brought with him a very nice rather plain young woman called Ella Rogers, of whom he seemed quietly fond. Katherine doubted if he felt for her what he had felt for Annabel, but perhaps that was just as well. He must never be hurt again in that soul-destroying fashion.

Charlotte, too, was busier than ever as her position on the administrative staff of Lynton's grew in responsibility. It was generally accepted now, even by an exacting Henry, that she had won her spurs. Her personal relationship with her father remained cool, but she had always been readier than her brothers to make allowances for him. She had taken to visiting him again in the Park Lane flat whenever she knew her stepmother to be away. And as Annabel had been living in Hollywood for the past three months, Charlotte had seen him more frequently of late. But that, of course, meant that she visited Katherine less. There were, as she pointed out, only so many hours in every day.

Katherine had raised no objection, although she never enquired after Henry, a still slumbering anger and a sense of loyalty to Nicholas smothering her curiosity and concern. As a result, however, her feeling of isolation increased as the months went by until one evening in late April, when Jonathan had again proposed to her over dinner, she had accepted without giving herself time to stop and think. It had seemed the sensible thing to do, and she was tired of her lonely bed. But she had gone home and cried herself to sleep.

This ambivalence towards her forthcoming marriage had remained with her. She liked Jonathan; she admired him and knew that he would make her a good husband, just as she would try to make him a good wife. At the same time she resented his aloofness, his never-failing sense of what was due to his position and his finicky, almost obsessive correct-

344

ness. He was a humourless man who never lost his temper, indicating any displeasure by quietly leaving the room. Katherine had never heard anyone call him Jon.

In reply to Jane's question, however, she merely said, 'Oh, I just thought it was time I settled down again.'

Jane, she thought, was running to fat. She looked sleek and contented, cramming sandwiches and chocolate cake into her mouth with a complete disregard for her figure. There was no doubt that she was happy. The Victorian house in Chelsea, which Robert had bought after their marriage, was full of Jane's elegant touches. The interior had been lightened by painting most of the walls in pale pastel colours, and the curtains were delicate, floral, Laura Ashley prints. There were flowers everywhere in tall glass vases, and the furniture was modern and light. It made The Lodge look even darker and dowdier by comparison, and Katherine was aware of a growing dissatisfaction. Another reason, perhaps, why she had accepted Jonathan's proposal: the desire to begin afresh.

The two men, who had finished their tea some time ago and, excusing themselves, had retired to Robert's study to talk business, now returned.

'You're not still eating, are you?' Robert asked fondly, leaning over the back of Jane's chair and kissing her upturned face.

He must be nearly sixty, Katherine thought to herself, suddenly jealous of the love which he and Jane so obviously shared. It would be nice if Jonathan could show her some similar mark of affection, but he sat down primly, a few feet away, on the chair he had vacated half an hour previously.

'Settled your business?' Jane enquired, raising a hand to pat her husband's cheek. She added reprovingly, 'This is a Bank Holiday, you know.'

345

Robert laughed indulgently, stroking her hand, giving Jane what Katherine privately dubbed 'the little woman treatment'. It wouldn't suit her. She had never wanted it and never been given it; not even, she reflected ironically, by Robert. But, looking back, she could see that that was probably the sort of wife he had always needed. And if only Sheila had let him comfort and support her after Iain's death, their marriage might possibly have survived.

But some display of affection was necessary, even vital, to any relationship, and Katherine glanced at Jonathan with renewed misgivings. He smiled at her; a reassurance, she felt, that she could rely on him not to embarrass her in public. At that moment, she wasn't sure that it was the sort of commitment that she wanted.

Her gaze strayed back to Jane, who gave her a slant-eyed grin, the moist parted lips displaying the marvels of American dentistry. She patted her stomach.

'Katherine thinks I'm getting fat,' she said to her husband. 'I am, aren't I, honey? And I shall be fatter still before I'm through.' She laughed delightedly at Katherine's incredulous expression. 'That's right! At long last, I'm going to have a baby.'

Katherine stammered her congratulations, conscious of an overwhelming jealousy, not because she wanted another child, but because she had lost the ability to bear one. It reminded her forcibly of the difference in age between herself and Jane MacNeice; and also that men remained potent long after Nature had arbitrarily decided that women should be infertile.

She was glad when Jonathan rose and said politely that they must go. They were going to the theatre that evening.

Driving her back to The Lodge so that she could bath and change, Jonathan remarked disapprovingly,

'Rather foolish, I should have thought, becoming a father again at Robert's age. But that, of course, is one of the penalties for marrying a much younger woman.' He added, after a momentary pause, 'You need have no fears that I shall bother you in that way. I envisage ours purely as a marriage of convenience.'

'Oh!' Katherine said blankly, uncertain whether she was dismayed or relieved.

He dropped her at The Lodge, refusing to come in for a drink with the reminder that they only had two hours before the play started.

'It would never do to be late. I shall call for you promptly at seven-thirty.'

Katherine went indoors, feeling depressed and with a nagging headache. The house was silent and gloomy, and she went into the drawing-room to pour herself a Scotch and soda. It was unusual for her to drink so early in the evening, but she suddenly felt in desperate need of a stimulant. She switched on the television . . .

It took her a minute or two to absorb what the news-reader was saying. Earl Mountbatten was dead, killed by a bomb planted on his yacht by the IRA. And if that were not sufficient horror for one day, eighteen young soldiers had been massacred in an ambush at Warren Point, near the Irish border.

Katherine found that she was crying and trembling, and had to sit down to steady herself. She took a large gulp of her Scotch, but felt no better. It was not normal for her to react like this to news, however disastrous. She hadn't even been able to shed tears over the tragedy at Aberfan, or when Kennedy was assassinated, and everyone she knew seemed heartbroken. She must be very low to let herself be so personally affected.

The doorbell was ringing. It couldn't be Jonathan, Katherine decided dazedly: he never changed his mind. And she wasn't expecting anyone. It must be one of the children; Guy, perhaps, home on an unexpected leave. If so, he would just have to fend for himself this evening.

'You look a mess,' Henry said roughly, regarding her across the lozenge-patterned dimness of the hall. 'You're not ill, are you?'

Katherine couldn't remember letting him in. He seemed to have materialized, like a genie out of a bottle. She wasn't even sure, at that moment, that he was real. She put a hand to her head, swaying slightly. The evening sun, filtering through the panes of coloured glass, was hurting her eyes.

'What are you doing here?' she asked vaguely. She was beginning to feel sick. Was it something she had eaten? She started to sweat.

'I came to see you,' Henry said, eyeing her narrowly. 'Here!' He put an arm about her waist and guided her, unresisting, into the drawing-room. 'Sit down, for God's sake. What's wrong with you?'

'I'm all right.' Katherine snapped. 'Just a bit tired, that's all. Why have you come? Why do you want to see me?' She added randomly, 'Mountbatten's dead. Blown up by the IRA.'

'I know. I heard it on a special news bulletin, mid-afternoon.' Henry paused, then went on, 'I've been making up my mind to come and see you for some weeks, ever since I got back to London. While we were in Cornwall, we saw Guy. His ship was at Devonport for a refit, and he came to Chapel Rock for the day.'

'Oh, yes. You've been unwell, haven't you?' Katherine frowned with the effort of concentration. She picked up her drink and took another gulp. She felt marginally better. 'Charlie told me. A heart attack, wasn't it? I'm sorry.'

'It wasn't serious, and I'm better now. Guy says you're getting married again, to Jonathan Anthony.'

Katherine nodded. The room was spinning gently round her. The sensation was not unpleasant and she leaned back in her chair, quite enjoying it.

'We're being married next month. Why? Do you and Annabel want an invitation?' She started to giggle. 'By the way, your former wife – your second former wife, that is – is pregnant. I had tea with her this aft ... afternoon.' Katherine realized that her speech was becoming slurred and looked accusingly at her empty glass.

'Don't do it, Kate,' Henry urged, sitting forward and gripping one of her knees. 'For pity's sake, don't do it! Jonathan Anthony's not the man for you. He's a stick!'

Katherine began to laugh crazily and found that she could not stop.

'What do you propose, then?' she asked. 'That I wait f ... for you? But you're married, Henry. You're always ... married.' She stood up suddenly, rocking on the balls of her feet. She had stopped laughing and was crying instead. 'Get out! Go on, get out! This is my house now. You gave it to me, remember? When we were ... When we were ...'

But somehow she couldn't pronounce the word 'divorced'; it stuck in her throat and she was feeling sick again. A yellow mist blotted out her vision. She knew Henry had his arms around her and was shouting something, but she was unable to hear what he said. He had gone a long way away. But why had he gone so far when she needed him; when she had always needed him? She wanted to ask him, but couldn't. She was submerged in darkness.

27

'It's certainly quiet here,' Charlotte said, looking out at the snowy heights of Mount Titlis from the *gasthaus* window. 'As long as you're prepared to be sensible, and don't go racketing around the shops in Lucerne, you should be completely fit by the time we leave.'

Katherine, sitting on the edge of one of the beds unpacking her case, smiled faintly at her daughter's maternal tone, but made no real objection to being mothered. She had been in bed for several weeks suffering from what the hospital doctors described as a state of exhaustion, and which her own GP had bluntly informed her was close to a nervous breakdown.

'More mental than physical, my dear,' he had said, pressing her shoulder affectionately. 'My advice to you would be a lot more practical than that of some of my more elevated colleagues in the profession.'

'And all the better for that,' she had said, buttoning her pyjamas, while he put away his stethoscope.

Charlotte, from the other side of the bed, had added her mite.

'You tell her, Doctor. A dose of common sense is what my mother needs, not medicine.'

'Well, I'd sell this house, for a start.' The doctor had glanced around him disparagingly. 'Very nice for a large family, or turned into flats, but too big and lonely for just one person. And then' – he had regarded her straitly, aware that he was about to overstep the professional boundaries, but determined to say his piece, all the same – 'I'd get my emotional life sorted out. I wouldn't force myself, however good or seemingly cogent the reasons, to marry someone I didn't want to marry.'

'He's right, you know,' Charlotte had said when the doctor had gone. She had indicated the telephone by Katherine's bed. 'Phone Jonathan now and tell him you've changed your mind.'

And Jonathan had, greatly to his credit, accepted her decision without question or recrimination.

'Your job's here when you want it,' he had told her gently. 'Come back as soon as you can. I'm lost without you. But not until you're perfectly fit.'

He continued to send fresh flowers almost daily: huge sheaves of tawny, shock-headed chrysanthemums and asters; elegant, late, tight-budded roses. Charlotte had moved back temporarily into The Lodge and said with a sniff that the place looked like a hothouse. Nicholas arrived, armed with chocolates and bunches of grapes, an expression of concern in his quiet grey eyes. Twice Ella Rogers had accompanied him, speaking to, and looking at him in such a proprietorial way that Katherine felt certain an engagement was in the offing. Guy telephoned regularly, and once arrived home unexpectedly on a forty-eight-hour pass. Jane MacNeice called, with an armful of glossily expensive magazines, and said that Robert sent his best wishes. Beryl Claypole dropped in, oozing goodwill and making Katherine laugh with her own brand of barbed and witty gossip. They were comfortable together, two old antagonists who had mellowed and were now good friends.

The only person who did not come, although Charlotte was aware that Katherine watched for him constantly, was Henry. He had telephoned for the ambulance and accompanied her to hospital, that

August Bank Holiday afternoon, but had gone befor
she recovered consciousness and had not been nea
her since.

Charlotte had walked unceremoniously into th
big office at the front of Lynton House, and demande
an explanation. She had never before, during wor
hours, traded on her position as the boss's daughte
but on this occasion she felt her actions to b
justified. The office itself had changed little sinc
Sandor Scott had once sat there, voicing his objec
tions to chemical warfare: the carpet, though new
remained traditional Axminster, and the brass lam
still decorated the top of the vast oak desk. The gree
velvet curtains had been replaced with red, whic
gave the room a warmer appearance, but that was th
single major alteration.

'Why haven't you been to see Mother?' Charlott
had demanded.

'Because she doesn't want to see me,' Henry ha
replied shortly, a bad-tempered frown between hi
eyes.

'Yes, she does.' Charlotte sat down, uninvite
crossing her shapely legs. 'She might pretend other
wise, but she doesn't fool me for a minute. And
know her quite as well as you do.'

Henry said nothing for a moment, then aske
more mildly, 'What good would it do either of us if
went to see her? I'm married. Now that I know she'
not going to marry Anthony, there's nothing else I ca
do. That was the only reason I called that day: to try t
dissuade her from ruining her life.'

'You've already done a pretty good job of doin
that for her,' Charlotte answered bluntly. 'And it'
not a bit of use glaring like that, because you don
frighten me. You never have. I realized from an earl
age that your bark's a damn sight worse than you
bite.' She uncrossed her legs and leaned forwar
gripping the edge of the desk. 'You and Mother lov

352

each other. You always have, although a bigger couple of bunglers it would be hard to imagine. Annabel's been away for months now. Is she ever coming home?'

'I don't know.' Henry fiddled absent-mindedly with the papers in front of him.

'Why don't you get a divorce? You can't go on like this, waiting ad infinitum.'

'I've suggested a divorce to Annabel, but for some reason she isn't keen. And I won't force her against her will, Charlie, so don't nag me. I owe her that much, at least.'

He had suddenly looked so ill, so old, now that the fire of his hair had turned to grey, that Charlotte said no more. She knew the impression of age was an illusion; that in spite of the hiccup in his health earlier in the year, he was still an active and virile man. But for days afterwards she could not rid herself of that picture of her father, defeated and sick-looking, as though he had come to the end of his tether. A moment later he had been his usual self, half-laughing, half-annoyed, ordering her out of his office, pressing the intercom button for Mrs Parsons, taking two telephone calls at once, speaking alternately to Geneva and Rome on two widely differing issues.

Nevertheless, it was the former picture which Charlotte remembered, as she turned away from the window of the Gasthaus Edelweiss and started to unpack her things.

'Why did you choose Engelberg?' she asked Catherine over lunch, a few days later. 'You've been here before, that's obvious. You know your way round.'

They had spent the morning walking to a place called, appropriately enough, the End of the World, where the strange, wild silence of the snow-capped

mountains had argued, Katherine felt, the need fo
some sort of belief in God. Later, when they returne
to Engelberg, she had slipped away from Charlot
to visit the local church; but its baroque interior, i
ornately fretted ceiling and gilded saints only di
pelled her mood. She had gone back to the *gastha*
feeling dispirited.

'I came here with Henry, years ago,' she sai
'before we were married. After I'd run away fro
Robert. We stayed at the main hotel, the Titlis, fo
a couple of nights, before going home to face tl
music.'

'You must have loved him very much,' Charlot
urged gently, 'to have left your husband.'

'Yes.' Katherine's reply was guarded. She adde
without raising her eyes from her plate, 'I had a lett
from Nick this morning. He wanted me to know rig
away that he and Ella are getting married.'

Charlotte grimaced. 'She'll probably suit him. Sl
has the chief requirement for a woman who wants
make a success of her marriage. She thinks Nick
wonderful and can do no wrong.'

Katherine laughed, but said, 'Don't be so cynica
Besides, it's not true. At least, not always.'

'Was it true for you and Dad?'

Katherine shook her head. 'No. But, then, o
marriage wasn't successful either, so perhaps you'
right, after all.'

Charlotte, who had finished her meal, propp
her elbows on the table and cupped her chin in h
hands.

'Would you have him back if he and Annab
were divorced?'

Katherine spooned up her last mouthful of i
cream and answered briskly, 'But they're not di
orced, are they? Shall we have our coffee in t
lounge? I think it's too cold for the terrace.'

In the afternoon, they went by ski-lift to the la

354

at Trübsee. It had been Katherine's suggestion; something she felt she must make herself do, to prove that she could retrace the steps of the thirty-year-distant holiday with Henry, and remain untroubled by ghosts. It was the reason why she had chosen this part of Switzerland when the doctor had ordered her to take a complete rest before returning to her job with Rosewall Foods.

'Get right away,' he had said. 'Go abroad. Get that bossy daughter of yours to go with you. She'll see that you don't overdo things, if anyone can.'

When she told him, a few weeks later, that she was going to Switzerland he had been delighted. She guessed that he would have been less pleased had he known her motives; that she was once again forcing herself through emotional hoops. It hadn't occurred to Charlotte yet, but Katherine braced herself for anger, once the realization dawned.

Trübsee was just the same: ageless, beautiful, an eternal ministration to the soul. Katherine experienced a return of the same sensation she had felt that morning, at the End of the World. *I will lift up mine eyes unto the hills from whence cometh my help.* Psalm 121. There was something, after all, to be said for a religious education. She wondered guiltily if she hadn't deprived her children of something vital by never making them go to church.

But Katherine had never been quite sure what she believed, and neither had Henry; except in each other and their mutual love. They had believed in that, all right. She remembered, as if it were yesterday, walking with him along the shore of this mountain lake, holding hands, stopping every now and then to look at one another, as though to reassure themselves that it was not some impossible dream from which they must awaken. She had left her husband, he had defied his uncle, and his future – the future that he so desperately wanted – was clouded

355

and uncertain. But they had been happy; far happier in the circumstances, than either of them had deserved to be.

Later on, they had found a secluded place in one of the folds of the surrounding hills, and made love. It was the first time Katherine had done this outside a bedroom, and she had been amazed at the sensation of freedom it had given her. She supposed that she must already have been carrying Charlotte, though she had not known it; Charlotte, who was Henry's favourite child, but who really belonged to Robert. Katherine had been bitter about Henry deceiving her with his women, but had she ever stopped to consider that she might be practising an even greater deception on him?

'What is it?' Charlotte asked, pausing and peering closely at her mother. 'You're crying. Aren't you feeling well?'

Katherine strove to control her voice. 'I'm perfectly all right. Perfectly.' The tears refused to be checked and she gave up the unequal struggle. She clung to her daughter, thankful on this chilly autumn day there were few people around to see her. 'Oh Charlie! Charlie! I'm sorry. I didn't want to make a scene. It's just that I was thinking about Henry.'

The cab dropped her high in the heart of Bel Air. When she had paid her fare, Charlotte pushed tentatively at the tall iron gates set in the equally forbidding-looking wall. The cab driver, about to restart his engine, leaned out of the off-side window.

'Lady! It ain't no good trying to get in that way.' He indicated an intercom system. 'Speak in there. Tell 'em who you are.'

'Thank you,' Charlotte said gratefully.

Two Alsatians suddenly raced out of nowhere barking like fiends, and positioned themselves on the other side of the gates. Their upper lips were drawn back in a perpetual snarl, and Charlotte could see that they both had excellent teeth. Behind her the taxi engine revved into life, and driver and vehicle hurriedly departed. Dear God! Charlotte thought, eyeing the two dogs with misgivings. Did all film stars have to live like this?

It was ten months since the holiday in Switzerland with her mother; ten months during which she had hoped that the situation between Henry and Annabel would resolve itself without her intervention. But nothing had happened. Annabel remained in Hollywood, working on her third – or was it fourth? – film, while Henry stayed in London, making no move to contact either her or Katherine. Katherine, meanwhile, had got rid of The Lodge, and now rented a pleasant flat not far from the Brompton Oratory. She had invested part of the money from the sale of the house in her father's old bungalow, which had fortuitously come on to the market at the precise moment when Katherine had been looking for somewhere to live.

'I'm going back to my roots,' she had told Charlotte, defending her decision to buy a permanent home in Plymouth.

'You won't be there all that much,' her daughter had objected. 'I hate this business of holiday homes. They play havoc with the indigenous population.'

'In three years' time, I shall be sixty,' Katherine had pointed out. 'Retirement age. I've had enough of London. As I said, I'm returning to my roots.'

It had sounded ominously final to Charlotte; a settled and solitary old age. Katherine was already spending most weekends in Devon, supervising structural alterations to the bungalow, overseeing the redecorations. Even Nicholas, busy as he was, complained that he rarely saw his mother these days.

'Let's hope', he had commented acidly, 'that she doesn't forget the wedding.'

Nicholas and Ella Rogers were married quietly at St Margaret's, Westminster, at the beginning of July, in a capital already celebrating the Queen Mother's eightieth birthday; although the birthday itself was not until the fourth of August.

'Today,' Charlotte thought with a little start of surprise, as she pressed the intercom button which would connect her with the house. England seemed so very far away, as, literally, she supposed it was. The Alsatians continued barking.

A man's voice said, 'Yes? Who is it?'

'My name's Charlotte Lynton. Mrs ... Miss Hardwicke's expecting me.'

'OK.' There was a faintly foreign intonation to the voice. The butler? Charlotte wondered. 'Are the dogs there?'

'Can't you hear the bloody things?' she snapped bad-temperedly. 'Don't you dare open these gates until someone has collected these hell-hounds.'

The man gave a high-pitched nasal laugh and the intercom went dead. A few moments later another man, plainly not the one she had been speaking to, shambled round a bend in the drive and, with much cursing, hauled the dogs away. After a decent interval, the gates swung open and Charlotte was able to go inside.

The garden was much bigger than she had expected, also lusher, thanks to half a dozen water sprinklers which played constantly over the lawns and shrubs. The house itself, when it came into view, was a long low hacienda-type building, with a green and blue tiled roof. A man stood waiting for her on the stone-flagged patio, tall and slender, black-haired and arrogantly good-looking.

Definitely not the butler, Charlotte told herself.

'Charlotte?' He pronounced her name, stressing the second syllable. She thought how much prettier it

358

sounded when spoken that way. 'Annabel is waiting for you.'

He led the way round the house to the inevitable swimming-pool, where the hot sun glanced off improbably blue water and caused hundreds of dancing lights to surface from the gold-painted tiles at the bottom. Cold drinks were set on a low table between striped loungers, on one of which Annabel was reclining, in a black bikini. She got up when she saw Charlotte and came towards her, revealing the lack of height and slight dumpiness which were so well concealed in her films.

'Charlie! How nice you could come to see me. Your call last night was quite a surprise.' She offered a sun-tanned cheek to be kissed.

Charlotte complied. 'I was in the States on business for the firm, and I suddenly thought, why not fly out to California and see Annabel? So here I am.'

Annabel's smile was brittle. 'It was your own idea, was it? I mean, Henry didn't ask you to check up on me while you were here?'

'Good God, no! Whatever gave you that impression?'

'I just wondered ... Although not seriously. It's not really Henry's style.' Annabel waved her guest to one lounger and resumed her former place on the other. She turned to look up at the young man who was hovering solicitously behind her. 'Carlo, darling, this is my stepdaughter, Charlotte. Be an angel and fetch up her cases.'

'Oh, I'm not stopping,' Charlotte said quickly. 'I've booked into a hotel downtown. It didn't seem worth bothering you for just one night. I'm flying back east tomorrow.'

She had the feeling that Annabel was far from sorry, even though her stepmother made all the usual noises of regret. But Annabel's manner relaxed as she

darted a sidelong glance at Carlo that palpabl[y]
expressed relief.

'Then, pour drinks for us, will you, darling?' Sh[e]
disregarded the young man's scowl. 'Lemonad[e]
Charlie? Or something stronger?'

'Lemonade's fine by me. It's not my time of day f[or]
serious drinking.'

As she spoke, Charlotte reflected that Annab[el]
had changed, and not for the better. There was a[n]
artificiality about her; a kind of feverish glitter. Th[e]
heavy make-up, the stagey conversation were i[n]
direct contrast to the blunt, rather prosaic girl sh[e]
remembered. And Carlo, where did he fit into th[e]
scheme of things? He was obviously living there an[d]
equally obviously, was more than just a part of th[e]
décor.

Annabel patted the young man's hand and sai[d]
'Carlo's my live-in houseboy. He attends to all m[y]
wants.'

Charlotte resisted the temptation to reply 'I bet h[e]
does!' and smiled politely instead.

Sulkily, Carlo poured lemonade for the three [of]
them, the ice chinking against the sides of the froste[d]
tumblers, and then lit cigarettes for himself an[d]
Annabel. Charlotte was surprised: she recalled tha[t]
Annabel had always been outspokenly anti-smoking

'What do you think of Anna's last film?' Carl[o]
asked. 'She was great, no? Magnificent, even.'

'I'm afraid I didn't see it,' Charlotte answere[d]
candidly. 'I don't go to the cinema much these days[.]

Carlo seemed far more offended than Annabel a[t]
this admission. Annabel merely laughed, revertin[g]
abruptly to her normal self.

'Go and take a swim, darling,' she said, giving hi[m]
a playful push. 'Charlie and I have a lot to talk about.[']

Carlo looked sulkier than ever, but in the end h[e]
went, pulling off shirt and trousers to reveal a pair o[f]
brief swimming trunks beneath.

Before Charlotte could say anything further, Annabel remarked, 'Nicholas is married, then.'

'Yes.' Charlotte raised her strongly marked eyebrows. 'How did you know?'

'For heaven's sake! We get all the English papers out here. And the wedding of one of the few new Labour candidates to win a seat at the last election merited a small paragraph in most of them.'

'Yes, of course. Silly of me. Sorry.'

'What's she like, this woman he's married?'

'Ella? She's a nice girl. Rather plain. A bit dull. But she'll make Nick an excellent wife, I have no doubt. She won't complain when he has an all-night sitting in the House, and she'll be a marvel in the constituency. She thinks the sun rises and sets on him.'

Annabel made no reply, staring out over the gold-spangled water. Her expression was blank. There was no way of telling what she was thinking.

'Well, that's nice for him,' she said brightly, after a while. 'Is he happy?'

'Yes ... Yes, I suppose so,' Charlotte said, taken aback by the question. 'I mean, who can really say? But he appears to be happy enough.'

Annabel drew deeply on the cigarette she was smoking, looked at it as though she wondered what she was doing with it and stubbed it out, almost furtively, in a green glass ashtray. She glanced at Charlotte and smiled. 'And to what, as they say, do I owe the honour of this visit?'

The feverish, over-excited look had returned, and Charlotte noted that the pupils of Annabel's eyes were dilated.

'I've come to talk about you and Father,' she replied, deciding on the direct approach. 'Why won't you divorce him? Or, alternatively' – her gaze flicked to Carlo's lean brown body effortlessly, lazily cleaving the water – 'let him divorce you?'

Annabel followed her glance and waved idly at

Carlo, who was now clambering on to an air-bed floating in the middle of the pool.

'Oh, I don't want to marry Carlo,' she said. 'I don't want to marry anyone. I've had enough of marriage.'

'In Hollywood?' Charlotte was incredulous. 'People here get married and divorced all the time.'

'I'm not like everyone else,' Annabel answered. 'Henry's my protection from men like Carlo, who, if I were single, would expect me to marry him tomorrow. As it is, he'll get tired of the situation in five or six months, and move on to someone else. And I shall be free to begin again with somebody new. Oh, no, my dear, a rich businessman husband, living on the other side of the Atlantic, is ideal as far as I'm concerned. The perfect protection from predatory males.'

'But you can't want to live like that for ever!'

'For ever?' Annabel was contemptuous. 'Who wants to think about for ever? One day at a time is enough for me. And you've been in no rush to get married. What are you now? Thirty? And still single.'

Charlotte ignored the rider and protested angrily, 'But what about Father? You're not playing fair by him. He's lonely. If you and he divorced, he could marry my mother again.'

'Ah!' Annabel smiled, her eyes half-closed. 'So that's it, is it? The little matchmaker.'

'You have no intention of divorcing him, then? Even though you're spoiling his life?'

Annabel laughed. It sounded wild and abandoned. Carlo turned his head on the air-pillow and looked at her. Without knowing what she was laughing at, he joined in. They both seemed a little . . . a little what? Charlotte wondered; not mad, exactly, but slightly off-balance.

Annabel stopped laughing and said, 'Henry doesn't need anyone to spoil his life. He's very good at doing that himself. And he spoils other people's lives

362

along with his own. I used to be fond of him, but I've had a lot of time to think since I've been out here. No, if Henry wants a divorce, he'll have to divorce me, and he won't do that. He's very old-fashioned in some ways. He's a mass of contradictions. But there again, aren't we all? Aren't we all?' Her eyes narrowed sleepily. 'So it seems Henry's stuck with me, Charlie, unless you can persuade him otherwise. Sorry to ruin your nice little dream.'

28

'Drugs,' Charlotte said. 'That's what it was. It must have been. Why didn't I think of it before?'

'What on earth are you talking about?' Katherine asked, stepping back to admire the curtains she had just finished hanging. 'I'm quite pleased with those. Don't you think they're a pretty colour?'

'Mmm? Oh, yes. Quite a pretty colour. I'm talking about Annabel. When I went to visit her last year, in California.' Charlotte gazed round the living-room of the bungalow – made larger by knocking the dining-room and old kitchen into one and building on a new kitchen at the back – momentarily diverted. 'You don't belong in a place like this,' she grumbled. 'You belong at Chapel Rock.'

'I grew up in this bungalow,' Katherine retorted, nettled. 'The vast majority of people in this country belong in a place like this. Bungalows, semis, suburbia; most of us aren't lucky enough to be brought up in the sort of homes that you were. You, my girl, were born with a golden spoon in your mouth. Don't knock what you know nothing about.'

'All right. All right,' Charlotte grinned placatingly.

She looked through the picture window, another new feature, at the china-clay mounds on the edge of Dartmoor, and at the newly tidied garden. She liked the early spring when crocuses pierced the borders with little flames of coloured light, when mornings were sharp with the scent of dew, when the bare trees began thickening to their summer green. She was glad for her own sake that she had managed to get out of London for this one weekend, leaving behind the increasing pressure of business life and her dissatisfaction with her current lover. She wondered sometimes if she might have lesbian tendencies, but was too idle and too indifferent to find out. What she enjoyed was work, vying with men in the boardroom instead of in bed. She looked forward to taking over Lynton's some time in the future. Nevertheless, she had the sense to realize that a break now and then was essential. Besides, she had special reasons for coming down to Plymouth this weekend.

'What were you saying just now?' Katherine enquired absent-mindedly. 'Something about drugs . . . I wonder if I was wise to have the whole bungalow fitted with this neutral-coloured carpet. It'll show the dirt.'

'You can always put rugs down later on,' Charlotte suggested, but without much enthusiasm. 'It'll look quite different, anyway, when the furniture's in.' She glanced at her watch. 'Isn't it time we were getting back to the hotel for dinner?'

'I suppose so. We've done quite well, getting all the curtains up this afternoon. And it'll soon be dusk, and the electricity hasn't been reconnected yet.' Katherine picked up her coat from where she had dropped it, in one corner. 'What were you nattering about just now? You still haven't told me.'

'Drugs. Annabel was on drugs. I've only just tumbled to it, fool that I am. It was those cigarettes she and her boyfriend were smoking.'

'Reefers,' Katherine said, dredging the word up from the depths of her memory. Her brain constantly surprised her by the things it knew. It did so again. 'Marijuana, that's what reefers are made from. Hemp. Not really the hard stuff, is it?'

'People have to start somewhere. Drug addiction can only get worse.'

'Or be cured,' Katherine argued. 'What did you go to see her for, anyway?'

'No particular reason,' Charlotte lied airily. 'I was in the States, and she is my stepmother. Talking of which – my ex-stepmother, that is – how's Robert and Jane's little boy?'

'He's lovely,' Katherine said warmly. 'He really is a delightful child, and Jane's the perfect mother. I'm so glad Robert had another son. Jamie can't replace Iain, of course, but he compensates.' She thought: Jamie's your half-brother and you don't even know it.

'Right,' Charlotte said briskly, pulling on her anorak over her shirt and jeans. 'Let's go, shall we? I'm famished. I hope it's something decent for dinner.'

'You go on out to the car. I'll make sure everything's locked up. Empty houses are such a target for vandals these days.'

Katherine went through to the back door, which was now in the new extension. Everything here smelt of freshly applied plaster and paint. What would Aunt Margery have said, she wondered, to all the alterations: the double glazing, the central heating, the disappearance of her beloved old kitchen? It was Aunt Margery who was closest to her in the bungalow; who kept her company as she wandered through the silent, empty rooms. Oddly, she rarely felt her father's presence, although his had been the stronger personality. Perhaps it was because, in her mind, she associated him with Chapel Rock, where, ironically, he had seemed so much more at home. In spite of his republicanism, Communism, whatever he liked to call it, Victor Grey had always had grandiose ideas. It had often occurred to Katherine that, paradoxically, if you were from the hopefully aspiring world of the lower middle class, it took a lot of self-assurance to vote Labour.

She went into what had once been Aunt Margery's bedroom, now silent and deserted in the gathering dusk. The pale fitted carpet, the eggshell-blue walls, the white plastic German window-frames and double glazing had nothing whatever to do with her aunt, and yet it remained Margery's room. If Katherine closed her eyes, her childhood came flooding back and she could see it exactly as it used to be: cluttered with furniture and dozens of ornaments, presents from St Ives and Penzance, or the more exotic bric-à-brac brought home by Victor from his travels. Katherine recalled a beautiful fringed sash made of thousands upon thousands of tiny glass beads, translucent gold, with a pattern of white and blue diamonds running through the centre, worked with endless patience and loving care by the Maoris of New Zealand. What had happened to it? Lost, she supposed; carelessly thrown out when the bungalow was cleared, along with the paper-thin Japanese tea-set, which every sailor, in those days, seemed to bring home as a matter of course . . .

Charlotte poked her head round the door. 'There you are! What on earth are you doing? I've been waiting in the car for ages. Come on! Dinner's at seven thirty and we have to get back and change.'

The hotel was on the Hoe, overlooking the Sound and Drake's Island. Katherine and Charlotte had a table in the bay window, and at night, with the curtains still undrawn, they could see the distant lights shining on the water.

Towards the end of the meal Katherine became aware that Charlotte was muttering something, looking embarrassed, fidgeting guiltily with the spoon on her empty plate.

'Sorry, darling,' Katherine said. 'I didn't catch what you said.'

'I said . . . would you like to have coffee in the

lounge? There's someone there waiting to see you.'

Katherine frowned. 'Who?' she asked, then her face brightened. 'Is it Guy?'

'No,' Charlotte snapped. 'He wouldn't waste his time dancing attendance on us. He'd be whooping it up in Union Street, in one of the clubs. Anyway, isn't he on exercises off the coast of Scotland?'

'Yes, of course. I forgot.' Katherine's eagerness faded. 'Who is it, then? Anyone I know?'

Charlotte's colour rose and she stared defensively at her mother.

'It's Dad. I asked him to come down this weekend and join us.'

'You did what?' Katherine asked slowly.

'It's OK. He isn't stopping here. He's booked in at the Holiday Inn. He rang me just before dinner to say he'd be here by nine. So what do you say? Will you see him?'

'You know, if you don't watch it,' Katherine said with some asperity, 'you'll turn into an interfering, busybodying old maid!'

'A very sexist remark, Mother dear,' Charlotte observed, unruffled, her composure returning as she detected undertones of capitulation in Katherine's voice. Her mother was not nearly as angry as she wished to be thought. 'Shall we go? Coffee in the lounge, please, for three,' she added to the hovering waitress.

There were very few people staying at the hotel in March, and the lounge was empty except for Henry, sitting in one corner of the deep chintz-covered settee, his eyes fixed anxiously, painfully almost, on the door. He got to his feet as Katherine and Charlotte came in.

'I want you to know that I don't approve of this meeting,' Katherine said by way of greeting. 'Charlie set this up entirely on her own. I knew nothing about it.'

'I'm aware of that,' Henry answered quietly. 'But

now you're here, won't you at least sit down? Please.'

Katherine nodded rather ungraciously, seating herself between Henry and Charlotte. She was shaking with emotion, and was glad of the enforced silence while the little red-headed waitress, who had served them at dinner, arranged the coffee things on the table in front of them. Charlotte, who saw that her mother's hands were unsteady, took over the task of pouring out.

'Why did you do it?' Katherine asked at last, looking at her daughter. 'What's the point?' She turned to Henry. 'I assume you're still married. I haven't heard any rumours of a divorce.'

'Yes, I'm still married, if you can call it that.' Henry's voice was unemotional. 'Annabel's still in Hollywood and shows no sign of coming home.'

'But you're not even legally separated,' Katherine persisted. 'So what do you want with me?'

'I've persuaded Dad it's time he stopped playing silly buggers,' Charlotte answered for him. 'He's going to divorce Annabel, after all. He's hired a private detective in Los Angeles to provide him with the necessary evidence. The man won't have much difficulty earning his fee from what I saw when I was out there.'

'I see.' Katherine sipped her coffee. 'But you still haven't explained how this affects me.'

'For Christ's sake, don't start being coy, Mother!' Charlotte exclaimed angrily. 'You know you're in love with Dad, just as much as he's in love with you! Isn't it time you two got your act together and stopped behaving, as Grandpa would have said, like a couple of Queen Mary's Gifts? Accept the truth! You're miserable apart; you always have been, you always will be. Do you want to go on hurting one another until it's too late to do anything about it?'

There was silence. After a moment or two, Katherine looked at Henry.

'It's a nice night,' she said. 'Quite warm. Moonlight. Would you like to go for a walk along the Hoe? If you'll give me a couple of minutes, I'll fetch my coat.'

In the quiet of her hotel bedroom Katherine paused, staring at her reflection in the wardrobe mirror. What on earth was she doing? She had put her life in order, made provision for her old age, accustomed herself to the idea of a solitary existence, even persuaded herself that she might rather like it. And, yet here she was, throwing it all away, preparing to get involved once again with Henry, who had brought her so much heartache and trouble in the past.

But he had also given her more happiness than she had ever known with anyone else, man or woman. And, anyway, who wanted the ordered, uneventful, monotonous, boring existence she had mapped out for herself? She was only fifty-seven: she wasn't in her dotage. And by the standards of 1981 she wasn't even old.

She remembered, earlier in the day, hearing one of the Beatles' songs blaring out from someone's transistor radio, and reliving the horror and shock which the world had felt at John Lennon's murder, the previous December. It was trite, but none the less true, that you never knew what was waiting for you round the next corner. Eat, drink and be merry . . . What was the point of planning, of self-denial, of caution and resentment, if tomorrow you might be lying dead?

'Never let the sun go down on your anger,' Aunt Margery had always told her when she was young. 'If you do; you might live to regret it tomorrow.' Homespun philosophy, no doubt, but not necessarily to be derided for all that.

Henry was in the hotel foyer when she got downstairs. Without saying anything, she took his arm and they went through the door and down the steps, directing their footsteps towards the Citadel.

Drake's statue and, to their right, Smeaton Tower stood out clear and stark, drenched in moonlight.

'I love you, you know,' Henry said quietly. 'No one else has ever meant anything to me compared with you.'

'No, I know. Shush!' Katherine squeezed his arm. 'We'll talk about it tomorrow. Tonight, it's just enough to be together. Let's look at the naval war memorial. It used to fascinate me as a child.'

They passed between the walls of stone, open to the sky, carved with name after name of sailors lost at sea during two world wars.

'Do you feel it?' she whispered as they stared at the inscriptions, each of which represented a husband, lover, son or brother. 'The silence, I mean. You can almost touch it. Even on the hottest summer day, when the Hoe's packed with trippers, you can stand between these walls and everything is quiet.' She began to cry, silently. 'So many of them,' she said, reading down the seemingly endless lists of names. 'Please God our young men never have to go to war again.'

'What did you talk about?' Charlotte wanted to know the following day as they sat up in bed, drinking their early-morning tea. 'What have you decided? What plans have you made?'

'We haven't decided anything,' Katherine answered repressively; then relented and smiled. 'We didn't say much at all, if you really want to know. We were just content, for the time being, to be in one another's company.'

It was Charlotte's turn to smile. 'That sounds promising. And what's the drill for today, then?'

'Henry's coming to the hotel this morning for a serious discussion. There are a lot of things to be settled between us.'

'Right.' Charlotte lay back against her pillows, her

hands linked behind her head. 'In that case, I'll make myself scarce. I might even go to church, as it's Sunday.'

'Church? You?' Katherine mocked, getting out of bed and going into the bathroom. 'That I should live to see the day!' She closed the door, but opened it again a moment later, a troubled frown puckering her brow. 'Charlie, do you believe in premonitions?'

Charlotte ceased her happy contemplation of the view beyond the window and turned her head.

'What sort of premonition?'

Katherine came back into the bedroom and sat on the edge of her daughter's bed.

'Last night, Henry and I were looking at the naval war memorial on the Hoe. All those names. All those dead, drowned sailors. And suddenly I felt as though someone was walking over my grave. I felt . . . Oh, I don't know! As though some disaster was imminent. I suppose nothing has happened to Guy?'

'For goodness' sake, Mother!' Charlotte exclaimed impatiently, sitting up higher in the bed. 'You don't believe in premonitions and auguries and rubbish like that, surely? If anything had happened to Guy, the Admiralty would have been on to you by now. You were just a bit emotional, that was all. That's the explanation for most of that kind of foreboding.'

'Yes. Of course you're right.' Katherine got up, grinning rather sheepishly. 'Although Robert's mother, old Mrs MacNeice, was a firm believer in the second sight.'

'Poppycock,' Charlotte responded, getting out of bed in her turn. 'And don't be all day in the bathroom. Remember, I want to get in. And if you're not quick, Dad will be here before you've finished breakfast.'

But when Katherine descended to the dining-room, half an hour later, she was told that Mr Lynton

372

had already arrived and was waiting for her at her table.

'He wouldn't have anything to eat, madam, but he's had some coffee.' The little red-haired waitress was plainly curious.

Katherine made her way to the table in the bay window where she was brought up short by the sight of Nicholas, sitting in Charlotte's place and staring out of the window at the view across the Sound.

'Nick!' Katherine tried not to let disappointment seep into her tone. 'How lovely to see you. What are you doing here? And so early in the morning.'

Nicholas rose and kissed her dutifully on the cheek. 'I had a constituency meeting yesterday evening and I had to stop in Bristol overnight. I thought I'd drive down to see you, as it was such a nice morning. I started very early and I was in Plymouth by half-past eight. I'll be going back to town after lunch.'

'How did you know where to find me? I haven't seen you for weeks.'

'I telephoned Jonathan before I left London. I guessed he'd know where you were staying. I thought, after breakfast, you could show me the bungalow. I think I might have been there once, when I was very small.'

Katherine hesitated. 'I ... I'm afraid I can't, darling, but Charlie will take you, if you're really curious. The thing is I may not be going to live there, after all. In fact, I'll probably be reselling it.'

'Not going to live there?' Nicholas looked astonished. Then his puzzled expression vanished and he smiled. 'You've come to your senses. You're going to marry Jonathan. I was only saying to Ella the other night that you'd be bound to change your mind again, eventually.'

'No, it's not that.' Katherine suddenly felt tongue-tied and was relieved to see Charlotte approaching.

Charlotte regarded her brother uncertainly. 'Oh,' she said, 'it's you. When they said Mr Lynton was here, I thought . . .' Her voice tailed off and she looked around for another chair, dragging one from beneath an empty, unlaid table.

'You thought what?' Nicholas was growing suspicious. 'What's going on? Neither of you is exactly delighted to see me, and Mother tells me she's thinking of selling the bungalow at Higher Compton. What are you two up to? Or is it a secret?'

'No, it's not a secret,' Katherine said, taking her courage in both hands. She ignored the red-haired waitress who was waiting impatiently to take their order. Food could come later when she felt more like eating. 'Your father and I are thinking – and, at the moment, it has proceeded no further than that – of getting back together again. He's . . . He's going to divorce Annabel.'

'I persuaded him,' Charlotte cut in. 'That marriage has been over in everything but name for ages.'

Nicholas replaced his coffee cup in its saucer with extravagant care. His face was very pale and tense.

'I see,' he said at last. After a long pause, he raised his head and met Katherine's eyes. His own were as blank as a sleepwalker's. Then he blinked two or three times in rapid succession, and the grey depths, so like his father's, were rekindled with life. He linked his bony hands together on the tablecloth. His voice was even. 'I'll tell you both why I really came down to Plymouth this morning. It was to tell you the news. Ella's expecting a baby. If all goes well, it will be born round about Christmas.' Nicholas looked steadily at his mother. 'I want to make it clear, however, that if you remarry my father, if you have anything whatsoever to do with him, you will never set eyes on your grandchild, nor will you ever see me again.' He rose to his feet, oblivious of Charlotte's horrified protests. 'I mean it, Mother. I'll never forgive him as long as I live, so you have a straight choice. It's between him and me.'

Katherine stood once again at the bungalow window, staring out over Dartmoor and the mounds of china clay. She would be living here, after all, when the time came for her to retire. She wouldn't be going back to Chapel Rock or the Park Lane flat. She would be ending where she began, along with her ghosts. What other decision could she possibly have come to?

It was no good ranting and raving, like Charlotte; calling down curses on Nicholas's head. Henry had understood right away, when she had told him.

'That's it, then,' he had said, holding both her hands in his. 'I won't be the instrument of separating you from our son and grandchild. My follies have cost you dear enough already.'

'For God's sake, stand up to Nick!' Charlotte had urged them. 'Don't let him ruin what's left of your lives! When he finds out you're really serious, he'll come round. He won't make good his threats. He couldn't be so unnatural.'

'Yes, he could.' Katherine had smiled faintly. 'You know your brother better than that. He can be extremely stubborn.'

'With reason, in this case,' Henry had added wryly. 'What I did to Nick was in itself unnatural. I'm getting what I deserve. Unfortunately, it also involves punishing your mother.'

'I'll talk to him as soon as I get back to town tomorrow.' Charlotte prepared to leave the hotel lounge where the three of them had been sitting. 'In fact, I think I'll go and phone Ella now, and tell her just what I think of her precious husband.'

But this both Katherine and Henry had expressly forbidden.

'It's not your business,' Katherine had said with finality.

So here she was, wandering once more through the empty rooms of the bungalow, herself a ghost, lost and desolate. After Henry had left she had felt the need to be on her own, and her old home had seemed the most appropriate place. Charlotte had wanted to go with her, but Katherine had refused her company.

'I shan't be very long. Only an hour or so. You settle the bill and do the packing. We'll go back to London this afternoon instead of tomorrow.'

She recalled the first occasion she had brought Henry to the bungalow. Victor had been in one of his moods, behaving outrageously. But Henry hadn't minded. His easy American charm had soon won her father over, and he had had Aunt Margery eating out of his hand.

It was all such a long time ago now: it had been another world and they had been different people. So much water had flowed under so many bridges since then . . . She felt tired; exhausted. All she wanted to do was sleep. It was time to go; back to the hotel, back to London, back to her lonely, loveless life.

Feeling sorry for herself wouldn't help. Katherine braced her shoulders, took a last look round and went outside, locking the front door behind her. She climbed into her waiting car and started the engine.

29

Deborah Katherine Lynton was born just before Christmas 1981, in time for some of the worst winter weather on record.

January came in with heavy falls of snow and high winds, causing blizzard conditions; but the child lay snug and warm in her cot, unaware of the Arctic world outside her parents' Queenhithe flat, overlooking the river.

'She's beautiful,' Katherine said, lingering by the cot, staring in awe at the the tiny, perfectly formed fingers which clutched aimlessly at the satin binding of the soft yellow blanket. 'However often I see a newborn baby, I still can't get over what miracles of perfection they are.'

'Don't give Mother any more to drink,' Charlotte said plaintively. 'She's waxing lyrical.'

They all laughed, Nicholas and Ella, Charlotte and her latest boyfriend, Katherine and Jonathan Anthony, gathered in the flat's living-room to see in the New Year at midnight. It had been Nicholas's intention to go to his constituency for the Parliamentary recess, but the weather, which had already begun to worsen, had dictated otherwise. He was proving to be a concerned, almost obsessively doting parent, a fact which amused and surprised Katherine. She fancied that her daughter-in-law was also surprised.

'Nick never struck me as being overly fond of

children before Debbie was born,' Ella had remarked earlier in the evening when the women had been in the kitchen, washing up after dinner. 'In fact, when I first discovered I was pregnant, I was doubtful about how he'd take the news.' But before Katherine could make any comment, she had changed the subject. 'I hope you didn't mind Nick inviting Jonathan. He knows you still see one another. Out of work as well as in, I mean.'

'No, of course I don't mind,' Katherine had said 'but there's nothing more to our relationship than what you see on the surface. Jonathan realizes that. I wish I could be sure that Nick does, too.'

'I'm sure he does, really.' Ella had carefully dried her hands and smoothed handcream into them from a bottle which stood ready on the window-ledge. She was an extremely precise and efficient young woman. 'But he tries to delude himself that you'll change your mind. He'd like to see you married again. He thinks you're lonely.'

'I am,' Katherine answered frankly, wondering how much Ella knew about the scene in Plymouth last spring. Had Nicholas told her? And, if so, did she endorse his behaviour?

'You're still in love with his father, aren't you?' Ella looked slightly disapproving. She did not condone infidelity in marriage. She was fully aware of the circumstances which had led Nicholas to propose to her, that she was in fact only second best, but she did not mind. If, however, her husband were now to betray her with another woman, she would leave him without a second's hesitation. Brought up in a strict Baptist family, she lived by a set of rules, a code of conduct, which, in its way, thought Katherine, was every bit as immutable as the laws of the Medes and the Persians.

'Yes, I'm in love with Henry,' Katherine answered

378

lightly. 'But he's still married to Annabel, so it's not likely to get me very far.'

'I thought Nick said . . . Wasn't there some talk of his divorcing her, earlier this year?'

'He changed his mind. And she doesn't seem eager to end the marriage. Right! That's done.' Katherine had wiped the last plate and hung up the tea-towel to dry. 'Shall we join the others?'

Looking now across the room at Ella, Katherine wished she had her daughter-in-law's moral courage and strength of purpose. Ella would never question her own judgement, or make the mistake of seeing things from another point of view. Not for her self-doubt or self-blame. It was all black and white in Ella's world; there were no tones of grey or neutral.

Katherine glanced at the silver-case clock on the shelf near the blocked-in chimney breast, a wedding present from Jonathan and incongruous amid the stacks of records and stereo equipment which filled that end of the room. It was nearly midnight. In a few minutes they would be drinking to 1982. Nicholas had switched on the television set. It was a programme about the events of the past year: the engagement and wedding of the Prince and Princess of Wales; the incident at the Trooping the Colour ceremony, in June, when a man had shot blanks at the Queen with a pistol; the intruder who had managed to enter Buckingham Palace; the assassination of President Sadat of Egypt . . .

She sat down beside Jonathan, who was talking to Nicholas, and picked up the telegram from Guy. It had arrived a few days earlier, Nicholas had said when he had shown it to her just before dinner.

'Congratulations both. Hope mother and child well,' it ran. 'Looking forward seeing niece April.' It was signed: 'Deborah's uncle'.

Guy's most recent promotion had posted him to

HMS *Sheffield*, and he was at present on a five-months tour of duty which would keep him at sea until the spring. Looking at the conventional words of greeting, Katherine was suddenly reminded of the premonition of disaster she had experienced that night when she and Henry had visited the naval war memorial on the Hoe. The feeling had been so real, so strong at the time; but in her ensuing unhappiness, she had forgotten it. Now, without warning, she felt again the same sense of foreboding.

She was being ridiculous. What could possibly happen to Guy or to any of them? And if the answer to that was, at that moment, being graphically displayed on the television screen — war, famine, bombings, hi-jackings, terrorist attacks — she resolutely closed her mind to the implications. Nothing could touch her or her family. These were catastrophes which only happened to other people.

The television pictures changed abruptly. The bloodstained sights of Northern Ireland and the Lebanon gave place to balloons, streamers, ringing bells and kilts, interspersed with scenes of the crowds in Trafalgar Square. Nicholas was on his feet, replenishing empty glasses. Charlotte's boyfriend — who must, Katherine reflected, be all of thirty-five — was trying to nibble Charlotte's ear.

The chimes of Big Ben filled the room, and everyone waited tensely for the first magic stroke of twelve. How arbitrary, how artificial a barrier it was, created so that man could at least have the illusion of putting the past behind him. Then they were all on their feet, chinking glasses, wishing one another a happy New Year.

On Thursday morning, the twenty-fifth of March, Katherine found herself riding up in the lift to her second-floor office with Robert. His hair was now completely grey, but other than that he showed little sign of ageing. He must be over sixty, but having a small child, Katherine supposed, kept him young. It must be like starting all over again.

'Hello, Kate,' he said, as she stepped inside and pressed the second-floor button. 'Cold this morning.'

She agreed, making polite enquiries about Jane and his son.

'Oh, they're fine. Blooming.' His manner seemed slightly odd, although she would have found it difficult to say in what precise way. Twice she caught him looking at her obliquely.

'Have you read the paper this morning?' he asked, as the lift rushed smoothly upwards. He indicated the *Guardian*, tucked under her arm.

'Not properly. I haven't had time. I overslept and left home in a hurry. There's some dispute going on with Argentina, I gathered from a cursory glance at the front page.'

'Oh, the Falklands! Yes.'

Robert was dismissive. Katherine didn't even know where the Falkland Islands were. Somewhere, she thought vaguely, in the South Atlantic.

'Why do you ask?' she wanted to know.

The lift came to a halt, the doors slid open and they both got out.

'No reason. No reason,' Robert said airily. 'See you later, at the meeting.' And he turned left along the corridor, in the direction of his office.

Katherine went into her own office, glad of the warmth of the central heating. She could hear the typist in the farther room already at work, and grimaced to herself. Such industry in a new girl seemed distinctly promising: she must be sure to give her due acknowledgement. Katherine took off her coat and gloves and tidied her hair, staring at her reflection in her handbag mirror. She would soon be fifty-nine, and looked it, she thought. She wondered where all the years had vanished . . .

Jonathan came in half an hour later, summoning her as soon as he had settled into his office. Katherine opened the communicating door, taking with her the letters she had typed the previous evening and which still lacked his signature.

'Leave those, my dear,' he said, waving her into a chair. He gave her a look which was as oblique as Robert's had been. 'Have you read the paper this morning?'

Katherine laughed in exasperation. 'No, I haven't. Only the headlines. What is this, a conspiracy? Robert asked me the same question, coming up in the lift.'

For an answer, Jonathan picked up *The Times* and folded it back to one of the middle pages. He halved, then quartered it, finally passing it to her across the desk.

'A couple of paragraphs,' he said, 'down in the right-hand corner.'

Katherine took the paper curiously, searching for the unspecified item. Jonathan evidently assumed that she would recognize it when she saw it.

He was right. The headline, 'Hollywood Star Dies of Drug Overdose', told its own story without her having to read a word of the text. It was Annabel, of course. She remembered the conversation she had once had with Charlotte. But she read the article, just the same, very slowly, very carefully, giving herself time to think.

'British star Annabel Hardwicke was found dead at her home in the Hollywood suburb of Bel Air yesterday morning. It is thought that the cause of death was an overdose of heroin. The actress was known to have been addicted to the drug for some time.

'Miss Hardwicke was a miner's daughter from Durham, and had not worked since her last film, *The Long, Long Road*, made more than three years ago. In

382

private life she was the wife of Henry Lynton, head of Lynton's Chemicals, but the couple had lived apart since 1978, although they were not divorced.'

Katherine put the newspaper on the desk and looked at Jonathan. He smiled, a little sadly.

'Henry's free,' he said at last. 'I hope most sincerely that you'll both find happiness.'

Katherine shook her head. 'You don't understand. It doesn't make any difference. All the same, I'd like to phone Charlie. I'd like to find out if there's anything I can do.'

'Of course. I shan't be needing you for the rest of the morning.'

Charlotte, when Katherine was at last able to contact her after several hours of trying, had little to add.

'Someone telephoned Dad yesterday afternoon, but he didn't let me know until late last night. I fully intended to get in touch with you this morning, but I've been so frantically busy. I'm sorry you had to read it like that, in the papers. I didn't think they'd get hold of the story so soon.'

'How's Henry taking it?' Katherine asked, wondering what she would feel if the answer was 'badly'. She had never been quite sure of the state of Henry's affection for Annabel.

'He's sad for her sake, naturally. He feels it's a waste of a life and a talent.' Charlotte paused, not so much choosing her words, Katherine thought, as sorting through her own impressions. 'He is upset, in a way. I think he had a genuine fondness for her, which he never had for Jane. That was solely a sexual attraction. Jane was just one of his women, whom he got pushed into marrying.'

'But with Annabel it was different,' Katherine prompted, not responding to her daughter's unspoken accusation.

'Oh, yes. I think so. There was some spark there,

383

between them. But he wasn't in love with her, and I'm sure his overriding emotion is one of relief. The marriage has been ended without him having to go through a third unpleasant and messy divorce. My guess is that in a month or two he'd be positively euphoric, if you'd only have the courage to stand up to Nick.'

Katherine didn't bother to argue the point. She could not give up her son and granddaughter, even for Henry. She loved them both too much, as she loved all her children. It would need exceptional circumstances to make her break that resolution.

Charlotte said, 'I must go. I've a million and one things to do. When is Guy home, by the way? This time, I really must make an effort to see him.'

'Next month. April sixth. They should be at Gib by the second. He's promised to spend a few days in London with me, so perhaps we can all get together.'

'Fine. Let's hope he doesn't get caught up in this Falklands thing.'

'What Falklands thing?' Katherine asked, puzzled

'The Argentinians are making warlike noises Haven't you read the headlines this morning?'

'They've been doing that for decades,' Katherine replied scornfully, vague memories stirring of earlier crises. Her father had told her about those in 1910 and 1927, although until this moment she had forgotten his little lectures on international banditry: Spanish, French and most certainly British. Much more recently, in 1965, the Argentinian government had lobbied the United Nations about the return of the islands. But nothing serious had ever developed, and Britain remained on relatively good terms with Argentina. 'It'll blow over in a couple of days,' she told her daughter cheerfully.

The following day, Friday, March the twenty-sixth, Argentinian commandos landed on South Georgia. A week later, on April the second, the

384

Argentinian flag flew over Government House in Port Stanley, and the Governor and his family were on their way back to London.

HMS *Sheffield* was near Gibraltar when the news was received, but the captain reassured his crew over the tannoy that, after four and a half months at sea, they would still be arriving home on April the sixth as planned. A few hours later he was obliged to tell them, 'Forget it. We're steaming south.'

Katherine, when she heard, was not particularly worried. Like most people, and in spite of the sailing of a naval task force for the South Atlantic, she did not really believe that the crisis would escalate into war. Britain had done no fighting since the end of the Korean affair, and had resolutely stayed out of the débâcle in Vietnam. War was a thing of the past, and possibly, more terrifyingly, a thing of the future. But it was laughable to think of it in the context of the present. The arrival of the task force would frighten General Galtieri and the Argentinian junta into withdrawing from the Falklands, and that would once again be that. The United States, in the person of Secretary of State Alexander Haig, was working night and day to get the two opposing sides round the negotiating table.

May the second was a Sunday and it rained hard. Katherine, who had gone down to Plymouth for the weekend, stayed indoors. The next day, the May Day Bank Holiday, was a little better and she decided to drive round the coast to Bigbury-on-Sea. It was while she was lunching at the ancient smugglers' inn, the Pilchard, on Burgh Island, that she heard about the sinking of the *General Belgrano*.

The Argentinian warship had been torpedoed the previous day by the submarine *Conqueror*, with a loss of three hundred and sixty-eight lives. Some people were cheering and singing 'Rule, Britannia', but many others, who had experienced the horrors of the Second World War, were silent, thinking of the dead and wounded.

'That'll put an end to the Argies' nonsense,' a woman said. 'That'll show them.'

Katherine got up and went outside. Not for a moment did she believe that this undeclared war was over, nor that the Argentinians would meekly accept defeat. There would be reprisals. Guy was down there, in the wastes of the South Atlantic, as were hundreds of other young British servicemen.

She wandered along the path, looking back at the clouded mainland; at the gentle, rolling hills, with their clusters of houses and tree-lined clefts; at the ploughed fields, the red Devonshire earth showing up like raw wounds against the soft, lush background of green. The wide expanse of sea was rimmed with gold, glossed by a sudden burst of sunlight, a little oasis of good weather amidst the storms. The sabre-like fronds of three small stunted palms, opposite the pub's main door, rattled in a rising wind. A finger of light touched the figurehead of some old man-of-war, perched on a knoll of ground, among brakes of as yet unflowering broom and gorse.

Katherine remembered, as though it were yesterday, being brought here as a child, first by her mother and, later, by Aunt Margery. She had loved Bigbury, with its little island which, at low tide, was linked to the mainland by a wide expanse of wet and glistening sand. And at high tide there had been the excitement of crossing by a weird and wonderful contraption – its successor was still in use – like an open-sided tent on stilts and wheels.

In her turn she had brought her own children here, making the longer journey across the Tamar from Chapel Rock, so that they, too, could sample the delights of playing on an island, pretending to be pirates and smugglers, watching the sea roll in between them and the safety of the beach. Katherine longed passionately to bring her grandchildren here, to this very English place; and if Charlotte maintained her refusal to marry, or become a mother, then Katherine's dependence must be all on Nicholas and Guy . . .

But at the thought of Guy she felt again the cold chill of fear, the premonition of disaster which had dogged her now for so many months . . .

The *Sheffield* was struck amidships by an Exocet missile the following day, Tuesday, May the fourth. Guy was among those killed.

The official notification did not arrive for some days; days during which Katherine alternately swung between hope and despair, struggling to ignore what she already knew to be the truth. Her sense of foreboding was now so strong as to preclude any other outcome.

Because of the divorce Guy had named her, and not his father, as next of kin. It was therefore up to Katherine to break the news to Henry. She walked to the Park Lane flat from her own in Brompton Road, but afterwards could recall absolutely nothing of the brief journey. There must have been a lot of people about on such a fine Saturday evening in May, but she could remember no one. Her first conscious thought, after leaving home, was that the Park Lane entrance hall looked exactly the same as when she had last seen it.

She had telephoned Henry to say that she was coming, and he was waiting for her. As she stepped out of the lift he came forward and put an arm around her shoulders, drawing her gently inside the flat and closing the door. One look at his face, and she knew that she had no need to tell him anything: he had already guessed. He opened his arms and she was folded inside their comforting embrace.

They clung to one another, disbelief and sorrow each struggling to get the upper hand. It had all happened so swiftly, with so little warning, that they found it difficult to comprehend.

Katherine started to cry, quietly at first, then in loud, noisy sobs as the anxiety and sleepless nights of the past week began to take their toll.

'He should have been home now,' she kept saying. 'Guy should have been home. The worst part, the awful part, is wondering if he suffered.'

She had nightmare visions, as all mothers did, of her children, lost and frightened, crying for her in vain in the eternal dark.

'Hush, hush,' Henry murmured. He forced her gently into the living-room and made her sit down, then poured her out a brandy. She drank it neat, coughing and gasping for breath, but it saved her from the hysteria which was threatening to engulf her. She sat up, drying her eyes, trying to regain her control.

'Why him? Why Guy?' she demanded angrily. 'He was always so full of life. Twenty-seven, that's no age to die. Why couldn't it have been someone else's son, instead of mine?'

Henry said nothing, but sat with his arms around her, letting her find some relief in the spate of swearwords and profanities she was suddenly spewing out, beating her fists impotently against his chest.

He understood how she felt. He kept remembering Guy, a bright, noisy, eager little boy; forgetting his faults, recalling only his virtues. Henry had not always liked his younger son, but it was not the moment for such recollections.

Later, when Katherine was a litle calmer, Henry asked, 'Have you told Charlie and Nicholas?' She shook her head. 'Would you like me to do it for you?'

She blew her nose defiantly, pushing her hair back from her hot damp forehead.

'No, I think I'd better do it. Nicholas, anyway. But not tonight. I don't want to see anyone but you tonight. You're the only person I can bear to have near me. You're such a part of me; you always have been. You know exactly what I'm thinking and how I feel. Put your arms around me again and hold me tight.'

30

On Monday, June the fourteenth, the day that Major-
General Menendez surrendered the Falkland Islands
to the British, Katherine had tea with Nicholas on the
terrace of the House of Commons. She had come
intending to be frank, and decided that to waste time
on more than the barest of preliminaries might
weaken her resolve. So, as soon as she had enquired
after Ella and the baby, she plunged straight in.

'Your father and I are getting married again next
week by special licence. It will be a very quiet
wedding, for obvious reasons, at Plymouth Register
Office. The actual day is the twenty-third. Wednesday. If you and Ella want to join Charlotte and
Jonathan Anthony, you know how happy it would
make us both. If you feel you can't, we shall, of
course, understand. Afterwards, we'll be spending a
week at Chapel Rock.'

She had said it. She had got it all out without
hesitation or apology. She had burned her boats. Now
it was up to Nicholas.

When Henry had asked her to marry him again,
that dreadful night when they had shared the grief of
Guy's death, Katherine's only impulse had been to
accept. She knew that it was the right decision to
make; that without one another each was merely half
a person. He had quoted Marvel: *Had we but world
enough and time* ... But that, at sixty and nearly
sixty, was what neither of them had. Nevertheless,

remembering Nicholas and his threat, Katherine had been unable to commit herself.

And then, a week ago, unpacking some of her books which had remained crated ever since her move to Brompton Road, she had come across the copy of Buchan's *Montrose* which Henry had bought for her in John Knox's house, all those years ago. She had sat, staring at it; at the gold lettering on the dark green binding, now rubbed and faded; fingering the rough, wartime economy paper and the untrimmed edges.

> He either fears his fate too much
> Or his deserts are small
> That puts it not unto the touch
> To win or lose it all.

James Graham had written those words over three hundred years ago, but she supposed they were as relevant today as ever. And in that moment, sitting there on the floor by the box of books, the summer day drawing to a close, the silence and emptiness of the flat all around her, Katherine had made up her mind. If Nicholas cut himself and his family off from her, then so be it. It would hurt, but she would have to learn to live with it.

She remembered Robert once saying that the death of a child either drew the bereaved parents closer together, or drove them apart. For him and Sheila it had sadly been the latter; but Guy's loss had forged a bond between herself and Henry stronger than ever before. She had no idea what the future held: Henry's eye would no doubt still rove each time he saw a pretty woman; she would continue to irritate his innate conservatism with her father's heretical views. But they would survive, and, more importantly, they would survive together. Her only regret would be if Nicholas refused to accept the marriage.

There was a long silence after she had finished speaking. All around them people were laughing and talking; a ship's siren sounded from the river. Famous faces, well-known voices mingled with the less familiar. Sunlight sparkled on the water.

At last, Nicholas said quietly, 'We'll be at the wedding. We'll bring the baby.' Katherine, not trusting herself to speak, not even sure that she had heard him correctly, sat mute, her throat constricted, her eyes brimming with tears. Nicholas went on in the same unemotional tone, which concealed his own sense of loss, 'I miss Guy, you know. I miss him far more than I should have thought possible. I didn't always like him, and we didn't always get on. He bullied me a lot when we were children, and he wasn't always kind. But, then, who is? And, if I'm honest, I very often used to go out of my way to annoy him, so that he'd thump me and get told off. We never had much in common, but I was used to him being there, in the background of my life. The navy had mellowed him; rubbed off the raw edges. We got on quite well the last time we met. So, you see, I do appreciate what you and . . . and' – he made a palpable effort – 'my father are going through. It wouldn't be fair, in the circumstances, to inflict any more grief and loss.'

Katherine reached out and touched her son's hand. She wanted to say so much, but she knew that any effusion would only embarrass Nicholas. All she said was, 'Thank you.'

He nodded abruptly. 'But don't expect me to be all over Father. Things are bound to be strained at first. You must give me time.'

All the time in the world, she thought happily; but in the same moment, she was filled with bitterness at the way Fate seemed to give with one hand and take with another. Had it really needed Guy's death to reconcile Nicholas with his father? Probably, human nature being what it was. The passage from Ecclesiastes came into her mind. *A time to be born, and a time to die . . . A time to weep, and a time to laugh; a time to mourn, and a time to dance . . . ; A time to love, and a time to hate . . .* Life, it seemed, had always been the same; never wholehearted, never without its conditions. There was no such thing as perfect happiness, but would anyone know what to do with it if there were? And for the second time that afternoon Katherine thought of Robert, who had to lose her to find Sheila, to lose his son to find Jane.

She looked across the table at Nicholas and smiled. Reluctantly, slowly, he smiled back.

'It went off better than I could ever have hoped for,' Henry said quietly, adding sombrely, 'And much better than I deserve.'

Katherine nodded. 'Nick behaved extremely well. Ella and the baby were just themselves.'

'My granddaughter,' Henry murmured. 'Our granddaughter. She's a darling, isn't she? Do you think there will be more children?'

'Maybe, but I don't ask.' Katherine turned to smile at him. 'You're still an old dynast at heart.'

They had arrived at Chapel Rock about tea-time, and now, four hours and one of Mrs Godfrey's excellent dinners later, they were standing beside the Tamar in the fading light, having walked down through the valley garden. Behind them the lime kilns rose grey and monolithic, museum pieces, whose ancient fires had long since gone out.

Katherine sighed with pleasure. 'It's so good to be back.'

'It's where you belong,' Henry said. 'You love it as I've grown to love it over the years. To begin with, when I first came from the States, Chapel Rock was just a status symbol. Something to impress visitors with, especially foreigners. "Come and see this

393

quaint old house I've got, in Cornwall." Jane felt the same way about the place. Annabel was never comfortable here. She resented Chapel Rock, just as she resented my money and her own success. I used to tell her that she was born out of time and out of context. She'd have been happier sitting around the guillotine, counting heads. But, of course, most of all, she resented me and what I'd made her do.'

'That wasn't altogether fair,' Katherine objected, 'although I can see why she felt that way.'

Henry smiled. 'I suppose I can, too. She was the real loser, not Nicholas; not even, as it turns out, me.' He gave Katherine's shoulders a squeeze and kissed her lightly on the top of her head. 'Nick seems very happy with his family. Ella's a nice girl. She'll make him an excellent wife. Much better than Annabel.'

'I think Nick knows that now. It's partly why he relented and came to the wedding today. I just wish Charlie would find a good man and settle down.'

Henry laughed. 'You know, Kate, you're very old-fashioned in some of your ideas. You used to accuse me of the same fault, but, after all, I've learned to move with the times better than you have. Marriage and motherhood aren't the be-all and end-all of life for women nowadays. If you think back, it wasn't for you, either. You were always fighting to have your own career. But in those days, if women wanted sex, most of them got married. Charlotte doesn't have to. She can have a succession of lovers and nobody cares. And, anyway, she's the soul of discretion. She never flaunts her men. She's going to be head of Lynton's one day, I've seen to that. And the day won't be that far distant. My body's given me one warning, and I don't intend to be carried out in a box. I'm sixty-plus, and I'm going to bow out gracefully in the next few years.' Henry turned towards the kilns and the rising path through the trees, his arm still about Katherine's shoulders. 'I've decided I want some time to live, to

394

be with you, to do all the things we want to do together. I'm not going to die with my boots on. I've made up my mind.'

The long June day was closing in a blaze of glory. The sun spread its ribbons of red and orange flame across the sky, touching the trees with fire. The little chapel of St Hyacinth loomed ahead of them.

Katherine stopped, forcing Henry to stop with her. She asked quietly, 'You've really made up your mind, then, to leave Lynton's to Charlie?'

'Why should that surprise you? You were the one who always maintained that women had as much business acumen as men. Once, I didn't believe you, but Charlie's changed my mind. And Nick certainly isn't interested in the company, any more than Guy would have been, had he lived.'

'A family business,' Katherine said, and her tone was sombre. 'Stephen's dream of a dynasty of Lyntons.'

'What's wrong with that? Family businesses are becoming few and far between. I don't know how long Lynton's can survive in this hyper-competitive age of the merger and the takeover and the giant monopoly. But it's worth a try. In case you don't know, we stopped doing work for the government quite some time ago. Sandor would have been pleased.'

The name echoed queerly here among the trees, evoking memories of a past which no longer seemed to have any meaning for her. But perhaps that was simply because she had other things on her mind.

'There's something I have to tell you,' Katherine said, holding tightly to both of Henry's hands. 'Something I should have told you a long, long time ago; certainly before I let you marry me again. Charlotte isn't your daughter, she's Robert's. She isn't really a Lynton.'

It was very quiet suddenly, as the darkness

gathered round them, concealing the expression in Henry's heavy-lidded eyes. The birds had gone to roost, but the scufflings and scurryings of the nocturnal animals had not yet begun. Very faintly, beyond the belt of trees, Katherine could hear the lapping of the river.

She waited with a kind of desperate calm for Henry's reaction, but this, when it came, wasn't at all what she had expected. He began to laugh, silently at first, then with a deep, full-throated chuckle.

'I'm telling you the truth, damn you!' Katherine exclaimed tearfully, shaking him. 'I'm not making it up. She could have been yours, so easily, and I prayed to God that she was. But as she grew older I could see her likeness to Robert. It truly wasn't my fault. He was drunk and forced himself on me the last night we were together. Will you stop laughing! What's so funny?'

Henry put his arms around her, folding her against the rough tweed of his jacket.

'I suppose I'm laughing', he said, 'because it's a case of the biter bit. You see, I'm not really a Lynton, either.'

Katherine forced herself away from his chest, tilting her head back to look at his face. 'What do you mean, you're not a Lynton?'

'What I say. Oh, Geoffrey Lynton accepted me and brought me up, but he knew, and made sure I knew, that he wasn't really my father. That gentleman, apparently, was the red-headed Irishman with whom my mother absconded six weeks after I was born. It always surprised me that Stephen accepted me so readily, considering I don't look anything like the Lyntons.'

'But ...' Katherine felt dazed. 'Then, Nicholas isn't a Lynton, either?'

'I'm afraid not. So you see, Charlotte being

396

Robert's child doesn't really matter. Have you ever told her the truth?'

'No . . . No, I haven't. But, Henry, are you sure? Your father . . . Geoffrey Lynton, I mean, he wasn't just having you on?'

They began walking again. Henry encircled her waist with one arm.

'Now, would he? On such a subject? C'mon, Kate, pull yourself together. Your wits have gone woolgathering. Does it matter all that much to you that I'm not a Lynton?'

'It doesn't matter at all,' Katherine answered, pausing to reach up and kiss him. 'It's you I love. What you are. Who you are isn't important. But I can't reconcile myself to the idea all in a moment. What did you feel about deceiving Stephen?'

'I didn't feel that I was. Geoffrey Lynton raised me as his son. My birth certificate shows him as my father. So, in law, he was my parent, as I'm Charlie's. I don't suppose Stephen would have seen it in that light, but by claiming to be his nephew I wasn't doing anything illegal. That was between me and my conscience; and I was young and ambitious enough to feel justified in suppressing the absolute truth. I was no less a Lynton than if my father had adopted me from an orphanage. In fact, I'd been a part of his life from the very first moment I was born. In my own eyes, I was his son. Geoffrey brought me up, imbued me with his ideas, talked to me about his family as if it were my own, treated me most of the time as if I were a Lynton. It was only when he was drunk that he'd abuse me with the truth. I must have been five or six the first time it happened.'

'What effect did it have on you?' Katherine wanted to know, as they began the steep ascent through the garden.

'It's so long ago, I can't remember.' Henry put a

hand under her elbow as she moved ahead of him on the narrow, stony path which led to the fish-pond. 'I don't suppose, at that age, I really knew what he was saying. By the time I was old enough to understand, I didn't think it mattered. Wasn't it St Ignatius Loyola who said: "Give me a child for the first five years of his life, and you can have him for the rest"? Or something along those lines? I was a Lynton by upbringing, if not by birth. I felt like a Lynton. In the same way, Charlie is my child, not Robert's. They've nothing in common, while she's a lot like me.'

'Stubborn, bossy and always certain that her way is the right one,' Katherine agreed. 'You can say that again! She surely is a lot like you.'

Henry grinned. 'From that description, I'd have to agree that she has more in common with her mother. No, no! Stop it, Kate! This path is uneven. You'll have us over.'

Katherine had turned, laughing, punching and attacking him in pretended fury. They both fell sideways into a bed of lupins, the crushed flowers smelling sweetly beneath Katherine's cheek. She picked herself up, brushing earth from the cotton dress into which she had changed before taking their walk after dinner. Henry followed suit, wincing and rubbing his left shoulder.

'We're getting too old for this sort of horseplay,' he admonished her. 'Honestly, Kate, you are a fool. We might have done ourselves serious damage.'

'Nonsense!' she retorted stoutly. 'Not a couple of battle-scarred warriors like us.' She sobered. She thought: Here we are, laughing and joking, and it's less than two months since Guy was killed. How could we have forgotten so quickly, even if it was only for a moment or so?

Henry mounted a step in the path and stood beside her, taking her in his arms again. He rocked her gently. 'I know what you're thinking,' he whispered. 'I was there, ahead of you. But just because we laugh now and then, it doesn't mean to say that we're callous. Guy was our son, but we can't mourn him every second of the day. It wouldn't be natural.'

'No.' She moved closer to him. From somewhere among the trees which shrouded the approach to the house, an owl hooted. Then it appeared like a shadow, skimming low and straight, down over the garden towards the river. Katherine raised her head to watch it go by, and turned to Henry.

'There wouldn't be any point, would there, in telling the children the truth? In Charlie's case, it would be doubly traumatic.'

'No point at all,' Henry agreed, kissing her.' And as far as I'm concerned it wouldn't be the truth, except in the most literal of senses. We're who we believe ourselves to be, that's the important thing, not who other people tell us we are. *That which we call a rose et cetera . . .*'

'Yes. You're right.' Katherine tapped his arm. 'And we're too advanced in years to play Romeo and Juliet out of doors. The air's getting damp. I can feel it. Come on, it's time we went in. We've the rest of our lives to indulge in philosophical discussions, and I don't want to shorten them with an inflammation of the lungs or, less romantically, a chill on the kidneys.'

At the top of the garden, by the wicket-gate, they paused and looked back, both breathing a little more heavily than they used to do after the climb. The garden, with its shadowy outlines of dovecot and summer-house nestling among the flat paper shapes of the darkened trees, lay silent and mysterious below them.

To everything there is a season, and a time to every purpose under the heaven . . .

Her purpose now, Katherine thought, was to pick up the pieces of her life and make the most of the years remaining to her and Henry. No one could foresee the future, but she was going to be happy, she could feel it in her heart, in spite of its present burden of sadness. Victor's spirit was here, more than in the bungalow, which she had now sold. Guy was here, too: she could hear the far-off echoes of his childish laughter. Nicholas would come here with his wife and child; and so, when time permitted, would Charlotte. And Henry, he would be with her. They would never let circumstances separate them again.

They smiled at one another.

'Let's go in,' Katherine said.

They had come home.

THE END